The Best of

The Hardy Boys®

CLASSIC COLLECTION

Volume 2

The House on the Cliff

The Ghost at Skeleton Rock

The Sting of the Scorpion

By Franklin W. Dixon

Grosset & Dunlap • New York

THE HOUSE ON THE CLIFF copyright © 1987, 1959, 1955,
1927 by Simon & Schuster, Inc. THE GHOST AT SKELETON
ROCK copyright © 1994, 1966, 1957 by Simon & Schuster, Inc.
THE STING OF THE SCORPION copyright © 1979 by Simon
& Schuster, Inc. All rights reserved. THE BEST OF THE
HARDY BOYS CLASSIC COLLECTION Volume 2 published in
2004 by Grosset & Dunlap, a division of Penguin Young Readers
Group, 345 Hudson Street, New York, New York 10014.
THE HARDY BOYS® is a registered trademark of Simon &
Schuster, Inc. GROSSET & DUNLAP is a trademark of
Penguin Group (USA) Inc. Printed in the U.S.A.

ISBN 0-448-43628-0   10 9 8 7 6 5 4 3 2 1

The Hardy Boys Mystery Stories®

THE HOUSE

ON

THE CLIFF

BY

FRANKLIN W. DIXON

GROSSET & DUNLAP
Publishers • New York
A member of The Putnam & Grosset Group

CONTENTS

CHAPTER I

Spying by Telescope

"So you boys want to help me on another case?" Fenton Hardy, internationally known detective, smiled at his teen-age sons.

"Dad, you said you're working on a very mysterious case right now," Frank spoke up. "Isn't there some angle of it that Joe and I could tackle?"

Mr. Hardy looked out the window of his second-floor study as if searching for the answer somewhere in the town of Bayport, where the Hardys lived. Finally he turned back and gazed steadfastly at his sons.

"All right. How would you like to look for some smugglers?"

Joe Hardy's eyes opened wide. "You mean it, Dad?"

"Now just a minute." The detective held up his

hand. "I didn't say capture them; I just said look for them."

"Even that's a big assignment. Thanks for giving it to us!" Frank replied.

The lean, athletic detective walked to a corner of the study where a long, narrow carrying case stood. Tapping it, he said:

"You boys have learned how to manipulate this telescope pretty well. How would you like to take it out onto that high promontory above the ocean and train it seaward? The place I mean is two miles north of the end of the bay and eight miles from here."

"That would be great!" said seventeen-year-old, blond-haired Joe, his blue eyes flashing in anticipation.

Frank, who was a year older than his brother and less impetuous, asked in a serious tone of voice, "Dad, have you any ideas about the identity of any of the smugglers?"

"Yes, I do," Mr. Hardy answered his tall, dark-haired son. "I strongly suspect that a man named Felix Snattman is operating in this territory. I'll give you the whole story."

The detective went on to say that he had been engaged by an international pharmaceutical company to trace stolen shipments of valuable drugs. Reports of thefts had come from various parts of the United States. Local police had worked on the case, but so far had failed to apprehend any suspects.

"Headquarters of the firm is in India," the detective told the boys. "It was through them that I was finally called in. I'm sure that the thefts are the result of smuggling, very cleverly done. That's the reason I suspect Snattman. He's a noted criminal and has been mixed up in smuggling rackets before. He served a long term in prison, and after being released, dropped out of sight."

"And you think he's working around Bayport?" Joe asked. He whistled. "That doesn't make this town a very healthy place to live in!"

"But we're going to make it so!" Mr. Hardy declared, a ring of severity in his voice.

"Just where is this spot we're to use the telescope?" Frank asked eagerly.

"It's on the Pollitt place. You'll see the name at the entrance. An old man named Felix Pollitt lived there alone for many years. He was found dead in the house about a month ago, and the place has been vacant ever since."

"It sounds as if we could get a terrific range up and down the shore from there and many miles across the water," Frank remarked.

Mr. Hardy glanced at his wrist watch. "It's one-thirty now. You ought to be able to go out there, stay a fair amount of time, and still get home to supper."

"Oh, easily," Joe answered. "Our motorcycles can really burn up the road!"

His father smiled, but cautioned, "This telescope happens to be very valuable. The less jouncing it receives the better."

"I get the point," Joe conceded, then asked, "Dad, do you want us to keep the information about the smugglers to ourselves, or would it be all right to take a couple of the fellows along?"

"Of course I don't want the news broadcast," Mr. Hardy said, "but I know I can trust your special friends. Call them up."

"How about Chet and Biff?" Joe consulted Frank. As his brother nodded, he said, "You pack the telescope on your motorcycle. I'll phone."

Chet Morton was a stout, good-natured boy who loved to eat. Next to that, he enjoyed being with the Hardys and sharing their exciting adventures, although at times, when situations became dangerous, he wished he were somewhere else. Chet also loved to tinker with machinery and spent long hours on his jalopy which he called Queen. He was trying to "soup up" the motor, so that he could have a real "hot rod."

In contrast to Chet, Biff Hooper was tall and lanky. To the amusement—and wonder—of the other boys, he used his legs almost as a spider does, covering tremendous distances on level ground or vaulting fences.

A few minutes later Joe joined his brother in the garage and told him that both Chet and Biff would go along. Chet, he said, had apologized for not being able to offer the Queen for the trip but her engine was "all over the garage." "As usual," Frank said with a grin as the two boys climbed on their motorcycles and set out.

Presently the Hardys stopped at Biff Hooper's home. He ran out the door to meet them and climbed aboard behind Joe. Chet lived on a farm at the outskirts of Bayport, about a fifteen-minute run from the Hooper home. The stout boy had strolled down the lane to the road and was waiting for his friends. He hoisted himself onto Frank's motorcycle.

"I've never seen a powerful telescope in operation," he remarked. "How far away can you see with this thing?"

"It all depends on weather conditions," Frank replied. "On a clear day you can make out human figures at distances of twenty-four miles."

"Wow!" Chet exclaimed. "We ought to be able to find those smugglers easily."

"I wouldn't say so," Biff spoke up. "Smugglers have the same kind of boats as everybody else. How close do you have to be to identify a person?"

"Oh, about two and a half miles," Joe answered.

The motorcycles chugged along the shore

road, with Frank watching his speedometer carefully. "We ought to be coming to the Pollitt place soon," he said finally. "Keep your eyes open, fellows."

The boys rode on in silence, but suddenly they all exclaimed together, "There it is!"

At the entrance to a driveway thickly lined with trees and bushes was a stone pillar, into which the name "Pollitt" had been chiseled. Frank and Joe turned into the driveway. The only part of the house they could see was the top of the roof. Finally, beyond a lawn overgrown with weeds, they came upon the tall, rambling building. It stood like a beacon high above the water. Pounding surf could be heard far below.

"This place sure looks neglected," Biff remarked.

Dank, tall grass grew beneath the towering trees. Weeds and bushes threatened to engulf the whole building.

"Creepy, if you ask me," Chet spoke up. "I don't know why anybody would want to live here."

The house itself was in need of repair. Built of wood, it had several sagging shutters and the paint was flaking badly.

"Poor old Mr. Pollitt was probably too sick to take care of things," Frank commented, as he looked at several weed-choked flower beds.

To the Hardys' disappointment, the sky had

become overcast and they realized that visibility had been cut down considerably. Nevertheless, Frank unstrapped the carrying case and lugged it around to the front of the house.

He unfastened the locks and Joe helped his brother lift out the telescope and attached tripod, pulling up the eye-end section first.

Biff and Chet exclaimed in admiration.

"Boy, that's really neat!" Chet remarked.

He and Biff watched in fascination as Frank and Joe began to set up the telescope. First they unfastened the tape with which the tube and tripod legs were tied together. Joe turned the three legs down and pulled out the extensions to the desired height. Then Frank secured the tripod legs with a chain to keep them from spreading.

"What's next?" Biff asked.

"To get proper balance for the main telescope tube we slide it through this trunnion sleeve toward the eye end, like this." After doing so, Frank tightened the wing nuts on the tripod lightly.

Joe picked up the balance weight from the carrying case and screwed it into the right side of the telescope tube about one third the distance from the eyepiece.

"This'll keep the whole thing from being top heavy," he pointed out.

"And what's this little telescope alongside the big one for?" Chet queried.

"A finder," Frank explained. "Actually, it's a small guide telescope and helps the observer sight his big telescope on the object more easily."

"It's as clear as mud," Chet remarked with a

grin. He squinted through the ends of both the large and the small telescopes. "I can't see a thing," he complained.

Joe laughed. "And you won't until I insert one

of the eyepieces into the adapter of the big telescope and put another eyepiece into the finder."

In a few minutes the Hardys had the fascinating device working. By turning a small knob, Frank slowly swung the telescope from left to right, and each boy took a turn looking out across the water.

"Not a boat in sight!" said Chet, disappointed.

Frank had just taken his second turn squinting through the eyepiece when he called out excitedly, "I see something!"

He now began a running account of the scene he had just picked up. "It's not very clear . . . but I see a boat . . . must be at least six miles out."

"What kind of boat?" Joe put in.

"Looks like a cruiser . . . or a cutter. . . . It's not moving. . . . Want to take a look, Joe?"

Frank's brother changed places with him. "Say, fellows, a man's going over the side on a ladder . . . and, hey! there's a smaller boat down below. . . . He's climbing into it."

"Can you see a name or numbers on the big boat?" Frank asked excitedly.

"No. The boat's turned at a funny angle, so you can't see the lettering. You couldn't even if the weather was clearer."

"Which way is the man in the small boat heading?" Biff asked.

"He seems to be going toward Barmet Bay."

Joe gave up his position to Biff. "Suppose you keep your eye on him for a while, and also the big boat. Maybe it'll turn so you can catch the name or number on the box."

Chet had been silent for several moments. Now he said, "Do you suppose they're the smugglers?"

"Could be," Frank replied. "I think we'd better leave and report this to Dad from the first telephone we—"

He was interrupted by the sudden, terrifying scream of a man!

"Wh-where did that come from?" Chet asked with a frightened look.

"Sounded as if it came from inside," Frank answered.

The boys stared at the house on the cliff. A moment later they heard a loud cry for help. It was followed by another scream.

"Somebody's in there and is in trouble!" Joe exclaimed. "We'd better find out what's going on!"

Leaving the telescope, the four boys ran to the front door and tried the knob. The door was locked.

"Let's scatter and see if we can find another door," Frank suggested.

Frank and Joe took one side of the house, Biff and Chet the other. They met at the rear of the old home and together tried a door there. This, too, was locked.

"There's a broken window around the corner," Biff announced. "Shall we climb in?"

"I guess we'd better," Frank answered.

As the boys reached the window, which seemed to open into a library, they heard the scream again.

"Help! Hurry! Help!" came an agonized cry.

CHAPTER II

Thief at Work

Joe was first to slide through the broken window. "Wait a moment, fellows," he called out, "until I unlock this."

Quickly he turned the catch, raised the window, and the other three boys stepped inside the library. No one was there and they ran into the large center hall.

"Hello!" Frank shouted. "Where are you?"

There was no answer. "Maybe that person who was calling for help has passed out or is unconscious," Joe suggested. "Let's look around."

The boys dashed in various directions, and investigated the living room with its old-fashioned furnishings, the dining room with its heavily carved English oak set, the kitchen, and what had evidently been a maid's bedroom in days gone by. Now it was heaped high with empty boxes and crates. There was no one in any of the rooms and the Hardys and their two friends met again in the hall.

"The man must be upstairs," Frank decided.

He started up the front stairway and the others followed. There were several bedrooms. Suddenly Chet hung back. He wanted to go with his pals but the eeriness of the house made him pause. Biff and the Hardys sped from one to another of the many rooms. Finally they investigated the last of them.

"Nobody here! What do you make of it?" Biff asked, puzzled.

Chet, who had rejoined the group, said worriedly, "M-maybe the place is haunted!"

Joe's eyes were searching for an entrance to the third floor. Seeing none, he opened three doors in the hall, hoping to find a stairway. He saw none.

"There must be an attic in this house," he said. "I wonder how you get to it."

"Maybe there's an entrance from one of the bedrooms," Frank suggested. "Let's see."

The boys separated to investigate. Suddenly Frank called out, "I've found it."

The others ran to where he had discovered a door behind a man's shabby robe hanging inside a closet. This in turn revealed a stairway and the group hurriedly climbed it, Chet bringing up the rear.

The attic room was enormous. Old newspapers and magazines were strewn around among old-fashioned trunks and suitcases, but there was no human being in sight.

"I guess that cry for help didn't come from the house at all," Biff suggested. "What'll we do now? Look outdoors?"

"I guess we'll have to," Frank answered.

He started down the steep stairway. Reaching the foot, he turned the handle of the door which had swung shut. To his concern he was not able to open it.

"What's the matter?" asked Chet from the top of the stairway.

"Looks as if we're locked in," Frank told him.

"Locked in?" Chet wailed. "Oh, no!"

Frank tried pulling and pushing the door. It did not budge.

"That's funny," he said. "I didn't see any lock on the outside."

Suddenly the full import of the situation dawned on the four boys. Someone had deliberately locked them in! The cries for help had been a hoax to lure them into the house!

"You think somebody was playing a joke on us?" Biff asked.

"Pretty rotten kind of joke," Chet sputtered.

Frank and Joe were inclined to think that there was more to it than a joke. Someone had seen a chance to steal a valuable telescope and two late-model motorcycles!

"We've got to get out of here!" Joe said. "Frank, put your shoulder to the door and I'll help."

Fortunately, the door was not particularly sturdy and gave way easily. Frank glanced back a moment as he rushed through and saw two large hooks which he had not noticed before. They had evidently been slipped into the eyes and had been ripped from the framework by the crash on the door.

The other boys followed, running pell-mell through the hallway and clattering down the stairway. They dashed out the front door, leaving it open behind them. To their relief, the telescope still stood at the edge of the cliff, pointing sea-ward.

"Thank goodness!" said Joe. "I'd hate to have had to tell Dad the telescope was gone!"

Frank rushed over to take a quick look through the instrument. It had occurred to him that maybe some confederate of the smugglers had seen them spying. He might even have tricked them into the house during the very time that a smuggling operation would be within range of the telescope!

When Frank reached the edge of the cliff and tried to look through the instrument, he gasped in dismay. The eyepieces from both the finder and the telescope tube had been removed!

As he turned to tell the other boys of his discovery, he found that they were not behind him. But a moment later Joe came running around the corner of the house calling out:

"The motorcycles are safe! Nobody stole them!"

"Thank goodness for that," said Frank.

Chet and Biff joined them and all flopped down on the grass to discuss the mysterious happenings and work out a plan of action.

"If that thief is hiding inside the house, I'm going to find him," Joe declared finally.

"I'm with you," said Frank, jumping up. "How about you, Biff, guarding the motorcycles and Chet taking charge of the telescope? That way, both the front and back doors will be covered, too, in case that thief comes out."

"Okay," the Hardys' friends agreed.

As Frank and Joe entered the front hall, Joe remarked, "There's a back stairway. If we don't find the person on the first floor, I'll take that to the second. You take the front."

Frank nodded and the search began. Not only the first, but the second and attic floors were thoroughly investigated without results.

"There's only one place left," said Frank. "The cellar."

This area also proved to have no one hiding

in it. "I guess our thief got away," Frank stated.

"And probably on foot," Joe added. "I didn't hear any car, did you?"

"No. Maybe he went down the cliff and made a getaway in a boat," Frank suggested.

In complete disgust the Hardys reported their failure to Biff and Chet. Then they packed up the telescope and strapped it onto Frank's motorcycle.

"We may as well go home," Joe said dolefully. "We'll have a pretty slim report for Dad."

"Slim?" said Biff. "I haven't had so much excitement in six months."

The boys climbed aboard the motorcycles. As the Hardys were about to start the motors, all four of them froze in the seats. From somewhere below the cliff came a demoniacal laugh. Involuntarily the boys shuddered.

"L-let's get out of here!" Chet urged.

Frank and Joe had hopped off the motorcycles, and were racing in the direction from which the eerie laughter was coming.

"It may be another trap!" Chet yelled after them. "Come back!"

But the Hardys went on. Just before they reached the edge of the cliff they were thunderstruck to hear the laughter coming from a completely different area. It was actually in back of them!

"What gives?" Joe asked.

"Search me," his brother answered. "The ghost must have a confederate."

The brothers peered over the edge of the cliff but could see only jagged rocks that led to the booming surf below. Frank and Joe returned to their chums, disappointed that they had learned nothing and had no explanation for the second laugh.

"I'm glad it stopped, anyhow," said Chet. "It gave me goose pimples and made chills run up and down my spine."

Biff looked at his wrist watch. "I really have to be getting home, fellows. Sorry to break up this man hunt. Maybe you can take me to a bus and come back."

The Hardys would not hear of this and said they would leave at once.

They had gone scarcely a mile when the motor on Frank's cycle sputtered and backfired, then died. "A swell time for a breakdown," he said disgustedly as he honked for Joe to stop.

Joe turned around and drove back. "What's the matter?"

"Don't know." Frank dismounted. "It's not the gas. I have plenty of that."

"Tough luck!" Joe said sympathetically. "Well, let's take a look at the motor. Better get out your tools."

As Frank opened the toolbox of his motorcycle, an expression of bewilderment came over his face.

"My tools!" he exclaimed. "They're gone!"

The others gathered around. The toolbox was indeed empty!

"Are you sure you had them when you left Bayport?" Chet asked.

"Of course I did. I never go anywhere without them."

Biff shook his head. "I suppose the guy who took the eyepieces stole your tools too."

Joe dashed to the toolbox on his own motorcycle and gave a cry of dismay.

"Mine are gone, too!"

CHAPTER III

Landslide!

"THAT's a shame, fellows," Chet Morton said. "This is sure your day for bad luck. First the eye-pieces from your telescope are taken and now the tools from your motorcycles."

"And all by the same person, I'm sure," Frank remarked grimly.

"Some slick operator, whoever he is," Joe added gloomily.

Chet put his hands into his trouser pockets and with a grin pulled out a pair of pliers, a screw driver, and a wrench.

"I was working on the Queen this morning," he explained. "Good thing I happened to put these in my pocket."

"I'll say," Frank declared gratefully, taking the tools which Chet handed over.

He unfastened the housing of the motor and

began checking every inch of the machinery. Finally he looked up and announced, "I guess I've found the trouble—a loose connection."

Frank adjusted the wires and a moment later the vehicle's motor was roaring normally. The housing was put back on, Chet's tools were returned with thanks, and the four boys set off once more.

"Let's hope nothing more happens before we get home," Biff said with a wry laugh.

"I'll second that," Joe said emphatically.

For five minutes the cyclists rode along in silence, their thoughts partly on the passing scenery, but mostly on the mystery in which they had become involved.

Joe's mind was racing with his throbbing motorcycle. In a few minutes he had far outdistanced his brother. Frank did not dare go any faster because of the telescope strapped onto his handle bars.

Presently Joe reached a spot in the road where it had been cut out of the hillside on the right. There was a sharp curve here. The motorcycle took it neatly, but he and Biff had scarcely reached the straightaway beyond when they heard a thunderous sound back of them.

"What's that?" Joe cried out.

Biff turned to look over his shoulder. "A landslide!" he shouted.

Rocks and dirt, loosened by recent heavy rainstorms, were tumbling down the steep hillside at terrific speed.

"Frank!" Joe cried out in horror. He jammed on his brake and disengaged the engine. As he ran back to warn his brother, Joe saw that he was too late. Biff had rushed up and both could only stare helplessly, their hearts sinking.

Frank and Chet came around the corner at good speed and ran full tilt into the landslide. Its rumbling sound had been drowned out by the pounding surf and their own roaring motor.

The two boys, the motorcycle, and the telescope were bowled over by the falling rocks and earth. As the rain of debris finally stopped, Joe and Biff reached their sides.

"Frank! Chet!" they cried out in unison. "Are you hurt?"

Frank, then Chet, sat up slowly. Aside from looking a bit dazed, they seemed to be all right. "Rock just missed my head," Frank said finally.

"I got a mean wallop on my shoulder," Chet panted gingerly, rubbing the sore spot.

"You fellows were lucky," Biff spoke up, and Joe nodded his intense relief.

"How about the telescope?" Frank asked quickly. "Take a look at it, will you, Joe?"

The battered carrying case, pushed out of the straps which had held it in place on the motorcycle, lay in the road, covered with stone and dirt. Joe opened the heavily lined box and carefully examined the telescope.

"It looks all right to me," he said in a relieved voice. "Of course we won't know for sure until we try other eyepieces in it. But at least nothing looks broken."

By this time Frank and Chet were standing up and Biff remarked, "While you two are getting your breath, Joe and I can take the biggest rocks out of the way. Some motorist may come speeding along here and break his neck or wreck his car unless this place gets cleaned up."

"Oh, I'm okay," Chet insisted. "The rock that hit me felt just like Bender, that big end on the Milton High team. He's hit me many a time the same way."

Frank, too, declared that he felt no ill effects. Together, the boys flung rock after rock into the field between the road and the water and, in pairs, carried the heavier rocks out of the way.

"Guess we're all set now," Frank spoke up. "Biff, I'm afraid you're going to be late getting home." He chuckled. "Who is she?"

Biff reddened a little. "How'd you guess? I have a date tonight with Sally Sanderson. But she's a good sport. She won't mind waiting a little longer."

Again the four boys straddled the motorcycles

and started off. A few minutes later a noise out in the ocean attracted Frank's attention and he peered across the rolling sweep of waters. A powerful speedboat came into view around the base of a small cliff about a quarter mile out. It was followed at a short distance by a similar, but larger craft. Both boats were traveling at high speed.

"Looks like a race!" Joe called out. "Let's watch it!"

The Hardys ran their motorcycles behind a clump of trees and stopped, then walked down to the shore line.

The boats did not appear to be having a friendly speed contest, however. The first boat was zigzagging in a peculiar manner, and the pursuing craft was rapidly overtaking it.

"See! That second boat is trying to stop the other one!" Frank exclaimed.

"It sure is. Wonder what's up," said Joe tensely. "I wish that telescope was working. Can any of you fellows make out the names on the boats?"

"No," the others chorused.

The two men standing in the bow of the pursuing craft were waving their arms frantically. The first boat turned as if about to head toward the shore. Then, apparently, the helmsman changed his mind, for at once the nose of his boat was pointed out into the ocean again.

But the moment of hesitation had given the

pursuers the chance they needed. Swiftly the gap between the racing craft grew smaller and smaller until the boats were running side by side. They were so close together that a collision seemed imminent.

"They'll all be killed if they aren't careful!" Frank muttered as he watched intently.

The lone man in the foremost craft was bent over the wheel. In the boat behind, one of the two men suddenly raised his right arm high. A moment later he hurled an object through the air. It landed in back of the engine housing in the center of the craft. At the same time the larger boat sped off seaward.

"What was that?" Chet asked. "I—"

Suddenly a sheet of flame leaped high into the air from the smaller boat. There was a stunning explosion and a dense cloud of smoke rose in the air. Bits of wreckage were thrown high and in the midst of it the boys saw the occupant hurled into the water.

Swiftly the whole boat caught fire. The flames raced from bow to stern.

"That man!" shouted Frank. "He's alive!"

The boys could see him struggling in the surf, trying to swim ashore.

"He'll never make it!" Joe gasped. "He's all in."

"We've got to save him!" Frank cried out.

CHAPTER IV

The Rescue

THE Hardy boys knew that they had no time to lose. It was evident that the man in the water had been injured by the explosion and could not swim much longer.

"We'll never reach him!" Chet said, as the four boys dashed across the rocks and grass to the shore.

Suddenly Frank cried out, "I see a rowboat up on the beach." His sharp eyes had detected a large rowboat almost completely hidden in a small cove at the bottom of the cliff. "We'd make better time in that!"

A huge rock jutting out of the water cut the cove off from the open part of the beach.

"We'd have to go up to that ridge and then down," Joe objected. "I'll swim out."

"I will too," said Biff.

The two plunged into the water and struck out for the stricken man.

Meanwhile, Frank and Chet sped up the slope, cut across a strip of grass, and began running down the embankment toward the rowboat.

"That man's still afloat," Frank shouted as he looked out over the water.

Joe and Biff were making good time but were a long way from the man, who seemed now to be drifting with the outgoing tide. The explosion victim, fortunately, had managed to seize a piece of wreckage and was hanging onto it.

Slipping and scrambling, Frank and Chet made their way down the slope. Rocks rolled and tumbled ahead of them. But finally they reached the bottom safely and examined the boat. It was battered and old, but evidently still seaworthy. There were two sets of oars.

"Grab hold!" Frank directed Chet.

The boys pulled the boat across the pebbles and into the water. Swiftly they fixed the oars in the locks and took their places. Pulling hard, Frank and Chet rowed toward the distressed swimmer. Presently they overtook Joe and Biff, who clambered aboard. The man had seen the boys and called feebly to them to hurry.

"Faster!" Joe urged. "He looks as if he'll go under any second!"

The motorboat in the background was still

blazing fiercely, flames shooting high in the air. The craft was plainly doomed.

The boys pulled harder and the rowboat leaped across the water. When it was only a few yards away from the man, he suddenly let go his hold on the bit of wreckage and slipped beneath the waves.

"He's drowning!" Chet shouted, as he bent to his oar again.

Joe made a tremendously long, outward dive and disappeared into the water where the man had gone down. Frank and Chet rowed the boat to the spot and leaned over the side to peer down.

Just then, Joe and the stranger broke the surface of the water, with the boy holding an arm under the man's shoulders. His head sagged.

"He's unconscious!" Biff whispered hoarsely, as he helped pull the victim into the boat. The man sprawled helplessly on the bottom, more dead than alive.

"We'd better revive him and get him to the hospital," said Frank.

He applied artificial respiration, forcing a little water from the man's lungs, but the stranger did not regain consciousness.

"I think he collapsed from exhaustion," Joe spoke up.

Frank and Chet took off their jackets and wrapped them around the wet figure.

"How about taking him to that farmhouse over there—along the road?" Chet suggested.

The others agreed. As Frank and Chet rowed toward the farm, the boys discussed the mystery. Who was the victim of the explosion and why had the men in the other motorboat tried to kill him?

The man they had rescued lay face downward in the bottom of the boat. He was a slim, dark-haired man with sharp, clean-cut features, and his clothes were cheap and worn. Biff looked in his pockets for identification but found none.

"Wonder if he's a local man," Joe said. "Never saw him around town."

The other boys declared they never had either.

By this time the boat was close to shore. Joe and Biff leaped out and dragged it part way up on the beach. Then the four boys carried the unconscious man up the rocky shore toward the farmhouse.

At their approach a plump woman came hurrying out of the house. From the orchard nearby a burly man in overalls came forward.

"My goodness! What has happened?" the woman asked, running toward them.

"We just pulled this man out of the water," Frank explained. "We saw your house—"

"Bring him in," boomed the farmer. "Bring him right in."

The woman ran ahead and held the door

open. The boys carried the stranger into the house and laid him on a bed in the comfortably furnished first-floor bedroom. The farmer's wife hastened to the kitchen to prepare a hot drink.

"Rub his ankles and wrists, and get those wet clothes off him," the farmer told the boys. "That will step up his circulation. I'll get him some pajamas."

"How about calling a doctor?" Frank asked.

"No need. He'll be okay," the farmer declared.

The victim was soon under the covers. Frank and Joe continued to massage his wrists and ankles.

At last the stranger stirred feebly. His eyelids fluttered. His lips moved, but no words came. Then his eyes opened and the man stared at those around him, as though in a daze.

"Where am I?" he muttered faintly.

"You're safe," Frank assured him. "You're with friends."

"You saved me?"

"Yes."

"Pretty near—cashed in—didn't I?"

"You nearly drowned, but you're all right now. When you feel like talking, you can tell us the whole story," said Frank. "But, in the meantime, we'll call the police or the Coast Guard and report those men who tried to murder you."

The man in the bed blinked and looked out the

window. Finally he said, "No, no. Don't do that."

The boys were shocked. "Why not?" Joe burst out.

The man was thoughtfully silent for a moment, then said, "Thanks, but I'd rather let matters stand as they are. I'll take care of it as soon as I get my strength back." The rescued man turned to the farmer. "Okay with you if I stay here overnight? I'll pay you, of course."

The farmer put out his hand. "The name's Kane and you're welcome to stay until you feel strong. Nobody can say I ever turned a sick man away. And what's your name?"

The patient hesitated a moment. "Jones. Bill Jones," he said at last.

It was so evidently a false name that the Hardys glanced knowingly at each other. Mr. Kane did not seem to realize that his guest was apparently trying to hide his identity.

Mrs. Kane appeared with hot broth and toast. She suggested that her husband and the boys let the patient rest for a while. When she joined them in the living room she invited the boys to have a snack. Chet readily accepted for all of them.

The snack consisted of sandwiches of home-cured ham with cheese, glasses of fresh milk, and rich lemon pie, frothy with meringue. Chet beamed. "Mrs. Kane, you ought to open a restaurant. I'd be a steady customer. You're the best pie maker I've ever met."

Frank, Joe, and Biff chuckled. How often they had heard their stout, food-loving chum make similar remarks! But in this case they had to agree with him and told Mrs. Kane so.

She smiled. "It's the least I can do for you boys who just saved someone's life."

Her young guests said nothing of their early afternoon's adventure inside the Pollitt house, but Frank casually asked the Kanes if they had known the deceased owner and if anyone were living there now.

"Sure I knew Felix Pollitt," the farmer replied. "Closemouthed old codger, but I did hear him once say somethin' about havin' a no-good nephew. Pollitt said he was his only livin' relative and he supposed he'd have to leave the property to him."

"But who'd want the place?" Mrs. Kane spoke up. "It's falling apart and would cost a mint of money to fix up."

Joe grinned. "Sounds like a haunted house," he remarked pointedly.

"Funny you should say that." Mrs. Kane looked at Joe. "There was a family stopped here the other day. Wanted to buy some eggs. One of the little girls said they'd had a terrible scare. They'd stopped at the old Pollitt place to have a picnic, and were scared out of their wits by moans and groans and queer laughs from the house."

Mr. Kane's face broke into a grin. "The kid's imagination sure was runnin' away with itself."

"I'm not so sure of that," his wife disagreed. "I think some boys were in there playing pranks."

After Frank and Joe and their friends had left the farmhouse, they discussed the strange noises at the Pollitt place from this new angle.

Biff frowned. "If those ghosts are from Bayport High, they'll sure have the laugh on us," he remarked.

"They sure will," Chet agreed. "I'd hate to face them on Monday."

Frank and Joe were not convinced. After they had dropped their chums at the Morton and Hooper homes, they discussed the day's strange and varied adventures all the way to the Hardy house.

"I'm sure that ghost business was meant to be something more than a prank," Frank stated.

"Right," his brother agreed. "I just had an idea, Frank. Maybe nobody was in the house, but he could have rigged up a tape recorder to make those sounds and a remote control to start it. What say we go back sometime and take a look?"

"I'm with you."

By this time the boys had turned into the long driveway of the Hardy home, a spacious, three-story clapboard house on the corner of High and Elm streets. The large two-story garage at the rear of an attractive garden had once been a barn.

Frank and Joe parked their motorcycles, unstrapped the telescope, and carried it to the back porch. As they entered the kitchen, they found their mother, a pretty, sweet-faced woman, with sparkling blue eyes, preparing supper.

"Hello, boys," she greeted them. "Did you have a good day? See any smugglers?"

They kissed her and Frank said, "We have a lot to tell you and Dad."

"He's in the study upstairs. I'll go up with you right away and we can talk while the chicken's roasting and the potatoes baking."

The three hurried up to the room where Mr. Hardy was busy looking in a large metal file in which he kept important records. The detective stopped his work and listened with rapt attention as Frank and Joe gave a detailed account of their adventures.

"We sure fell for that cry for help," Joe explained. "I'm sorry about the stolen eyepieces from the telescope."

"And I hope it wasn't damaged when I had my spill," Frank added. He smiled wanly. "You'll probably want to dismiss us from your detective force."

"Nothing of the kind," his father said. "But

now, let's discuss what you saw through the telescope. You said you spotted a man who climbed down the ladder of a boat and went off in a smaller one. Could he have been this same fellow who calls himself Jones?"

"We couldn't identify him," Joe replied, "but he might be."

Frank snapped his fingers. "Yes, and he could be one of the smugglers."

"But who threw that hand grenade at him?" Joe asked. "Not one of his own gang, surely. And those guys in the other speedboat—they couldn't have been Coast Guard men, even in disguise. They wouldn't use grenades."

"Joe's right on the second point," Mr. Hardy agreed. "But Jones may still be a smuggler."

"You mean he might have done something to make his boss mad and the boss sent out a couple of men to get him?" Joe asked.

The detective nodded. "If this theory is right, and we can persuade Jones to talk before he either rejoins the gang or starts trying to take revenge, then we might get him to turn state's evidence."

The boys were excited. Both jumped from their chairs and Joe cried out eagerly, "Let's go talk to him right away! By morning he'll be gone!"

CHAPTER V

Pretzel Pete

"Just a minute!" Mrs. Hardy said to her sons. "How about supper?"

"We can eat when we come back from our interview with Jones," Joe answered. "Mother, he may decide to leave the farmhouse any time."

Despairingly Mrs. Hardy returned to her husband. "What do you think, Fenton?"

The detective gave his wife an understanding smile, then turned to Frank and Joe. "Didn't you say Jones was in pretty bad shape?"

"Yes, Dad," Frank replied.

"Then I doubt very much that he'll try to leave the Kanes' home before the time he set—tomorrow morning. I'm sure that it'll be safe for us to eat Mother's good supper and still see our man in time."

Joe subsided, and to make his mother feel better, said with a smile, "Guess I let this mystery go to my brain for a minute. As a matter of fact, I have an empty space inside of me big enough to eat two suppers!"

Mrs. Hardy tweaked an ear of her energetic son, just as she had frequently done ever since he was a small boy. He smiled at her affectionately, then asked what he could do to help with supper.

"Well, suppose you fill the water glasses and get milk for you and Frank," Mrs. Hardy said, as she and Joe went downstairs together.

At the table, as often happened at meals in the Hardy home, the conversation revolved around the mystery. Frank asked his father if he had made any progress on his part in the case concerning the smugglers.

"Very little," the detective replied. "Snattman is a slippery individual. He covers his tracks well. I did find this out, though. The law firm which is handling old Mr. Pollitt's affairs has had no luck in locating the nephew to whom the property was left."

"Mr. Kane said he'd heard Mr. Pollitt call his nephew a no-good," Frank put in.

"That's just the point," Mr. Hardy said. "The lawyers learned from the police that he's a hoodlum and is wanted for burglary."

Frank whistled. "That puts the nephew in a

bad spot, doesn't it? If he shows up to claim the property, he'll be nabbed as a criminal."

"Exactly," Mr. Hardy answered.

"What will become of the property?" Joe queried.

His father said he thought the executors might let the house remain vacant or they might possibly rent it. "They could do this on a month-to-month basis. This would give added income to the estate."

"Which wouldn't do the nephew much good if he were in jail," Mrs. Hardy put in.

"That would depend on how long his sentence was," her husband said. "He may not be a dangerous criminal. He may just have fallen into bad company and unwittingly become an accessory in some holdup or burglary."

"In that case," Frank remarked, "he may realize that he wouldn't have to stay in prison long. He may appear to claim the property, take his punishment, and then lead a normal, law-abiding life out at his uncle's place."

"Well, I sincerely hope so," Mr. Hardy replied. "The trouble is, so often when a young man joins a group of hoodlums or racketeers, he's blackmailed for the rest of his life, even though he tries to go straight." The detective smiled. "The best way to avoid such a situation is never to get into it!"

At this moment the phone rang and Frank went to answer it. "It's for you, Dad!" he called, coming back to the table.'

Mr. Hardy spent nearly fifteen minutes in conversation with the caller. In the meantime, the boys and Mrs. Hardy finished their supper. Then, while Mr. Hardy ate his dessert, he told his family a little about the information he had just received on the phone.

"More drugs have disappeared," he said tersely. "I'm positive now that Snattman is behind all this."

"Were the drugs stolen around here?" Frank asked.

"We don't know," his father answered. "A pharmaceutical house in the Midwest was expecting a shipment of rare drugs from India. When the package arrived, only half the order was there. It was evident that someone had cleverly opened the package, removed part of the shipment, and replaced the wrapping so neatly that neither the customs officials nor the post office was aware that the package had been tampered with."

"How were the drugs sent to this country?" Joe queried.

"They came by ship."

"To which port?"

"New York. But the ship did stop at Bayport."

"How long ago was this?"

"Nearly two months ago. It seems that the pharmaceutical house wasn't ready to use the drugs until now, so hadn't opened the package."

"Then," said Joe, "the drugs could have been removed right on the premises, and have had nothing to do with smugglers."

"You're right," Mr. Hardy agreed. "Each time drugs are reported missing, there's a new angle to the case. Although I'm convinced Snattman is back of it, how to prove this is really a stickler."

Mr. Hardy went on to say that the tip he had received about Snattman being in the Bayport area had been a very reliable one. He smiled. "I'll tell you all a little secret. I have a very good friend down on the waterfront. He picks up many kinds of information for me. His name is Pretzel Pete."

"Pretzel Pete!" Frank and Joe cried out. "What a name!"

"That's his nickname along the waterfront," Mr. Hardy told them. He laughed. "During the past few years I've munched on so many of the pretzels he sells, I think I'm his best customer."

By this time the boys' father had finished his dessert, and he suggested they leave at once for the Kane farmhouse. He brought his black sedan from the garage and the boys hopped in. It did not take long to cover the six miles to the place where Jones was spending the night.

"Why, the house is dark," Frank remarked, puzzled.

"Maybe everyone's asleep," Joe suggested.

"*This* early?" Frank protested.

Mr. Hardy continued on down the lane. There was no sign of anyone around the place. Frank remarked that perhaps the farmer and his wife had gone out for the evening. "But I'm surprised that they would leave Jones alone in his condition," he added.

"I'm quite sure they wouldn't," his father averred. "If they're asleep, I'm afraid we'll have to wake them."

He pulled up in front of the kitchen entrance. Frank was out of the car in an instant, the others followed. He rapped on the door. There was no answer.

"Let's try the front door," Joe suggested. "Maybe that has a knocker on it."

The boys walked around to the ocean side of the house. Although they banged loudly with the brass door knocker, there was still no response.

"The Kanes must have gone out," said Joe.

"But what about Jones? Surely he's here."

"And too weak to come to the door," Frank surmised. "But he *could* call out. I can't understand it."

The brothers returned to the back door and reported to their father. Then, as Joe rapped several more times without response, a sinking feeling came over the brothers.

"I guess Jones recovered fast and has gone," Joe said dejectedly. "We've goofed."

"Try the knob. The door may not be locked," Mr. Hardy ordered. From his tone the boys knew that he shared their fears.

Frank turned the knob and the door swung open. Mr. Hardy felt around for a light switch on the wall.

"We'll go in," he murmured. "If Jones is here we'll talk to him."

By this time the detective had found the switch. As the kitchen became flooded with light, the boys gasped, thunderstruck. On their previous visit they had been impressed by the neatness of the room. Now the place looked as though an earthquake had shaken it.

Pots and pans were scattered about the floor. The table was overturned. A chair lay upside down in a corner. Shattered bits of cups and saucers were strewn on the floor.

"What happened?" Frank exclaimed in bewilderment.

"There's been a fight—or a struggle of some kind," said Mr. Hardy. "Let's see what the rest of the house looks like."

The boys opened the door to the adjoining living room. Frank snapped on the wall switch.

The farmer and his wife were bound and gagged

There a horrifying sight met the Hardys' eyes.

The farmer and his wife, bound and gagged, were tied to chairs in the middle of the room!

Swiftly Frank, Joe, and their father rushed over to Mr. and Mrs. Kane. They had been tied with strong ropes and so well gagged that the couple had been unable to utter a sound. In a minute the Hardys had loosened the bonds and removed the gags.

"Thank goodness!" Mrs. Kane exclaimed with a sigh of relief, stretching her arms.

Her husband, spluttering with rage, rose from his chair and hurled the ropes to one side. "Those scoundrels!" he cried out.

Frank hastily introduced his father, then asked, "What happened?"

For several moments Mr. and Mrs. Kane were too upset to tell their story. But finally the farmer staggered over to the window and pointed down the shore road.

"They went that way!" he roared. "Follow them!"

"Who?"

"Those thugs who tied us up! They took Jones!"

CHAPTER VI

The Strange Message

"How long ago did those kidnapers leave?" Frank asked the Kanes quickly.

"About ten minutes," replied the farmer. "Maybe you can catch them if you hurry!"

"Come on, Dad!" Frank cried. "Let's go after them!"

Mr. Hardy needed no further urging. He and his sons ran out of the house and jumped into the car.

"That's rough stuff," Joe said to his father as they turned onto the shore road, "barging into a house, tying up the owners, and kidnaping a guy!"

"Yes," Mr. Hardy agreed. "It looks as though your friend Jones *is* mixed up in some kind of racket. Those men must have been pretty desperate to risk breaking into an occupied house."

The boys' father was able to follow the tracks of the car from the tread marks in the dusty road. But soon there were signs that another car had turned onto the shore road from a side lane and the trail became confused.

The Hardys passed the lane that led into the Pollitt place and continued on until they came to a hilltop. Here they could get a clear view of the road winding along the coast for several miles. There was no sign of a car.

"We've lost them, I guess," said Frank in disappointment, as Mr. Hardy brought the sedan to a stop.

"They had too much of a head start," Joe remarked. "If only we'd gotten to the farm sooner. Well, we may as well go back."

Mr. Hardy agreed, turned the car around, and once more the Hardys headed for the farm. On the way they discussed the mysterious kidnaping, and speculated on the identity of those responsible.

"I'll bet those men in the other motorboat saw us rescue Jones, or else they heard somehow that he'd been taken to the farmhouse," Joe surmised.

"If they *are* the kidnapers, I wonder what will happen to Jones now," Frank said gravely. "They tried to kill him once."

"Maybe they'll just hold him prisoner," Mr. Hardy stated thoughtfully. "They were probably afraid he'd tell all he knew, and couldn't afford to leave him at the farmhouse."

When they got back to the Kanes', they found the farmer and his wife somewhat recovered from their harrowing experience. Mrs. Kane was busy straightening up the kitchen.

"We couldn't catch them," Frank reported sadly.

"Well, those hoodlums had a high-powered car and they weren't wastin' any time. I could see 'em from the window as they went down the lane," the farmer remarked, frowning angrily at the recollection.

"Please tell us exactly what happened, Mr. Kane," Joe urged.

"Well, Mabel and I were here in the kitchen," the man began. "Mabel was washin' the supper dishes when this fellow came to the door. He was a tall chap with a long, thin face."

"He asked us if we were looking after the man that was almost drowned earlier," the farmer's wife took up the tale. "When we said we were, the fellow told us that Mr. Jones was his brother and he had come to take him away."

"I got suspicious," Mr. Kane broke in. "He didn't look nothin' like Jones. I asked him where he lived."

"At that," Mrs. Kane said, "he walked in the house with another fellow right at his heels.

They grabbed my husband. Henry put up an awful good fight but he was outnumbered. When I tried to help, a third man appeared from nowhere and held me back."

"They dragged us into the livin' room, tied us to those chairs, and put the gags in our mouths," the farmer continued. "Then we heard 'em goin' into Jones's room. Pretty soon they carried him out to a car where a fourth fellow was sittin' at the wheel."

"Did Jones put up a fight when they took him away?" Frank asked.

"He tried to. He hollered for help, but of course I couldn't do anythin' and he was too weak to struggle much."

"This whole affair is very peculiar," Mr. Hardy observed. "Perhaps Jones is mixed up in the smuggling going on around here. But who were those four men, I wonder?"

Mrs. Kane shook her head. "All I know is, we're sure glad you and your sons came out tonight. There's no telling how long we'd have been tied up before somebody found us!"

"We're glad, too, that we got here," Frank replied.

"You folks say your name's Hardy?" said the farmer. "Any relation to Fenton Hardy?"

"Right here." The detective smiled.

"Pleasure to know you!" exclaimed Kane

heartily, putting out his hand. "If anyone can get to the bottom of this business, you can."

"I'll certainly try," the boys' father promised.

The Hardys bade the farmer and his wife good-by. They promised to call again at the Kane farm as soon as they had any further information, and Mr. Kane, in turn, said he would notify them if he found any trace of Jones or his kidnapers.

When they returned home the boys followed their father into his study.

"What do you make of all this, Dad?" Joe asked.

Mr. Hardy sat down at his desk. He closed his eyes and leaned back in his chair a few moments without speaking.

"I have only one theory," he said at last. "The kidnapers probably are Snattman's friends. That means you boys may have uncovered the fact that there is a whole gang of smugglers around here."

The brothers were pleased with their progress. "What do we do next, Dad?" Joe asked eagerly.

"I want to evaluate this case from every angle," their father replied. "I'll think about it and talk to you later." With this the boys had to be content for the rest of the week end.

When the brothers came downstairs Monday morning, Mrs. Hardy was putting their breakfast on the table.

In answer to the boys' inquiries, she replied, "Your father went out early this morning in his car. He didn't say when he would return. But your dad didn't take a bag with him, so he'll probably be back today." Mrs. Hardy was accustomed to her husband's comings and goings at odd hours in connection with his profession and she had learned not to ask questions.

Frank and Joe were disappointed. They had looked forward to resuming a discussion of the case with their father.

"I guess we're left on our own again to try finding out something about those smugglers," Frank remarked, and Joe agreed.

Later, when they reached Bayport High School, the brothers saw Iola Morton standing on the front steps. With pretty, dark-haired Iola was her best friend Callie Shaw. Callie, a blond, vivacious, brown-eyed girl, was Frank's favorite among all the girls in his class.

"How are the ghost hunters this morning?" she asked with a mischievous smile. "Iola told me about your adventures on Saturday."

"Chet was really scared," Iola chimed in. "I think somebody played a good joke on all of you."

"Well, whoever it was had better return the telescope eyepieces and our motorcycle tools," Joe said defiantly.

But as the day wore on and none of their classmates teased them or brought up the subject, the Hardys became convinced that the "ghost" had been serious and not just playing pranks.

"It was no joke," Joe said to Frank on the way home. "If any of the fellows at school had done it, they'd have been kidding us plenty by now."

"Right," Frank agreed. "Joe, do you think the smugglers had anything to do with what happened at the Pollitt place?"

"That's a thought!" exclaimed Joe. "That house on the cliff would be a great hide-out. If the smugglers could make the house appear to be haunted, everyone would stay away."

"I wish Dad would get home, so we could take up this idea with him," Frank said thoughtfully.

But Mr. Hardy did not come home that day. He had often been away for varying lengths of time without sending word, but on this occasion, since he had not taken a bag, the boys felt uneasy.

"Let's not worry Mother about this," Frank said. "But if Dad's not back by Wednesday—at the latest—I think we should do some inquiring. Maybe Pretzel Pete will be able to help us."

Joe agreed. Wednesday was the start of their summer vacation and they could give full time to trying to locate their father.

On Tuesday afternoon the mystery of Mr. Hardy's absence took a strange turn. Frank and Joe came home from school to find their mother seated in the living room, carefully examining a note that she evidently just had received.

"Come here, boys," Mrs. Hardy said in an apprehensive tone. "Look at this and tell me what you think." She handed the note to Frank.

"What is it?" he asked quickly. "Word from Dad?"

"It's supposed to be."

The boys read the note. It was typed on a torn sheet of paper and the signature looked like Fenton Hardy's. It read:

I won't be home for several days. Don't worry. Fenton.

That was all. There was nothing to indicate where the detective was; nothing to show when the note had been written.

"When did you get this, Mother?" asked Frank.

"It came in the afternoon mail. It was addressed to me, and the envelope had a Bayport postmark."

"Why are you worried?" Joe asked. "At least we've heard from Dad."

"But I'm not sure he sent the note."

"What do you mean?"

"Your father and I have an agreement. Whenever he writes me, he puts a secret sign beneath his signature. Fenton was always afraid that someone would forge his name to a letter or note, and perhaps get papers or information that he shouldn't have."

Frank picked up the note again. "There's no sign here. Just Dad's signature."

"It *may* be his signature. If not, it's a very good forgery." Mrs. Hardy was plainly worried.

"If Dad didn't write this note," Joe asked, "who did and why?"

"Your father has many enemies—criminals whom he has been instrumental in sending to prison. If there has been foul play, the note might have been sent to keep us from being suspicious and delay any search."

"Foul play!" exclaimed Frank in alarm. "Then you think something has happened to Dad?"

CHAPTER VII

The Hidden Trail

JOE put an arm around his mother. "Frank and I will start a search for Dad first thing tomorrow," her son said reassuringly.

Next morning, as the boys were dressing, Joe asked, "Where shall we start, Frank?"

"Down at the waterfront. Let's try to find Pretzel Pete and ask him if Dad talked to him on Monday. He may give us a lead."

"Good idea."

The brothers reached the Bayport waterfront early. It was the scene of great activity. A tanker was unloading barrels of oil, and longshoremen were trundling them to waiting trucks.

At another dock a passenger ship was tied up. Porters hurried about, carrying luggage and packages to a line of taxicabs.

Many sailors strolled along the busy street.

Some stepped into restaurants, others into amusement galleries.

"I wonder where Pretzel Pete is," Frank mused. He and Joe had walked four blocks without catching sight of the man.

"Maybe he's not wearing his uniform," Joe surmised. "You know, the one Dad described."

"Let's turn and go back the other way beyond the tanker," Frank suggested.

The boys reversed their direction and made their way through the milling throng for six more blocks.

Suddenly Joe chuckled. "Here comes our man."

Strolling toward them and hawking the product he had for sale came a comical-looking individual. He wore a white cotton suit with a very loose-fitting coat. Around his neck was a vivid red silk handkerchief, embroidered with anchors.

The vendor's trousers had been narrowed at the cuff with bicycle clips to keep them from trailing on the ground, with the result that there was a continuous series of wrinkles from the edge of his coat to his ankles.

The man wore a white hat which came down to his ears. On the wide brown band the name *Pretzel Pete* was embroidered in white letters.

"Boy, that's some gear!" Frank murmured.

Pretzel Pete's garb was bizarre, but he had an

open, honest face. He stopped calling "Pretzels! Hot pretzels! Best in the land!" and smiled at the Hardys. He set down the large metal food warmer he carried. From the top of it rose three short aerials, each ringed with a dozen pretzels.

"You like them hot, or do you prefer them cold?" he asked the brothers.

Joe grinned. "If they're good, I can eat them any way." Then he whispered, "We're Mr. Fenton Hardy's sons. We'd like to talk to you."

At that moment a group of sailors brushed past. Pretzel Pete did not reply until they were out of earshot, then he said to the boys, "Come into this warehouse."

The brothers followed him down the street a short distance and through a doorway into an enormous room which at the moment was practically empty.

"You've brought a message from your pop?" the vendor asked.

Quickly Frank explained to him that their father seemed to be missing. "We thought you might have heard this."

"Yes, I did," Pretzel Pete answered. "But I didn't think nothing about it. I always thought detectives disappeared—sometimes in order to fool people they were after."

"They sometimes do," Joe told him. "But this time seems to be different. Dad said he often came

down here to get information from you—because
you always give him good tips—and we wondered
if you had seen him lately."

"Yes."

"When?"

"Monday morning."

"Dad has been gone ever since."

"Hmm." The man frowned, picked up a pretzel from one of the aerials, and began to munch
on it. "Help yourselves, fellows."

Frank and Joe each took one of the pretzels.
They had just bitten into the delicious salted
rings when Pete continued, "Now you got me
worried. Your pop's a fine man and I wouldn't
want to see anything happen to him. I'll tell you
a place you might look for him."

Pretzel Pete said that he had picked up a bit
of information that led him to think an East Indian sailor named Ali Singh might be engaged in
some smuggling. The vendor did not know what
ship he sailed on, but he understood that the man
had come ashore for a secret meeting of some gang.

"This here meeting," Pretzel Pete explained,
"was being held out in the country somewhere
off the shore road. It was to be in a deserted farmhouse on Hillcrest something or other. I don't
remember whether it was 'road' or 'street' or
what."

"Was this last Monday?" Frank asked eagerly.

"Oh, no," the vendor answered. "This was about three weeks ago, but when I told your pop he seemed real interested and said he guessed he'd go out there and look around."

Joe broke in, "Dad must have thought the rest of the gang might be living there. Maybe they're holding him a prisoner!"

"Oh, I hope not," Pretzel Pete said worriedly. "But you fellows had better get right out there and take a look."

"We certainly will," Frank told the man.

The brothers thanked Pretzel Pete for the information, then hurried home. Mrs. Hardy was not there, so they did not have a chance to tell her about their plans.

"We'll leave a note," Frank decided and quickly wrote one.

Their hopes high, the brothers set off on their motorcycles on the search for their father. By now they were very familiar with the shore road but did not recall having seen any sign reading Hillcrest.

"Suppose it's not marked," said Joe. "We'll never find it."

Frank gripped his handle bars hard. "If Dad found it, we won't give up until we do."

The motorcycles chugged past side road after side road. The farther away from Bayport the boys went, the farther apart these roads became.

After a while they came to the Kanes' farmhouse and were tempted to stop to see if they might know where Hillcrest was. But just then, a short distance ahead, Joe saw a small car suddenly turn into the shore road. It seemed to have come right out of a clump of bushes and trees.

"Come on, Frank! Let's investigate that place."

The boys pushed ahead, hoping to speak to the driver of the car. But he shot down the road in the opposite direction at terrific speed. When Frank and Joe reached the place from which he had just emerged, they saw that it was a road, though hardly noticeable to anyone passing by.

"I'll take a look and see where it goes," Frank said, shutting off his motorcycle and walking up the grassy, rutted lane. Suddenly he called back, "We're in luck, Joe. I see a homemade sign on a tree. It says Hillcrest Road."

Frank returned to his brother and the boys trundled their machines up among the trees to hide them. Then they set off afoot along the almost impassable woods road.

"There aren't any tire tracks," Joe remarked. "I guess that fellow who drove out of here must have left his car down at the entrance."

Frank nodded, and then in a low tone suggested that they approach the deserted farmhouse very quietly, in case members of the gang were there.

"In fact, I think it might be better if we didn't stay on this road but went through the woods."

Joe agreed and silently the Hardys picked their way along among the trees and through the undergrowth. Five minutes later they came to a clearing in which stood a ramshackle farmhouse. It looked as if it had been abandoned for many years.

The young sleuths stood motionless, observing the run-down building intently. There was not a sound of activity either inside or outside the place. After the boys had waited several minutes, Frank decided to find out whether or not anyone was around. Picking up a large stone, he heaved it with precision aim at the front door. It struck with a resounding thud and dropped to the floor of the sagging porch.

Frank's action brought no response and finally he said to Joe, "I guess nobody's home. Let's look in."

"Right," Joe agreed. "And if Dad's a prisoner there, we'll rescue him!"

The boys walked across the clearing. There was no lock on the door, so they opened it and went inside. The place consisted of only four first-floor rooms. All were empty. A tiny cellar and a loft with a trap door reached by a ladder also proved to have no one in them.

"I don't know whether to be glad or sorry Dad's

not here," said Frank. "It could mean he escaped from the gang if he *was* caught by them and is safely in hiding, but can't send any word to us."

"Or it could mean he's still a captive some-where else," Joe said. "Let's look around here for clues."

The boys made a systematic search of the place. They found only one item which might prove to be helpful. It was a torn piece of a turkish towel on which the word *Polo* appeared.

"This could have come from some country club where they play polo," Frank figured.

"Or some stable where polo ponies are kept," Joe suggested.

Puzzled, Frank put the scrap in his pocket and the brothers walked down Hillcrest Road. They brought their motorcycles from behind the trees and climbed aboard.

"What do you think we should do next?" Joe asked.

"See Police Chief Collig in Bayport," Frank replied. "I think we should show him this towel. Maybe he can identify it."

Half an hour later they were seated in the chief's office. The tall, burly man took a great in-terest in the Hardy boys and often worked with Fenton Hardy on his cases. Now Chief Collig gazed at the scrap of toweling for a full minute, then slapped his desk.

"I have it!" he exclaimed. "That's a piece of towel from the *Marco Polo!*"

"What's that?"

"A passenger ship that ties up here once in a while."

Frank and Joe actually jumped in their chairs. Their thoughts went racing to Ali Singh, smugglers, a gang at the deserted farmhouse!

At that moment Chief Collig's phone rang. The Hardys waited politely as he answered, hoping to discuss these new developments with him. But suddenly he put down the instrument, jumped up, and said:

"Emergency, fellows. Have to leave right away!" With that he rushed out of his office.

Frank and Joe arose and disappointedly left headquarters. Returning home, they reported everything to their mother, but upon seeing how forlorn she looked, Frank said hopefully, "That note you received with Dad's name on it *could* have been on the level."

Mrs. Hardy shook her head. "Fenton wouldn't forget the secret sign. I just know he wouldn't."

Word quickly spread through Bayport that the famous Fenton Hardy had disappeared. Early the next morning a thick-set, broad-shouldered young man presented himself at the front door of the Hardy home and said he had something to tell them. Mrs. Hardy invited him to step inside and he stood in the hall, nervously twisting a cap in his hands. As Frank and Joe appeared, the man introduced himself as Sam Bates.

"I'm a truck driver," he told them. "The reason I came around to see you is because I heard you were lookin' for Mr. Hardy. I might be able to help you."

CHAPTER VIII

A Cap on a Peg

"You've seen my father?" Frank asked the truck driver.

"Well, I did see him on Monday," Sam said slowly, "but I don't know where he is now."

"Come in and sit down," Frank urged. "Tell us everything you know."

The four walked to the living room and Mr. Bates sat down uneasily in a large chair.

"Where did you see Mr. Hardy?" Mrs. Hardy asked eagerly.

But Sam Bates was not to be hurried. "I'm a truck driver, see?" he said. "Mostly I drive in Bayport but sometimes I have a run to another town. That's how I come to be out there that mornin'."

"Out where?"

"Along the shore road. I'm sure it was Monday,

because when I came home for supper my wife had been doin' the washin' and she only does that on Monday."

"That was the day Dad left!" Joe exclaimed.

"Well, please go on with the story," Frank prodded Sam Bates. "Where did you see him?"

The truck driver explained that his employer had sent him to a town down the coast to deliver some furniture. "I was about half a mile from the old Pollitt place when I saw a man walkin' along the road. I waved to him, like I always do to people in the country, and then I see it's Mr. Hardy."

"You know my father?" Frank asked.

"Only from his pictures. But I'm sure it was him."

"Dad left here in a sedan," Joe spoke up. "Did you see one around?"

"No, I didn't."

"What was this man wearing?" Mrs. Hardy asked.

"Well, let's see. Dark-brown trousers and a brown-and-black plaid sport jacket. He wasn't wearin' a hat, but I think he had a brown cap in one hand."

Mrs. Hardy's face went white. "Yes, that was my husband." After a moment she added, "Can you tell us anything more?"

"I'm afraid not, ma'am," the trucker said. "You

see, I was in kind of a hurry that mornin', so I didn't notice nothin' else." He arose to leave.

"We certainly thank you for coming to tell us, Mr. Bates," Mrs. Hardy said.

"Yes, you've given us a valuable lead," Frank added. "Now we'll know where to look for Dad."

"I sure hope he shows up," the driver said, walking toward the door. "Let me know if I can help any."

When the man had left, Joe turned to Frank, puzzled. "Do you suppose Dad hid his car and was walking to the Pollitt house? If so, why?"

"Maybe he picked up a clue at that deserted farmhouse on Hillcrest Road," Frank suggested, "and it led to the old Pollitt place. If he left his car somewhere, he must have been planning to investigate the haunted house without being seen."

"Something must have happened to him!" Joe cried out. "Frank, I'll bet he went to Pollitt's and that fake ghost got him. Let's go look for Dad right away!"

But Mrs. Hardy broke in. Her expression was firm. "I don't want you boys to go to that house alone. Maybe you'd just better notify the police and let them make a search."

The brothers looked at each other. Finally Frank, realizing how alarmed she was, said, "Mother, it's possible Dad is there spying on some activities offshore and he's all right but can't leave to phone you. The Pollitt line must have been disconnected. If Joe and I go out there and find him we can bring back a report."

Mrs. Hardy gave a wan smile. "You're very convincing, Frank, when you put it that way. All right. I'll give my permission, but you mustn't go alone."

"Why not, Mother? We can look out for ourselves," Joe insisted.

"Get some of the boys to go with you. There's safety in numbers," his mother said.

The boys agreed to this plan and got busy on the telephone rounding up their pals. Chet Morton and Biff Hooper agreed to go, and they suggested asking Tony Prito and Phil Cohen, two more of the Hardys' friends at Bayport High. Phil owned a motorcycle. He and Tony said they could go along.

Shortly after lunch the group set out. Chet rode with Frank, Biff with Joe, and Tony with Phil. The three motorcycles went out of Bayport, past the Tower Mansion, and along the shore road.

They passed the Kane farmhouse, Hillcrest Road, and at last came in sight of the steep cliff rising from Barmet Bay and crowned by the rambling frame house where Felix Pollitt had lived. All this time they had watched carefully for a sign of Mr. Hardy's car, but found none.

"Your dad hid it well," Chet remarked.

"It's possible someone stole it," Frank told him.

As the boys came closer to the Pollitt property, Phil said to Tony, "Lonely looking place, isn't it?"

"Sure is. Good haunt for a ghost."

When they were still some distance from the lane, Frank, in the lead, brought his motorcycle to a stop and signaled the other two drivers to do likewise.

"What's the matter?" Chet asked.

"We'd better sneak up on the place quietly. If we go any farther and the ghost is there, he'll hear the motorcycles. I vote we leave them here under the trees and go the rest of the way on foot."

The boys hid their machines in a clump of bushes beside the road, and then the six searchers went on toward the lane.

"We'll separate here," Frank decided. "Three of us take one side of the lane and the rest the other side. Keep to the bushes as much as possible, and when we get near the house, lay low for a while and watch the place. When I whistle, you can come out of the bushes and go up to the house."

"That's a good idea," Joe agreed. "Biff, Tony, and I will take the left side of the road."

"Okay."

The boys entered the weeds and undergrowth on either side of the lane. In a few minutes they were lost to view and only an occasional snapping and crackling of branches indicated their presence. The six sleuths crept forward, keeping well in from the lane. After about ten minutes Frank raised his hand as a warning to Chet and Phil. He had caught a glimpse of the house through the dense thicket.

They went on cautiously until they reached the edge of the bushes. From behind the screen of leaves they looked toward the old building. An expression of surprise crossed Frank's face.

"Someone's living here!" he exclaimed in astonishment.

From where the boys stood they hardly recognized the old place. Weeds that had filled the flower beds on their last visit had been completely cleared away. Leaves and twigs had been raked up and the grass cut.

A similar change had been wrought in the house. The hanging shutters had been put in place and the broken library window glass replaced.

"What do you suppose has happened?" Chet whispered.

Frank was puzzled. "Let's wait a minute before we go any farther."

The boys remained at the edge of the bushes, watching the place. A short time later a woman came out of the house carrying a basket of clothes. She walked over to a clothesline stretched between two trees and began to hang up the laundry.

Shortly afterward a man came out, and strode across the yard to a shed where he started filling a basket with logs.

The boys looked at one another in bewilderment. They had expected to find the same sinister and deserted place they had visited previously. Instead, here was a scene of domestic tranquillity.

"There's not much use in our hiding any longer," Frank whispered. "Let's go out and question these people." He gave the prearranged whistle.

The other three boys appeared, and the entire group walked boldly up the lane and across the yard. The man in the woodshed saw them first and straightened up, staring at them with an expression of annoyance. The woman at the clothesline heard their footsteps and turned to face them, her hands on her hips. Her gaunt face wore an unpleasant scowl.

"What do you want?" demanded the man, emerging from the shed.

He was short and thin with close-cropped hair, and he needed a shave. His complexion was swarthy, his eyes narrow under coarse, black brows.

At the same time another man came out of the kitchen and stood on the steps. He was stout and red-haired with a scraggly mustache.

"Yeah, who are you?" he asked.

"We didn't know anyone was living here," Frank explained, edging over to the kitchen door. He wanted to get a look inside the house if possible.

"Well, we're livin' here now," said the red-haired man, "and we don't like snoopers."

"We're not snooping," Frank declared. "We are looking for a man who has disappeared from Bayport."

"Humph!" grunted the woman.

"Why do you think he's around here?" the thin man put in.

"He was last seen in this neighborhood."

"What does he look like?"

"Tall and dark. He was wearing a brown suit and sports jacket and cap."

"There hasn't been anybody around here since we rented this place and moved in," the red-haired man said gruffly.

There seemed to be no prospect of gaining information from the unpleasant trio, so the boys started to leave. But Frank had reached the kitchen door. As he glanced in he gave a start. Hanging on a peg was a brown sports cap!

It looked exactly like the one his father owned, and which he had worn the morning that he had disappeared.

CHAPTER IX

Plan of Attack

"I'm very thirsty," Frank said quickly to the occupants of the Pollitt house. "May I have a
drink?"

The red-haired man and the woman looked at
each other. They obviously wished to get rid of
their visitors as soon as possible. But they could
not refuse such a reasonable request.

"Come into the kitchen," said the man grudgingly.

Frank followed him through the door. As he
passed the cap he took a good look at it. It *was* his
father's, and there were stains on it which looked
like blood!

The redheaded man pointed to a sink on the
other side of the room. On it stood a plastic cup.
"Help yourself," he said gruffly.

Frank went across the room and ran some water
from the faucet. As he raised the cup to his lips,

his mind was racing. On his way out he glanced again at the peg.

The cap was gone!

Frank gave no sign that he had noticed anything amiss. He walked out into the yard and joined the other five boys.

"I guess we may as well be going," he said nonchalantly.

"You might as well," snapped the woman. "There's no stranger around here, I tell you."

The boys started off down the lane. When they were out of sight of the house, Frank stopped and turned to his companions.

"Do you know what I saw in that kitchen?" he asked tensely.

"What?"

"Dad's cap hanging on a peg!"

"Then he *has* been there!" cried Joe. "They were lying!"

"Yes," Frank continued, "and—and there were bloodstains on the cap!"

"Bloodstains!" Joe exclaimed. "That means he *must* be in trouble. Frank, we've got to go back!"

"We sure do!" his brother agreed. "But I wanted to tell you all about it first."

"What do you think we should do?" Chet asked.

"I'll ask those people in the house about the cap and force a showdown," Frank declared tersely. "We've got to find out where Dad is!"

Resolutely the boys started back to the Pollitt house. When they reached the yard they found the two men and the woman standing by the shed talking earnestly. The woman caught sight of them and spoke warningly to the red-haired man.

"What do you want now?" he demanded, advancing toward the boys.

"We want to know about that sports cap in the kitchen," said Frank firmly.

"What cap? There's no cap in there."

"There isn't now—but there was. It was hanging on a peg when I went in for a drink."

"I don't know anythin' about no cap," persisted the man.

"Perhaps we'd better ask the police to look around," Joe suggested.

The redhead glanced meaningly at the woman. The other man stepped forward. "I know the cap this boy means," he said. "It's mine. What about it?"

"It isn't yours and you know it," Frank declared. "That cap belongs to the man we're looking for."

"I tell you it *is* my cap!" snapped the swarthy man, showing his yellowed teeth in a snarl. "Don't tell me I'm lyin'."

The red-haired man intervened. "You're mistaken, Klein," he said. "I know the cap they mean now. It's the one I found on the road a few days ago."

"Guess you're right, Red," Klein conceded hastily.

"You found it?" asked Frank incredulously.

"Sure, I found it. A brown cap with bloodstains on it."

"That's the one. But why did you hide it when I went into the kitchen?"

"Well, to tell the truth, them bloodstains made me nervous. I didn't know but what there might be some trouble come of it, so I thought I'd better keep that cap out of sight."

"Where did you find it?" Joe asked.

"About a mile from here."

"On the shore road?"

"Yes. It was lyin' right in the middle of the road."

"When was this?"

"A couple of days ago—just after we moved in here."

"Let's see the cap," Chet Morton suggested. "We want to make sure of this."

As Red moved reluctantly toward the kitchen, the woman sniffed. "I don't see why you're makin' all this fuss about an old cap," she said. "Comin' around here disturbin' honest folks."

"We're sorry if we're bothering you," said Joe, "but this is a very serious matter."

Red came out of the house holding the cap. He tossed it to Frank.

The boy turned back the inside flap and there he found what he was looking for—the initials F. H. printed in gold on the leather band.

"It's Dad's cap all right."

"I don't like the look of those bloodstains," said Joe in a low voice. "He must have been badly hurt."

"Are you sure you found this on the road?" Frank asked, still suspicious.

"You don't think I'd lie about it, do you?" Red answered belligerently.

"I can't contradict you, but I'm going to turn this over to the police," Frank told him. "If you know anything more about it, you'd better speak up now."

"He doesn't know anything about it," shrilled the woman angrily. "Go away and don't bother us. Didn't he tell you he found the cap on the road? I told him to burn up the dirty thing. But he wanted to have it cleaned and wear it."

The boys turned away, Frank still holding the cap. "Come on, fellows," he said. "Let's get out of here."

As the boys started down the lane they cast a last glance back at the yard. The woman and the two men were standing just where the young sleuths had left them. The woman was motionless, her hands on her hips. Red was standing with his arms folded, and Klein, the swarthy man, was lean-

"He doesn't know anything about the cap,"
the woman shrilled

ing against a tree. All three were gazing intently and silently after the departing boys.

"I'm sure that those people know more about Dad's cap than they're telling," Frank said grimly, as the boys mounted their motorcycles and rode back toward Bayport.

"What are you planning to do next?" Phil asked as he pulled his machine alongside Frank's.

"I'm going right to Chief Collig and tell him the whole story."

"Okay, we're with you!"

The boys rode directly to police headquarters and left their motorcycles in the parking lot. Chief Collig looked up as his six visitors were ushered into his office.

"Well," he said heartily, "this is quite a delegation! What can I do for you?"

As Frank and Joe took turns, with an occasional graphic illustration from one of the other boys, they told the full story and showed him the blood-stained cap.

Chief Collig looked grave. "I don't like the sound of this at all," he said finally. "We must find your father at once! This cap is a good clue." Then he went on, "Of course you realize that the area where the Pollitt house is located is outside the limits of Bayport, so my men can't go there. But I'll get in touch with Captain Ryder of the State Police at once, so he can assign men to the case."

The boys thanked the chief for his help and left. Chet, Tony, Biff, and Phil went their separate ways while Frank and Joe turned toward home. They decided not to upset their mother about the bloodstained cap, but merely tell her that the State Police would take over the search for her husband.

"I still think there's some connection between Dad's disappearance and the smuggling outfit and the house on the cliff," Frank declared.

"What I've been wondering," said Joe, "is where those two motorboats came from that day Jones was attacked. We didn't see them out in the ocean earlier—at least not both of them."

"That's right. They could have come right out from under the cliff."

"You mean, Frank, there might be a secret harbor in there?"

"Might be. Here's the way it could work. Dad suspects smugglers are operating in this territory from a base that he has been unable to find." Frank spread his arms. "The base is the old Pollitt place! What more do you want?"

"But the house is on top of a *cliff*."

"There could be a secret passage from the house to a hidden harbor at the foot of the cliff."

"Good night, Frank, it sure sounds reasonable!"

"And perhaps that explains why the kidnapers got away with Jones so quickly on Saturday. If they left the Kane farmhouse just a little while before we did, we should have been able to get within sight of their car. But we didn't."

"You mean they turned in at the Pollitt place?"

"Why not? Probably Jones is hidden there right now."

"And maybe Dad too," Joe cried out excitedly.

"That's right. I'm against just sitting and waiting for the state troopers to find him. How about asking Tony if he will lend us his motorboat, so we can investigate the foot of that cliff?"

"I get you!" Joe agreed enthusiastically. "And if we pick up any information we can turn it over to the State Police and they can raid the Pollitt place!"

CHAPTER X

A Watery Tunnel

WHEN the brothers arrived home Frank and Joe assured their mother that the State Police would soon find Mr. Hardy. Some of the anxiety left her face as she listened to her sons' reassuring words.

When she went to the kitchen to start preparations for supper, the boys went to phone Tony Prito. After Frank explained their plan to him, he agreed at once to let them use the *Napoli*, provided they took him along.

"I wouldn't miss it for anything," he said. "But I can't go until afternoon. Have to do some work for my dad in the morning. I'll meet you at the boathouse at two o'clock."

"Swell, Tony. I have a job of my own in the morning."

Chet called a few minutes later. As Frank finished telling him about the plan, he whistled.

"You fellows have got your nerve all right. But count me in, will you? I started this thing with you and I'd like to finish it. We've got to find your father!"

After Chet had said good-by, Joe asked his brother, "What's on for the morning?"

"I want to go down to the waterfront and talk to Pretzel Pete again. He might have another clue. Also, I want to find out when the *Marco Polo* is due back here."

Joe nodded. "I get it. You think something may be going on then?"

"Right. And if we can find Dad and lead the Coast Guard to the smugglers before the boat docks—"

"Brother, that's a big order."

By nine o'clock the following morning Frank and Joe were down at the Bayport docks. Pretzel Pete was not in evidence.

"We'd better be cagey about asking when the *Marco Polo's* coming in," Frank cautioned. "The smugglers probably have spies around here and we'd sure be targets."

Acting as if there were no problems on their minds, Frank and Joe strolled along whistling. Once they joined a group of people who were watching a sidewalk merchant. The man was demonstrating little jumping animals. Frank and Joe laughed as they bought a monkey and a kangaroo. "Iola and Callie will get a kick out of these," Joe predicted.

"Say, Frank, here comes Pretzel Pete now!" Joe whispered.

The Hardys went up the street, saying in a loud voice in case anyone was listening, that they were hungry and glad to see Pete.

"Nobody can make pretzels like yours," Joe exclaimed. "Give me a dozen. Two for my mouth and ten for my pockets."

As Pretzel Pete laughed and pulled out a cellophane bag to fill the order, Frank said in a whisper, "Heard anything new?"

"Not a thing, son." Pete could talk without moving his lips. "But I may know something tomorrow."

"How come?"

"The *Marco Polo's* docking real early—five A.M. I heard Ali Singh is one of the crew. I'll try to get a line on him."

"Great! We'll be seeing you."

The boys moved off, and to avoid arousing any suspicion as to why they were in the area, headed for a famous fish market.

"Mother will be surprised to see our morning's catch," Joe said with a grin as he picked out a large bluefish.

The brothers did not discuss the exciting information Pretzel Pete had given them until they were in the safety of their own home. Then Joe burst out, "Frank, if the *Marco Polo* gets offshore during the night, it'll have to lay outside until it's time to dock!"

"And that'll give those smugglers a real break in picking up the stolen drugs!" Frank added. "Maybe we should pass along our suspicions to the Coast Guard."

"Not yet," Joe objected. "All we have to go on is Pretzel Pete's statements about Ali Singh. Maybe we'll learn more this afternoon and then we can report it."

"I guess you're right," Frank concluded. "If those smugglers are holding Dad, and find out that we've tipped off the Coast Guard, they'll certainly harm him."

"You have a point."

When Frank and Joe reached the Prito boathouse at two o'clock, Tony and Chet were already there. Tony was tuning up the motor, which purred evenly.

"No word from your dad yet?" Tony asked. The Hardys shook their heads as they stepped aboard.

The *Napoli* was a rangy, powerful craft with graceful lines and was the pride of Tony's life. The boat moved slowly out into the waters of Barmet Bay and then gathered speed as it headed toward the ocean.

"Rough water," Frank remarked as breaking

swells hit the hull. Salt spray dashed over the bow
of the *Napoli* as it plunged on through the white-
caps. Bayport soon became a speck nestled at the
curve of the horseshoe-shaped body of water.
Reaching the ocean, Tony turned north. The boys
could see the white line of the shore road rising
and falling along the coast. Soon they passed the
Kane farm. Two miles farther on they came within
sight of the cliff upon which the Pollitt house
stood. It looked stark and forbidding above the
rocks, its roof and chimneys silhouetted against
the sky.

"Pretty steep cliff," Tony observed. "I can't see
how anyone could make his way up and down that
slope to get to the house."

"That's probably why nobody has suspected the
place of being a smuggling base," Frank replied.
"But perhaps when we look around we'll find an
answer."

Tony steered the boat closer toward the shore,
so that it would not be visible from the Pollitt
grounds. Then he slackened speed in order that
the sound of the engine would be less noticeable,
and the craft made its way toward the bottom of
the cliff.

There were currents here that demanded skill-
ful navigation, but Tony brought the *Napoli*
through them easily, and at last the boat was chugging along close to the face of the cliff.

The boys eagerly scanned the formidable wall of rock. It was scarred and seamed and the base had been eaten away by the incessant battering of waves. There was no indication of a path.

Suddenly Tony turned the wheel sharply. The *Napoli* swerved swiftly to one side. He gave it power and the craft leaped forward with a roar.

"What's the matter?" Frank asked in alarm.

Tony gazed straight ahead, tense and alert. Another shift of the wheel and the *Napoli* swerved again.

Then Chet and the Hardys saw the danger. There were rocks at the base of the cliff. One of them, black and sharp, like an ugly tooth, jutted out of the water almost at the boat's side. Only Tony's quick eye had saved the *Napoli* from hitting it!

They had blundered into a veritable maze of reefs which extended for several yards ahead. Tony's passengers held their breaths. It seemed impossible that they could run the gantlet of those rocks without tearing out the bottom of the craft.

But luck was with them. The *Napoli* dodged the last dangerous rock, and shot forward into open water.

Tony sank back with a sigh of relief. "Whew, that was close!" he exclaimed. "I didn't see those rocks until we were right on top of them. If we'd ever struck one of them we'd have been goners."

Frank, Joe, and Chet nodded in solemn agreement. Then, suddenly, Frank cried out, "Turn back! I think I saw an opening!"

Tony swung the boat around. The opening which Frank had spotted was a long, narrow tunnel. It led right through the cliff!

"This might be the secret entrance!" Joe exclaimed.

"I think it's large enough for the boat to go through," said Tony. "Want me to try it?"

Frank nodded tensely. "Go ahead."

The *Napoli* slipped through the opening and in a few moments came out into a pond of considerable extent. The boys looked about expectantly. Steep slopes covered with scraggly trees and bushes reached to the water's edge. But there was no path or indication that any human being ever came down to the pond.

Suddenly Frank gave a gasp of surprise and said, "Look to my right, fellows."

Among the thickets at the base of the steepest slope stood a man. He was very tall, his face was weather-beaten, and his lips thin and cruel. He stood quietly, looking at the boys without a shadow of expression on his sinister face.

Upon realizing he had been observed, the man shouted, "Get out of here!"

Tony throttled the engine and Frank called, "We aren't doing any harm."

"I said 'Get out!' This is private property."

The boys hesitated. Instantly the man, as though to back up his commands, reached significantly toward the holster of a revolver.

"Turn that boat around and beat it!" he snapped. "And don't ever come back here! Not if you know what's good for you."

The boys realized that nothing would be gained by argument. Tony slowly brought the boat around.

"Okay," Joe called cheerfully.

The stranger did not reply. He stood gazing fixedly after them, his left hand pointing to the exit, his right tapping the gun holster, as the motorboat made its way out through the tunnel.

"Looks as if he didn't want us around," remarked Tony facetiously, as soon as the *Napoli* was in open water again.

"He sure didn't!" Frank exclaimed. "I expected him to start popping that gun at any moment!"

"He must have an important reason. Who and what do you suppose he is?" Tony asked in bewilderment.

"Fellows," Frank said thoughtfully, "I think that man might have been Snattman!"

CHAPTER XI

Cliff Watchers

"FRANK!" Joe exclaimed. "I think you've hit it! That man had no reason to act the way he did unless he's covering up something."

"Something like smuggling, you mean," said Chet. "He must be Snattman or one of his gang."

"And," Frank went on, "the fact that he was in that cove must mean he has some connection with the house on the cliff."

"Snattman, king of the smugglers!" Tony whistled. "You guys really get in some interesting situations!"

"I'll bet that he's one of the fellows who chased Jones that day in the motorboat," Joe cried.

"And tried to kill him," Frank continued the thought.

"Let's get away from here!" Chet urged.

"Why should we go now?" Frank demanded.

"We've stumbled on something important. That hidden pond may be the smugglers' base."

"But if they use the house how do they get to it?" Tony asked. "Those cliffs up from the pond were mighty steep."

"There must be some other way that we couldn't see," Joe said. "What say we hang around here for a while and find out what we can?"

Tony caught the Hardys' enthusiasm and agreed to keep the motorboat in the vicinity of the cliff.

"That fellow may be keeping his eye on us and we don't want him to know that we're watching the place," Frank observed. "Let's run back to the bay and cruise up and down a while, then return."

Chet sighed. "I'm glad none of you argued with that armed man."

"Right," Joe replied. "As it is, he must think we were simply out for a cruise and wandered into that tunnel by mistake."

"Yes," his brother agreed. "If he'd known we're hunting for Dad, he might have acted very differently."

In the late afternoon Tony took the *Napoli* back to the suspected shore spot. Keeping well out from the breaking waves, he cruised along the cliff. The boys kept a sharp eye on the location of the tunnel. As the boat passed it they were just able to distinguish the narrow opening in the rocks.

"I won't be able to go in there after a while," Tony remarked. "The tide's coming in. At high tide I'll bet that tunnel is filled with water."

Suddenly Tony swung his craft so hard to the right that the other boys lost their balance.

"Sorry, fellows," he said. "Saw a log—oh!"

He shut off his engine in a flash and leaned over the gunwale. His companions picked themselves up and asked what had happened.

"Propeller started to foul up with some wire on that log." Tony began to peel off his clothes. "Get me some pliers, will you?"

Frank opened a locker and found a pair. Taking them, Tony dived overboard. A minute later he reappeared and climbed in. "I'm lucky," he said. "Just plain lucky. Two seconds more and all that wire would have been wound around the prop and the log would have knocked it off."

"Good night!" Chet exclaimed. "It would have been a long swim home."

Joe slapped Tony on the back. "Good work, boy. I'd hate to see the *Napoli* out of commission."

Chet and Frank hauled the log aboard, so it would not damage any other craft. "This is a fence post with barbed wire!" Chet said. "Wowee! It's good you spotted that log, Tony."

Tony dressed, then started the engine. He

cruised around for more than an hour, but the boys saw no sign of life about the base of the cliff. They could see the Pollitt house, but to their amazement no lights appeared in it as twilight came.

"How much longer do you think we should stay out here?" Chet asked. "I'm getting hungry."

"I have a few pretzels and a candy bar, but that's not much for four of us," Joe remarked.

"Aha!" crowed Tony. "I have a surprise for you! I stowed away a little food before we took off." With that he pulled a paper bag from the locker and passed each boy a large sandwich, a piece of chocolate cake, and a bottle of lemon soda.

"You deserve a medal," Chet remarked as he bit into a layer of ham and cheese.

"You sure do!" Frank agreed. "I think we should stay right here for a while and watch. It's my guess the smugglers will be on the job tonight. Don't forget that the *Marco Polo* is docking tomorrow morning."

"I get it," said Chet. "If she lays offshore or steams in slowly, it'll give Ali Singh a chance to drop the stolen drugs overboard to Snattman."

"Correct," said Frank.

Tony looked intently at the Hardys. "Is it your idea to keep Snattman from meeting Ali Singh? But what about your father? I thought we came out here to get a line on how to rescue him."

The brothers exchanged glances, then Joe said, "Of course that's our main purpose, but we hope that we can do both."

Twilight deepened into darkness and lights could be seen here and there through the haze. The cliff was only a black smudge and the house above was still unlighted.

Suddenly the boys heard a muffled sound. Tony slowed the *Napoli* and they listened intently.

"Another motorboat," Tony whispered.

The sound seemed to come from near the cliff. Straining their eyes in that direction, the four were at last able to distinguish a faint moving light.

"Can you head over that way, Tony?" Frank asked in a low voice. "And could you take a chance on turning off our lights?"

"Sure. Here goes. The wind's blowing from the land, so our engine won't be heard from the shore."

The boys were tense with excitement as the *Napoli* moved slowly toward the light. As the boat crept nearer the cliff, they could barely distinguish the outline of a motorboat. The craft seemed to be making its way carefully out of the very face of the cliff.

"It must have come from that tunnel!" Joe whispered to Frank.

"Yes."

The *Napoli* went closer, in imminent danger of being discovered or of being washed ashore onto the rocks. Finally the other boat slowed to a crawl. Then came the faint clatter of oars and low voices. The motorboat had evidently met a rowboat.

The next moment, with an abrupt roar, the motorboat turned and raced out to sea at an ever-increasing rate of speed.

"Where can it be going?" said Tony, in amazement. "Out to meet the *Marco Polo?*"

"Probably," Frank replied, "and we'd never catch it. I wonder where the rowboat's going."

The four boys waited in silence for several minutes. Then the rattle of oars came again. This time the sound was closer. The rowboat was coming toward them!

"What'll we do now?" Tony asked.

"Turn off your engine," Frank whispered. Tony complied.

Through the gloom suddenly came snatches of conversation from the rowboat. "—a hundred pounds—" they heard a man say harshly, and then the rest of the sentence was lost. There was a lengthy murmur of voices, then, "I don't know. It's risky—"

The wind died down just then and two voices could be heard distinctly. "Ali Singh's share—" one man was saying.

"That's right. We can't forget him," the gruff voice replied.

"I hope they get away all right."

"What are you worryin' about? Of course they'll get away."

"We've been spotted, you know."

"It's all your imagination. Nobody suspects."

"Those boys at the house—"

"Just dumb kids. If they come nosin' around again, we'll knock 'em on the head."

"I don't like this rough stuff. It's dangerous."

"We've got to do it or we'll end up in the pen. What's the matter with you tonight? You're nervous."

"I'm worried. I've got a hunch we'd better clear out of here."

"Clear out!" replied the other contemptuously. "Are you crazy? Why, this place is as safe as a church." The man laughed sardonically. "Haven't we got all the squealers locked up? And tonight we make the big cleanup and get away."

"Well, maybe you're right," said the first man doubtfully. "But still—"

His voice died away as the boat entered the tunnel.

Joe grabbed Frank's arm. "Did you hear that? All the squealers locked up? I'll bet Dad's one of them and he's a prisoner somewhere around here."

"And this is the hide-out of Snattman and

the other smugglers he was after," Frank added.

"I don't like this," Chet spoke up. "Let's leave here and get the police."

Frank shook his head. "It would take so long we might goof the whole thing. Tell you what. Joe and I will follow that rowboat through the tunnel!"

"How?"

"On foot or swim. I don't think it's deep along the edges."

"You mean Chet and I will wait here?" Tony asked.

"No," Frank answered. "You two beat it back to Bayport and notify the Coast Guard. Tell them we're on the track of smugglers and ask them to send some men here."

"And tell them our suspicions about Ali Singh and the *Marco Polo*," Joe added. "They can radio the captain to keep an eye on him."

"Okay," said Tony. "I'll do that. First I'll put you ashore."

"Don't go too close or you'll hit those rocks and wreck the boat," Frank warned. "Joe and I can swim to shore. Then we'll work around into the tunnel and see what we can find. If we do discover anything, we'll wait at the entrance and show the men from the Coast Guard where to go when they get here."

Tony edged the boat in as close to the dark

shore as he dared without lights. Quickly Frank and Joe took off their slacks, T shirts, sweaters, and sneakers. They rolled them up, and with twine which Tony provided, tied the bundles on top of their heads. Then they slipped over the side into the water. The *Napoli* sped off.

Frank and Joe were only a few yards from the rocks and after a short swim emerged on the mainland.

"Well, here goes!" Joe whispered, heading for the tunnel.

CHAPTER XII

The Secret Passage

CAUTIOUSLY Frank and Joe made their way across the slippery rocks. Suddenly there was a loud splash as Joe lost his footing.

"Are you all right?" Frank whispered, as he came up to where his brother was standing in the shallow water at the edge of the cliff.

"Yes. For a moment I sure thought I'd sprained my ankle," Joe replied tensely, "but it seems to be okay now."

"Give me your hand," Frank whispered and quickly pulled Joe back onto the rocks.

The Hardys had landed at a point some twenty-five yards from the tunnel opening, but the climb over the treacherous rocks was so difficult that the distance seemed much longer. It was very dark in the shadow of the steep cliff. The waves breaking against the rocks had a lonely and foreboding sound.

"Good night!" Joe muttered. "Aren't we ever coming to that tunnel?"

"Take it easy," Frank advised. "It can't be much farther."

"I hope Tony and Chet will hurry back with help," Joe said. "This is a ticklish job."

"If anybody's on guard here, we'll certainly be at a disadvantage," Frank remarked in a barely audible tone. "Watch out!"

By this time they had reached the entrance to the tunnel. After a few cautious steps they discovered that the narrow piece of land between the water and the base of the cliff was covered by a thick growth of bushes.

Frank turned to Joe. "If we try to walk through all that stuff," he whispered, "we're sure to be heard. That is, if those men are in here some place."

Joe grunted in agreement. "What shall we do?"

Tentatively, Frank put one foot into the water from the rock on which he was standing.

"It isn't deep," he said. "I guess we can wade through."

The boys hugged the wall and started off. Fortunately, the water came only to their knees because there was a shelf of rocks all the way along. The brothers' hearts beat wildly. What would they find ahead of them?

The boys had not heard a sound since entering

the tunnel. It appeared that the men in the rowboat had gone on to some secret hiding place.

"I think I'll risk my flashlight," Frank said in a low voice as they reached the pond. "We can't find out anything without it."

He pulled one he always carried from its waterproof case and snapped it on. The yellow beam shone over the pond. There was no sign of the rowboat.

"How do you think those men got out of here?" Joe asked. "Do you suppose there's another opening?"

Frank turned the flashlight onto the steep sides surrounding the water. "I don't see any. My guess is that those men hid the boat some place. Let's make a thorough search."

Slowly the brothers began to walk around the edge of the pond, brushing aside the heavy growth and peering among the bushes. They had about given up in despair as they reached the section by the far wall of the tunnel. Then, as Frank beamed the flashlight over the thicket, he exclaimed hoarsely, "Look!"

"A door!" Joe whispered tensely.

The door had been so cleverly concealed that it would not have been seen in full daylight except at close quarters. The glare of the flashlight, however, brought the artificial screen of branches and leaves into sharp relief against the dark cliffside.

"This explains it," Joe said. "The men in the boat went through here. I wonder where it goes."

In order to avoid detection, Frank extinguished his light before trying to open the door. He swung it open inch by inch, half expecting to find lights and people beyond. But there was only darkness. Luckily the door had made no noise. Frank turned on his light again.

Ahead was a watery passageway some ten feet wide and twenty-five feet long, with a ledge running along one side. At the end was a tiny wharf with a rowboat tied to a post.

"This is fantastic!" Joe whispered. "And it must have been here a long time. Do you suppose it's connected with the Pollitt place?"

"If it is, it could mean old Mr. Pollitt was mixed up with the smugglers!" Frank answered. "Hey, do you suppose Snattman is his nephew?"

Excited over this possible new angle to the case, Frank and Joe stepped onto the ledge. They dressed, then quietly inched forward. Reaching the wharf, they looked about them as Frank beamed his flashlight on the walls.

"Hold it!" Joe whispered.

Directly ahead was a crude arch in the rock. Beyond it, the boys could see a steep flight of stone steps. Their hearts pounded with excitement.

"We've found it!" Frank whispered. "This must be the secret passageway!"

"Yes," Joe agreed, "and from the distance we've come I'd figure that we're right underneath the house on the cliff."

"Let's go up."

The light cast strange shadows in the passage through the rocks. Water dripped from the walls. The boys tiptoed forward and stealthily began the ascent.

As they crept up the stairs, Frank flashed the light ahead of them. Shortly they could see that the steps ended at a heavy door. Its framework was set into the wall of rock. Above them was only a rocky ceiling.

When Frank and Joe reached the door, they hesitated. Both were thinking, "If we go through that door and find the gang of smugglers, we'll never get out. But, on the other hand, we *must* find Dad!"

Frank stepped forward, pressed his ear against the door, and listened intently. There was not a sound beyond.

He turned off his light and looked carefully around the sides of the door to see if he could catch a glimmer of any illumination from the other side. There was only darkness.

"I guess there's no one inside," he said to Joe. "Let's see if we can open it."

Frank felt for the latch. The door did not move. "It must be locked," he whispered.

"Try it again. Maybe it's just stuck."

Frank put his hand on the latch, this time also pushing the door with his shoulder. Suddenly, with a noise which echoed from wall to wall, the latch snapped and the door swung open.

Joe stepped forward, but Frank put out a restraining hand. "Wait!" he cautioned. "That noise may bring someone."

Tensely, they stood alert for the slightest sound. But none came. Hopeful that there was no one in the area beyond, Frank switched on the flashlight.

The vivid beam cut the darkness and revealed a gloomy cave hewn out of the rock in the very center of the cliff. The boys wondered if it had been a natural cave. It was filled with boxes, bales, and packages distributed about the floor and piled against the walls.

"Smuggled goods!" Frank and Joe thought.

The fact that the majority of the boxes bore labels of foreign countries seemed to verify their suspicions.

Convinced that the cave was unoccupied, the boys stepped through the doorway and looked about for another door or opening. They saw none. Was this the end of the trail?

"But it couldn't be," the young sleuths thought. "Those men went *some* place."

Bolts of beautiful silk had been tossed on top

of some of the bales. Valuable tapestries were also lying carelessly around. In one corner four boxes were piled on top of one another. Frank accidentally knocked the flashlight against one of these and it gave forth a hollow sound.

"It's empty," he whispered.

An idea struck him that perhaps these boxes had been piled up to conceal some passage leading out of the secret storeroom. He mentioned his suspicion to Joe.

"But how could the men pile the boxes up there after they went out?" his brother questioned.

"This gang is smart enough for anything. Let's move these boxes away and maybe we'll find out."

Frank seized the topmost box. It was very light and he removed it from the pile without difficulty.

"I thought so!" Frank said with satisfaction. The flashlight had revealed the top of a door which had been hidden from view.

The boys lost no time in moving the other three boxes. Then Frank and Joe discovered how it was possible for the boxes to be piled up in such a position, in spite of the fact that the smugglers had left the cave and closed the door behind them.

Attached to the bottom of the door was a thin

wooden platform that projected out over the floor of the cave and on this the boxes had been piled.

"Very clever," Joe remarked. "Whenever any one leaves the cave and closes the door, the boxes swing in with the platform and it looks as though they were piled up on the floor."

"Right. Well, let's see where the door leads," Frank proposed.

He snapped off his light and with utmost caution opened the door. It made no sound. Again there was darkness ahead.

"What a maze!" Frank whispered as he turned on his flash and beamed the light ahead.

Another stone-lined passage with a flight of steps at the end!

Suddenly Frank stiffened and laid a warning hand on his brother's arm. "Voices!" he said in a low tone and snapped off his light.

The boys listened intently. They could hear a man's voice in the distance. Neither could distinguish what he was saying, for he was still too far away, but gradually the tones grew louder. Then, to the brothers' alarm, they heard footsteps. Hastily they retreated into the secret cave.

"Quick! The door!" Frank urged.

They closed it quietly.

"Now the boxes. If those men come in here

they'll notice that the boxes have been moved!"
He turned on the light but shielded it with his
hand.

Swiftly Joe piled the empty boxes back onto the
platform that projected from the bottom of the
door. He worked as silently and quickly as possible,
but could hear the footsteps drawing closer and
closer.

Finally the topmost box was in place.

"Out the other door!" Frank hissed into Joe's
ear.

They sped across the floor of the cave toward
the door opening onto the stairs they had recently
ascended. But hardly had they reached it before
they heard a rattle at the latch of the door on the
opposite side of the cave.

"We haven't time," Frank whispered. "Hide!"

The beam of the flashlight revealed a number
of boxes close to the door. On top of these someone had thrown a heavy bolt of silk, the folds of
which hung down to the floor. The brothers
scrambled swiftly behind the boxes, pressing
themselves close against the wall. They had just
enough time to hide and switch out Frank's light
before they heard the other door open.

"There's a bunch of drugs in that shipment that
came in three weeks ago," they heard a husky
voice say. "We'll take it upstairs. Burke says he
can get rid of it for us right away. No use leaving

it down here. Got to make room for the new shipment."

"Right," the Hardys heard someone else reply. "Anything else to go up?"

"No. I'll switch on the light."

There was a click, and suddenly the cave was flooded with light. It had been wired for electricity.

Frank and Joe crouched in their hiding place, holding their breaths in terror. Would they be discovered?

Footsteps slowly approached the boxes behind which they were concealed!

CHAPTER XIII

A Startling Discovery

FRANK AND JOE tried to crowd themselves into the smallest space possible as the men came nearer to their hiding place. The electric light bulb hanging from the center of the ceiling cast such a strong illumination over the cave that the boys felt certain they would be discovered.

The boxes were placed a small distance apart, and only the fact that folds of silk hung down over the open spaces between the boxes prevented the boys from being seen immediately. However, through a crack in one of the crates, the Hardys could just make out two husky-looking figures.

"Here's some o' that Japanese silk," the boys heard one of the men say. "I'd better take a bolt of that up too. Burke said he could place some more of it."

Instantly the same thought ran through both

the brothers' minds. If the man picked up the silk, they would surely be found!

"Don't be crazy!" the other man objected. "You know you won't get any credit for pushin' a sale. Why break your arm luggin' all that stuff upstairs?"

"Well," the first man explained in a whining tone, "I thought maybe we could get rid of some more of this swag and make ourselves a little extra dough."

"Naw," his companion snarled. "I can tell you ain't been with this gang long. You never get any thanks around here for thinkin'. If Burke don't take the extra stuff, the boss'll make you bring it all the way down again."

"Maybe you're right."

"Sure I'm right! My idea for the rest of us in this gang is to do just what Snattman tells us to and no more."

"You got somethin' there, Bud. Okay. We'll just take up the package of drugs and leave the rest."

To the boys' relief the men turned away and went over to the other side of the room. Frank and Joe did not dare peer out, but they could hear the sound of boxes being shifted.

Then came the words, "All set. I've got the packages. Let's go!"

The switch was snapped and the cave was

plunged into darkness. The Hardys began to breathe normally again. The door to the corridor closed and faintly the boys could detect the men's footsteps as they ascended the stairs at the end of it.

When they had died away completely, Frank switched on the flashlight. "Wow!" he said, giving a tremendous sigh of relief. "That was a close call! I sure thought they had us."

"Me too," Joe agreed. "We wouldn't have had a chance with that pair. Looked like a couple of wrestlers."

"Do we dare follow them?"

"You bet. I'd say we've solved the smuggling mystery, but we've still got to find out if they're holding Dad," Joe said grimly.

"We'll have to watch our step even more carefully. We don't want to walk right into the whole ring of smugglers," Frank reminded him.

"Right. I don't crave anything worse than what we've just gone through," said Joe. "I thought I'd die of suspense while that pair was in here."

They crossed the room, opened the door, and started up the dark passageway. Presently they were confronted by the flight of steps. Part way up there was a landing, then more steps with a door at the top.

"I'll go first," Frank offered. "Stick close behind me. I think I'll keep the flash off."

"That's right," Joe agreed. "Snattman might

have a guard at the top and there's no use advertising our presence."

Step by step, the boys crept upward in the inky blackness. Then they found themselves on a crude landing of planks. Carefully they felt their way along the side of the rock wall until they reached the next flight of steps.

Here the brothers stopped again to listen. Silence.

"So far, so good," Frank whispered. "But somehow I don't like this whole thing. I have a feeling we're walking into a trap."

"We can't quit now," Joe answered. "But I admit I'm scared."

Still groping in the dark, the boys climbed up and up until they were nearly winded.

"Where are we?" Joe panted. "I feel as if I've been climbing stairs for an hour!"

"Me too," Frank agreed. "The cliff doesn't look this high from the outside."

They rested a minute, then continued their journey. Groping around, they finally reached another door. Frank hunted for the door handle. Finding it, he turned the knob ever so slightly to find out if the door was locked.

"I can open it," Frank said in Joe's ear, "but we'd better wait a few minutes."

"Every second is vital if Dad's a prisoner," Joe objected.

Frank was about to accede to his brother's urging when both boys heard footsteps on the other side of the door. A chill ran down their spines.

"Shall we run?" Joe said fearfully.

"It wouldn't do us any good. Listen!"

There came a queer shuffling sound and a sigh from somewhere beyond the door. That was all.

"Someone's in there," Frank breathed. Joe nodded in the darkness.

The boys did not know what to do. The gang might have posted a sentry. If there was only one, the Hardys might be able to jump the man and disarm him. However, they probably could not do it without making some noise and attracting the attention of the rest of the smugglers.

Frank and Joe gritted their teeth. They couldn't give up now!

As they were trying to decide how to proceed, the situation took an unexpected turn. A door slammed in the distance. Then came the murmur of voices and the sound of advancing footsteps.

"This nonsense has gone far enough," a man said angrily. "He'll write that note at once, or I'll know the reason why."

The boys started. The voice was that of the man who had ordered them to leave the pond during the afternoon.

"That's right, chief!" another voice spoke up.

"Make him do as you say and get the heat off us until we've got all the loot moved."

"If he doesn't write it, he'll never get out of here alive," the first man promised coldly.

Instantly Frank and Joe thought of the note their mother had received. Was the man these smugglers were talking about their father? Or was he someone else—maybe Jones, who was to be forced to obey them or perhaps lose his life?

The speakers went a short distance beyond the door behind which Frank and Joe were standing. Then they heard the click of a switch. A faint beam of yellow light shone beneath the door. The brothers figured there was a corridor beyond and three or four men had entered a room opening from it.

"Well, I see you're still here," said the man who had been addressed as chief. "You'll find this an easier place to get into than out of."

A weary voice answered him. The tones were low, so the boys pressed closer to the door. But try as they might, they could not distinguish the words.

"You're a prisoner here and you'll stay here until you die unless you write that note."

Again the weary voice spoke, but the tones were still so indistinct that the boys could not hear the answer.

"You won't write it, eh? We'll see what we can do to persuade you."

"Let him go hungry for a few days. That'll persuade him!" put in one of the other men. This brought a hoarse laugh from his companions.

"You'll be hungry enough if you don't write that letter," the chief agreed. "Are you going to write it?"

"No," the boys barely heard the prisoner answer.

The chief said sourly, "You've got too much on us. We can't afford to let you go now. But if you write that letter, we'll leave you some food, so that you won't starve. You'll break out eventually, but not in time to do us any harm. Well, what do you say? Want some food?"

There was no reply from the prisoner.

"Give his arm a little twist," suggested one of the smugglers.

At this the Hardys' blood boiled with rage. Their first impulse was to fling open the door and rush to the aid of the person who was being tormented. But they realized they were helpless against so many men. Their only hope lay in the arrival of the Coast Guard men, but they might come too late!

"Chief, shall I give this guy the works?" one of the smugglers asked.

"No," the leader answered quickly. "None of

that rough stuff. We'll do it the easy way—starvation. I'm giving him one more chance. He can write that note now or we'll leave him here to starve when we make our getaway."

Still there was no reply.

To Frank's and Joe's ears came a scraping sound as if a chair was being moved forward.

"You won't talk, eh?" The leader's voice grew ugly.

There was a pause of a few seconds, then suddenly he shouted, "Write that note, Hardy, or you'll be sorry—as sure as my name's Snattman!"

CHAPTER XIV

Captured

JOE gave a start. "It *is* Dad!" he whispered hoarsely. "He found the smugglers' hide-out!"

Frank nudged his brother warningly. "Not so loud."

The boys' worst fears were realized—their father was not only a prisoner of the smugglers, but also his life was being threatened!

"Write that note!" Snattman demanded.

"I won't write it," Fenton Hardy replied in a weak but clear voice.

The chief persisted. "You heard what I said. Write it or be left here to starve."

"I'll starve."

"You'll change your mind in a day or two. You think you're hungry now, but wait until we cut off your food entirely. Then you'll see. You'll be ready to sell your soul for a drop of water or a crumb to eat."

"I won't write it."

"Look here, Hardy. We're not asking very much. All we want you to do is write to your wife that you're safe and tell her to call off the police and those kids of yours. They're too nosy."

"Sooner or later someone is going to trace me here," came Mr. Hardy's faint reply. "And when they do, I can tell them enough to send you to prison for the rest of your life."

There was a sudden commotion in the room and two or three of the smugglers began talking at once.

"You're crazy!" shouted Snattman, but there was a hint of uneasiness in his voice. "You don't know anything about me!"

"I know enough to have you sent up for attempted murder. And you're about to try it again."

"You're too smart, Hardy. That's all the more reason why you're not going to get out of here until we've gone. And if you don't co-operate you'll *never* make it. Our next big shipment's coming through tonight, and then we're skipping the country. If you write that letter, you'll live. If you don't, it's curtains for you!"

Frank and Joe were shaken by the dire threats. But they must decide whether to go for help, or stay and risk capture and try to rescue their father.

"You can't scare me, Snattman," the detective

said. "I have a feeling your time is up. You're never going to get that big shipment."

The detective's voice seemed a little stronger, the boys felt.

Snattman laughed. "I thought you were smart, but you're playing a losing game, I warn you. And how about your family? Are you doing them a service by being so stubborn?"

There was silence for a while. Then Fenton Hardy answered slowly:

"My wife and boys would rather know that I died doing my duty than have me come back to them as a protector of smugglers and criminals."

"You have a very high sense of duty," sneered Snattman. "But you'll change your mind. Are you thirsty?"

There was no reply.

"Are you hungry?"

Still no answer.

"You know you are. And it'll be worse. You'll die of thirst and starvation unless you write that note."

"I'll never write it."

"All right. Come on, men. We'll leave him to himself for a while and give him time to think about it."

Frank squeezed Joe's arm in relief and exhilaration. There was still a chance to save their father!

Footsteps echoed as Snattman and the others

left the room and walked through the corridor. Finally the sounds died away and a door slammed.

Joe made a move toward the door, but Frank held him back. "We'd better wait a minute," he cautioned. "They may have left someone on guard."

The boys stood still, listening intently. But there were no further sounds from beyond the door. At length, satisfied that his father had indeed been left alone, Frank felt for the knob.

Noiselessly he opened the door about an inch, then peered into the corridor which was dimly lighted from one overhead bulb. There was no sign of a guard.

Three doors opened from the corridor—two on the opposite side from where the brothers were standing and another at the end.

The passage was floored with planks and had a beamed ceiling like a cellar. Frank and Joe quickly figured where their father was and sped across the planks to the room. They pushed open the door of the almost dark room and peered inside. There was a crude table and several chairs. In one corner stood a small cot. On it lay Fenton Hardy. He was bound hand and foot to the bed and so tightly trussed that he was unable to move more than a few inches in any direction. He was flat on his back, staring up at the ceiling of his prison. On a chair beside the cot was a sheet of paper and a

pencil, evidently the materials for the letter Snattman had demanded he write.

"Dad!" Frank and Joe cried softly.

The detective had not heard the door open,
but now he looked at his sons in amazement and
relief. "You're here!" he whispered. "Thank
goodness!"

The boys were shocked at the change in their
father's appearance. Normally a rugged-looking
man, Fenton Hardy now was thin and pale. His
cheeks were sunken and his eyes listless.

"We'll have you out of here in a minute," Frank
whispered.

"Hurry!" the detective begged. "Those demons
may be back any minute!"

Frank pulled out his pocketknife and began to
work at the ropes that bound his father. But the
knife was not very sharp and the bonds were thick.

Joe discovered that he did not have his knife
with him. "It probably slipped out of my pocket
when we undressed on the *Napoli*," he said.

"Mine's gone too," Mr. Hardy told them.
"Snattman took everything I had in my pockets,
including concentrated emergency rations. Have
you anything sweet with you?"

Joe pulled out the candy bar from his pocket
and held it, so Mr. Hardy could take a large bite
of the quick-energy food. Meanwhile, his eyes
roamed over the room in search of something

sharp which he might use to help Frank with the ropes. He saw nothing.

Mr. Hardy finished the candy bar, bite by bite. Now Joe started to help Frank by trying to untie the knots. But they were tight and he found it almost impossible to loosen them.

Minutes passed. Frank hacked at the ropes, but the dull blade made little progress. Joe worked at the obstinate knots. Fenton Hardy could give no assistance. All were silent. The only sound was the heavy breathing of the boys and the scraping of the knife against the ropes.

At last Frank was able to saw through one of the bonds and the detective's feet were free. His son pulled the ropes away and began to work on the ones that bound his father's arms. As he reached over with the knife there came a sound that sent a feeling of terror through the Hardys.

It was a heavy footstep beyond the corridor door. Someone was coming back!

Frank worked desperately with the knife, but the ropes still held stubbornly. The dull blade seemed to make almost no impression. But at last a few strands parted. Finally, with Fenton Hardy making a mighty effort and Joe clawing at the rope with his fingers, it snapped.

The detective was free!

But the footfalls of the approaching smuggler came closer.

"Quick!" Frank whispered, as he flung the ropes aside.

"I—I can't hurry!" Mr. Hardy gasped. "I've been tied up so long my feet and legs are numb."

"But we've got to hurry, Dad!" Frank said excitedly. "See if you can stand up."

"I'll—I'll do my best," his father replied, as the boys rubbed his legs vigorously to restore full circulation.

"We must run before those crooks come!" Joe said tensely.

Fenton Hardy got to his feet as hastily as he could. But when he stood up, the detective staggered and would have fallen if Frank had not taken his arm. He was so weak from hunger that a wave of dizziness had come over him. He gave his head a quick shake and the feeling passed.

"All right. Let's go," he said, clinging to both boys for support.

The three hastened out the door of the room and across the corridor to the cave. As they entered it, Mr. Hardy's knees buckled. In desperation his sons picked him up.

"You go on," he whispered. "Leave me here."

"I'm sure all of us can make it," Joe said bravely.

They reached the far door, but the delay had been costly. Just as Frank opened it, clicking off his flashlight, the corridor door was flung open and the ceiling light snapped on.

Frank leaped directly at the smuggler

Frank and Joe had a confused glimpse of the dark man whom they had seen at the pond that afternoon. Snattman! Two rough-looking companions crowded in behind him.

"What's going on here?" Snattman exclaimed, apparently not recognizing the group for a moment.

"It's the Hardys!" one of the other men cried out.

The fleeing trio started down the steps but got no farther than the landing when the smugglers appeared at the stairway and rushed down after them.

"Stop!" cried Snattman, jumping down the last three steps and whipping an automatic from his hip pocket. The place was flooded with light.

As Snattman drew closer, Frank crouched for a spring, then leaped directly at the smuggler. He struck at the man's wrist and the revolver flew out of his grasp. It skidded across the landing and clattered down the steps. Frank closed in on the man. Snattman had been taken completely by surprise. Before he could defend himself, Frank forced him against the wall.

Joe, in the meantime, with a swift uppercut had kayoed one of the other men. And Mr. Hardy, whose strength had partially returned, was battling the third as best he could.

But at this moment the boys saw their father's

adversary dodge to the wall and press a button. In an instant an alarm bell sounded in the corridor. Within seconds a new group of Snattman's gang appeared. As some held drawn revolvers, others overpowered the three Hardys.

In the face of the guns, father and sons were forced to surrender and return to the room where Mr. Hardy had been held captive before.

Within five minutes Fenton Hardy was bound again to the cot, while Frank and Joe, trussed up and unable to move, were tied to two chairs.

CHAPTER XV

Dire Threats

SNATTMAN, once he had recovered from his first consternation and surprise at finding the Hardy boys in the underground room, was in high good humor. He turned to his men.

"Just in time," he gloated, rubbing his hands together in satisfaction. "If we hadn't come here when we did, they'd have all escaped!"

The Hardy boys were silent, sick with despair. They had been sure they were going to succeed in rescuing their father and now the three of them were prisoners of the smuggling gang.

"What are we goin' to do with these guys?" asked one of the men.

The voice sounded familiar to the boys and they looked up. They were not surprised to see that the man was the red-haired one they had met at the

Pollitt place when Frank had discovered his father's cap.

"Do with them?" Snattman mused. "That's a problem. We've got three on our hands now instead of one. Best thing is to leave them all here and lock the door."

"And put gags in their traps," suggested a burly companion.

Red objected. "As long as the Hardys are around here, they're dangerous. They almost got away this time."

"Well, what do you suggest?"

"We ought to do what I wanted to do with the old man in the first place," Red declared doggedly.

"You mean get rid of them?" Snattman asked thoughtfully.

"Sure. All of them!"

"Well—" Snattman gazed at Mr. Hardy with a sinister look.

"I should think you have enough on your conscience already, Snattman!" the detective exclaimed. "I don't expect you to let me go," he added bitterly. "But release my boys. They haven't done anything but try to rescue their father. You'd do the same thing yourself."

"Oh yeah?" Snattman sneered. "Don't bother yourself about my conscience. Nobody—but nobody ever stands in my way.

"As to letting these boys go, what kind of a fool do you take me for?" Snattman shouted. "If you three are such buddies, you ought to enjoy starving together."

The smuggler laughed uproariously at what he considered a very funny remark.

Frank's and Joe's minds were racing with ideas. One thing stood out clearly. Snattman had said the Hardys almost escaped. This meant that no one was guarding the secret entrance!

"If we can only hold out a while," they thought, "the Coast Guard will arrive. There'll be nobody to stop them from coming up here."

Then, suddenly, a shocking possibility occurred to the boys. Suppose the Coast Guard could not find the camouflaged door opening from the pond!

During the conversation four of the smugglers had been whispering among themselves in the corridor. One of them now stepped into the room and faced Snattman.

"I'd like a word with you, chief," he began.

"What is it now?" The smuggler's voice was surly.

"It's about what's to be done with the Hardys, now that we've got 'em," the man said hesitantly. "It's your business what you do to people who make it tough for you when you're on your own. But not in our gang. We're in this for our take out of the smugglin', and we won't stand for too much rough stuff."

"That's right!" one of the other men spoke up.

"Is that so?" Snattman's upper lip curled. "You guys are gettin' awful righteous all of a sudden, aren't you? Look out or I'll dump the lot of you!"

"Oh, no, you won't," replied the first man who had addressed him. "We're partners in this deal and we're goin' to have our full share of what comes in. We ain't riskin' our lives for love, you know."

"We've got another idea about what to do with these three prisoners," a third smuggler spoke up. "I think it's a good one."

"What is it?" Snattman asked impatiently.

"We've been talkin' about Ali Singh."

Frank and Joe started and listened intently.

"What about him?" Snattman prodded his assistant.

"Turn the prisoners over to him. He's got a friend named Foster who's captain of a boat sailin' to the Far East tonight. Put the Hardys on board that ship," the first smuggler urged.

Snattman looked thoughtful. The idea seemed to catch his fancy.

"Not bad," he muttered. "I hadn't thought of Ali Singh. Yes, he'd take care of them. They'd never get back here." He smiled grimly.

"From what he told me about that friend of his,

the captain'd probably dump the Hardys overboard before they got very far out," the man went
on smugly. "Seems like he don't feed passengers
if he can get rid of 'em!"

"All the better. We wouldn't be responsible."

"Leave them to Ali Singh." Red chuckled evilly.
"He'll attend to them."

Snattman walked over to the cot and looked
down at Mr. Hardy. "It's too bad your boys had to
come barging in here," he said. "Now the three of
you will have to take a little ocean voyage." He
laughed. "You'll never get to the Coast Guard
to tell your story."

The detective was silent. He knew further attempts at persuasion would be useless.

"Well," said Snattman, "haven't you anything
to say?"

"Nothing. Do as you wish with me. But let the
boys go."

"We'll stick with you, Dad," said Frank quickly.

"Of course!" Joe added.

"You sure will," Snattman declared. "I'm not
going to let one of you have the chance of getting
back to Bayport with your story."

The ringleader of the smugglers stood in the
center of the room for a while, contemplating his
captives with a bitter smile. Then he turned suddenly on his heel.

"Well, they're safe enough," he told Red. "We

have that business with Burke to take care of. Come on, men, load Burke's truck. If any policemen come along and find it in the lane we'll be done for."

"How about them?" asked Red, motioning to the Hardys. "Shouldn't they be guarded?"

"They're tied up tight." Snattman gave a short laugh. "But I guess we'd better leave one guard, anyway. Malloy, you stay here and keep watch."

Malloy, a surly, truculent fellow in overalls and a ragged sweater, nodded and sat down on a box near the door. This arrangement seemed to satisfy Snattman. After warning Malloy not to fall asleep on the job and to see to it that the prisoners did not escape, he left the room. He was followed by Red and the other smugglers.

A heavy silence fell over the room after the departure of the men. Malloy crouched gloomily on the box, gazing blankly at the floor. The butt of a revolver projected from his hip pocket.

Frank strained against the ropes that bound him to the chair. But the smugglers had done their task well. He could scarcely budge.

"We'll never get out of this," he told himself ruefully.

Joe was usually optimistic but this time his spirits failed him. "We're in a tough spot," he thought. "It looks as if we'll all be on that ship by morning."

To lighten their spirits the Hardys began to talk, hoping against hope to distract the guard and perhaps overpower him.

"Shut up, you guys!" Malloy growled. "Quit your talking or I'll make it hot for you!" He tapped his revolver suggestively.

After that, a melancholy silence fell among the prisoners. All were downhearted. It looked as if their fate truly were sealed.

CHAPTER XVI

Quick Work

IN DESPAIR the boys glanced over at their father on the cot. To their surprise they saw that he was smiling.

Frank was about to ask him what he had found amusing about their predicament when his father shook his head in warning. He looked over at the guard.

Malloy was not watching the prisoners. He sat staring at the floor. Occasionally his head would fall forward, then he would jerk it back as he struggled to keep awake.

"Snattman sure made a poor selection when he chose Malloy as guard," the boys thought.

Several times the burly man straightened up, stretched his arms, and rubbed his eyes. But when he settled down again, his head began to nod.

In the meantime, the boys noticed their father struggling with his bonds. To their amazement he did not seem to be so tightly bound as they had thought. Both of them tried moving but could not budge an inch.

The boys exchanged glances, both realizing what had happened. "Dad resorted to an old trick!" Frank told himself, and Joe was silently fuming, "Why didn't we think of it?"

Mr. Hardy had profited by his previous experience. When the smugglers had seized the detective and tied him to the cot for the second time, he had used a device frequently employed by magicians and professional "escape artists" who boast that they can release themselves from tightly tied ropes and strait jackets.

The detective had expanded his chest and flexed his muscles. He had also kept his arms as far away from his sides as he could without being noticed. In this way, when he relaxed, the ropes did not bind him as securely as his captors intended.

"Oh, why were Frank and I so dumb!" Joe again chided himself.

Frank bit his lip in utter disgust at not having remembered the trick. "But then"—he eased his conscience—"Dad didn't think of it the first time, either."

Mr. Hardy had discovered that the rope binding his right wrist to the cot had a slight slack in it. He began trying to work the rope loose. This took a long time and the rough strands rubbed his wrist raw. But at last he managed to slide his right hand free.

"Hurray!" Frank almost shouted. He glanced at the guard. Malloy appeared to be sound asleep. "Hope he'll stay that way until we can escape," Frank wished fervently.

He and Joe watched their father in amazement, as they saw him grope for one of the knots. The detective fumbled at it for a while. It was slow work with only his one hand free. But the boys knew from his satisfied expression that the smugglers in their haste apparently had not tied the knots as firmly as they should have.

At this instant the guard suddenly lifted his head, and Mr. Hardy quickly laid his free hand back on the cot. He closed his eyes as if sleeping and his sons followed his example. But opening their lids a slit, they watched the smuggler carefully.

The guard grunted. "They're okay," he mumbled. Once more he tried to stay awake but found it impossible. Little by little his head sagged until his chin rested on his chest. Deep, regular breathing told the prisoners he was asleep.

Mr. Hardy now began work again on the knot of the rope that kept his left arm bound to the cot. In a matter of moments he succeeded in loosening it and the rope fell away from his arm.

After making sure the guard was still asleep, the detective sat up on the cot and struggled to release his feet. This was an easier task. The smugglers had merely passed a rope around the cot to hold the prisoner's feet. A few minutes' attention was all that was necessary for the boys' father to work his way loose.

"Now he'll release us," Joe thought excitedly, "and we can escape from here!"

As Fenton Hardy tiptoed toward his sons, the board floor squeaked loudly. The guard muttered again, as if dreaming, shook his head, then sat up.

"Oh, no!" Frank murmured, fearful of what would happen. He saw his father pick up a white rag someone had dropped.

A look of intense amazement crossed Malloy's face. As he opened his mouth to yell for help, Fenton Hardy leaped across the intervening space and flung himself on the smuggler.

"Keep quiet!" the detective ordered.

Malloy had time only to utter a muffled gasp before the detective clapped a hand over the guard's mouth, jammed the rag in it, and toppled him to the floor. The two rolled over and over in a desperate, silent struggle. The boys, helpless, looked on, their fears mounting. They knew their father had been weakened by his imprisonment and hunger, and the guard was strong and muscular. Nevertheless, the detective had the advantage of a surprise attack. Malloy had had no time to collect his wits.

Frank and Joe watched the battle in an agony of suspense. If only they could join the fight!

Mr. Hardy still had the advantage, for he could breathe better than his opponent. But suddenly Malloy managed to raise himself to his knees. He reached for the revolver at his hip.

"Look out, Dad!" Frank hissed. "He's got his gun!"

Quick as a flash the detective landed a blow on the guard's jaw. Malloy blinked and raised both hands to defend himself as he fell to the ground. Mr. Hardy darted forward and pulled the revolver out of the man's side pocket.

"No funny business!" the detective told him in a low voice.

Without being told, Malloy raised his hands in the air. He sat helplessly on the floor, beaten.

"He's got a knife too, Dad," Joe said quietly. "Watch that."

"Thanks, Joe," his father replied. Then, motioning with the pistol, he said, "All right. Let's have the knife!"

Sullenly the guard removed the knife from its leather sheath at his belt and handed it to Mr. Hardy.

Frank and Joe wanted to shout with joy, but merely grinned at their father.

Still watching Malloy, the detective walked slowly backward until he reached Joe's side. Without taking his eyes from the smuggler, he bent down and with the knife sliced at the ropes that bound his son. Fortunately, the knife was sharp and the ropes soon were cut.

"Boy, that feels good, Dad. Thanks," Joe whispered.

He sprang from the chair, took the knife, and while his father watched Malloy, he cut Frank's bonds.

"Malloy," Mr. Hardy ordered, "come over here!"

He motioned toward the bed and indicated by gestures that the smuggler was to lie down on the cot. Malloy shook his head vigorously, but was prodded over by Joe. The guard lay down on the cot.

The ropes which had held Mr. Hardy had not been cut. Quickly Frank and Joe trussed up Malloy just as their father had been tied, making certain that the knots were tight. As a final precaution they pushed in the gag which was slipping and with a piece of rope made it secure.

The whole procedure had taken scarcely five minutes. The Hardys were free!

"What now?" Frank asked his father out of earshot of Malloy. "Hide some place until the Coast Guard gets here?" Quickly he told about Tony and Chet going to bring the officers to the smugglers' hide-out.

"But they should have been here by now," Joe whispered. "They probably haven't found the secret door. Let's go down and show them."

This plan was agreed upon, but the three Hardys got no farther than the top of the first stairway when they heard rough, arguing voices below them.

"They can't be Coast Guard men," said Mr. Hardy. "We'll listen a few seconds, then we'd better run in the other direction. I know the way out to the grounds."

From below came an ugly, "You double-crosser, you! This loot belongs to the whole gang and don't you forget it!"

"Listen," said the second voice. "I don't have to take orders from you. I thought we was pals. Now you don't want to go through with the deal. Who's to know if we got ten packages or five from that friend o' Ali Singh's?"

"Okay. And the stuff'll be easier to get rid of than those drugs. They're too hot for me. Snattman can burn for kidnapin' if he wants to—I don't."

The voices had now become so loud that the Hardys did not dare wait another moment. "Come on!" the boys' father urged.

He led the way back to the corridor and along it to the door at the end. Suddenly Frank and Joe noticed him falter and were afraid he was going to faint. Joe recalled that his father had had no food except the candy bar. Ramming his hands into his pockets, he brought out another bar and some pieces of pretzel. Quickly he filled both his father's hands with them. Mr. Hardy ate them hungrily as his sons supported him under his arms and assisted him to the door.

As Frank quietly opened it, and they saw a stairway beyond, the detective said, "These steps will bring us up into a shed near the Pollitt house. There's a trap door. That's the way Snattman brought me down. Got your lights? We haven't any time to lose." Mr. Hardy seemed stronger already. "I'll take the lead."

As they ascended, Frank and Joe wondered if they would come out in the shed where they had seen the man named Klein picking up small logs.

When the detective reached the top of the stairs he ordered the lights out and pushed against the trap door. He could not budge it.

"You try," he urged the boys. "And hurry! Those men we heard may discover Malloy."

"And then things will start popping!" Frank murmured.

The boys heaved their shoulders against the trap door. In a moment there came the rumble of rolling logs. The door went up easily.

Frank peered out. No one seemed to be around.

He stepped up into the shed and the others followed.

The three stood in silence. The night was dark. The wind, blowing through the trees, made a moaning sound. Before the Hardys rose the gloomy mass of the house on the cliff. No lights could be seen.

From the direction of the lane came dull, thudding sounds. The boys and their father assumed the smugglers' truck was being loaded with the goods which were to be disposed of by the man named Burke.

Suddenly the Hardys heard voices from the corridor they had just left. Quickly Frank closed the trap door and Joe piled up the logs. Then, silently, the Hardys stole out into the yard.

CHAPTER XVII

Hostages

LITHE as Indians the three Hardys hurried across the lawn and disappeared among the trees. They headed for the road, a good distance away.

"I hope a bus comes along," Frank said to himself. "Then we can get to a phone and report—"

His thought was rudely interrupted as the boys and their father heard a sound that struck terror to their hearts—the clatter of the logs tumbling off the trap door!

An instant later came a hoarse shout. "Chief! Red! The Hardys got away! Watch out for them!"

"He must be one of the men we heard coming up from the shore," Joe decided. "They must have found Malloy trussed up!"

Instantly the place became alive with smugglers flashing their lights. Some of the men ran from the truck toward the road, shouting. Others began to comb the woods. Another man emerged from the trap door. He and his companion dashed to the ocean side of the house.

Two burly smugglers flung open the kitchen door and ran out. One shouted, "They ain't in the house!"

"And they're not down at the shore!" the other yelled. "I just talked to Klein on the phone down there."

"You guys better not let those Hardys get away!" Snattman's voice cut through the night. "It'll be the pen for all of you!"

"Fenton Hardy's got a gun! He took Malloy's!" came a warning voice from the far side of the house. The two men who had gone to the front now returned. "He never misses his mark!"

When the fracas had started, the detective had pulled his sons to the ground, told them to lie flat, face down, and not to move. Now they could hear the pounding steps of the smugglers as they dashed among the trees. The boys' hearts pounded wildly. It did not seem possible they could be missed!

Yet man after man ran within a few yards of the three prone figures and dashed on toward the road. Presently Mr. Hardy raised his head and looked toward the Pollitt mansion.

"Boys," he said tensely, "we'll make a run for

the kitchen door. The men won't expect us to go there."

The three arose. Swiftly and silently they crossed the dark lawn and slipped into the house. Apparently no one had seen them.

"When Snattman doesn't find us outdoors," Joe whispered, "won't he look here to make sure?"

"Yes," Mr. Hardy replied. "But by that time I hope the Coast Guard and State Police will arrive."

"Joe and I found a hidden stairway to the attic," Frank spoke up. "Snattman won't think of looking in it. Let's hide up there."

"You forget the ghost," Joe reminded his brother. "*He* knows we found that stairway."

"Nevertheless, Frank's suggestion is a good one," Mr. Hardy said. "Let's go to the attic. Were any clothes hanging in the closet that might be used to conceal the door?"

"Yes, a man's bathrobe on a rod."

The Hardys did not dare use a light and had to make their way along by feeling walls, and the stair banister, with Frank in the lead and Mr. Hardy between the boys. Reaching the second floor, Frank looked out the rear window of the hall.

"The smugglers are coming back!" he remarked in a low voice. "The lights are heading this way!"

The Hardys doubled their speed, but it was still slow going, for they banged into chairs and a wardrobe as Frank felt his way along the hall toward the bedroom where the hidden staircase was.

Finally the trio reached it. Just as Frank was about to open the door to the attic, a door on the first floor swung open with a resounding bang.

"Scatter and search every room!" Snattman's crisp voice rang out.

"We're trapped!" Joe groaned.

"Maybe not," Frank said hopefully. "I have a hunch Klein was the ghost. It's possible that he's the only one who knows about this stairway and he's down at the shore."

"We'll risk going up," Mr. Hardy decided. "But not a sound." He slid the bathrobe across the rod, so that it would hide the door.

"The stairs creak," Joe informed him.

Mr. Hardy told his sons to push down the treads slowly but firmly with their hands and hold them there until they put one foot between them and then raised up to their full weight.

"And lean forward, so you won't lose your balance," he warned.

Fearful that he could not accomplish this, Frank opened the door carefully and started up in the pitch blackness. But the dread thought of capture made him use extreme caution and he reached the attic without having made a sound.

After closing the door, Joe and his father quickly followed. The three moved noiselessly to a spot out of sight of the stairway behind a large trunk.

They sat down and waited, not daring even to whisper. From downstairs they could hear running footsteps, banging doors, and loud talk.

"Not here!"

"Not here!"

"Not here!"

The search seemed to come to an end, for the second-floor group had gathered right in the room where the secret stairway was.

"This is it! The end! They're going to search up here!" Frank thought woefully.

His father reached over and grasped a hand of each of his sons in a reassuring grip. Someone yanked open the closet door. The Hardys became tense. Would the robe over the entrance to the secret stairway fool him?

"Empty!" the man announced and shut the door. The smugglers went downstairs.

There were fervent handshakes among the detective and his sons. Other than this they did not move a muscle of their bodies, although they inwardly relaxed.

Now new worries assailed the Hardys. It was possible that Snattman and his gang, having been alerted, would move out and disappear before the police or Coast Guard could get to the house on the cliff.

Frank's heart gave a jump. He suddenly realized that his father was hiding to protect his sons. Had he been alone, the intrepid detective would have been downstairs battling to get the better of Snattman and break up the smuggling ring.

"What a swell father he is!" Frank thought. Then another idea came to him. "Maybe being here isn't such a bad plan after all. Dad might have been fatally shot if he'd been anywhere else on the property."

A moment later the Hardys again became aware of voices on the second floor. They recognized one as Snattman's, the other as Klein's.

"Yeah, there's a secret stairway to the attic," Klein announced. "I found it when I was playin' ghost. And them Hardy boys—they found it too. I'll bet my last take on those rare drugs we're gettin' tonight that the dick and his sons are up in that attic!"

The Hardys' spirits sank. They were going to be captured again after all!

They heard the door at the foot of the stairway open. "Go up and look, Klein," ordered Snattman.

"Not me. Fenton Hardy has Malloy's gun."

"I said go up!"

"You can't make me," Klein objected in a whining tone. "I'd be a sure target 'cause I couldn't see him. He'd be hiding and let me have it so quick I'd never know what hit me."

Despite the grave situation, Frank's and Joe's

faces were creased in smiles, but they faded as Snattman said, "I'll go myself. Give me that big light!"

Suddenly a brilliant beam was cast into the attic. It moved upward, accompanied by heavy footsteps.

"Hardy, if you want to live, say so!" Snattman said, an evil ring in his voice.

No answer from the detective.

"We've got you cornered this time!"

Mr. Hardy did not reply.

"Listen, Hardy!" Snattman shouted. "I know you're up there because you moved that bathrobe. I'll give you just one minute to come down out of that attic!"

Still no answer and an interval of silence followed.

Then came Snattman's voice again. "This is your last chance, Hardy!"

Nearly a minute went by without a sign from the two enemy camps. Then Snattman moved up the stairs a few more steps.

"Hardy, I have a proposition to make to you," he said presently. "I know you don't want to die and you want those boys of yours to live too. Well, so do I want to live. So let's call it quits."

The detective maintained his silence and Snattman continued up the steps. "Give you my

"You are my hostages!" the smuggler sneered

word I won't shoot. And I know you never fire first unless you have to."

A moment later he appeared at the top of the stairs, empty-handed except for the light. In a moment he spotted the Hardys with his high-powered flashlight.

"Here's the proposition—your lives in exchange for mine and my gang's."

"How do you mean?" Mr. Hardy asked coldly.

"I mean," the smuggler said, "that you are my hostages."

"Hostages!" Frank and Joe exclaimed together.

"Yes. If my men and I can get our stuff moved away before the police or the Coast Guard might happen in here, then you can leave a little later."

"But if they do come?" Frank asked.

"Then I'll bargain with them," Snattman answered. "And I don't think they'll turn me down. They don't know where you are, but I'll make them understand I mean business. If they take me, you three die!"

Frank and Joe gasped. The famous Fenton Hardy and his sons were to be used as a shield to protect a ruthless gang of criminals!

The boys looked at their father in consternation. To their amazement he looked calm, but his mouth was drawn in a tight line.

"It won't do you any good to shoot me, Hardy," the smuggler said. "Mallory said all the chambers in that gat are empty but one. If the gang hears a shot, they'll be up here in a minute to finish you all off properly."

The Hardys realized that if Snattman's remark about the gun were true, they were indeed at the mercy of this cunning, scheming, conniving smuggler. He now started backing toward the stairway.

"I think I'm a pretty fair guy," he said with the trace of a satisfied smile.

"And one to be hated and feared!" Joe thought in a rage. "We've *got* to outwit this man somehow!" he determined.

But at the moment the possibility of this looked hopeless.

CHAPTER XVIII

Coast Guard Action

WHILE the Hardy boys had been investigating the smugglers' hide-out and had been captured, together with their father, Tony and Chet were trying their best to accomplish the errand which Frank and Joe had given them.

During the early part of their trip back to Bayport to contact the Coast Guard, the *Napoli* had cut through the darkness like a streak. Then suddenly Tony exclaimed, "Oh, oh! My starboard light just went out."

Chet turned to look at the portside. "This light's all right. Must be the bulb in the other one."

"That's what I was afraid of," said Tony. "I'll bet I haven't another bulb."

"You mean, somebody might not see the *Napoli* and ram us?" Chet asked fearfully.

"We'll have to be careful," Tony replied.

"Chet, take the wheel, will you? I'll see if I can find an extra bulb."

Chet changed places with Tony, throttled the motor, and gazed intently ahead. The moon had not yet risen and it was difficult to see very far ahead.

"Find anything?" Chet called out, as Tony finished his round of the lockers and was now rummaging in the last one.

"Not yet." Tony pulled out a canvas bag, a pair of sneakers, and some fishing tackle. As he reached in for the last article in the locker, he gave a whoop of joy. "Here's one bulb—just one—keep your fingers crossed, pal. If this isn't any good, we're in a mess."

"And breaking the law besides," Chet added.

He held his breath as Tony went forward and crawled inside the prow of the *Napoli*. With a flashlight, Tony found the protecting shield for the bulb and unfastened it. After removing the dead bulb, he screwed in the new one. As the light flashed on, Tony breathed a sigh of relief and started to crawl out of the prow.

"Good work!" Chet said. "It's lucky we—"

Chet never finished the sentence. At this instant he saw another speedboat loom up in front of him. Like lightning he swung the wheel around, missing the oncoming craft by inches!

"You fool!" the driver of the other boat

shouted. "Why don't you look where you're going?"

Chet did not reply. He was quivering. Besides, he had stalled the motor, which had been throttled so low it had not been able to take the terrific swerving. "Oh, now I've done it!" the stout boy wailed.

There was no response from Tony for several seconds. He had been thrown violently against the side of the boat and was dazed. But he quickly collected his wits and crawled down beside Chet.

"What happened?" he asked.

Chet told him, then said, "You'd better take over. I'm a rotten pilot."

Tony took the seat behind the wheel, started the motor, and sped off toward Barmet Bay.

"We've sure wasted a lot of time," he remarked. "I wonder how Frank and Joe are making out."

"Hope they found Mr. Hardy," Chet added.

There was no more conversation until the boys turned into the bay. The Coast Guard station for the area was a short distance along the southern shore of the bay and Tony headed the *Napoli* directly for it. He pulled up at the dock, where two patrol boats and a cutter were tied.

The two boys climbed out and hurried up to the white building. As they were about to enter it, Chet and Tony were amazed to find Biff Hooper and Phil Cohen coming out of it. Jerry Gilroy, another Bayport High friend, was with them.

"Well, for Pete's sake!" the three cried out, and Biff added, "Boy, are we glad to see you! Where are Frank and Joe?"

"Still hunting for the smugglers," Chet replied. "What brings you here?"

Biff explained that an hour ago Mrs. Hardy had telephoned him to see if he had heard from Frank and Joe. She confessed to being exceedingly worried about her sons. Mrs. Hardy knew they had gone to look for their father and she was in a panic that they had been captured by the same men who were possibly holding her husband.

"I told her I'd round up a couple of the fellows and go on a hunt," Biff went on. "Jerry thought maybe Frank and Joe had come back to town and were somewhere around. We looked, but we couldn't find them anywhere, so we borrowed Mr. Gilroy's car and came out here to tell the Coast Guard. They're going to send out boats. You'd better come in and talk to Chief Warrant Officer Robinson yourself."

The boys hurried inside. Quickly Chet and Tony told of the Hardys' suspicion that they had found the entrance to the smugglers' hide-out.

"Can you send help out there right away?" Chet asked. "We'll show you where the secret tunnel is."

"This is astounding," said Chief Robinson. "I'll order the *Alice* out. You can start within five minutes."

"I'll phone Mrs. Hardy right away," Jerry offered. "I'm afraid, though, that the news isn't going to make her feel too good."

While Jerry was gone, Chet told the chief warrant officer that the Hardys thought they knew the names of two of the men who were involved in the smuggling racket. Chet revealed the Hardy suspicions about Snattman being one and Ali Singh the other.

"We think Ali is a crewman on the *Marco Polo* that's going to dock early tomorrow morning in Bayport," Chet continued. "Frank and Joe got a tip that makes them think this is the deal: While the ship is offshore, Ali Singh pitches stolen drugs overboard and one of the smugglers picks the package up in a speedboat."

Robinson raised his eyebrows. "Those Hardy boys certainly take after their father," he remarked. "They have the makings of good detectives."

Biff told the Coast Guard officer of the boys' adventure at the haunted house on their first visit to the Pollitt place. "Frank and Joe are sure there is some connection between the house and the smugglers."

"And they are probably right," the chief remarked. "I'll call the State Police at once and tell them the latest developments in this case."

The boys waited while he made the report. Jerry, who had just finished telephoning Mrs. Hardy, said that she seemed even more worried than before but relieved that the Coast Guard was going to take a hand.

The chief warrant officer then told the boys he would get in touch with the captain of the *Marco Polo* at once by ship-to-shore telephone. The connection was made and the boys listened with great interest to the conversation. The captain had a booming voice which they could hear plainly.

"Yes, I have a sailor named Ali Singh," he replied in answer to Chief Robinson's question. "He's a member of the kitchen crew."

After he had been told that Ali Singh was suspected of stealing drug shipments and dropping them overboard to a confederate, he said, "That would be pretty easy for him to do. Singh probably throws them out when he dumps garbage into the water, even though he's not supposed to do it. The drugs could be in an inflated waterproof bag."

"Captain, will you have someone keep an eye on this Ali Singh without his knowing he's being watched?" Chief Robinson requested. "I'll send a patrol boat out from here to watch for any of his gang who may be in a small boat waiting to pick up something he dumps overboard. How far offshore are you?"

"About sixteen miles from your headquarters," was the answer.

"Will you keep in touch with the patrol boat?" Robinson requested. "It's the *Henley,* in charge of Chief Petty Officer Brown."

"I'll do that."

"Ali Singh can be arrested when your ship docks."

As the conversation was concluded, a uniformed coastguardman came in. He was introduced as Chief Petty Officer Bertram in charge of the *Alice,* which would follow Tony and Chet to the smugglers' hide-out.

"I'm ready, sir," he told his chief, after a short briefing. He turned to the boys. "All set?"

Chet and Tony nodded. As they turned to follow Bertram, Biff, Phil, and Jerry looked glum.

Noting the expressions on the three boys, Chief Robinson leaned across his desk and said, "I guess you fellows were hoping to be in on this too. How would you like to go on the *Henley* with Chief Petty Officer Brown and watch the fun?"

The eyes of the three boys lighted up and Phil said, "You mean it?"

"Do you want a formal invitation?" Chief Robinson asked with a laugh.

He rang for Chief Petty Officer Brown, and after introducing the boys, he explained what the mission of the *Henley* was to be.

"I understand, sir," Brown replied. "We'll leave at once."

The three boys followed him down to the dock and went aboard. They met the other Coast Guard men and the fast patrol boat set off. It seemed to the boys as if the sixteen miles were covered in an incredibly short time. The lights of the *Marco Polo* loomed up in the distance.

"She's moving very slowly, isn't she?" Biff asked their skipper.

"Yes, she's making only about four knots."

"So it would be easy for a small boat to come alongside and take something from her?" Phil suggested.

"Yes, it would." Quickly the officer picked up a telescope and trained it on the large craft. "The galley hatches are on the left and the tide is coming in," he reported. "Anything thrown overboard will float toward shore."

He ordered the wheelsman to go past the *Marco Polo,* come down the other side, and approach within three hundred yards, then turn off the engine and lights.

When they reached the designated spot, Petty Officer Brown ordered everyone on board the *Henley* not to talk or to move around. The *Marco*

Polo's decks, as well as the water some distance from the craft, was illuminated by light from some of the stateroom portholes. Biff, Phil, and Jerry crowded close to the chief as he trained his powerful binoculars on the galley hatches, so he could give them a running account of anything that might happen. The officer reported little activity aboard the *Marco Polo* and the boys assumed that the passengers either were asleep or packing their luggage in anticipation of landing the next morning.

Suddenly Petty Officer Brown saw one of the hatches open. A small man, with a swarthy complexion and rather longish coal-black hair, appeared in the circular opening. He looked out, then raised a large pail and dumped its contents into the water. Quickly he closed the hatch.

"Ali Singh!" the three boys thought as Brown reported what he had seen.

They watched excitedly to see what would happen now.

Suddenly Biff grabbed Phil's arm and pointed. Vaguely they could see a long pole with a scooping net fastened to the end of it appear from outside the circle of light and fish among the debris. Petty Officer Brown reported that apparently the person holding the pole had found what he wanted, for he scooped something up and the pole vanished from sight.

The boys strained their ears for the sound of a small boat. It did not come and they were puzzled. They also wondered why Petty Officer Brown seemed to be doing nothing about trying to apprehend the person.

The tense skipper suddenly handed the binoculars to Phil. Without a word the puzzled boy looked through them at the spot where Brown had been gazing. To his amazement he could make out the dim shape of a speedboat with two figures in it. Each held an oar and was rowing the small boat away from the *Marco Polo* as fast as possible.

"We've got the smugglers dead to rights!" Petty Officer Brown whispered to the boys.

"Aren't you going to arrest them?" Phil asked.

"Not yet," the officer told him. "I'm afraid we can't do it without some shooting. I don't want to scare the passengers on the *Marco Polo*. We'll wait a few minutes."

Suddenly the engine of the smugglers' speedboat was started. Tersely, Brown began issuing orders to his men. The motors roared into action.

The chase was on!

CHAPTER XIX

The Chase

IN A few minutes the *Henley's* brilliant search-light was turned on. It picked up the speedboat which was racing toward shore at full power. But gradually the Coast Guard boat lessened the distance between them.

Chief Petty Officer Brown picked up a mega-phone and shouted for the fleeing men to stop. They paid no attention.

"We'll have to show them we mean business," the officer told Biff, Phil, and Jerry. "We'll shoot across their bow."

He ordered the boys out of the line of fire, in case the smugglers should attempt to retaliate. They obeyed, and though from their shelter the three could not see the speedboat, they listened intently to what was going on.

The *Henley* plowed ahead and presently the boys heard a shot whistle through the air.

"Stop your engine!" Brown commanded. A second later he added, "Drop those guns!"

The smugglers evidently did both, for Skipper Brown said to the boys, "You fellows can come forward now."

The three scrambled to his side. Biff was just in time to see one of the two captured men half turn and slyly run his hand into the large pocket of his sports jacket. Biff expected him to pull out a gun and was about to warn Brown when the smuggler withdrew his hand and dropped something into the water.

"The rare drugs!" Biff thought.

Instantly he began peeling off his clothes, and when the others asked him what he was doing this for, he merely said, "Got an underwater job to do."

Biff was over the side in a flash and swimming with strong, long strokes to the speedboat. He went beyond it and around to the far side.

In the meantime, Petty Officer Brown had ordered the smugglers to put their hands over their heads. As the *Henley* came alongside, two of the enlisted coastguardmen jumped across and slipped handcuffs on them. Brown instructed one of the enlisted men to take their prisoners back to Coast Guard headquarters in the smugglers' boat.

"You got nothin' on us! You ain't got no right to arrest us!" one of the captured men cried out.

At that moment Biff Hooper's head appeared over the side of the speedboat and a moment later he clambered aboard. He called out, "You've got plenty on these men! Here's the evidence!"

He held up a waterproof bag, tightly sealed. It was transparent and the printing on the contents was easily read. "I happen to know that what's in here is a rare drug," Biff added. "I heard our doctor mention it just a few days ago."

This announcement took the bravado out of the smugglers. The two men insisted they were only engaged to pilot the speedboat and deliver the drugs. But they would not give the name of the person who had hired them, nor the spot to which they were supposed to go.

"We know both the answers already," Petty Officer Brown told the smugglers. Then he said to his wheelsman, "Head for the house on the cliff! They may need a little more help over there."

Biff was hauled aboard, and as he put his clothes back on, the *Henley* shot through the water. He whispered to his pals, "We'll see some more excitement, maybe."

Some time before this, Chet and Tony had reached the area where the secret tunnel was. The patrol boat which had been following them turned on its great searchlight to pick out the exact spot.

"Look!" Chet cried out.

A speedboat with two men in it had just entered

the choppy, rocky waters in front of the tunnel.

"Halt!" Skipper Bertram of the *Alice* ordered.

The man at the wheel obeyed the command and turned off his motor. But instead of surrendering, he shouted to his companion, "Dive, Sneffen!"

Quick as a flash the two smugglers disappeared into the water on the far side of their boat. When they did not reappear, Chet called:

"I'll bet they're swimming underwater to the tunnel. Aren't we going after them?"

"We sure are," Petty Officer Bertram replied. "Tony, can you find the channel which leads to that tunnel?"

"I think so," Tony answered, eying the smugglers' speedboat which now, unattended, had been thrown violently by the waves onto some rocks.

"Then we'll come on board your boat," the chief petty officer stated. He left two of his own men aboard the *Alice* to guard it and to be ready for any other smugglers who might be arriving at the hide-out.

The rest of the crew, including Bertram himself, climbed aboard the *Napoli*, and Tony started through the narrow passage between the rocks leading to the tunnel. One of the enlisted men in the prow of the boat operated a portable searchlight. Everyone kept looking for the swimmers, as they went through the tunnel, but did not see them. When the *Napoli* reached the pond, the man swung his light around the circular shore line.

"There they are!" Chet cried out.

The two smugglers, dripping wet, had just opened the secret door into the cliff. They darted through and the door closed behind them.

Tony pulled his boat to the ledge in front of the door, turned off the engine, and jumped ashore with the others. To their surprise the door was not locked.

"I'll go first," Bertram announced.

"But be careful!" Chet begged. "There may be a man with a gun on the other side!"

The officer ordered everyone to stand back as he pulled the door open. He beamed the searchlight inside. No one was in sight!

"Come on, men!" the skipper said excitedly.

The group quickly went along the route the Hardys had discovered earlier. When they reached the corridor and saw the three doors, Tony suggested that they look inside to see if the Hardys were prisoners. One by one each room was examined but found to be empty.

The searchers hurried on down the corridor and up the stairway which led to the woodshed of the Pollitt place. They pushed the trap door but it did not open. Their light revealed no hidden springs or catches.

"The two smugglers that got away from us may have sounded an alarm," Bertram said. "They probably set something heavy on top of this trap door to delay us."

"Then we'll heave it off!" Chet declared.

He and Tony, with two of the enlisted men, put their shoulders to the trap door and heaved with all their might. At last it raised a little, then fell back into place.

"It isn't nailed shut from the other side at any rate," Bertram said. "Give it another shove!"

The four beneath it tried once more. Now they all could hear something sliding sideways.

"All together now!" Chet said, puffing. "One, two, three!"

The heave that followed did the trick. A heavy object above toppled with a crash, and the trap door opened. As before, Chief Petty Officer Bertram insisted upon being the first one out. There was not a sound from the grounds nor the house and not a light in evidence. He told the others to come up but cautioned:

"This may be an ambush. Watch your step and if anything starts to pop, you two boys go back down through the trap door."

Suddenly there was a sound of cars turning into the lane leading to the Pollitt place. The vehicles' lights were so bright that Bertram said, "I believe it's the police!"

A few moments later the cars reached the rear of the old house and state troopers piled out. Chief

Petty Officer Bertram hurried forward to introduce himself to Captain Ryder of the State Police. The two held a whispered conversation. From what the boys overheard, they figured that the troopers planned to raid the house.

Just as the men seemed to have reached a decision, everyone was amazed to see a man appear at the rear window of the second-floor hall. He held a gun in his right hand, but with his left he gestured for attention.

"My name's Snattman," he announced with a theatrical wave of his hand. "Before you storm this place, I want to talk to you! I know you've been looking for me and my men a long time. But I'm not going to let you take me without some people on your side getting killed first!" He paused dramatically.

"Come to the point, Snattman," Captain Ryder called up to him. He, too, had a gun poised for action should this become necessary.

"I mean," the smuggler cried out, "that I got three hostages in this house—Fenton Hardy and his two sons!"

Chet and Tony jumped. The boys had found their father, only to become captives themselves. And now the three were to be used as hostages!

"What's the rest?" Captain Ryder asked acidly.

"This: If you'll let me and my men go, we'll clear out of here. One will stay behind long

enough to tell you where the Hardys are." Snattman now set his jaw. "But if you come in and try
to take us, it'll be curtains for the Hardys!"

Chet's and Tony's hearts sank. What was going
to be the result of this nightmarish dilemma?

In the meantime Frank, Joe, and their father,
for the past hour, had despaired of escaping before
Snattman might carry out his sinister threat. After
the smuggler left the attic, they had heard hammering and suspected the smugglers were nailing
bars across the door. The Hardys tiptoed to the
foot of the stairway, only to find their fears confirmed.

"If those bars are made of wood," Frank whispered, "maybe we can cut through them with our
knives without too much noise."

"We'll try," his father agreed. "Joe, take that
knife I got from Malloy."

As Detective Hardy sat on the steps, leaning
weakly against the wall, his two sons got to work.
They managed to maneuver the knives through
the crack near the knob. Finding the top of the
heavy crossbars, the boys began to cut and hack
noiselessly. Frank's knife was already dull and it
was not long before Joe's became so. This greatly
hampered their progress.

Half an hour later the boys' arms were aching
so badly that Frank and Joe wondered how they
could continue. But the thought that their lives

were at stake drove them on. They would rest for two or three minutes, then continue their efforts. Finally Joe finished cutting through one bar and started on the second of the three they had found. Ten minutes later Frank managed to cut through his.

"Now we can take turns," he told his brother.

Working this way, with rest periods in between, the boys found the task less arduous.

"We're almost free!" Joe finally said hopefully.

Just then, the Hardys heard cars coming into the driveway. They were sure that the police had arrived because of the illumination flooding the place even to the crack under the attic door.

It was less than a minute later that they heard the cars come to a stop outside and then Snattman's voice bargaining for his own life in exchange for his hostages!

"Let's break this door down and take our chances," Frank whispered hoarsely.

"No!" his father said. "Snattman and his men would certainly shoot us!"

At this instant Frank gave a low cry of glee. His knife had just hacked through the last wooden bar. Turning the knob, he opened the door and the three Hardys stole silently from their prison.

From the bedroom doorway they peered out to where Snattman was still trying to bargain with the police. No one else was around. The boys and their father looked at one another, telegraphing a common thought.

They would rush the king of the smugglers and overpower him!

CHAPTER XX

The Smuggler's Request

As THE three Hardys crept forward, hoping to overpower Snattman before he saw them, they heard a voice outside the house say, "You'll never get away with this, Snattman! You may as well give up without any shooting!"

"I'll never give up!"

"The house is surrounded with troopers and Coast Guard men!"

"What do I care?" Snattman shouted, waving his arms out the window. "I got three hostages here, and I've got one of the Coast Guard."

"He's in the house too?"

Snattman laughed. "Trying to catch me, eh? Well, I'm not going to answer that question."

There was silence outside the house. This seemed to worry the man. He cried out, "It won't do you any good to talk things over! I got you where I want you and—"

Like three stalking panthers Frank, Joe, and their father pounced upon the unwary smuggler. Mr. Hardy knocked the man's gun from his hand. It flew out the window and thudded to the ground below. The boys pinned his arms back and buckled in his knees.

From below came a whoop of joy. "The Hardys have captured Snattman!" The voice was Chet Morton's.

"My men will never let you in here!" the victim screamed. He snarled, twisted, and turned in his captors' grip.

Mr. Hardy, fearful that Snattman would shout to order his men upstairs, clamped a hand over the smuggler's mouth. By this time there was terrific confusion inside and outside the Pollitt place. State troopers and the Coast Guard men had burst into both the front and rear doors.

Others guarded the sides of the house to prevent any escape from the windows. A few shots were fired, but soon the smuggling gang gave up without fighting further. The capture of their leader and the sudden attack had unnerved them.

The Hardys waited upstairs with their prisoner. In a few moments Chet and Tony appeared and behind them, to the utter astonishment of Frank and Joe, were Biff, Phil, and Jerry.

Stories were quickly exchanged and Mr. Hardy praised Frank's and Joe's chums for their efforts.

All this time Snattman glowered maliciously.

In a few moments chief petty officers Bertram and Brown appeared in the second-floor hall with Captain Ryder. Immediately the state trooper fastened handcuffs onto the prisoner. He was about to take him away when Frank spoke up:

"There's someone else involved in this smuggling who hasn't been captured yet."

"You mean the man who got away from here in the truck?" Officer Ryder asked. "We've set up a roadblock for him and expect to capture him any minute."

Frank shook his head. "Ali Singh, the crewman on the *Marco Polo,* has a friend who owns a small cargo ship. Right now, it's lying somewhere offshore. Snattman was thinking of putting my dad, Joe, and me on it and arranging things so that we never got home again."

The king of the smugglers, who had been silent for several minutes, now cried out, "You're crazy! There's not a word of truth in it! There isn't any boat offshore!"

The others ignored the man. As soon as he stopped yelling, Joe took up the story. "I have a hunch you'll find that your Coast Guard man is a prisoner on that cargo ship. The name of the captain is Foster."

"You mean our man Ayres is on that ship?" Petty Officer Brown asked unbelievingly.

"We don't know anyone named Ayres," Frank began. He stopped short and looked at his brother. They nodded significantly at each other, then Frank asked, "Does Ayres go under the name of Jones?"

"He might, if he were cornered. You see, he's sort of a counterspy for the Coast Guard. He pretended to join the smugglers and we haven't heard from him since Saturday."

"I found out about him," Snattman bragged. "That name Jones didn't fool us. I saw him make a sneak trip to your patrol boat."

Frank and Joe decided this was the scene they had seen through the telescope. They told about their rescue of "Jones" after a hand grenade had nearly killed him. They also gave an account of how his kidnapers had come to the Kane farmhouse, bound up the farmer and his wife, and taken "Jones."

Skipper Brown said he would send a patrol boat out to investigate the waters in the area and try to find Captain Foster's ship.

"We'll wait here for you," Captain Ryder stated. "This case seems to be one for both our branches of service. Two kidnapings on land and a theft from the *Marco Polo,* as well as an undeclared vessel offshore."

While he was gone, the Hardys attempted to question Snattman. He refused to admit any guilt in connection with smuggling operations or the shipment of stolen goods from one state to another. Frank decided to talk to him along different lines, hoping that the smuggler would inadvertently confess something he did not intend to.

"I heard you inherited this house from your uncle, Mr. Pollitt," Frank began.

"That's right. What's it to you?"

Frank was unruffled. "I was curious about the tunnel and the stairways and the cave," he said pleasantly. "Did your uncle build them?"

Snattman dropped his sullen attitude. "No, he didn't," the smuggler answered. "My uncle found them all by accident. He started digging through his cellar wall to enlarge the place, and broke right through to that corridor."

"I see," said Frank. "Have you any idea who did build it?"

Snattman said that his uncle had come to the conclusion that the tunnel and pond had been discovered by pirates long, long ago. They apparently had decided it would be an ideal hide-out and had built the steps all the way to the top of the ground.

"Of course the woodshed wasn't there then," Snattman explained. "At least not the one that's here now. The trap door was, though, but there was a tumble-down building over it."

"How about the corridor? Was it the same size when your uncle found it?"

"Yes," the smuggler answered. "My uncle figured that was living quarters for the pirates when they weren't on their ship."

"Pretty fascinating story," Tony Prito spoke up.

Several seconds of silence followed. Snattman's eyes darted from one boy to another. Finally they fastened on Frank Hardy and he said:

"Now that I'm going to prison, the eyepieces to your telescope, and your motorcycle tools, won't do me any good. You'll find them in a drawer in the kitchen."

"Thanks a lot," said Frank.

There was another short silence. Then the smuggler went on, his head down and his eyes almost closed, "Mr. Hardy, I envy you. And I—I never thought I'd be making this kind of a confession. You know almost everything about what I've been doing. I'll tell the whole story later. Since they're going to find that Coast Guard officer, Ayres, on Foster's ship there's no use in my holding out any longer.

"I said I envy you, Mr. Hardy. It's because you brought up two such fine boys and they got swell friends. Me—I wasn't so lucky. My father died when I was little. I was pretty headstrong and my mother couldn't manage me. I began to make the

wrong kind of friends and after that—you know
how it is.

"My uncle, who owned this place, might have
helped me, but he was mean and selfish and never
gave us any money. The most he would do was invite my mother and me here once in a while for a
short visit. I hated him because he made my
mother work very hard around the house all the
time we were here. It wasn't any vacation for her.

"One of the times when I was here my uncle
showed me the pirates' hide-out and I never forgot it. After I got in with a gang of hoods I kept
thinking about this place, and what a swell hide-
out it would be for smugglers. I was afraid to try
it while my uncle was alive. But when I heard he
was dead, I thought that was my chance.

"You see, I didn't dare go to claim the property as the rightful heir. But now I'm planning to
take it over. Of course it won't do me any good,
because I know I'll have to do a long stretch in the
pen. But I'm going to ask those executors to use
my uncle's money to run this place as a boys'
home—I mean a place where boys without proper
home training can come to live."

The group listening to Snattman, king of the
smugglers, were too overwhelmed by his complete
change of heart to say anything for a few seconds.
But when the man looked up, as if pleading for
his hearers to believe him, Mr. Hardy said, "That's

a very fine thing for you to do, Snattman. I'm sure that the boys who benefit from living here will always be grateful to you."

The solemn scene was suddenly interrupted by the return of Chief Petty Officer Brown. He reported that another patrol boat had picked up his message about Captain Foster's ship and within a few minutes had reported sighting it. Then, within a quarter of an hour, word came that Captain Foster had been put under arrest, and that the missing Coast Guard man had been found on the ship, as well as a quantity of merchandise which the captain had expected Snattman to remove.

The prisoners were now taken away from the Pollitt home and the Hardys and their friends found themselves alone.

Chet asked suddenly, "How do we get home?"

Tony grinned. "I guess the *Napoli* will hold all of us."

The group went to the woodshed, opened the trap door, and started down the secret passageway to the pond below. They climbed into the *Napoli* and Tony slipped behind the wheel. The Coast Guard men thoughtfully had left the portable searchlight on the prow and Tony was able to make the trip through the tunnel and the narrow channel out to the ocean without accident.

Suddenly Frank spoke up, "Dad, what happened to your car?"

Mr. Hardy smiled. "It's in Bayport in a garage. I was being followed, so I shook off the shadowers and took the bus." He added ruefully, "But it didn't do me much good. Snattman's men attacked me and took me prisoner on the road."

The famous detective now said, "While I have the chance, I want to thank each of you boys individually for what you did. Without the seven of you, this case might never have been solved and I might not have been found alive."

Modestly Frank and Joe and their friends acknowledged the praise, secretly hoping another mystery would come their way soon. One did and by learning *The Secret of the Old Mill* the Hardy boys encountered a cunning gang of counterfeiters.

Suddenly Joe remarked, "Compliments are flying around here pretty thick, but there's one person we forgot to mention. Without him, Frank and I might never have found Dad."

"Who's that?" Biff asked.

"Pretzel Pete!" Joe replied.

"That's right," said Frank. "All together, fellows! A rousing cheer for Pretzel Pete!"

The Hardy Boys Mystery Stories®

THE GHOST AT SKELETON ROCK

BY

FRANKLIN W. DIXON

GROSSET & DUNLAP
Publishers • New York
A member of The Putnam & Grosset Group

CONTENTS

CHAPTER I

A Puzzling Message

"LET's see if you can get us down in one piece, Frank!" Blond, seventeen-year-old Joe Hardy leaned forward in the airplane as his brother circled in for a landing at the Bayport airfield.

"Don't worry, Joe. If we crack up the first time, I'll try again," the dark-haired boy quipped. Frank, who was a year older than Joe, grinned as he eased the craft downward in a graceful turn.

A third occupant of the plane, the regular pilot, smiled and said, "You're doing fine, Frank." Jack Wayne, lean-faced and tanned, was Mr. Hardy's pilot on all his chartered flights. Today Jack was teaching the boys how to fly the six-place, single-engine plane which their father had purchased recently.

"There's a gusty wind, so come in at a slightly higher airspeed," Jack reminded his pupil.

Frank's pulse quickened as he lined up on the

1

runway and reduced power. The beautiful blue-and-white craft descended in a normal glide.

The landing strip and parked planes below seemed to rush up at them, the details growing larger as Frank headed toward the ground.

"Watch out for those telephone lines!" Joe cried out.

The wires loomed squarely in front of the plane's nose. If Frank had judged his glide angle correctly, the wires should be dropping below his field of vision. Instead, they seemed to be coming straight at the plane!

Frank gulped with panic. *Would they crash?* Trying hard to keep cool, he eased back on the wheel. With barely a split second to go, the ship nosed upward and cleared the wires!

Moments later, the plane's wheels touched down in a perfect landing and the craft rolled to a stop. Frank climbed out after the others, feeling a bit weak.

"Quick thinking, boy!" Joe slapped his brother on the back. "Only next time, please don't shave it so close!"

Frank heaved a sigh. "I didn't think—I just acted! How come you didn't take over, Jack?"

"I figured you'd do the right thing"—the pilot chuckled—"and you did!" Suddenly his face clouded and he snapped his fingers. "I clean forgot to tell you!"

"What?" the boys chorused.

"A message your father gave me just before I took off from San Juan." Early that morning Jack had returned after flying Mr. Hardy to Puerto Rico the previous day on a top-secret case. "Sorry. Giving flying lessons must make me absent-minded." He handed the boys a piece of paper.

" 'Find Hugo purple turban,' " Frank and Joe read aloud. They stared at the paper, completely baffled by the cryptic message.

Jack went on to explain that Mr. Hardy had quickly jotted down the strange words, then handed the paper to him. "He did say," Jack added, "that he couldn't give any more details right then. He'd spotted a man he wanted to shadow."

The boys racked their brains for a moment in silence. Neither could think of anyone in Bayport named Hugo.

"Oh, well," Frank said, smiling, "we'll try to figure it out later. Thanks for the flying lesson, Jack."

After arranging for their next flight, the boys went to the parking lot, where they had left their convertible.

"I'll drive," said Frank. In a few minutes the boys were headed toward their pleasant, tree-shaded home at Elm and High streets.

The dazzling June sun shone down on them as they talked over the odd message Jack had relayed.

"We'll have to twirl our brains for this one," Joe commented as they pulled into the Hardys' gravel driveway. "I wonder who Hugo is. Someone in Bayport, maybe?"

"Let's try the phone book," Frank suggested. "Hugo could be someone's last name."

As the boys strode in through the kitchen door, their mother was trimming the crust on an apple pie. Each son gave her a quick kiss on the cheek, then Frank said, "We're trying to figure out a code message from Dad. Have you any idea who 'Hugo purple turban' might be?"

Mrs. Hardy, slim and pretty, shook her head as she slid the pie into the oven. "Not the faintest, but it sounds like the start of another interesting case."

Her husband, Fenton Hardy, had been a crack detective for years in the New York City Police Department. Later, when he retired and moved to the coastal town of Bayport, Mr. Hardy had become internationally famous as a private investigator. His two sons had skillfully assisted him on many of his cases.

Frank, intrigued by his father's newest assignment, hurried to the telephone book, Joe at his heels, and leafed through the pages of names beginning with H.

"Let's see now." Frank moistened his finger. "Hugo . . . Hugo . . . Here we are! Just three of them," he added after a moment. "It should be simple to find the right man."

Joe dialed the first number. The quavering, high-pitched voice of an elderly woman answered the phone. In reply to Joe's question, she snapped suspiciously, "A purple turban? What on earth are you talking about?"

Joe tried to explain. But the woman's reaction was unfriendly, as if she suspected some kind of a hoax.

"Young man, I can't make head nor tail of what you're saying. Sounds to me as if you're trying to be funny—or else you've got the wrong number!"

With a loud sniff, she hung up.

"Whew! Guess I didn't do too well on that one," Joe told his brother. "Next time remind me not to sound like such a crackpot!"

Joe dialed another number. The listing on this one was "Hugo's Meat Market."

"*Yah*, I'm Hugo," said a voice in a heavy German accent.

Joe explained that he was doing some private detective work and was trying to locate a person named Hugo who had some connection with a purple turban—or maybe someone known as "Hugo Purple Turban."

"*Ach*, no, I never hear of anyone like that," the butcher replied. "But if you like some good knackwurst, just drop around any time!"

Frank chuckled as Joe hung up the phone. "We're getting nowhere fast. Let me try."

The third Hugo listed was a Wilfred K., a jeweler and watch-repair expert.

" 'Hugo purple turban?' Hmm," the man responded thoughtfully. "Sounds to me as if it might refer to that fortuneteller."

"Fortuneteller?"

"The Great Hugo, he calls himself—at least that's the name painted on his trailer. He has a tent pitched beside the road, on Route 10, just north of town."

"Thanks a lot, sir!" Frank exclaimed, with a surge of excitement. "Sounds like a swell lead!"

As he cradled the phone, a peppery feminine voice spoke up from behind the boys. "Before you get too deep in another mystery, take my advice and—"

"Oh, hi, Aunt Gertrude!" Joe smiled and turned around.

Frank said mischievously, "Aunt Gertrude's just jealous, Joe, because she doesn't know all the facts!"

"Nonsense!" retorted their aunt, a tall, angular woman, who was Mr. Hardy's maiden sister.

Although Aunt Gertrude would never admit it, Frank and Joe knew that she was just as deeply intrigued by the Hardys' cases as the boys and their father.

Frank told her about Mr. Hardy's puzzling

communication "Hugo purple turban" and went on, "The man I just talked to on the phone seemed to think it might refer to some fortune-teller called The Great Hugo."

"The Great Hugo! Why, of course!" Aunt Gertrude's eyes narrowed with a look of suspicion.

"Do you know him?" Joe asked eagerly.

"I've heard about him—and what I've heard isn't good!" Miss Hardy explained that two women she knew had gone to have The Great Hugo tell their fortunes. After leaving his tent, they had discovered money missing from their handbags, which they had hung on the backs of their chairs.

"You mean Hugo stole it?" Frank asked.

"Who else? Naturally, the women couldn't *prove* it," Miss Hardy added, pursing her lips, "but there's no doubt in their minds."

The two boys exchanged glances. "He could be the man we're looking for," Frank remarked.

Joe nodded. "Let's check with Chief Collig."

As head of the Bayport Police Department, Chief Collig had cooperated with the Hardys on many of their cases. When Frank telephoned him, the chief said that he was acquainted with The Great Hugo and had had complaints about him.

"He's as phony as a nine-dollar bill, but so far we haven't enough evidence to take him in."

Frank thanked the chief, hung up, and passed the information to his brother.

"Come on! Let's go have a look at Hugo!" Joe urged.

Frank backed the car out of the drive and headed for Route 10. North of town, they sighted a bright, orange-colored tent just off the road.

"There it is," Frank murmured, slowing down. The tent bore a sign reading:

THE GREAT HUGO
WORLD-FAMOUS MYSTIC
Private Readings by Appointment

Near the tent stood a house trailer of the same orange color. It was hitched to a battered but powerful-looking black hardtop coupé of an expensive make.

Frank parked the convertible under a tree and the boys walked toward the tent. As they were about to enter, a man, at least six and a half feet tall, and with an extremely large head, loomed up in front of them, barring the way.

His swarthy, hook-nosed face gave the man a menacing air. But what jolted both boys were his clothes. He wore baggy trousers, Oriental slippers with pointed, curled-up toes, and a purple turban!

"What is it you wish?" he demanded in a deep, harsh voice.

"We came to have our fortunes told," Joe said evenly.

"I do not tell fortunes—I am only Abdul, a

"What is it you wish?" he demanded, barring the way

helper," the man grunted. "You wait outside. I go see if The Great Hugo will receive you."

Abdul entered the tent, dropping the flap across the entrance. Tense with excitement, the young detectives waited, but not for long. A moment later Abdul reappeared.

"I bring good news! The Great Hugo will see you at once!" he announced.

He drew aside the tent flap, bowed low, and invited the boys to enter. Cautiously they stepped into the gloomy interior. The walls of the tent were hung with dark draperies. Only the pale glow of a shaded lamp suffused the gloom. Soft rugs lay underfoot.

At a table covered with a silver-fringed black velvet cloth sat a slim, short man with a pointed brown beard. Before him on the table lay a crystal ball.

"So—you have come to have your fortunes told," he murmured. "Please be seated."

As the boys sank down onto two leather hassocks, Hugo's queer yellowish eyes seemed to be sizing them up shrewdly.

Stalling for time in order to observe the place carefully, Frank said, "Before you start, sir, perhaps you'd better tell us how much it's going to cost."

The Great Hugo waved his hand carelessly. "My usual fee is five dollars. But since I am not busy today I will take you both for two dollars."

The boys reached for their wallets and produced one dollar apiece. Hugo whisked the bills out of sight, then concentrated his gaze on the crystal ball. In a few moments he seemed to go into a trance.

"I see an airplane—a trip over water," the fortuneteller said in a droning voice. "The scene in the crystal ball is changing. . . . I see trouble! Danger!"

Suddenly Frank felt a hand groping into his pocket. Gripping the thief's wrist, he whirled around. It was Abdul!

"Oh, no, you don't!" Frank exclaimed, jumping up and forcing the man backward. But with lightning speed the brawny fellow stunned him with a blow on the chin. Frank staggered groggily.

Joe leaped to his brother's aid. But he was quickly grabbed by Abdul. As Joe struggled to get away from the giant, he knocked over the table and crystal ball.

In one end of the tent Hugo the Mystic was shouting commands to Abdul, and edging toward a position behind the three. A moment later black hoods were thrown over the boys' heads.

"Let's get rid of them, Abdul, and leave—quick!" Hugo growled.

CHAPTER II

The Suspicious Trailer

THEIR heads covered, Frank and Joe were hurled to the ground. Resistance was futile. Quickly their hands and feet were bound. Then they were dragged out of the tent and into some bushes. Footsteps indicated their attackers had left.

"Joe! Joe, can you hear me?" Frank shouted. The hood muffled his voice, but he was able to make out Joe's response.

"Right here, Frank."

From a short distance away came confused sounds as if the tent were being quickly taken down and stowed in the trailer. Soon the engine of a car roared to life and the vehicle went rumbling off down the highway.

Meanwhile, the boys twisted and turned in a frantic effort to loosen their bonds. This was not the only time they had found themselves in a predicament like this one.

Ever since their first big case, *The Tower Treasure,* the brothers had often been in tight spots. But always their quick, cool thinking had enabled them to outwit their adversaries. In their most recent mystery, they had survived underwater spear-gun attacks and other dangers to learn *The Secret of Pirates' Hill.*

By the time Frank got his hands free, his wrists were rubbed nearly raw. He jerked the black hood off his head and saw Joe still straining to free himself.

"Here! I'll do it!" Frank offered.

Quickly he removed his brother's hood. In a few moments both were free and on their feet.

Joe peered at the tire tracks of the vanished car and trailer. "They made a neat getaway," he said bitterly.

"Which means The Great Hugo must have been the Hugo we want!" Frank said grimly.

"Then what are we waiting for?" Joe sprinted toward the convertible. "Let's go after him!"

Before leaving, Frank insisted that they examine the tire treads of both the vanished car and the trailer. Then the boys ran to their convertible. Frank gunned the engine and they took off in a spurt of sand and gravel. Luckily, Route 10 ran straight north for almost twelve miles before intersecting another major highway.

En route there were several dirt-road turnoffs. Frank and Joe stopped at each one and got out to inspect all tire marks on them. But they found no sign of the vehicles belonging to Hugo and Abdul.

"Probably they're heading out of the county," Joe remarked.

"Wait a minute. Let's try this trailer court up ahead," Frank suggested. It was located less than half a mile from the highway intersection.

He braked the car and swung over onto the shoulder of the road. Again the boys climbed out.

"It's a hundred-to-one shot," Frank admitted, "but Hugo might have turned in here to throw us off the trail."

"He'll have a tough time hiding that orange trailer," Joe said. "Say look!" He broke off with a gasp and grabbed Frank's arm. "Over there!"

Frank turned to face the direction in which his brother was staring. An orange trailer!

Though partly hidden from view by other vehicles, the trailer looked like the one used by Hugo and Abdul. The boys approached it casually, trying not to attract any attention.

Their hopes, however, were soon dashed. Frilly lace curtains showed in the windows of the trailer. In front of it a fat, baldheaded man in Bermuda shorts lounged in a deck chair. A moment later a woman came out, carrying a baby.

Frank smiled to hide his disappointment. "Okay. So our long shot didn't pay off."

"Now what?"

Frank considered. "Once Hugo hits the cross-road, there's no telling which way he'll head. Guess we better notify the police."

Across the highway from the trailer court was a roadside store with a gasoline pump. The boys hurried over and put through a call to Chief Collig on the store's pay phone.

"I'll send out a radio alert," the officer promised, after hearing Frank's story. "Maybe the highway patrol can pick those men up before they cross the state line."

"Thanks, Chief! We'll keep in touch," said Frank.

Somewhat dejectedly, the boys plodded back to their convertible. "What a wild-goose chase!" Frank groaned.

On the way back to Bayport, Joe brightened suddenly as a thought struck him. "Maybe we could spot Hugo's trailer from the air. That bright-orange trailer ought to stand out on any road!"

Frank agreed. "We can ask Jack Wayne to take us up," he said.

When they reached home, Frank parked the convertible in the driveway and the boys hurried into the house. Before they were halfway through the kitchen, the telephone rang.

"Maybe it's Chief Collig with some news!" Joe exclaimed. He reached the hall first and scooped up the phone. "Hello."

"This is Chet, Joe," came a breathless voice over the wire. "Something's up! I need help right away—over at my place."

Chet Morton, a chubby pal of the Hardys, attended Bayport High with them. Good-natured and fond of eating, he was usually slow moving and easy going. But now his voice throbbed with fearful urgency.

"Chet! What's this all about?" Joe demanded.

"I can't explain over the phone, but get here fast," his friend pleaded. "This is important!"

"Okay. We'll be there pronto."

"What's wrong?" Frank asked as Joe hung up.

"Search me. Chet seems to be all worked up. Sounds as if he's in real trouble. He wants us to come out to the farm on the double."

"All right. But first let me call Jack Wayne."

Snatching up the phone, Frank dialed Jack's cubbyhole office at the airport. When the pilot answered, Frank gave him a quick account of their adventures with Hugo and Abdul. Jack was thunderstruck to learn that the brothers were already on the trail of "Hugo purple turban."

"Joe and I figure," Frank went on, "that the quickest way to spot the trailer is from the air. Could you go up and reconnoiter a bit?"

"Sure," Jack replied.

Frank described the hardtop coupé and orange trailer, then hung up and hurried out to the car with Joe. Twenty minutes later they reached the

Morton farmhouse on the outskirts of Bayport.

The boys ran up to the front door and rang the bell. Two pretty girls answered the door. One was Chet's dark-haired sister, Iola. The other, a blonde with sparkling brown eyes, was her chum, Callie Shaw. The two girls often double-dated Frank and Joe.

"Well! Imagine meeting you two here!" said Iola in pleased surprise.

"You're just in time," Callie said. She held up a puppet dressed like Little Red Ridinghood. "We were just practicing for a puppet show we're going to give at the hospital bazaar. You two can help us—"

"Where's Chet?" Joe interrupted.

"Why, out in the barn," said Iola. "But—"

"Come on, Frank!"

Without waiting to explain, Frank and Joe rushed outside and headed around the side of the barn to the rear. Voices became more audible at every step. Suddenly both boys pulled up short and stared at each other in amazement.

"Did you hear somebody mention the name Hugo?" Joe whispered breathlessly.

Freezing in their tracks, the Hardys listened intently.

"We'll get the Hardys and get 'em good, Hugo!" said a rough voice.

"Yeah," came the chuckling reply. "We'll ambush them tonight!"

CHAPTER III

The Hijacked Dummy

"AMBUSH?" Joe flashed his brother a startled glance.

Frank clenched his fists. "I don't know what's going on back there, but let's find out!"

With their hearts thumping and their fists ready for trouble, the Hardys dashed around the corner of the barn, then stopped dead in open-mouthed astonishment. The only person in sight was Chet Morton, propped up against the back of the barn.

"Hi, fellows!" he greeted them, lifting his eyebrows in an innocent, deadpan look. "Expecting someone else?"

"But where are those two men we heard?" Joe asked in surprise.

"You're looking at 'em, pal. Both of 'em!" Chet replied.

To prove this, he switched over to his two "tough guy" voices and uttered a few more blood-curdling threats.

"You?" Frank could hardly believe his ears.

"That's right." The stout boy chuckled. "A slight case of ventriloquism, gentlemen. Learned it from books. Thought it might come in handy helping you fellows on your cases." He burst into laughter. "Oh, boy, did you two ever fall for my act—hook, line, and sinker!"

"And that phone call begging for help?" Joe growled. "That was just a trick, too, to get us over here?"

Chet nodded. "But don't hold it against me."

The Hardy boys grinned, then Frank said, "You sure fooled us. I'll say you're good."

"I sure am!" Chet agreed. "In fact, I may make a career out of ventriloquism," he went on, turning serious. "Man, I can see myself now, doing a big show on television! Chet Morton, Man of Many Voices—World's Greatest Imitator!"

This time it was the Hardys' chance to needle their friend. "World's Greatest Appetite, you mean!" Joe hooted. "Otherwise known as Chet Morton, Man of Many Helpings!"

Chet's moonface took on a hurt look. "Okay, okay. Just because I happen to appreciate good food," he sulked. "If you fellows don't think I'm ready for the big time, just listen to this."

He jerked his thumb toward the house and

whispered, "Here comes my pesky cousin, Jinny."

A moment later a little girl's shrill, whiny voice seemed to come drifting around the corner of the barn:

"Oh, Chet! Your mother says you better get in the house right this minute and start cleaning up the basement! Y'hear me? You better come quick, or I'm gonna tell her just where you're hiding!"

The boys were amazed at the demonstration. Chet's lips had hardly moved.

"That's pretty convincing, Chet," said Frank.

Chet looked somewhat mollified. "It ought to be good," he bragged. "I've been studying and practicing secretly a whole month. I'm even thinking of buying a Hugo!"

"A Hugo?" Frank and Joe gasped together.

"Sure," Chet said calmly. "The same kind of dummy Professor Fox uses."

"Oh!" The Hardys relaxed as they recalled the act to which Chet was referring. Professor Fox was a star ventriloquist on TV. His dummy, Hugo, had become so popular that it was being copied and sold on a large scale. The dummy came in various-priced models.

"I'm going to get the most expensive Hugo on the market," Chet bragged. "I've been saving to buy it by doing extra chores around the farm. I have enough money now."

Just then Chet's bull terrier, Spud, came wandering out to see what was going on.

"Watch me fool him," Chet said with a wink at his friends. "Over there, boy!"

He pointed to a clump of bushes and threw his voice once again:

"Here, Spud! Come on, boy! Got a nice thick juicy steak for you! Come on, fella!"

Instead of responding, the bull terrier stood still, eyeing his master quizzically.

Chet lost his temper. "Well, go on, dopey. What're you waiting for?" The bull terrier merely panted and wagged his tail.

"Wow! Did you ever fool him!" Frank gibed. Both he and Joe doubled up with laughter.

Chet turned beet red and grumpily threw his dog a stick to chase. Then he casually suggested, "Let's get some lemonade and cookies."

On the way back to the house, Joe said thoughtfully, "Some of those Hugos come with Oriental turbans, don't they, Chet?"

"The better models do," replied the stout boy. "Why?"

"Oh, just a hunch I had about something." Turning to his brother, Joe went on, "Do you suppose Dad's message might have referred to one of those dummies?"

Frank nodded. "It's an idea."

"Don't tell me you fellows are wrestling with another mystery?" Chet inquired uneasily.

"Right. And you're just the one to help us solve it," Joe told Chet, slapping him on the back.

"Not me!" Chet protested with a shudder.

Getting involved in the Hardys' crime cases always gave Chet the jitters, although the roly-poly high-school boy had already been through several dangerous adventures with Joe and Frank.

"This won't get you into any danger," Joe assured him. Hastily he explained about the puzzling message which Mr. Hardy had sent from Puerto Rico.

"Where do I come in?" Chet asked suspiciously.

"When you go shopping for a Hugo dummy, just keep your eyes open. Better yet, let us go with you. Maybe we'll run across some kind of a clue."

"We-e-ell . . . I guess I can go along that far with you," Chet agreed grudgingly.

"Where did you plan on buying your dummy?" Frank asked.

"Bivven's Novelty Shop. That's where I've been getting all my books on ventriloquism."

"Okay. Let's go!"

After stopping in the house for lemonade with the girls and to pick up Chet's wallet, the three boys piled into the convertible and drove off. A few minutes later they pulled up in front of the novelty shop on King Street.

A bell tinkled as they walked in and Mr. Bivven, the squat, baldheaded proprietor, came out of the back room to greet them.

He beamed at the trio across the counter. "Something you'd like, boys?"

Chet said he wanted to look over the store's stock of ventriloquist's dummies.

One by one, Mr. Bivven showed his stock, but Chet turned them all down and asked for a Hugo dummy. The proprietor went to his storeroom and emerged presently with a cardboard box. It contained a Hugo dummy, clad in a tuxedo and red turban.

"I just received this today," Mr. Bivven said. Taking out the dummy, Chet set it on the counter and began putting on an impromptu ventriloquist act.

Frank watched, chuckling, for a moment. Then he picked up the instruction sheet which was lying in the box and began to read it. The simple directions were printed in three languages—English, French, and Spanish.

The doorbell tinkled again and two men entered the shop. One was tall and rough-looking, with large ears that stuck out from his head; the other was short and swarthy-complexioned.

Joe, who was standing alongside Chet and Frank, watched the men out of the corner of his eye. They stopped in front of a trayful of water pistols and began picking them over. It looked as though they were killing time until the proprietor could wait on them.

"Okay. I guess I'll take this one," Chet decided finally.

As he pulled out his wallet to pay for the

dummy, Mr. Bivven put the figure back in the box and started to wrap it.

"Good thing you stopped in today, son," he remarked chattily. "This here's the only Hugo in stock. If you'd waited any longer, I reckon you'd have been plumb out o' luck."

"Just a minute!" said the tall man, stepping forward. "That dummy is exactly what I been lookin' for. How much is the kid payin' for it?"

"Eighteen dollars and ninety-five cents."

"Then I'll give you twenty bucks!"

Mr. Bivven hesitated. He hated to lose the extra profit, but Chet was a good customer and he didn't want to offend him.

"Nope. I'm sorry, the deal's already closed."

"Twenty-five!"

Mr. Bivven gulped and shook his head. "I told you before, mister, it's no go. First come, first served. Dummy's already sold to Chet here."

Grinning triumphantly, Chet counted out the money. But as the proprietor turned to ring up the sale on the cash register, the short man suddenly whipped out a shiny, blue-steel revolver.

"It's a cinch *that* gun's no toy!" thought Joe, wincing.

"We want that dummy!" snarled the short man.

As Chet stood quaking, the tall fellow grabbed Hugo off the counter!

CHAPTER IV

A Double Burglary

THE armed intruders kept the boys and Mr. Bivven covered as they backed hastily toward the door with the Hugo dummy.

"Don't try any hero stuff and don't call the cops after we leave," warned the swarthy gunman. "If you do, you'll sure regret it!"

Then the tall man jerked open the door and the two dashed out to a car parked at the curb. Frank and Joe rushed to the window just in time to see the short man slide behind the wheel.

"Watch it, fellows," Chet begged.

Pale and trembling with excitement, he half expected to see the store's show window shattered by a hail of bullets. Instead, the engine roared and the car, a green sedan, sped away.

"No luck on the license number!" Joe groaned. "The rear plate was caked with mud."

"After them!" Frank cried, dashing out the door.

The Hardys leaped into their convertible and took off. Luckily, traffic was light. In the distance Joe caught a glimpse of the getaway car. "There it is!" he yelled.

Frank speeded up. The green car whined in a turn to the right at the next intersection. As the convertible followed, the other car suddenly put on a fresh burst of speed.

"They must have spotted us in their rear-view mirror," Frank muttered through clenched teeth.

As the chase continued, the green car shot through a stop sign. When the boys reached the crossing, a stream of traffic barred the way. Then a huge tank truck halted for a left turn, completely blocking the intersection. By the time the route was clear, the getaway car was nowhere in sight.

"What luck!" Joe groaned.

The boys cruised around for a while, hoping to locate the trail again, but finally gave up.

"Guess we may as well go back and get Chet," Frank sighed.

A police squad car was parked in front of the novelty shop. When the Hardys walked in, Mr. Bivven was relating the details of the holdup to the officers.

"These are the boys," he said, nodding at Frank and Joe.

"Any luck tracing the thieves?" one of the officers asked.

Frank shook his head glumly. "We couldn't even get their license number."

He gave a detailed description of the green sedan, and also reported the general route which the thieves had taken.

"I'll put it on the radio right away," said the other policeman. "There's still a chance we can stop 'em before they get out of town." He hurried outside to the squad car.

The other officer took down the names and addresses of everyone involved, then left the shop.

"Too bad, Chet," Joe sympathized. "Looks as if you're out of luck for a dummy today."

"You're telling me," the young ventriloquist answered gloomily.

"Don't be too sure of that," put in Mr. Bivven with a grin.

"Huh?" Chet's eyes popped. "What do you mean?"

"I mean there might just be another Hugo back in the storeroom. Dummies have been selling quickly, but while I was talking to those officers, I suddenly remembered tucking another box up on the top shelf. But don't get your hopes too high till I make sure."

Chet waited in eager suspense. A few moments later Mr. Bivven reappeared, beaming triumphantly. "Yes! Got one right here."

"Hot ziggety!" Chet pounced on the box in delight, ripping off the cover. As he pulled out the dummy, both Frank and Joe gave a yelp of excitement.

This one wore a purple turban!

"My stars!" Mr. Bivven chuckled. "Seems like you two are just as het-up as your friend here about finding this extra Hugo. But I reckon that's only natural, seeing as how you took your lives in your hands trying to save the other one."

Frank and Joe merely smiled and made no effort to explain their jubilation. But the same thought was passing through both their minds. Could this be the "Hugo purple turban" referred to in their father's message? And had the two men made off with the wrong dummy?

Meanwhile, Chet was putting the new Hugo through its paces. "Boy, this is for me!" he gloated. "I'll work with it at home this evening!"

As the proprietor wrote out the sales check, Joe examined the dummy but could find nothing unusual about it. Frank again glanced at the instruction sheet. This one was also printed in the same three languages.

Suddenly Frank's eyes narrowed. "That's funny," he muttered under his breath.

"What's funny?" Joe asked.

"These directions. The ones in French and English are the same as those which came with the other dummy. But the directions in Spanish are different."

Both boys could read French and Spanish.

"You're sure?" Joe asked.

"Positive." After Mr. Bivven finished writing out the sales check and tore off a copy for Chet, Frank asked the man, "Does any other store in Bayport sell the Hugo dummies?"

"You'd like one too, eh?" The proprietor smiled. "Well, now, let me think." He paused and scratched his chin. "Might try Hanade's over on Bay Street."

"Hanade's?"

"That's right. Nice elderly Japanese. Runs a puppet-repair shop, and handles all kinds of interesting doodads."

The Hardys thanked him and left the store with Chet. Outside, their stout pal asked Frank why he was so interested in finding another dealer.

"Don't tell me you're going to take up ventriloquism, too?" he teased.

"Not a chance," Frank replied, and explained about the curious difference in the instructions. He added, "It might be a fluke, or it might mean something. Anyhow, I'd like to check another set of instructions."

Hanade's Puppet Repair Shop did, indeed, carry "all kinds of doodads." The tiny store was crammed with Oriental trinkets, samurai swords, brass Buddhas, dolls' heads hanging on the wall, birds and bird cages, aquariums with darting tropical fish, and numerous other items.

Mr. Hanade was a small, bespectacled, pleasant gentleman. "Ah, yes," he replied to Frank's question. "I carry the Hugo puppets. Made by a very fine company. Every puppet carefully inspected by owner before he sends it out. Which kind do you wish to see?"

"The model with a turban, like this one my friend has," replied Joe as Chet displayed his Hugo.

"You wait, please. I check."

Mr. Hanade returned shortly with a box containing a Hugo similar to Chet's, but it wore a green turban. Ignoring the dummy, Frank took out the instruction sheet and compared it with the one in Chet's box.

"You're right," Joe muttered, reading over Frank's shoulder. "The Spanish wording *is* a little different!"

Frank asked if he might borrow Mr. Hanade's sheet of instructions overnight, and offered to leave a dollar on deposit. Though puzzled, the man agreed politely.

"You take, please. No deposit necessary."

"Thank you," said Chet, and the boys left the shop.

Before dropping Chet at the farm, Joe said impulsively, "Say, fellows, do you think Professor Fox could be mixed up in anything shady?"

Chet declared that the TV performer had a fine

reputation, and he was sure that the man was above suspicion. Frank agreed with this.

That evening after supper Frank and Joe huddled around the study lamp in their room, with the two sets of instructions in front of them. They were identical in every way, except for the change in the Spanish wording.

"What do you make of it?" Joe asked his brother.

Frank furrowed his brow. "Might be some kind of a code. Let's compare all the word changes and see what we get."

They had barely started on this job when the hall telephone rang. Joe took the call.

"This is Chief Collig," came a crisp voice. "Understand you and your brother were at Bivven's Novelty Shop this afternoon when the owner got robbed."

"That's right. In fact, we chased the holdup men."

"Anything to do with a case your father's working on, Joe?"

"Could be, sir. We're not sure."

"Well, if you're interested, the place was robbed again tonight. Or, anyhow, it was broken into and ransacked."

"What!" Joe cried out.

"Happened just about twenty minutes ago," the chief went on. "A patrolman walking past heard some noises and figured something funny was going on. When he went to investigate, the burglars ducked out the back way."

"Thanks for the tip, Chief," Joe said. "Frank and I will go right over there."

Frank was equally startled when he heard about the burglary. "I wonder if those men stole the wrong Hugo, and came back for another try!"

"Sure sounds that way," Joe agreed, "but they must have heard Mr. Bivven say it was his last Hugo in stock."

The two boys drove through the darkened streets of Bayport to the novelty shop on King Street. The store was ablaze with light, but no squad car stood at the scene. Apparently the police detectives had already left, but there was a patrolman on guard at the door.

The Hardys identified themselves, and Frank added, "Chief Collig just phoned us the news."

"He called me too," said the patrolman, and let them enter.

Mr. Bivven was busy straightening up the store. "Oh, it's you boys," he murmured, glancing up as the door's bell tinkled.

Most of the toys, dolls, and scale models had already been neatly replaced on the shelves.

"Sorry to hear the news, Mr. Bivven," Frank said. "Exactly what happened?"

The proprietor shrugged and sighed. "Place was ransacked but nothing taken. Dratted nuisance! Burglars twice in one day! I just can't figure it out. Still, I reckon I'm lucky it wasn't any worse."

"Mind if we look around for clues?" Frank asked.

"Go ahead, but the police have already done so."

As the boys poked about the store, Mr. Bivven bent down behind the counter. A moment later he stood up.

"Now that's strange," he remarked with a puzzled frown. "Seems as though someone's been fiddling with my sales checks."

"Sales checks!" Frank was struck by a sudden fear.

"Yes. Had 'em stashed away in order down here. Now they're all messed up."

"Any missing?"

Mr. Bivven scratched his bald head. "Well, now, that's a mite hard to say without checking the cash-register tape."

Frank said urgently, "Never mind the rest. Just look for the one you wrote up for our friend this afternoon. The name was Morton—Chet Morton."

"Sure, sure, I remember. Let me see." Mr. Bivven brought out the sheaf of slips, thumbed through them several times, then looked up in surprise. "By jingo, that one's gone. Those burglars must have taken it!"

"That's what I surmised," Frank said. "They came back to check on who had purchased other dummies lately and found out Chet had one!"

"That means Chet's in danger!" Joe said grimly. "And maybe Iola and their dad and mother!" Turning to Mr. Bivven, he asked, "May I use your phone?"

"Sure thing."

Thoroughly alarmed by now, Joe scooped up the telephone and dialed Chet's number. At the other end of the line, he could hear a steady series of rings. But after a minute he gave up.

"No answer," he reported to Frank. "Come on! Let's get out there fast!"

The boys dashed out of the store, leaped into the convertible, and headed for the Morton farm. Once outside of town, Frank switched on the long-range lights. The twin beams probed the darkness as they sped along.

Neither boy spoke, but both were gripped by the same fear. Was the Morton family in trouble? Why had no one answered the phone when Chet had said he would be at home?

Presently the farmhouse loomed up against the night sky. The windows were dark.

"I don't like this," Frank said grimly.

CHAPTER V

A Startling Discovery

FRANK jammed on the brakes and the convertible lurched to a halt in the Mortons' driveway. The boys jumped out and sprinted up the front-porch steps.

As Joe rang the doorbell, Frank noticed that the front door stood slightly ajar.

"It's open!" he whispered.

Fearful of some danger, Frank and Joe cautiously entered the hall. Like all the rest of the house, the living room was shrouded in darkness. Frank, in the lead, groped for the light switch.

Joe's scalp bristled when he heard some faint, whimpering noises. The sounds were muffled and scarcely seemed human.

Frank found the light switch and clicked it on. As the room leaped into brilliance, both boys exclaimed aloud.

Chet, Iola, and Mr. and Mrs. Morton were lying on the floor, bound and gagged!

"Jumpin' catfish!" Joe gulped.

The Hardys rushed forward and quickly started to untie the victims.

"Oh, my gracious! Thank you, thank you!" Chet's mother gasped as Frank removed her gag and undid the ropes.

"Luckily none of you were harmed, Mrs. Morton," he replied. Gently he helped her to her feet and then to the sofa.

Chet, however, was not so grateful. "I thought you fellows promised me there wouldn't be any rough stuff on this case!" he grumbled while Joe worked on a knot.

"What happened?" Frank asked.

The story tumbled out in a confused babble as the whole Morton family gave the details. They had been watching a television show in their living room when two masked men burst in. The intruders had tied up the Mortons, then searched the house and made off with something tucked under one man's arm.

"I'm willing to bet they're the same ones who held up the novelty shop this afternoon," Chet asserted. "One was a tall man and the other short. The tall guy's ears stuck out!"

Frank and Joe looked at each other in dismay. "I guess that means they took Hugo," said Joe.

Frank nodded, then said to the Mortons, "Please check and make sure what was stolen."

The family scattered through the rooms of the

rambling farmhouse to inspect the results of the burglary. Iola was the first to report.

"I know one thing they took!" she cried out, running downstairs from her bedroom.

"What?" asked Joe.

"One of my big puppets. It looked something like Chet's new dummy—even wore a purple turban."

"Hot dog!" Joe snapped his fingers. "I'll bet those burglars were in such a hurry they grabbed the wrong doll!"

The boys' hopes skyrocketed, but Frank added cautiously, "Let's not count our chickens till we hear from Chet."

The words were hardly spoken when Chet came lumbering joyfully onto the scene. He was clutching Hugo in one hand. "Look! He's still here!" Chet gloated. "I had him stowed in my closet, inside a pillowcase, and those men passed it up!"

The boys let out a whoop of triumph. Then Joe put in a wry afterthought:

"Now all we have to do is find out why those thieves were so eager to get hold of Hugo."

While Frank telephoned a report to Chief Collig, Iola made hot cocoa for everyone. As they sat in the living room drinking it, Chet gulped down three cupfuls. Then he laid his cup and saucer aside and picked up Hugo.

"And now, ladies and gentlemen," the young

ventriloquist announced, "we'll forget what happened and have a quick performance to show you what's to come later on my full-time television show!"

He set the dummy on his knee and proceeded to roll its huge popeyes from side to side. Then, as he manipulated Hugo's head and jaws, Chet went into his act. Many of his gags drew laughs from his audience.

Gaining confidence, Chet launched into a long, windy speech—at the same time working Hugo's head, arms, and legs in a wildly comical manner. Leaning forward with excitement, Chet grinned at his amused audience and perched the dummy on the edge of his knee.

Suddenly he jerked Hugo's limbs a bit too hard. The dummy slid off his knee and crashed to the floor, face down, amid a sound of shattering glass!

Chet went white. "Hugo!" he wailed mournfully. "I've ruined you!"

Frank and Joe rushed forward to assay the damage. "Don't worry," Joe consoled his friend. "It's not too bad."

"Those big, beautiful eyes—they're broken!" Chet groaned, kneeling on the floor.

"You can probably get new ones," Frank assured him. Cautiously he started picking up the glassy slivers and fragments. "Gosh," he remarked, "those eyes were even bigger than I—Oh, oh!"

"What's the matter?" asked Joe as Frank broke off with a gasp of amazement.

"This stuff isn't glass—at least not all of it."

"Then what is it?" asked Chet.

Frank's voice quivered with excitement. "This may sound crazy, but I think some of these pieces are uncut diamonds!"

"*What!*" Everyone in the room jumped up in astonishment and clustered around Frank.

"D-did you say *diamonds?*" Chet stuttered.

"That's what they look like." Frank held up some of the stones, which resembled tiny, greasy pebbles.

"Are you sure?" Iola asked. "They don't sparkle much!"

"Rough stones look this way before they're cut," Frank explained. "At least that's what I've read. What do you think, Joe?"

His brother nodded. "I think you're right. And that explains the burglaries. No wonder those men were so eager to grab Hugo!"

Picking up the dummy in one hand, Joe borrowed a bobby pin from Iola and began probing into the hollow eye shells. Several more uncut diamonds came tumbling out.

"I can't believe it!" Chet exclaimed. "Any more of them?"

"No, but here's something else."

Joe extracted a tiny, rolled-up wad of paper. When spread open, it revealed a strange printed notation:

Skeleton Rock 176

"How odd!" exclaimed Mrs. Morton, and Iola added, "It's positively spooky!"

Her father frowned uneasily. "Frank, you and Joe have had experience with this sort of thing. What do you think we should do?"

"If you don't mind, Mr. Morton, I'd like to take both the dummy and the diamonds home with us, so we can investigate them further."

"All right, you do that!" From the tone of his voice, Chet's father sounded relieved to have the disturbing objects removed from his house before the thieves might pay a return visit.

Before leaving, Frank telephoned his father's top investigator, Sam Radley, and asked him to meet the brothers at the Hardy home.

"I'll start at once," the detective promised.

Soon after the boys reached their house, they heard Sam's car pull into the driveway. Joe hurried to let him in.

"What's up, boys?" asked the muscular, sandy-haired detective as soon as he was seated in the living room.

Frank briefed him quickly, then showed Sam the dummy and the curious-looking stones. The

"D-did you say *diamonds?*" Chet stuttered

detective picked up one of the gems and held it to the light. Then he took a jeweler's loupe from his pocket and scrutinized the stone carefully.

"It's an uncut diamond, all right," Sam announced. He examined the others. "Several carats altogether; the lot of them should be worth a good sum of money." He advised the boys to notify Mr. Hardy about their find as soon as possible.

Joe warmed up the short-wave radio transmitter and tuned to the Hardys' special frequency for secret communications. He spoke into the mike:

"Bayport calling Fenton H. in Puerto Rico! Come in, please!"

Again and again Joe repeated the call. But transmitting conditions were poor and he failed to make contact.

"Never mind," said Frank. "We'll try again tomorrow."

"Which reminds me," Sam Radley put in. "I have news for you two."

He reported that Jack Wayne had spotted a car, tent, and trailer which might belong to Hugo and Abdul. He had made the discovery while flying over a wooded area fifty miles away.

"He couldn't get any answer to a phone call here, so he contacted me," Sam explained. "Told me he was planning to take you up for a look-see at five tomorrow morning. He didn't think the trailer would pull out before that."

The boys were jubilant at the news, and called Jack to say they would be on hand promptly for the take-off.

Early the next morning Frank and Joe hopped out of bed the instant their alarm clock rang. After breakfast they drove to the airport.

Jack Wayne had his own ship, *Skyhappy Sal,* fueled and ready on the runway. He was talking to Tony Prito, a good friend of the Hardy boys. During the summer the handsome, dark-eyed, olive-skinned boy drove a truck for his father's construction firm.

"Hi, fellows!" Tony greeted them. "Dad gave me the morning off. I decided to get some exercise and hike out here to see your dad's new plane. Boy, it's a real beauty! Say, you Hardys are on the job early. Another case?"

Frank explained briefly what their mission was, and Jack asked, "Want to come up with us? I have room for another passenger and we'll be back soon."

Tony enthusiastically accepted, and a few minutes later they took off. As the plane soared high above Bayport, Jack turned to Joe.

"Here, take over," the pilot said. "Might as well get a lesson out of this while you're in the air."

Joe proved to be a good pilot and navigated the craft on a straight course toward the spot where Jack had sighted Hugo's trailer.

"We're getting close," Jack said as a wooded area came into view. "Drop down a little, Joe."

Soon Frank cried out. "There they are! That's Hugo's outfit all right."

Joe swooped lower to get a better look at the fortuneteller's camp. The drone of the plane's engine must have aroused the occupants, for a man came rushing out of the trailer.

"Abdul!" Frank exclaimed.

Shaking his fist, the giant rushed back into the trailer and emerged with a high-powered rifle.

"He's going to shoot at us!" Tony cried out.

"Gun it!" Jack ordered.

Joe began to climb for altitude. Seconds later there was a flash from the rifle muzzle. Almost at the same instant, sheets of flame billowed from under the engine cowling and smoke began to seep into the cabin.

"He hit a gas line!" Jack shouted. "The engine's on fire!"

CHAPTER VI

Musical Password

Instinctively Joe pulled the control wheel back and lowered the wing into a steep left bank. He jammed the right rudder pedal to its full limit. The plane descended rapidly and skidded sideways in a "slip."

"Good work!" Jack said to Joe. "The plane's side motion will keep the flames away from the cabin!"

Joe reached down between the seats and turned the fuel selector valve to the "off" position, thus cutting off the flow of fuel from the tanks to the engine.

"Keep her slipping toward that clearing just to your left!" Jack ordered. "We should make it in there easy!" Joe nodded.

With the fuel valve turned off, the engine used the remaining gas in the lines. It then sputtered and quit.

Joe and his companions watched anxiously as the plane slipped toward the clearing. When just a few feet above it, the young pilot kicked the rudder pedals into neutral and leveled the wings. There was a jolt as he pulled the wheel back hard and the plane touched down on the grassy clearing. Joe then pressed hard on the wheel brakes. The craft rolled ahead for several yards and came to a halt with a lurch.

"Handled like a veteran!" Jack gave Joe a broad grin.

At that moment Frank caught sight of Abdul and Hugo sprinting toward their car. "Those men are getting away!" he yelled.

The Hardys and the others hopped out of the plane and dashed after them. But the men had too big a lead. They jumped into their car while the pursuers were still fifty yards away. The car roared down the woods road and disappeared.

Though disappointed, Frank pointed out that at least the suspects had had to abandon their tent and trailer. "Maybe they left some clues."

A quick search revealed little of interest. Besides some costumes, the crystal ball, and fortune-telling paraphernalia, Hugo and Abdul's gear consisted of food, street clothing, and cooking utensils. The searchers turned their attention to smaller articles.

"What's this?" Tony asked, unrolling a flag which he had found tucked away on a shelf of the trailer. On the left was a white circle on a red triangular field, and five green and white stripes running horizontally.

"A foreign flag!" Frank exclaimed.

"What about this?" Jack asked, pointing to a black cloth skeleton on the lower right-hand corner.

"Some kind of a Jolly Roger," Joe suggested.

"But why would petty thieves use a pirate flag?" Tony queried.

"Perhaps Hugo and Abdul belong to some rebel group," Frank mused.

Tony remarked, "Maybe they're just a couple of petty fakers."

Frank shook his head thoughtfully. "In that case, why all the rough stuff when we first saw them, and the rifleshot just now? If you ask me, they're mixed up in something big—and this skeleton flag may be a clue."

The group headed back to *Skyhappy Sal*. Jack Wayne removed part of the cowling and made a quick examination of the damage caused by Abdul's bullet. The shot had almost severed the slender copper tubing of the fuel line.

"What's the verdict?" Frank inquired.

Jack shrugged, frowning. "I can make a temporary repair with a plastic line—good enough to get us in the air, anyhow. But I doubt that it would hold as far as Bayport."

"How about the Eastern City airport?" Tony

suggested. "We could install a new fuel line there."

Jack nodded. "That's what we'll have to do."

He made the repair quickly, then everyone piled in. With Joe at the controls, the plane headed toward Eastern City. Located less than twenty miles away, this thriving city was a terminus for half a dozen airlines. Jack explained their plight to the tower and received permission to land. A mechanic guided him as he taxied the plane to a repair hangar.

"How long do you figure it'll take to put in the new line?" Joe asked as they climbed out.

"Oh, not too long, once I get the right size tubing," the pilot replied. "Fifteen, twenty minutes—if Tony will help me."

"Sure, be glad to!" Tony, an expert with tools, loved to tinker over an engine.

"In that case," said Frank, "Joe and I will find a phone booth and call the police."

They strode quickly to the terminal building. As they skirted the magazine stand on their way to the telephone booths, they noticed a man seated alone in a corner. Olive-skinned, with long, shiny black hair, he looked to be a Latin American. The man slouched on the bench, chin in hand, listening to music which apparently was issuing from a small portable radio on his lap.

Joe grinned at the catchy tune. "Boy, I go for that stuff," he said.

"What stuff?" Frank asked.

"Hot calypso!" Joe said.

His reply seemed to electrify the man on the bench. Jumping to his feet, he darted toward the boy and hissed in his ear, "Where are your gloves, you fool? You might leave fingerprints."

Joe blinked and stared. The man's next move was even more astounding. He pulled a pair of gloves from his pocket and stuffed them into Joe's hand!

The boy was taken completely by surprise, but instinct warned him not to betray his reaction. The stranger watched him closely.

Joe swallowed hard and looked at the gloves. They were made of gray fabric with a small label sewn to the hem of one, reading *Made in Tropicale*. Acting on a hunch, Joe pulled them on.

This seemed to please the stranger, who gave a tight smile. "Ah, *bueno!*" He produced a small key and slipped it into Joe's gloved hand, adding, "You have been instructed!"

Without another word the man turned, switched off the music, and strode away. For the first time, Frank and Joe noticed that what they had thought was a portable radio was actually a small portable record-player.

"Let's follow him!" Joe said.

"Better not," Frank advised. "I think we've stumbled onto something big. We've done the right thing so far. Let's not spoil it."

"You're right. 'Hot calypso' must be a password. Let's look at this key."

Joe held it up for examination. The key was inscribed with the number 176.

Frank repeated the number excitedly. "That wadded note we found in the dummy's eye!" he exclaimed. "It said 'Skeleton Rock 176'!"

"But what does it stand for?" Joe asked.

Frank thought a moment. "I can't answer that, but I'll bet this key opens one of those public lockers over there."

The boys hurried to the south wall of the air terminal, honeycombed with metal lockers.

"Here it is," said Frank.

Joe glanced around cautiously. The Latin American was not in sight and no one else seemed to be looking at the boys. Joe inserted the key in the lock. *It fitted!*

He turned the key and the door swung open. The locker contained a black-leather zippered case.

Joe reached in and pulled out the case. The next instant, both boys jumped in alarm as a voice behind them barked:

"You're under arrest!"

CHAPTER VII

Twin Clues

As THE Hardys whirled around from the airport lockers, they saw a dark-haired, hard-jawed man of medium build eyeing them coldly.

He flipped open his coat and flashed a detective's badge. "Now, then, who are you and what's your game?"

"We're Frank and Joe Hardy," Frank said coolly. "Our father is Fenton Hardy, the investigator. While we're at it, maybe you wouldn't mind telling us who *you* are?"

"Shanley, airport detective!" the man replied crisply. Opening his wallet, he showed them his detective's license. "You two still haven't told me what you're up to," he prodded.

"We're not 'up to' anything," Joe said tersely.

Shanley was annoyed. "Let's have a look at that leather case," he demanded.

But Frank interposed. "If you want to see the contents, let's go to police headquarters."

"Okay," the detective grumbled. "Come on. We'll go in my car."

The Hardys agreed and the trio headed out through the glass doors of the terminal building, with Joe clutching the brief case.

"Car's over there at the far end of the lot." Shanley pointed.

As they started across the parking area, Joe caught his brother's eye. He made a slight gesture toward the zippered case. Frank nodded.

Turning to Shanley, Frank started chattering casually. "Do you have an office here in Eastern City?" he inquired.

While Frank distracted the detective's attention, Joe gave the zipper a quick jerk. Inside, he caught a glimpse of several thin, flat boxes sealed in cellophane. They bore a drug manufacturer's label with the name *Variotrycin*.

Joe pulled the zipper shut before Shanley noticed anything. The young detective's mind was racing.

"Variotrycin's that new wonder drug I read about in the papers," Joe thought. "But what has a new wonder drug to do with dummies and diamonds—or *Skeleton Rock 176?*"

Joe, deeply engrossed in trying to find an answer to the puzzle, was taken off guard by three men who suddenly darted out from between two cars parked nearby.

"We'll take that case!" snarled the leader, a burly, baldheaded man in a polo shirt.

"Oh, no, you won't!" Joe ducked, and threw up an arm to protect himself.

Frank leaped to his assistance, fists flying, as the hoodlums tried to grab the case.

To their astonishment, Shanley had disappeared. But there was no time to speculate about what had happened to him as Frank drove home a punch that split the lip of his adversary, while Joe gave another of the men a blow that sent him reeling.

In doing so, Joe dropped the case he had held under his left arm. As the young detective stooped to pick it up, he was amazed to have it snatched from the ground by none other than Shanley! The detective had crept up from behind.

"Thanks!" Shanley sneered, and sprinted for his car.

The Hardys were powerless to stop him. With the odds three against two, their attackers were pressing the boys harder than before.

Furiously, Frank and Joe swung their fists with telling effect. One of their opponents howled with pain as Joe caught him on the nose. A second later the baldheaded leader winced and groaned under the walloping impact of Frank's fist under his chin.

Even so, the fight began to go against the boys.

Step by step, they were being driven back and hemmed in against the bumper of a parked car.

Then, suddenly, the tide of battle turned. The burly baldheaded man was jerked around and struck on the jaw by a blow that rocked him on his heels.

"Tony!" Joe cheered. Heartened by the unexpected help, the Hardys put forth a fresh surge of fighting fury.

Their assailants lost heart rapidly. "These guys are too tough! I'm gettin' outta here!" gasped one of the ruffians. Pulling loose from the fray, he turned and ran, with Tony after him.

The baldheaded ringleader followed, with Frank at his heels. As the third hoodlum tried to join in the getaway, Joe dropped him with a flying tackle.

But the leader and the other ruffian kicked off their pursuers and leaped into a car that was waiting for them on the road beyond the parking area. At the wheel was Shanley!

Discouraged by this latest development, Frank and Tony went back to Joe, who was holding their prisoner. The fellow was bony and pinched-faced, and wore a cheap-looking pinstriped suit.

"We're taking you to police headquarters," Joe told him.

The sullen man shifted uneasily, but kept quiet as the group headed for the taxi stand.

"By the way, fellows," said Tony, "would you mind telling me what this is all about?"

Frank gave him a quick account of the phony detective and the unexpected attack. "Thanks for coming to our rescue. You really saved the day!"

"Ditto!" put in Joe. "If it hadn't been for you, we wouldn't have this prisoner. By the way, Tony, you'd better go tell Jack Wayne what happened. We'll be back soon."

"Okay," Tony agreed. "But don't let buster boy here pull any more fast ones!"

As he headed back to the hangar, Frank and Joe hustled their prisoner into one of the waiting taxis.

"Police headquarters," Frank directed the driver.

A few minutes later the taxi pulled up in front of the brick building.

The sergeant in charge led the Hardys and their prisoner into the office of Inspector Moon, a friend of Fenton Hardy. He greeted the boys warmly, then said to a detective, "Take this man into the interrogation room and get the facts." Inspector Moon turned back to Frank and Joe. "Now give me the whole story."

The boys related everything that had happened at the airport terminal, including the way Shanley had led them into an ambush and then stolen the leather case.

"What did Shanley look like?" the officer asked. As Frank gave a description of the man, the inspector frowned and shook his head. "That wasn't Shanley."

"He was impersonating him, you mean?" Frank asked. "We saw his detective's license."

"Sure, *they* were the real Shanley's all right. His house was broken into last night and all his credentials stolen," the inspector explained.

Frank and Joe asked to read the report of the robbery, but found no clues of interest. In answer to Inspector Moon's questions, they explained that they were helping their father on a case and described their brush with Hugo and Abdul at the wooded site.

"I'll put out a call for them right away," Inspector Moon said. He picked up his phone and ordered that an alarm be sent to all radio cars.

"One thing I don't understand is why that Latin American fellow at the airport slipped me the gloves and key," said Joe, after the officer hung up. "Couldn't he tell just by looking at me that I wasn't the right guy?"

"Maybe you *do* look like the right guy," Inspector Moon pointed out.

"Wow! I never thought of that!"

Despite the seriousness of the situation, Frank suddenly grinned. "Good night! My brother looking like some underworld character!" Then he sobered. "If this is some kind of a racket—like a theft ring for passing stolen goods—we now have a good description of one of the members."

"Right," the inspector agreed. "I'll pass the word around for the men to be on the lookout for a fellow answering Joe's description."

"But of the criminal type, please," Joe pleaded.

Just then the door of the interrogation room opened, and the plainclothesman came out with the prisoner.

"Learn anything?" Inspector Moon asked the detective.

"No," he replied. "He won't even tell us his name."

"Any identification?" the inspector queried.

"Not even a driver's license. Only thing that might help is this tattoo." The detective pulled up the prisoner's sleeve to show a pineapple tattoo on his left forearm.

"Hmm. It's not much to go on," the inspector said, "but check the files. Anything else?"

"Yes, sir. This prisoner was carrying these in his pocket, together with a ticket to Mexico."

With a baffled look, the detective held up a pair of doll's glass eyes! Instantly the Hardys realized they were just like the dummy's eyes which had contained uncut diamonds!

CHAPTER VIII

Spanish Code

FRANK and Joe were excited. Here was a definite clue that tied the Eastern City holdup men to the Hugo dummy racket!

"I'd like to speak to you privately," Frank said to the police inspector. "And bring the doll's eyes along, please."

When they were alone in a rear office, Frank declared, "These doll's eyes prove the man you're holding and his gang are mixed up in the case Dad's working on!"

"And what about the boxes of Variotrycin in the brief case?" Joe asked.

Inspector Moon looked thoughtfully at both boys and said that he would follow through on this angle in a few minutes, then he held up the doll's eyes to the light.

"No diamonds here," he announced. "These eyes are empty. But we still have plenty to hold

Mr. Pineapple on. Maybe he'll change his mind later about talking."

Inspector Moon asked the boys to wait while he tried to find out about the Variotrycin. He telephoned first to Watkins Pharmacy. The boys could hear both sides of the conversation.

"That stuff's pretty new," Mr. Watkins told the inspector, "and very expensive. Far as I know, the Lexo Drug people that make it won't be supplying it in quantity until they can lower the price."

"Where is Lexo Drug?"

Mr. Watkins said the company had a plant in Hartsburg. "If you have a prescription, I could put in a special order—"

"No, thanks," the inspector interrupted.

Hartsburg was less than a hundred miles from Bayport. Inspector Moon then placed a long-distance call to the company.

"I'd like to speak to the plant manager," he told the switchboard girl.

A man's gruff voice came on the line. "McCardle speaking."

Inspector Moon introduced himself and said, "I'm calling to find out if any shipments of Variotrycin have been stolen recently."

The plant manager asked with a sharp note of interest, "Who did you say you were?"

"Inspector Moon of the Eastern City Police Department."

Mr. McCardle cleared his throat, then said that

a special messenger carrying a consignment of their new product had been attacked and robbed late the day before.

"Where?"

"Not far from here."

"Have you contacted your local police?" Inspector Moon asked.

"No. We just heard about the robbery. But I'll do so right away," McCardle replied.

He asked why the inspector had called him, and was told about the boxes in the brief case. "Well, we hope that you find the thief!" the manager said, then said good-by.

Inspector Moon turned to the Hardys. "How about you fellows helping on this?"

"We will!" the young sleuths promised.

Before leaving headquarters, Frank asked if he and his brother might borrow the doll eyes for further examination. Inspector Moon readily agreed.

The boys taxied back to the airport. Before the group took off for Bayport, Tony telephoned his father to tell what had happened. As he returned to the others, he said, "Lucky break! Dad says I can have the rest of the day off!"

On the flight back, the Hardys brought Jack and Tony up to date on the developments in the mystery.

"Things certainly worked fast," Jack remarked.

"Yes, and thanks a lot for your help," Joe said as they landed at Bayport. Frank echoed his words.

The pilot grinned. "Any time, fellows."

As the boys drove off, Joe suggested that they stop at Mr. Hanade's puppet-repair shop to see if he could tell them anything about the glass eyes, and to return his instruction sheet, which they had copied.

A few minutes later the trio pulled up outside Mr. Hanade's shop. The pleasant Japanese proprietor greeted the Hardys and Tony politely. "You learn something from instruction sheet for Hugo dummy?" he asked as Joe thanked him for lending it to them.

"Not yet, but we have something to show you," Joe replied. He took out the glass eyes. "Ever seen any like these before?"

Hanade studied them curiously. "Very old," he murmured. "Nowadays, manufacturers do not make dolls' eyes like this. Too expensive to make out of colored glass. Besides, glass breaks too easily."

He explained that eyes for modern dolls are normally made of plastic with a metal rod running through them. The rod is usually hinged, with a small counterweight to make the eyes open and close.

Frank murmured to Joe, "With a rod running

through them, there wouldn't be much room inside for hiding anything."

Joe nodded and said aloud, "If they're plastic, they're probably solid instead of hollow."

"That is correct," said Mr. Hanade.

"Do your Hugo dummies have solid plastic eyes?" Frank queried.

"Yes. Modern merchandise, of course."

"Any idea where these glass eyes might have come from?" Joe went on.

"Would be hard to say. Most likely from some old-fashioned American dolls or puppets."

"One more question," said Frank. "Where are the Hugo dummies made?"

"Mexico," said Mr. Hanade. At once the boys thought of the prisoner who had a ticket to Mexico. The man went on, "The dummies are fashioned of papier-mâché."

The boys thanked him for his help and left. As they drove home, the group exchanged views on the mystery.

"I still can't figure out why those guys in Eastern City were so anxious to get their hands on that Variotrycin," Joe remarked. "Maybe there's a connection between the drugs and the diamonds."

"And how about that pirate flag in Abdul's trailer?" Tony reminded them. "Where does that come in?"

Frank shrugged. "You've got me, pal!"

When they reached the Hardy home, Chet

Morton was rocking himself in the glider on the front porch.

"Hey, watch it, boy! You want that thing to collapse?" Joe called out laughingly.

"Where've you fellows been?" Chet complained. "I've been waiting here so long I'll bet I've missed my lunch."

Frank sniffed the appetizing aroma of freshly baked cake that floated out through the open windows. "Better come in and eat with us, Chet."

The stout teen-ager needed no urging. Soon all four boys were seated around the dining-room table, with Mrs. Hardy and Aunt Gertrude, spooning up hearty servings of delicious onion soup and enjoying crusty French bread.

"How did things go, boys?" Mrs. Hardy asked.

After hearing all about the exciting adventures, both women gasped and Aunt Gertrude said, "I warned you! If you'd only pay attention to me, you wouldn't risk your lives that way."

Mrs. Hardy looked troubled. "Please be careful," she cautioned.

After luncheon the four boys trooped upstairs to Frank and Joe's room. Once again the young sleuths took out the two instruction sheets for the Hugo dummies and began to compare them.

"I'll read off the extra words included on Chet's sheet that are different, Frank, and you write them down," Joe suggested.

"Okay, shoot!"

Frank wrote the words in a column with the translation opposite each one:

Cuerpo	body
ahora	now
bajo	low or under
escena	stage, scene
zapato	shoe
ojo	eye
necesitar	to want or need
aqui	here
Número	number

"What is it—a code?" asked Tony.

"Perhaps," said Frank. After a couple of minutes of trying various combinations, he added, "I can't make any sense out of them."

"Let's try the first letters of each Spanish word reading down," suggested Joe. "C,a,b,e,z,o, n,a,n—"

"The first word, *Cuerpo*," said Tony, "and the last word, *Número*, both have capital letters. Maybe that means the N should be separated from the rest."

Frank wrote it down this way:

Cabezona N

"I believe you're right," he commented, and consulted a Spanish dictionary. He read aloud:

" 'Cabezon, na, *adj. big-headed; stubborn; n.*

*collar of a shirt; opening in a garment for the
passage of the head; noseband (for horses) .'* "

"Doesn't make sense to me," said Frank, "unless the code refers to the Hugo dummy's big
head."

"That's it!" Joe exclaimed. "The instructions
might point out that the diamonds were secreted
in the dummy's head! And the N could stand for
north, which is the position the dummy's eyes are
located on its face."

Excited, the boys warmed up their short-wave
radio and beamed out a call over the Hardys' special frequency. After several minutes Mr. Hardy
answered.

"Fenton to Bayport. Can you read me?"

"Sure can, Dad!" Joe replied into the mike.
"We have some important news for you!"

"Better not tell it now," Mr. Hardy warned
hastily. "Someone may be listening!"

"Then tell us where to reach you and we'll send
it in code by airmail," Joe told his father.

"I have a better idea, son. Suppose you and
Frank fly down here to Puerto Rico and join me. I
can use your help. Call Jack Wayne right away
and make the arrangements."

Chet and Tony had listened to the invitation
with envy. "Ask your dad if he can use us," said
Chet. "We could be a big help!"

"It sure would be a lot of fun," Joe agreed.

"It's okay. Bring your pals along." Mr. Hardy

chuckled, having heard the whole conversation.

At once Chet and Tony dashed to the hall phone to call their parents. First Chet received permission to take a vacation from his summer work on the farm, then Tony's father agreed to give him time off.

The boys were jubilantly talking over their plans when the telephone rang sharply. It was Inspector Moon calling from Eastern City.

"I have some bad news," he told Joe, who answered. "That prisoner you and your brother captured this morning has just escaped by overpowering a guard."

"Escaped!" Joe echoed.

"I thought I'd better warn you two," the officer said.

"Thanks, Inspector. We'll be on our guard."

Frank was gravely alarmed when he learned of the escape. "Now we're in real trouble," he pointed out. "That man will pass along word to the gang that we have valuable information and they may try to harm us!"

"Good night!" Joe exclaimed. "If they come here while we're gone, Mother and Aunt Gertrude will be in danger!"

"We'd better call Sam Radley and ask him to guard the house," Frank decided.

Mr. Hardy's operative readily agreed not only to stand guard himself at night, but to provide around-the-clock protection for the Hardy home.

A call to Jack Wayne brought the promise that Mr. Hardy's new six-seater cabin plane would be fueled and ready for take-off at six the next morning.

"I'll be there at five to have everything in order," the pilot promised.

At dawn the brothers bounced out of bed, showered, dressed hastily, and had a quick breakfast.

"Now take your time and chew your food properly," Aunt Gertrude told them tartly. "I doubt that the island of Puerto Rico will sink out of sight if you don't get there in the next few hours!"

After good-bys and warnings to be careful, the boys flung their suitcases into the convertible and drove off. They picked up Chet and Tony, then set off for the airport.

It was a few minutes before six, and shreds of morning mist still clung to the ground when they arrived at the airport. Jack Wayne was nowhere in sight. A line-boy was refueling the blue-and-white Hardy plane at the gas pit. The young detectives asked him if he had seen Jack Wayne.

"I did, just a little while ago," the line-boy answered. "The last time I saw him he was headed for Hangar B. He asked me if I'd help him tow your father's plane out and refuel it. When I went over to the hangar a few minutes later, Jack was nowhere around. So I just went ahead and towed the plane out on my own."

The boys waited anxiously, but twenty minutes later, their pilot still had not arrived.

Frank's face clouded with worry. "I'm afraid that something has happened to Jack. He'd never be this late without letting me know."

"Yes," said Joe. "It looks as if our enemies may have already started their newest attack."

CHAPTER IX

The Ticking Suitcase

"MAYBE Jack went to the shop to get something," Tony said.

In pairs the boys began their hunt. When they met again a short time later, their faces registered failure.

"I'll call the motel where Jack lives," Frank decided. "He might have gone to his room to get something."

Hopefully the four boys hurried to the waiting room. Frank made the call.

"Is he there?" Joe asked anxiously when his brother emerged from the booth.

Frank shook his head. "The manager said Jack left a couple of hours ago."

For a moment the boys were silent, wondering what their next move should be. Suddenly Joe snapped his fingers. "We haven't checked Jack's plane. Let's go look!"

With quick strides the boys headed for Hangar

B, where their father and Jack kept their planes. Jack's sleek, silver-winged craft stood in one corner of the big corrugated-iron building.

Frank reached the plane first, climbed up, and jerked open the cabin door. He stopped short and gasped. Slumped on the floor was the huddled form of Jack Wayne!

"He's here, unconscious!" Frank reported.

"Good night!" cried Joe.

Gently the boys lifted the pilot out of the plane and laid him on a pile of tarpaulins.

"Is he badly hurt?" Chet asked.

"I think not," Frank replied, taking Jack's pulse, which was even. "Just knocked out. In fact, I believe I smell chloroform in here."

Jack moaned and stirred. "Thank goodness it's nothing worse," said Joe.

A few minutes later, though still woozy, Jack was able to sit up. "W-what—? W-where—?" he murmured, shaking his head from side to side.

"Take it easy," Frank advised.

"Oh, hello, fellows," Jack said shakily.

Chet Morton brought him a drink of water. While the pilot was sipping it, Frank and Joe went off to question the man in charge of the airport at the time, Burt Hildreth.

"Did you notice strangers prowling around early this morning?"

"Don't recall seeing any," said Hildreth, a tall man with a weather-beaten face. "In fact, no one's been out to the field this morning—except when this young man showed up at five o'clock." He pointed to Joe.

"Me?"

"Sure. Don't tell me you've forgotten our conversation."

Frank and Joe looked at each other, startled. *The early-morning visitor to the airfield must have been the one who resembled Joe—the contact man for the theft ring!*

Hildreth was puzzled. "What goes on here?" he asked. "You fellows mixed up in a mystery?"

"Yes," said Frank. "Joe and I didn't arrive until a few minutes ago." He explained that the police were looking for a suspect who resembled Joe. He might even be made up to look like him.

"Well, I'll be doggoned!" Hildreth exclaimed. "That fellow sure is your double! He asked if Wayne had filed the take-off time for your flight. I said, 'No, not yet, but he told me last night you'd be leaving around six.' Then he walked off toward the hangar."

Joe's eyes widened as a frightening thought struck him. "I have a hunch we'd better check our plane and check it good!"

The boys hurried back to the hangar, where they found Jack Wayne fully recovered. He told them he had been about to step into the Hardy plane when someone had sneaked up behind him and put a rag with chloroform under his nose.

"That's the last I remember. But why would anyone want to knock me out?"

"So he could sabotage our plane before take-off!" Frank replied grimly, and related Hildreth's story.

"Good night!" exclaimed Jack. "If that's the deal, we'd better go over the ship with a fine-toothed comb, or we may wind up in the drink!"

Worried, the group towed the big blue-and-white craft out onto the hangar apron. Under Jack's supervision, they began a thorough check.

Engine, landing gear, control cables, elevators, ailerons, trim tabs—everything seemed to be in order. Even the radio and flight instruments showed no signs of tampering.

Frank relaxed a bit. "I guess my hunch was wrong. Anyhow, I'm glad we made sure."

"But we still don't know why Jack was attacked," Joe pointed out.

While the pilot went off to file his flight plan, the others refreshed themselves with some hot cocoa at the airport lunch counter. Later, as Jack warmed up the engine for take-off, the boys lugged their baggage out to the ship.

Frank squatted just inside the cargo compartment in the rear of the plane and checked off each item as the others passed them in to him.

"Two bags for Joe and me," he sang out. "Three bags for Chet. One suitcase for Tony, and a bag and two suitcases for Jack already stowed aboard!"

Jack turned around. "Hey, did you say three for me? I brought only two."

"I'll bet Chet slipped in an extra one full of chow!" Tony joked.

"Either that, or he's trying to sneak his dummy aboard as a stowaway." Joe chuckled.

Suddenly Frank turned pale. "Say, what if that fellow who chloroformed Jack planted the extra bag! It could mean—"

The pilot had already jumped up from his seat and hurried aft. "These are my two suitcases," he said, pointing them out.

Frank grabbed the extra bag from the cargo space and held it to his ear.

"It's ticking!" he cried. "A time bomb!"

There was an instant of near panic as Jack and the boys stood frozen with fear. Should they leap from the plane and leave it to blow up when the bomb went off? Or should they take a chance and try to carry the bag to a safe distance?

Frank glanced at his watch. It was 6:33. "The person who planted the bomb probably figured we wouldn't be airborne just yet, so the bomb must be set to explode a few minutes from now. Out of my way, boys!" he cried.

Before anyone could stop him, Frank jumped from the plane, bag in hand, and sprinted down

the runway. Near the edge of the field, he paused and hurled the bag toward a vacant, brush-covered lot beyond.

He was halfway back to the plane when the

whole airport rocked under a sudden explosion.
Frank was hurled to the ground by the tremendous blast. Joe and the others ran to help him as
dirt, brush, and debris rained down on all sides of
the blast area.

"Frank! Are you all right?" Joe cried, reaching his brother and kneeling down beside him.

"Sure. Just a little shaken up."

"And m-me too!" said Chet. "Man alive, I thought you were a goner!" The stout boy's face was ash white and the rest of the group looked equally shocked.

By this time, the airport was in an uproar and it was some time before everyone was reassured that the bomb planter had directed his venom only toward the Hardys.

Meanwhile, Frank made a full report over the phone to Chief Collig. Finally a signal for departure was given and the graceful blue-and-white plane took off on its flight to Puerto Rico.

Everyone relaxed as the plane headed out over the Atlantic. The boys sat quietly and thought about the case. What sort of a racket were they up against? Obviously its members would stop at nothing to gain their objectives. The young sleuths had already had enough close scrapes to be sure of that!

Frank and Joe each took turns at the controls as Jack instructed them in long-range flying and navigation. It was nearing lunchtime when a voice came crackling over the plane's radio navigation frequency.

"*Sky Sleuth* One-One-Eight-Howe-Baker! This is Tancho radio! Do you read?"

Frank clicked the plane's transmitter to the

proper frequency. He then picked up the microphone and spoke into it. "Tancho radio! This is *Sky Sleuth* One-One-Eight-Howe-Baker! Read you loud and clear! Go ahead!"

"Eight-Howe-Baker! This is Tancho radio! Bayport tower has requested us to convey a message to you from Mrs. Hardy! You are requested to land at Centro in Tropicale! Repeat—land at Centro in Tropicale! Over!"

The boys were puzzled. Why land at the new Caribbean island democracy? Frank decided to check.

"Tancho radio! This is Eight-Howe-Baker! Would you please contact Bayport tower and have them call Mrs. Hardy? We would like to verify that message!"

"Stand by!"

Several minutes passed before the communicator's voice again crackled from the loudspeaker.

"Eight-Howe-Baker! This is Tancho radio! Bayport tower reports they called your home! No answer! Can we be of further assistance? Over!"

"This is Eight-Howe-Baker! Negative! We are proceeding to Centro. Please change our flight plan accordingly! Over and out!"

Shifting course to the right, Jack headed southwest toward Tropicale. Finally the lush green shores of the island came into view. The pilot consulted a map as they flew inland and soon they sighted the bustling city of Centro.

Arrowing in toward the airfield on the outskirts of town, Jack cleared with the tower and made a smooth landing. Almost before the plane rolled to a stop, a man in a white suit came running out to meet them. He was tall and dark with a long, drooping mustache.

As the boys climbed out of the plane, the stranger shoved a note into Frank's hand, then dashed off the field. Puzzled, Frank unfolded the paper and read the typewritten message. It said:

Danger. Do not come.
Dad

CHAPTER X

Cross Fire

CHET groaned in dismay at Mr. Hardy's message. To have come all this way and not go on to Puerto Rico.

Jack had a different idea. "Maybe it's a trick," he suggested.

"Yes, and the radio message too," Frank agreed.

"Then let's find that guy and make him talk!" Joe urged.

"Okay. Anybody see where he went?" Frank asked.

He and the others stared around the field. With several airliners loading and discharging passengers, the place throbbed with activity. Tourists swarmed about the terminal building.

"There he is!" cried Tony, pointing to a tall figure in a white suit talking earnestly to a group of men. They were standing near the roadway that bordered the field.

Joe took off at a fast sprint. All the others but Jack raced after him. As the boys ran, they caught a stir of movement in other parts of the field. Several uniformed men were pushing through the throng of people.

Suddenly a shot rang out, then another! The white-suited man and his companions jerked around, their hands flying toward their hip pockets.

"La policia!" one of them shouted.

Whipping out revolvers and automatics, they began shooting back. In an instant the Hardys and their friends found themselves caught in a fusillade of cross fire as bullets whined back and forth through the air.

"Wow!" Tony exclaimed as one whistled close to his ear.

"We've walked into a war!" Chet wailed.

Following Joe and Frank's example, the others fanned out, but kept on running—in an effort to escape the deadly exchange and catch up to the deliverer of the note.

One of the gunmen spotted the Americans. He let out a sharp cry in Spanish, which seemed to throw his companions into a panic. The men ran toward two parked cars.

Bringing up the rear was the mustached man in the white suit who had delivered the note. Joe was now within a couple of yards of him. With a lunge the boy hurled himself in a fierce flying tackle.

The white-suited man went down with a thud.

The other gunmen, already in the parked cars, made no effort to rescue their comrade. They sped off with a roar of exhaust!

By this time, the police had reached the scene in jeeps to give chase. But a lieutenant and several others stayed behind to take over the prisoner from the Americans.

"Caramba, señores!" the lieutenant exclaimed to Frank and Joe. "You are brave young men to capture, unarmed, such a gunman. In fact, you are all brave señores and I offer you my thanks!"

"Glad to help, but who are these men?" Frank asked.

"Rebels plotting against the Tropicale Government," said the lieutenant. "But if you will be so kind, you will tell me why you were mixed up in this."

Frank told his story briefly and the officer urged the boys to accompany him to police headquarters and repeat what had happened.

When they arrived at headquarters, he introduced them to Lieutenant Garcia and once more the boys told their story. Before the officer could take action, five other members of the rebel group were brought in, two of them injured. One of the getaway cars had smashed into a lamppost while making a turn. All the occupants had been captured.

"A bad business, señores! You see, there have

been several uprisings lately," Lieutenant Garcia explained to the Hardys. "The first took place at Santia, on the southeast coast of our island, but each new raid occurs farther west. We fear the rebels may be moving toward Savango."

He explained that the police had learned only a few hours earlier about the group's latest plan to seize or blow up the airport.

"But why?" Frank asked. "What's their purpose?"

The lieutenant shrugged. *"Quién sabe?* Perhaps they are criminals, crazy for power, trying to overthrow the lawfully elected government."

Meanwhile, the prisoners were being questioned in another room. Frank and Joe were allowed to be present at the interrogation. It was disappointing, because none of the captured men would talk.

"I'll bet the one we caught won't tell *us* anything, either," Joe whispered to his brother.

As Frank nodded, the man suddenly raised his hand to mop the sweat from his brow. Joe gasped and clutched his brother by the arm.

"Look!" he whispered.

On the prisoner's left forearm, just above the wrist, was a pineapple tattoo!

The Hardys exchanged excited glances. Did this sign mean that the man was a member of the same racket as the one in Eastern City with the tattoo on the left arm? The boys decided the chances were too slim for them to mention their suspicion to the Tropicale police.

After the prisoner had been taken to a cell, Lieutenant Garcia turned to the Hardys and said, "May I see the note, please, that was handed to you on the field?"

When the officer finished studying it, Frank added, "I have a hunch the radio message we got in the plane was a fake, but I'd like to make sure."

He asked permission to place a long-distance telephone call to Bayport. In a few minutes Mrs. Hardy's voice came through.

"Is everything all right?" she asked quickly.

"There's nothing to worry about, Mother," Frank reassured her, then asked if she had sent the radio message.

"Why, no, son."

Somewhat upset, Mrs. Hardy begged her sons to take care of themselves. "And that goes for Chet and Tony and Jack!" she added.

When Lieutenant Garcia heard Frank's report, he frowned. "It would appear, señores, that this gang was trying to lure you into some kind of trap. Fortunately their plan failed."

He summoned the prisoner who had delivered the note. The man glibly said a stranger had asked him to do the errand. Frank and Joe were sure he was lying, but he refused to change his story and was taken away to a cell.

After making signed statements, the Hardys

were driven back to the airport in a police car. Here they ate a hearty lunch, then took off again for Puerto Rico.

"I certainly hope we have no more delays," Joe said, heaving a great sigh.

It was late afternoon when they came in sight of the beautiful Caribbean island. From the air, it looked like a paradise of emerald green. White beaches with waving palms rimmed the shore line. Farther inland, cool blue mountains reared upward from the coastal plain.

"Ah me! W.at a place in which to relax and dream!" Chet said as he peered down from the cabin window.

"You mean with a well-filled lunch basket?" Tony put in, chuckling.

To the southeast of the International Airport near San Juan a green-clad mountain peak soared against the sky. "That's *El Yunque*—The Anvil," Jack pointed out. "It's a tropical rain forest with ferns as high as houses."

They landed and admired the large white modernistic terminal building as they walked toward it. The structure seemed to be poised on stilts.

Mr. Hardy was waiting to greet the travelers as soon as they cleared customs. "Good flight?" he asked.

"Wait'll you hear!" Joe grinned. "We stopped off in Tropicale and barged smack into a revolution!"

"Well, I'm glad you came through it alive!" Though eager to hear all the news, Mr. Hardy cautioned everyone not to talk freely until they were in their hotel rooms.

The group managed to squeeze into a single taxi. Soon they were whisked through a beautiful residential area of pink and white villas, then out onto a wide boulevard lined by palms, in clear view of the sea.

"Pretty nice place," Chet remarked. "Let's have some fun while we're here and not get mixed up with a bunch of crooks."

The others smiled. When they reached the hotel, the boys went at once to Mr. Hardy's room for a conference.

Frank and Joe quickly related everything that had happened to them since receiving his message of "Find Hugo purple turban."

Mr. Hardy was amazed. "So there were diamonds in the dummy! This case is even more complex than I realized," he declared, his face grave. "And you've done a good job. I thought that message might be a clue to a smuggling racket. It was written on a piece of paper left in a hastily vacated house."

The detective confided to the boys that he was working for the United States Government on the theft of some rare isotopes—materials which could be used in the manufacture of atomic weapons.

"The FBI believes they were stolen here in Puerto Rico, en route to foreign countries," he added. "It looks as if we may be up against a gang of air-freight thieves and smugglers who deal in other things besides isotopes!"

"Any leads so far?" Frank asked.

"Just one. My next job is to keep watch at a freight warehouse near the airport."

Joe jumped up from his chair in excitement. "How about Frank and Chet and Tony and myself doing a stakeout at the warehouse?"

The other boys were equally enthusiastic about the idea, and Mr. Hardy finally agreed. They soon devised a plan. The boys would hide in crates to be carted to the warehouse that evening.

After dinner the boys started out for a trucking company on a street called Calle Pacheco. The owner of the firm was cooperating with the police on the freight robberies.

"Don't look now," said Tony a few minutes later, "but I think a car's tailing us."

Frank leaned forward to watch the taxi's rear-view mirror. "You're right," he muttered. "Maybe we'd better split up."

Quickly he arranged with Chet and Tony to stay in the taxi and try to shake off their pursuer. "If you lose him, meet us at the trucking company in half an hour."

Three blocks down, the driver stopped for a red light. Quickly the Hardys jumped from the taxi and lost themselves in the passing throng of pedestrians.

They had not gone far when Frank and Joe noticed that a tall man seemed to be trailing them. His face was almost hidden by the pulled-down brim of his slouch hat. The Hardys were struck by something familiar about the fellow! But there was no time to mull this over.

"Better shake him," Frank muttered.

Joe agreed. Quickly the boys hailed a taxi and resumed their ride to the trucking company. When they arrived, the owner said:

"Ah, *si,* I have the boxes all prepared. The covers, of course, will not be nailed down."

A few minutes later Chet and Tony joined them. The boys took their places in the big crates, which were loaded aboard a truck. Soon they were bumping and rattling through the streets of San Juan.

When the truck arrived at the warehouse, the boxes were carried inside to the main room. As closing time neared, the workmen's voices died away and everything became quiet.

The first half hour of the boys' vigil went slowly. Cramped and tense in their hiding places, they sweated out each passing moment.

Then Frank heard a noise!

CHAPTER XI

Warehouse Marauders

FRANK strained his ears, wondering if he was mistaken. Then he heard it again—a faint scratchy noise which he could not identify.

Raising the lid of his box, he beamed a flashlight toward the sound. A large sheet of dirty wrapping paper lay a few yards away. On it crouched a small, brown furry creature.

"What gives?" came a whisper from Joe's box.

"Just a rat."

The rodent froze for a few seconds in the glare of light, its beady eyes shining with reflected brilliance. Then it scampered off into a dark hole nearby—apparently the opening to a small tunnel for an electrical conduit, but large enough for a person to crawl into.

The boys resumed their wait, shifting occasionally to exercise their cramped muscles. The warehouse lay wrapped in gloom, pierced only by a faint glow from the moon through a skylight.

Some time later another noise broke the stillness. It was a faint curse in Spanish! The voice sounded oddly hollow and muffled.

Frank and Joe raised the lids of their crates a crack. A moment later they saw two figures wriggle through the tunnel opening. Both snapped on flashlights and played them around the room. Then the intruders, whose faces were in shadow, separated and began examining the shipping labels on the boxes and crates.

One of the men approached the spot where the Hardys were hiding. The boys closed the lids noiselessly and held their breaths. Through a knothole, Joe could make out one man's legs, scarcely inches away. Apparently he was examining the label on Joe's box!

A cold sweat broke out on the youth's forehead. *What if he opened the lid?*

"Hey, come here!" called out a raspy voice.

"*Qué quieres?*" said the man near Joe.

"Think I've found somethin' good—a box of fine Swiss watches! Should make a real haul!"

"Ah, *bueno!*"

As the Spanish-speaking intruder moved away, Joe gave a noiseless sigh of relief.

The boys could hear muttered conversation as the thieves discussed the loot. Cautiously Frank and Joe raised the lids of their boxes. A moment later Chet and Tony lifted theirs.

They could see the figures of the two burglars

silhouetted by their own flashlights. They were squatting in front of a small crate, their backs to the boys. One of them seemed to be holding a bag.

Scarcely daring to breathe, the four boys watched tensely. One of the men produced a fine saw and began cutting deftly along the label of the box containing the watches.

In a few minutes an opening was made. The thief reached in and removed the packaged watches. Then his partner began filling the box with sand and rubble from the bag to equal its previous weight.

"Okay. Now!" hissed Frank, giving the signal to attack.

Moving silently, the four boys started to climb out of their crates. Chet was the first to emerge completely. But, in his eagerness, he let the crate lid slip from his sweaty fingers.

B-a-a-ang!

Instantly the burglars sprang to their feet. "Somebody's here!" cried one of them.

The other shrilled, *"Vámonos!* Let's go!"

Clicking off their flashlights, the two thieves darted off into the darkness. But the boys snapped on their own lights and managed to pin the fleeing men for a moment in the yellow beams.

One of the thieves was heavy-set, dark, and swarthy. The other, slim and blond, bore a startling resemblance to Joe!

The Hardys became tense with excitement.

Was this the contact man of the gang—the one who had chloroformed Jack Wayne back at the Bayport airfield?

"I'll guard the tunnel," Frank told his brother. "The rest of you scatter!"

The two thieves had already taken cover among the barrels and crates.

"One of 'em's over there!" shouted Tony. But a crash of boxes indicated that their quarry was already plunging off.

Joe, Tony, and Chet lost no time in pursuing him. Soon the darkened warehouse was a scene of bedlam.

"I wonder where the watchman is," thought Frank. "He must have been knocked out."

Crates were banged over, piles of goods and boxes sent toppling as hunters and quarry blundered about in the darkness.

"Help! I've got him!" Chet panted, in a far corner of the warehouse.

Tony sprinted to aid him. His beam picked out the blond man, struggling in Chet's bearlike embrace. Instantly Tony tackled the fellow around the knees just as he jerked loose from Chet. The stout boy flashed his light square on the prisoner.

"It's the one who looks like Joe!" Chet cried out triumphantly.

"I *am* Joe!" howled the captive.

"Oh, *no!*" babbled Chet in nervous confusion. Just then a yell from Frank brought the others whirling to attention. "They're getting away! Come quick!"

The three boys raced in the direction of Frank's voice. But it was too late. During the melee between Chet, Joe, and Tony, the two suspects had grabbed Frank and pinned him behind a stack of barrels. Then they had wriggled through the tunnel.

"Come on! Let's go after them!" cried Joe.

He started to crawl into the tunnel headfirst, but Tony dragged him back.

"No, Joe. Don't try it! Those guys have the advantage."

"But we can't let 'em get away!" Joe protested in exasperation.

In the meantime, Chet had released Frank and they ran forward.

"Let's try the door!" Frank suggested. "Maybe we can nail the men when they come out the other end of the tunnel."

He led the way eagerly toward the door. The others hurried after him, and tried to push it open.

"Locked!" he cried.

The boys hurried to a door leading to the office and let themselves outside. Back of a bench an elderly man was groggily getting to his feet.

"You the watchman here?" Frank asked.

"*Sí*. I—I think—someone—knock me out."

"You're right. Two thieves who've just robbed

this place. We're after them now. Where's the exit to the tunnel?"

The dazed watchman led the boys to the marauders' point of exit, an open manhole with its cover overturned. The discovery brought fresh groans.

"Of all the rotten breaks!" Joe grumbled.

Just then Frank heard the sound of a car starting up in the distance. "There they go!" he shouted, as twin headlights swept a path through the darkness.

Joe glanced around frantically for some way to take up the chase. He spotted a small motorcycle. "Whose is that?"

"It is mine, señor," the bewildered watchman admitted.

"May I borrow it?"

"*Sí, sí!* But be careful—*por favor!*"

Joe dashed toward the motorcycle, leaped into the saddle, and kicked the starter. The engine sputtered to life. With a blast of exhaust, he took off after the fleeing car.

The noise of the motorcycle gave warning to the thieves that they were being followed. At top speed they careened through the darkened residential district of Santurce, then into the old town of San Juan.

Most of the way, Joe managed to keep the car clearly in view. But after passing San Cristóbal fortress on the right, he emerged into the Plaza

Colón to find that the burglars' automobile was no longer in sight.

In the center of the square on a tall pillar, a bronze statue of Christopher Columbus loomed against the night sky.

"Oh, brother! If you could only talk!" Joe muttered helplessly.

Obviously the thieves had disappeared down one of the narrow, cobblestoned streets leading off the square. But which one?

Wheeling over to a parked taxi, Joe questioned the driver about a speeding car. "Ah, *si*, señor. It went that way!" replied the driver, pointing down one of the streets.

"Thanks! *Muchas gracias!*" Joe exclaimed.

So that the warehouse thieves wouldn't hear him approaching, he parked the motorcycle near the entrance to the narrow street and then continued on foot. He had gone scarcely a hundred yards when he gasped jubilantly. Ahead in the moonlight stood the thief who resembled Joe!

He was putting something into a basket which had been lowered by rope from a balcony. Joe had seen the same method being used earlier that evening when people purchased fruit or vegetables from street vendors.

Sprinting forward, Joe tried to take the man by surprise. Unfortunately, the fellow spotted him and darted into a narrow, twisting street.

Quickly Joe reached up and managed to grab

the basket. But the man on the balcony gave it a hard yank, jerking it free. The basket shot up out of Joe's grasp.

The young sleuth tried to find an entrance to the building, but apparently there was none facing the street. He retraced his steps part way to the square and found an alley which led back to the houses. Cautiously he made his way through the shadowy, musty passageway.

Counting the buildings, Joe found the one from which the basket had been lowered. It was a three-story building of pink stucco, with shuttered windows and a wrought-iron balcony on each of the two upper stories. An outside flight of steps led up to its gloomy-looking interior.

Joe started up the steps on tiptoe. But he did not get far. Suddenly he was struck on the head. Joe slumped to the ground, unconscious.

CHAPTER XII

The Tattooed Prisoner

BACK at the warehouse, Frank, Chet, and Tony waited anxiously for Joe to return. The police had come and gone. The boys had given the watchman first aid and he was now feeling better.

"Joe's been gone almost an hour," muttered Frank, glancing worriedly at his watch.

"Why don't we get a taxi," Tony suggested, "and see if we can find him?"

"Second the motion!" Chet responded.

But finding a taxi at that hour was not easy and the boys finally had to go to the airport to round one up. Since the thieves' car had sped away in the direction of Santurce, Frank ordered the driver to try that part of the city first. But fifteen minutes of cruising up and down the darkened streets proved fruitless.

"Take us into Old San Juan," Frank said.

As they drove into Columbus Plaza, Chet exclaimed, "There's the motorcycle Joe borrowed!"

It was standing parked at the curb where Joe had left it, but the young sleuth was nowhere in sight. Frank paid their driver, and gave him an extra dollar to take the motorcycle back to the watchman at once.

The three boys began a search of the surrounding streets for Joe. But the hunt was unsuccessful and finally they gave up in despair.

"Guess we may as well go back to the hotel," Frank said glumly. "But I sure hate to tell Dad that Joe's missing."

Mr. Hardy was greatly dismayed by the news. "With the gang we're up against, anything may have happened to Joe!" he declared.

Before he could formulate a plan of action, there was a knock on the door of the hotel room.

"You are Señor Fenton Hardy?" a Puerto Rican police officer asked.

"That's right."

"You have a son named Joe Hardy?"

"I certainly do. You have news of him?" Mr. Hardy asked anxiously.

"I regret to inform you, señor, that your son is in jail."

The officer, expecting to hear alarmed protests from the group, was amazed to see looks of relief on their faces.

"We'll go to see him at once," Mr. Hardy told the officer.

A police car took them to San Juan Police Headquarters. Here they learned, to their amazement, that Joe was being held for attempted burglary. A turnkey took them to his dimly lighted cell.

"There he is, señor," said the jailer.

The blond figure inside was slumped dejectedly on his cot, a livid bruise on one temple. But at sight of Mr. Hardy and the others, he brightened and jumped to his feet.

"Am I ever glad to see *you* people!"

Mr. Hardy was about to greet his son when Chet cried out in alarm. "Look! It's not Joe! It's that fellow who resembles him!"

Chet pointed out that on the prisoner's left forearm was a pineapple tattoo! To everybody's surprise, the prisoner merely laughed.

"Had you fooled, Chet," he said. "It's only a joke. I put the pineapple on myself with this indelible pencil I borrowed from the guard."

Frank chuckled with relief. "You're Joe, all right. Someday that stunt may come in handy."

"Now that you have been identified," said Mr. Hardy, "suppose you tell us why you're here."

Joe told about the basket incident and how he had tried to enter the house by a rear stairway. "Someone conked me. When I came to, the guy claimed I was a burglar and called the police!"

"Hmm." Mr. Hardy regarded his son with a

wry smile. "I suppose you can hardly blame the fellow for being suspicious."

"That's if he's on the level," said Joe. "But I have a hunch he was more interested in keeping me from finding out what was in the basket!"

"We'll check up on the place," Mr. Hardy said.

After showing his credentials, the detective obtained Joe's release. Although the officer in charge was a bit dubious, he issued a search warrant and dispatched a police car to take the group to the house in question.

They ascended the stairs to the rear entrance and knocked. A thin old man opened the door.

The policeman said in Spanish that they had a warrant to search the house for stolen goods.

The old man seemed bewildered, but allowed them to enter. He informed them that a separate family lived on each floor. Mr. Hardy and the policeman questioned all the occupants and searched every room with the help of the boys. Nothing suspicious was found and the man who had charged Joe with burglary was not at home.

"Looks like a wild-goose chase," Chet murmured as the searchers reached the top floor.

Frank, too, was about ready to give up when he caught sight of a small white card on the floor. He took out his handkerchief, wiped some dust off his hands, then dropped the handkerchief on the floor as if accidentally. He picked it up casually and returned the handkerchief to his pocket. A few minutes later the group left.

When they gathered later in Mr. Hardy's hotel room, the private investigator tossed his Panama hat on the bed with a sigh.

"Well, boys, it was a good try," he told them, "but we seem to have run into a blind alley."

Frank grinned. "Maybe not, Dad."

He pulled out the handkerchief and extracted the small white card. "I found this on the top floor," he explained, "but I didn't want to mention it in front of the people who lived there."

Mr. Hardy and the others read the card in amazement. It bore the words, crudely printed by hand:

CABEZONA N

Joe whistled loudly. "It's the same code message we worked out from those dummy instructions back in Bayport!" he exclaimed. "This house may be a hideout for the gang!"

"You're probably right, son," said his father, furrowing his brow. "But we may have a hard time convincing the police of that."

He and the boys discussed the mystery for nearly an hour before retiring, but arrived at no solution. The next morning they breakfasted together in the pleasant hotel dining room.

"Mmm, boy, this iced pineapple juice is sure good!" Chet smacked his lips.

Just then a bellhop came to their table. He informed Mr. Hardy that a visitor was waiting in the lobby. The detective asked to be excused and left. When he returned, there was a grave expression on his face.

"Who was it, Dad?" Frank asked.

"A United States federal agent," Mr. Hardy replied quietly. "Something new and serious has come up on my case. I'm not free to tell you any more just now, but it looks as though you boys will have to carry on here by yourselves."

Frank, Joe, Chet, and Tony enthusiastically said they were ready. Mr. Hardy informed them that he and Jack Wayne would have to take off at once for a secret destination. He quickly finished his meal and said good-by.

After breakfast the four boys assembled in Frank and Joe's room.

"It seems to me," said Joe, "that the house we searched last night is still our best lead. I think we ought to watch it."

"Check and double check," Tony said.

Frank agreed but said that to avoid suspicion they should not all take on the job at once. "We'd surely be spotted. Tony, how about you taking the first watch? With your olive complexion, you could pass for a native."

Tony grinned. "That's fine with me." He promptly left by taxi for Columbus Plaza.

The other three boys decided to look through

the telephone directory on the off-chance that "Cabezona" might be a person's name. Chet offered to check on this.

"Only one person in the whole city of San Juan named Cabezona," he informed the others after he ran his finger down the page. "And his initials are F. X.—not N."

"Let's talk to him, anyhow," urged Joe.

The boys left the hotel and asked the doorman for directions to the Avenida Ponce de Leon. At the address Chet had jotted down was a haberdashery shop. The owner, Señor F. X. Cabezona, was a stout, jolly man who spoke excellent English.

"And what may I show the young men? Shirts? Socks?" He beamed at his three customers.

"A necktie," Frank replied.

The proprietor showed them an assortment of gay ties, then said there were some that they might like in a new shipment just unpacked. He disappeared into a back room.

While he was gone, Chet whispered, "This can't be the right Cabezona."

"He sure doesn't look like a racketeer," Joe agreed.

When the owner returned, Frank said casually, "Your name is rather unusual."

"Ah, *sí!*" The jolly man chuckled. "In Puerto Rico the word means the big pineapples which grow on the south coast."

Pineapples! The Hardys and Chet were elated. They had picked up another clue! Maybe the word in the Hugo instructions and on the card Frank had found referred to the pineapple tattoo! It must be the gang's identification!

The affable haberdasher went on, "So far as I know, my wife and young son Carlos and I are the only Cabezona family on the island."

Frank and Joe wondered if there could be another Cabezona in Puerto Rico, perhaps living there secretly and leading the underground group.

After buying a tie, the boys returned to their hotel. When they reached their room, the phone was ringing. Joe answered. It was Tony calling.

"I just saw a tall guy with a large head sneak into the alley back of the house. How about you fellows getting over here? I have a hunch something's up!"

"We're on our way!" Joe promised. "Meet you at the statue of Columbus."

He put down the phone and relayed the news to Frank and Chet. Both were jubilant.

"That man might be the one who trailed us on our way to the trucking company last night," Joe pointed out.

"Not only that," said Frank, "but maybe his nickname is Cabezona!"

CHAPTER XIII

Pursuit at El Morro

WHEN the Hardys and Chet reached Columbus Plaza in a taxi, they saw Tony standing in the doorway of a small souvenir shop. It was on the corner of the narrow street to which Joe had traced the mystery man.

"Okay, right here, driver!" said Frank. The passengers got out and Tony came over to join them.

"Now tell us everything, Tony," Joe requested when the group walked off a distance, out of anyone else's hearing.

"Well, first of all, I want to tell you I've hired a swell observation post for us. Cost a buck," Tony explained. "It's a room in a house right across the street from the hideout. We'll have a clear view of both the pink stucco place and the alley."

"Good work!" said Joe.

The boys hurried down the narrow, cobblestoned street, then ducked into the side entrance of the house where Tony had rented a room. They posted themselves at the front windows of the room. Latticed shutters enabled them to peer out without being seen. Almost an hour went by without results.

"You sure you weren't seeing things?" complained Chet, who was getting warm.

"Positive!" said Tony. "Give the man in there a chance. If he went in, he's bound to come out *some* time!"

"Unless we've already missed him," Chet retorted.

The words were hardly out of his mouth when Tony exclaimed in a low voice, "There he is!"

A tall man, with an unusually large head, emerged from the alley. He was swarthy and had an aquiline-shaped nose.

"Abdul!" Frank exclaimed excitedly. *"He's* the fellow who was shadowing us, Joe."

His brother nodded. "We couldn't place him then with that hat over his face, plus not wearing his fancy Oriental getup."

The assistant to Hugo the fortuneteller, hatless now, wore dungarees and a striped jersey.

"There *is* a hookup between those Hugo-dummy smugglers and the freight thieves!" said Frank.

"Let's follow him!" Joe urged.

The four started out at once, keeping a safe distance behind the man. Abdul headed away from Columbus Plaza. At Calle San Justo he turned right and walked for several blocks, then walked to the left on the Boulevard del Valle.

Eventually he came to a broad iron gate standing open to visitors. It was the entrance to Fort Brooke, the big United States military post at the western tip of Old San Juan. With a casual salute to the soldier on guard, Abdul strolled on through.

"Gallopin' gooseberries!" Chet burst out. "What's he up to now? Is he going to steal some military secrets?"

"Only one way to find out," Frank replied, hurrying toward the fort.

As the boys passed through the gate, a grassy green plateau stretched ahead of them. It swept out toward the ocean and was used as a golf course. Men and women were playing golf. Tourists' cars stood parked along the road, which curved to the left of the course. Facing this was a row of Army buildings and officers' homes.

"Let's separate and act like sightseers," Frank advised his companions.

Each of them started wandering around alone, but kept a wary eye on Abdul. The man headed straight for the old Spanish battlements of El Morro. This ancient fort stood poised on a bluff jutting out over the sea, beyond the end of the golf course.

When Abdul reached the massive stone walls of

the fortress, he glanced around for a moment. Seemingly satisfied that no one was following him, he ducked hastily into a round, stone sentry house at the very tip of the rock-walled point. Below it, the surf pounded itself into foam over the coral rocks.

"Now why did he do that?" Chet asked himself, puzzled.

The boys began closing in. Frank reached the spot first and made his way along the wall of the steep parapet where an ancient bronze cannon offered a convenient hiding place. Frank crouched down behind it to watch Abdul.

Inside the sentry box the man took a mirror from his pocket and aimed it to catch the sun. Then he began shooting flashes of light out to sea. Frank had a clear view.

"He's signaling in international code!" the boy realized with a gasp of excitement.

Slowly the message was spelled out: "3–4–8–9–P–M–Skeleton."

Frank wondered what it meant and who was receiving the message. He stood up and glanced across the water. Half a mile out he could see a blue speedboat.

Just then Abdul turned to leave the sentry house. With a start he noticed Frank standing behind the cannon. At the same moment, the other three boys burst from their hiding places.

Muttering a threat, Abdul took off like a bolt of

lightning, heading for the road. Joe tried to nail him with a flying tackle, but the huge man swept the boy aside with a single blow of his great arm.

"Stop him!" yelled Frank to a soldier and several sightseers. "He's wanted by the police!"

Most of the tourists were bewildered by the sudden commotion, but some of the onlookers grabbed for the fugitive too late. Startled golfers watched the chase wonderingly.

By this time, Abdul was streaking across the links with the boys in hot pursuit. Despite his weight, the man covered the ground with amazing speed. Even Joe and Frank, who were track stars at Bayport High, could not catch up to him.

Abdul gained the road just as a delivery truck passed. He leaped on the tailboard, and in a matter of seconds, the vehicle rumbled through the gate.

"He's getting away!" Joe shouted, clenching his fists in bitter disappointment.

At that moment one of the golfers rushed forward. "Jump in my car!" he cried, sprinting toward a white convertible.

Panting their thanks, Frank and Joe piled in with him. As the car shot forward, the boys poured out their story in bits and snatches.

"That fellow's wanted by the police," Frank explained. "He's part of a smuggling ring."

"I hope we can catch him," the driver said.

Fortunately, due to the town's narrow streets,

Frank wondered who was receiving the signals

traffic had to move slowly. Swinging down Calle Cristo, they soon caught sight of the delivery truck. It had turned left into Calle Sol only to find the way blocked by a pushcart peddler.

"This'll do!" Joe said to their driver. "A million thanks."

The boys leaped from the car and ran toward the truck, Joe in the lead. To his dismay, Abdul was no longer aboard!

"Pardon me," Joe said to the man at the wheel. "Where's the big fellow who hitched a ride with you?"

The driver leaned out of his cab and pointed down the street. "He jumped off the truck and went into that restaurant, señor! *Caramba!* What kind of game is going on here?"

Without waiting to explain, the boys dashed off. A moment later they pulled up to a sliding halt as Joe caught sight of the restaurant's name.

"Look!" he gasped. *"El Calypso Caliente*—Hot Calypso! It's the password used at the airport back in Eastern City!"

"Hold it a second," Frank cautioned as his brother started inside. "Tony, you and Chet wait outside in case Abdul tries another fast one. If you see him come out, grab him."

"Right!"

Frank and Joe entered the restaurant and glanced around swiftly. Abdul was not in sight, so they headed toward the rear of the place.

The white-jacketed proprietor bustled forward to bar the way. He was a rather sinister-looking man with a heavy beard.

"You wish something to eat, señores?"

"We're looking for a man who's wanted by the police," Frank told him. "He came in here a few minutes ago."

"What did he look like?"

"A big fellow in a striped jersey."

The proprietor bared his teeth in a wide smile. "You are wrong, señores. No one of that description has entered the restaurant."

"Suppose we look in the kitchen, just in case," Frank suggested.

The owner hesitated, then raised his voice slightly and said in Spanish, "Visitors coming to the kitchen." To the boys he added, *"Muy bien,* señores. You may go in, if you wish."

He gestured toward the swinging doors that led to the kitchen.

"Thanks," Frank said crisply, and strode forward, ahead of Joe.

But as Frank pushed the doors open, his face suddenly blanched in alarm.

CHAPTER XIV

The Unseen Enemy

"Look out, Joe!" Frank yelled as he ducked to the floor of the restaurant's kitchen.

A sheet of boiling water flew at the boys, just as Joe dropped to his knees. Both boys barely avoided being scalded, as the water passed harmlessly over their heads.

The burly cook who had thrown the water stood holding a huge empty kettle in both hands. Joe was white-faced with anger. He jumped to his feet, ready to fly at the man with both fists.

"Why, you big—!" he exploded.

Frank interrupted with a shout, "Look! There goes Abdul!"

The man was darting out the back door. Frank and Joe started after him, but the stout chef blocked their way, saying, "Ah, I am so sorry about the water, *amigos!*"

He stepped back with a look of dismay as he spied the tattoo of indelible pencil still visible on Joe's arm.

"Please, Beppo!" he trembled. "I did not mean to—"

"Shut up, you fool!" the proprietor snarled.

The chef's words ended in a gulp, but he kept on staring at Joe with a strange look.

"Who's Beppo?" Frank demanded.

The cook said nothing, pretending not to understand.

"Maybe he's my double," said Joe.

Once more the owner assumed his pleasant expression. "He is confused, señor. I fear this little accident has greatly upset him. And now if you will kindly leave—"

"Not yet!" snapped Frank. "You two are mixed up in some kind of racket and we intend to find out what it's all about. If you don't want to tell us, maybe you'd rather talk to the police."

"The police!" Obviously dismayed by Frank's threat, the proprietor suddenly became nervously polite.

"I will tell you everything. That big man—he rushed in here and said he wanted to hide. And if we told someone called Beppo, who has a pineapple tattoo, or anyone else that he was here, he would kill us. So I gave you a lie. I am so sorry."

"But what about that hot water?" Joe asked.

The cook spoke up. "The big man made me

throw it. He held me at gunpoint—otherwise I would not do such a terrible thing!"

Frank and Joe did not know whether to believe the story, but they could not refute it. Finally Frank said, "Okay. We'll go now."

Both the cook and the proprietor looked relieved.

Outside, Tony and Chet were waiting eagerly. The Hardys related what had happened.

"You fellows should have crowned 'em both with that empty kettle!" Chet exploded indignantly.

"What now?" said Tony. "Go to the police?"

Frank shook his head. "Those men in there just *might* be telling the truth. Anyhow, we have plenty of other leads to keep us busy."

"How about that motorboat Abdul might have been signaling from El Morro?" Joe asked.

"I'd say it was worth checking up on. With that blue color, it should be easy to spot, if it's still in this area."

"Let me handle that end of it," Tony suggested. "I'm really aching for a chance to do some power-cruising in these waters!"

Back in Bayport, Tony owned a boat called the *Napoli II,* in which he spent most of his spare time.

The boys took a taxi to the oceanfront. It was a beautiful day and the sea sparkled in the sunshine. The four sleuths ate lunch at a restaurant specializing in seafood, then Frank rented a trim little speedboat.

"Oh, boy, I can hardly wait to take her out!" Tony gloated as he warmed up the motor.

"We should stick in pairs to be on the safe side," Joe said thoughtfully. Chet would accompany Tony.

A few moments later the two boys *put-putted* out across the water. Frank and Joe returned to the hotel, eager to work further on the clue of the pineapple tattoo, and, if possible, to link it with the word *Cabezona*. While there Joe scrubbed the indelible mark from his arm.

"Let's talk to the hotel manager," Frank suggested. They found him in his office and engaged him in conversation.

"Does the word *Cabezona* mean anything to you?" Frank inquired.

"It means a large head," the manager responded. He looked at the boys quizzically. "Why do you ask?"

"Is Cabezona ever used to mean a pineapple?" Joe questioned.

The manager scratched his head in thought for a moment. "I don't know," he said. "But I suppose the word could be used when referring to a large pineapple. If you are interested in pineapples, a friend of mine could give you information on the subject. He is Juan Delgado and owns a pineapple plantation at Manati."

"We'd sure appreciate it if you could arrange for us to make a visit," said Frank.

"I will call him at once."

The manager put through the call and carried on a rapid, pleasant conversation in Spanish. When he hung up, he turned to the boys with a smile.

"It is all arranged. He will expect you early this afternoon."

"Thank you," said Frank. "You've been a great help."

The brothers went to a car-rental agency, and made arrangements for hiring a coupé.

The attendant provided them with a road map of the island, saying, "Just follow the directions I have marked, señores."

The drive was thoroughly enjoyable, with a cool trade wind steadily blowing in from the sea. On their left, the blue-green mountains rose toward the cloudless sky.

The lush coastal plain was dotted with waving seas of sugar cane, interspersed here and there with fields of pineapple planted in orderly rows.

In places the road became hilly, with shade trees arching overhead. Some were *flamboyantes,* the flame trees with gorgeous red blossoms.

"Things really grow here!" Joe said admiringly.

"Like living in a flower garden!" Frank remarked. "Mother and Aunt Gertrude would love this."

Arriving in Manati, the boys inquired the way to the Delgado plantation and were told it was located a mile north of town. When they reached it, Señor Delgado greeted them cordially on the steps of his long, low white bungalow.

"Welcome, *amigos!* I understand you have come to learn about pineapples."

"Yes, Señor Delgado," Frank said as he and Joe shook hands with the man. "Cabezona pineapples."

The plantation owner drove the boys around, pointing out the fields of spiked plants in various stages of growth. Men were busy in one section cutting off huge pineapples with long, sharp knives. Then, after showing Frank and Joe the huge cannery, he took them into his office. A white-jacketed Puerto Rican boy brought glasses and a pitcher of iced pineapple juice on a tray.

"And now, perhaps you would like to ask me some questions," said Señor Delgado as they all sipped the fruit juice.

Shooting a quick glance at his brother, Frank decided to take the plantation owner into their confidence. When the servant left, he explained that they were trying to solve a mystery.

"We have an idea," Frank said, "that a certain dangerous group in Puerto Rico may use a pineapple as a sort of insignia. Have you ever heard of anyone wearing a pineapple tattoo on his left forearm?"

Señor Delgado shook his head. "I have never heard of such a thing, señores, but it is certainly possible."

Joe inquired if Cabezona were the name of a place somewhere in Puerto Rico. Again Señor Delgado replied in the negative.

But the native servant, returning just in time to hear the question, interrupted politely, "Excuse me, señores, but I have heard of a small place called Punta Cabezona on the coast north of here. The people call it this because the land is thickly overgrown, and looks like a huge pineapple. It is near the La Palma sugar *central*."

"Sugar *central?*" Joe repeated as both boys tried hard to conceal their excitement.

"A mill where the sugar cane is ground up and crushed," Señor Delgado explained. "I have never heard of this Punta Cabezona, but I can at least give you a note of introduction to the owner of the *central,* and he can give you exact directions."

He quickly wrote the note, then the boys drove off. Some time later the mill came into view, in the midst of vast fields of sugar cane. A tall stack, jutting up from the mill's corrugated iron roof, belched a steady plume of smoke.

"The whole air smells sweet around here," Joe observed.

Frank stopped the car and they got out at a small building with a sign marked *Office*. Inside, they found the manager and gave him Señor Delgado's note. After reading it, the man rubbed his chin and looked puzzled.

"I am sorry, but I myself am new in this district. However, I am sure that my foreman, Rodriguez, could direct you to this Punta Cabezona. You will find him working the cane crusher in the mill."

The boys walked over to the main *central* building. Trucks and tractor-trains loaded with cane were drawn up outside. Huge cranes lifted the stalks and dumped them into a chute.

Frank and Joe entered and found themselves in a dark bedlam of noise. Giant rollers ground the cane into juice, which was then pumped into hot, spinning kettles to be granulated into sugar.

A flight of steel steps led up to a narrow catwalk. At the far end was an enclosed cab, where the operator controlled the crushers.

"That must be Rodriguez up there." Frank had to shout to make himself heard.

The boys climbed the stairs and made their way along the catwalk, clinging to a slender handrail. They were fascinated by the scene below. On their left were the huge rollers. On the right there was a steep drop past the giant flywheel into a pit of churning machinery.

Suddenly Frank and Joe were shoved from behind. Taken off guard, they lost their balance. With wild yells, the boys toppled over the left rail!

CHAPTER XV

Atomic Cargo

As Frank went over the railing, he managed to clutch an iron upright with one hand. Joe grabbed his brother's belt. White with fear, the two boys hung dangling above the pit of sugar-crushing machinery!

"Help! Help!" they shouted. But the thundering machinery drowned out their voices.

Would Señor Rodriguez hear their cries in time to save them from a horrible fate?

Joe reached up, and by stretching was able to grasp a bar and let go the belt. The boys' last ounce of strength was ebbing fast when Frank saw a figure in tan work clothes running along the catwalk toward them.

"Hang on, Joe!" he gasped. "Someone's coming!"

An instant later Frank's wrist was seized in a

strong grip, while another brawny arm reached down to grab Joe's. Singlehanded, the foreman hauled the boys across the rail.

By the time the Hardys were dropping weakly onto the catwalk, two other workmen arrived on the scene to lend a hand.

"*Santa Maria!*" gasped the boys' rescuer, who had turned pale himself. "Never have I seen such a narrow escape!"

The men helped Frank and Joe down the iron steps and out into the fresh air.

"Thank you. Thank you very much," Frank said to the man who had saved their lives. "Are you Señor Rodriguez?"

"*Sí*, I am Rodriguez," the foreman replied. "And now do you mind telling me the reason why you came so close to killing yourselves?"

Joe explained what had happened, adding that the boys had not seen the person who had shoved them. The brawny foreman exploded with anger. "If I get my hands on that killer, I will wring his neck!"

Turning to the workers, he asked in Spanish if any of them had witnessed the incident. One man told of having seen a man run down from the catwalk and flee out the door. Through the mill window, he had seen him drive off in a car.

Rodriguez said to the boys, "I can assure you none of my men would try such a hideous trick!"

"I believe you," Frank said quietly, then after a

pause, he asked, "We came here to get directions to a place called Punta Cabezona."

"Ah, *sí*," said Rodriguez. "It is about five or six miles from here, but the road there is rather rough." He gave the boys careful directions, and expressed the hope they would meet again under pleasanter circumstances.

Frank and Joe thanked him, then walked back to the *central* office. As they entered, the manager looked up.

"Did your friend find you, señores?" he inquired.

"What friend?" Joe asked in surprise.

"I did not catch his name, but he was a very tall man with a large head. I told him you had just gone over to the mill."

Frank and Joe exchanged knowing glances. *Abdul!* But how did he know they were here?

After telling briefly about their close brush with death, Frank asked if he might use the telephone to call Señor Delgado. The manager, distressed that he had unwittingly helped the would-be killer, hastily agreed.

"I—I do not know what to say, señores!" he gasped.

"It wasn't your fault," Frank assured him.

The manager helped to put through the call, and Frank spoke to Señor Delgado.

"This is Frank Hardy," he told the plantation

owner. "Did anyone come there looking for us after we left?"

Joe saw his brother's face tighten as he listened to the reply. When he hung up, Frank's eyes were grim.

"Well, that explains it," he said. "Abdul must have trailed us to the pineapple plantation. He arrived there right after we left and said he had an urgent message for us. So of course Señor Delgado told him where we'd gone."

"He must be a bad enemy," the manager commented.

"We agree," the Hardys chorused.

Realizing that they were still in grave danger, the Hardys drove cautiously to Punta Cabezona. The dirt road twisted through palm groves and canopies of dense green vegetation. When the boys arrived, Frank stopped the car and they got out.

"Easy to see how this place got its name," he remarked, peering ahead.

The spit of land, jutting out to sea, ended in a bulging mound. This was topped with bushy green foliage, which sprouted outward from the crown of the hill, giving the place the appearance of a huge pineapple.

"But I wonder how it ties in with the gang," Joe said with a puzzled frown. "The place appears to be deserted."

The boys strolled out on the tiny peninsula, and climbed the hill. Reaching the top, they poked about among the bushes and vegetation. But the thick underbrush showed no sign of having been trampled by human feet!

The Hardys were baffled. "I was sure we were on to something," Frank said, disappointed. "Let's walk along the shore."

They encountered several natives on the way. When questioned, none of them could recall having seen anybody lurking around the point.

"Why should a person go out there, señor?" said one old man in Spanish, shrugging his shoulders. "Without a machete to chop down brush, there is hardly even a place to sit down!"

A few moments later a plane droned overhead. Frank looked up and noted that it was flying due north. Suddenly he snapped his fingers.

"Cabezona N!" he whispered excitedly. "Say, Joe, that N might be a directional signal, meaning north of here. Maybe it leads to the gang's hideout!"

"In the middle of the ocean?" Joe questioned dubiously.

"No! It could be some island north of Puerto Rico!" Frank explained.

Joe was impressed by his brother's theory. "Maybe you've hit it," he admitted. "Well, locating it will be our next trip, I suppose."

Elated over the clue, the boys returned to San

Juan. By the time they reached the hotel, it was seven o'clock. Tony and Chet had not returned yet.

"They must be doing some real sleuthing," Frank commented, a little worried.

The Hardys waited a while, but finally went down to the hotel dining room. Frank and Joe, growing anxious about their friends, had little appetite for their meal. As they forced themselves to eat, they discussed the message which Abdul had flashed out to sea: "3-4-8-9-P-M-Skeleton."

"That 'PM' part sounds like a time signal to me," Joe remarked.

"Sure, but a signal for what?"

Joe mulled over the problem. "Well, this is a shot in the dark," he admitted, "but how about a rendezvous at the airport? After all, if the racket we're investigating is the theft of air-freight shipments, there might be some flight coming in that the gang is watching for."

Frank nodded. "That makes sense."

After finishing their supper, the two boys sat in the lobby and waited another half hour for Chet and Tony, but they failed to appear.

"I think I'll phone the police," Frank said.

He put in a call and asked if any boat had been reported in trouble. The answer was No.

"That's a relief," Frank told Joe. "But I'd feel better if Chet and Tony were here."

"I'm getting the creeps waiting," said Joe. "Suppose we go out to the airport and look over cargo flights."

"Okay."

After leaving a message for their friends, they took a taxi to the field. On the schedule board inside the air-freight operations office all incoming flights were posted.

Frank gave a gasp. "You hit the nail on the head, Joe!" he exclaimed. "Look there!"

According to the board, cargo flight No. 348, en route from New York to South America, would stop at the field at 9 P.M.

Joe glanced at his watch. "Almost that now. Let's go out and take a look."

The boys strolled up and down. Soon the green and red lights of a plane came into view overhead. Moments later, a large cargo ship thundered down out of the sky and taxied to a halt.

The boys moved closer, acting like casual sightseers. They watched as an unloading ramp was wheeled out to the plane and the crew disembarked.

"No one seems to be meeting any of them," Frank remarked. "That must mean that the message I picked up refers to the cargo." He added excitedly, "Maybe it's on the plane and the gang is planning to steal it!"

Joe nodded. "Keep your eyes on things. I'll try to contact the airport manager, or a guard."

"Roger!"

Left to himself, Frank strolled as close to the plane as he felt was safe, without attracting attention. Just then the pilot and copilot walked past him, heading for the flight operations office.

"I'll be glad when the run is over," Frank heard the pilot say. "I don't like carrying this kind of top-secret cargo."

"No," said the copilot. "But at least it's well locked up."

Frank wondered if the pilot could mean component parts for atomic weapons. At that moment, out of the corner of his eye, Frank noticed two men who seemed to be watching the ship closely. They were standing perfectly still in the shadow of the cargo warehouse which extended from the rear of the terminal building.

"I wonder who they are," Frank thought. "Probably detectives!"

At that moment two cargo handlers drove a forklift to the cargo compartment door which stood open. After removing several crates and boxes, they went off, leaving the door wide open.

Frank looked for the men in the shadows. They were gone!

"Could they have been security guards assigned to watch the plane," Frank reasoned, "or were they freight thieves?"

Frank wondered, too, if the handlers might have been bribed by the thieves not to close the cargo door! There might be a robbery of the ship's top-secret cargo at any moment!

With no help in sight, Frank decided on a bold move. He hurried toward the plane and climbed into the cargo hold, reasoning that his presence alone might balk an attempted robbery. On the other hand, if the thief tried force, Frank could put up a fight and perhaps pin the man down until Joe arrived with the airport guards.

Just forward of the cargo hatch was a metal-gated section, enclosing large steel-strapped boxes. Frank found the gate open and went forward to inspect the cargo.

Flicking on his pocket flashlight, he played the beam over the crates and boxes. Suddenly Frank was startled by a sound behind him. Looking up, he saw Joe a few feet away. In relief he said:

"I thought you'd gone for help. If those thieves are getting ready to rob this—"

Frank got no further. Too late he realized that the person was not Joe, but the smuggler who looked like him! The fellow's fist shot out, caught Frank on the jaw, and sent him sprawling.

Just before the young sleuth blacked out, he heard the door slam shut.

Frank was a prisoner!

CHAPTER XVI

Island of Danger

INSIDE the cargo compartment Frank slowly revived. When he realized the plane was airborne, he was seized with terror. The ship was soaring higher and higher and the cargo hold was not pressurized! Frank shuddered at the thought of blacking out for an indefinite time through lack of enough oxygen at high altitudes. Also, there was the danger of freezing to death!

At the airport, meanwhile, Joe had managed to locate the night manager, a husky balding man named Mr. Lopez. Though somewhat doubtful about the boy's story, he promised to alert both the tower and the airport detectives for any sign of a disturbance. Joe returned to the field just in time to see the cargo plane take off. Apparently there had been no trouble.

Frank was nowhere in sight. Joe walked through the waiting room, looking up and down.

Suddenly an alarming thought struck Joe. Was Frank, by any chance, in the plane? Joe hurried back to the manager's office. Hastily he reported his brother's disappearance.

"Please call the plane back, Mr. Lopez!" he exclaimed. "I'm sure Frank's locked in the cargo compartment."

The man looked puzzled. "Why you told me yourself your brother had climbed out of the plane and reported everything was all right."

"What?"

"Look! Are you playing a game?" snapped Mr. Lopez.

Joe turned pale. "I haven't been back here in your office since I first talked to you."

Breathlessly Joe explained how a man they thought was a smuggler was practically his double. "That faker has already posed as me once!" Joe went on. "He did it so he could sabotage our plane before we flew here. Now he's done it again, so they could trap my brother! Mr. Lopez, you must bring that plane back!"

Though startled by what Joe had told him, Lopez hesitated.

"I can't bring back the ship just on your say-so," he protested. "Maybe your brother is still here. I'll have him paged on the loudspeaker."

In a moment the public-address system was blaring out Frank's name, asking him to call the manager's office at once. There was no response, but suddenly a startling bit of news was relayed to Lopez. The two detectives assigned to watch the cargo plane had been found unconscious.

Mr. Lopez needed no further convincing about Frank's plight. He called the tower. "Radio Flight 348 to return to San Juan immediately. Emergency."

Up in the control tower, the operator barked the orders into his mike. Then he added, "Attention, all planes. An emergency landing is expected. All other ships in the air, circle the field until further notice. Repeat—circle the field."

An ambulance with oxygen equipment was rushed out on the field. Joe found the tension almost unbearable as he waited. At last the green and red lights of the cargo craft were sighted. A few minutes later the big plane landed and taxied down the runway.

Even before the landing wheels slowed to a halt, the ambulance roared out to meet it. Doctor, stretcher-bearers, and ground crew stood ready as the door of the cargo hatch was unlocked.

Joe, forced to watch from the apron, saw a still figure being carried out onto the stretcher. *Frank!* Breaking away from the manager and guards, Joe raced out on the field.

"Frank! Frank!" he cried frantically.

"Take it easy, son," said one of the ground crewmen, restraining him gently. "Doc's doing everything he can."

The stretcher was lifted into the ambulance and Joe jumped in after it. The doctor applied an oxygen mask to Frank, then he filled a hypodermic and injected a stimulant.

Badly shaken, Joe could only watch and hope. After what seemed hours, he saw the color seeping back into his brother's cheeks. Soon Frank became conscious, but he appeared dazed.

Joe flashed an anxious look at the doctor, who nodded reassuringly. "He's all right now. But it was a mighty close call! Fortunately for him the plane had not remained at high altitudes for too long."

A few minutes later Frank, with a rueful grin, told his story. "I sure am glad the plane was called back," he remarked.

"Thank your brother," said the physician. "Now, young man, I want you to rest in our infirmary for an hour."

While Frank relaxed on a hospital bed, word came that there had been no theft of freight from the plane, but the two cargo handlers had admitted accepting money from some man to leave the cargo door open.

"I have a hunch you foiled a robbery," Joe told Frank. "That shipment of parts for an atomic weapon will reach its destination now."

"I hope so. But we didn't capture any of the gang. What's more, they'll probably make it tougher than ever for us."

Joe nodded in agreement.

When the doctor discharged Frank, the boys started back to their hotel. "I sure hope Chet and Tony are there," said Joe.

To their relief, the Hardys found that their two friends had just returned. They were sweaty and disheveled. Tony had a cut on his forehead and Chet was hobbling on one leg.

"It looks as if you'd run into trouble," Joe remarked in alarm.

"Real trouble," Chet confessed.

He said that after an hour of cruising, he and Tony had spotted the suspicious blue speedboat and given chase. Suddenly, though the blue craft was outrunning their own, it had turned around and deliberately sideswiped Tony's boat!

"As they went by," Tony took up the story, "the men in the boat hid their faces."

"You mean you didn't get a look at them?" Joe asked.

"Not a peek," Tony replied. "And, boy, did they really let us have it!"

The collision had stove in the side of Tony's boat and disabled the propeller. Both Chet and Tony had been hurled from their seats and almost swept overboard by the speedboat's powerful wake.

"We managed to signal the harbor police by waving our shirts," Chet said. "They towed us into shore, then went to hunt for the blue boat."

"Any luck?" asked Frank.

"Not a bit," Chet replied. "We hung around the dock waiting for word till it got dark, but the police couldn't find any trace of the blue speedboat."

"I'll bet I know why," Joe said grimly. "Instead of coming back to port, those men made for an island offshore. That's probably the reason they smashed up Tony's boat—so you couldn't find out which way they were heading."

For the first time the four friends grinned and Frank said, "But they didn't fool us. Tomorrow we'll get another boat and head north of Cabezona."

"And now," said Tony, "tell Chet and me what you fellows have been doing."

When they heard the Hardys' story, their grins faded, and Chet said woefully, "All I wanted was a ventriloquist's dummy and look what happened!"

After another hour of conversation the four boys went to bed. The next morning they felt none the worse for their previous day's experiences. After a hearty breakfast of bacon and eggs, they took a taxi to the boat dock.

"Wonder how much that man'll charge us for damages," Tony said uncomfortably.

The boat owner, however, was quite cordial. "Do not worry, señores," he assured the boys. "The police have told me the whole story, and I know it was not your fault. Besides, the boat was covered by insurance."

This time, Frank rented a much faster speedboat and filled the tank with enough fuel for a long run. Heading westward, they cruised along the Puerto Rican coast until Frank sighted a pineapple-shaped hill at the tip of a small spit of land.

"There's Punta Cabezona," he told Tony. "Now steer a course due north."

As they headed out to sea, the water was almost glassy calm. About twenty miles out, they sighted a small island, green and palm-fringed.

Joe gave a whoop of triumph. "Frank, I believe your hunch about a hideout north of Cabezona is paying off!"

"Where to now?" Tony asked. "Do we make a landing?"

"That's what we came for," Frank said grimly as he shaded his eyes to peer shoreward.

The tiny island was narrow and stringbean-shaped, with its long axis lying north and south. Tony cruised cautiously until he found an opening in the coral reef surrounding the islet. Then he steered toward the beach through the gentle breakers, and anchored in shallow water. The boys kicked off their sneakers and waded ashore.

"I wonder if any of the gang is lurking around," Joe murmured when they reached the sandy beach, which sparkled bone-white in the sunshine. "Maybe we should have—"

He broke off, startled, as a horde of wild-eyed natives sprang from a dense thicket of greenery. Waving clubs and knives, they charged at the boys with blood-chilling yells!

"Run for it!" yelled Frank.

The boys plunged into the water and plowed back to the boat. As Chet, in the rear, squirmed aboard, Frank gunned the engine and steered out to a safe distance. Back near shore, the natives stood waist-deep in water, still yelling and shaking their weapons.

"Wow!" Joe gulped. "What started all that?"

"W-we did!" said Chet, trembling with fright. "We must have landed right in the middle of the gang's hideout. Those cannibals are standing guard for 'em!"

"Cannibals nothing!" said Tony. "I'll bet those are Carib Indians. Isn't that what they call the original inhabitants of these parts?"

"Call 'em anything you like," Chet replied. "They're still heap bad medicine!"

The stout boy was all for returning to San Juan. But the other three managed to persuade him that they should explore further.

With Frank at the helm, they cruised along the western shore of the island. Presently they came to a small cove, which formed a snug little natural harbor. Alongside a pier which jutted out into the water a red motorboat was moored. Back of the shore lay a palatial white villa.

"Must be some millionaire's vacation home,"
Chet remarked. "But I wouldn't want to be that
close to those natives!"

On higher ground back of the estate the boys
glimpsed an airstrip with a plane on it much like
the Hardys' craft, except that it was silver in
color.

"Should we tie up and look around?" Chet
asked.

"Not yet," said Frank. "Let's cruise a bit farther first, and get the lay of the land."

Continuing along the coast, they circled the
northern tip of the island. It was covered with
pineapple fields, but there was no sign of workers
or natives.

"Guess we may as well go back," Frank remarked.

He reversed course and steered back around the
island. As they neared the tiny harbor, a man
waved cheerfully from the pier.

"Hi, there!" he shouted. "Come on in!"

Frank brought the boat to shore, and they tied
up to the dock on the opposite side from the red
motorboat. The man who had called to them was
a stout and affable-appearing person, wearing an
immaculate white suit and puffing on a cigar.

"Glad to see you," he greeted the boys as they
climbed onto the pier. "We don't often have visitors. Durling Hamilton's my name," he added.

The boys shook hands and introduced themselves. They learned that Hamilton was a retired sportsman, who spent most of his time on the island estate.

"What brings you boys out here?" he queried.

"We're hunting for a gang of thieves," Chet blurted before Frank or Joe could stop him.

Hamilton appeared not to notice the awkward silence that followed. "Well, I wish you luck." He smiled. "Got quite a problem myself. Confounded natives just south of here have made trouble for me ever since I built my home on Calypso Island."

The Hardys and their friends tried not to look startled at this remark. Casually Frank asked, "Did you say Calypso Island?"

Hamilton nodded. "That's what the natives call it. They're descendants of Carib Indians with some mixed blood. They practice voodoo and worship a small flat stone—*Skeleton Rock.*"

CHAPTER XVII

Voodoo Vengeance

HERE at last was a real clue! Frank and Joe figured that probably the natives of Calypso Island were being used as a screen by the smugglers. So it was only natural that they should try to drive Durling Hamilton off the island.

"Have the natives been doing anything unusual lately?" Joe asked the sportsman. "I mean, have you noticed mysterious ceremonies?"

Hamilton puffed his cigar for a moment. "Well," he replied, "I did see a blue speedboat put in on the natives' side of the island yesterday."

"A blue boat!" Tony's eyes flashed excitedly.

"That's right," Hamilton went on. "Four men came ashore."

"Did you get a good look at them?" Frank asked eagerly.

"Yes. I watched them through binoculars.

About all I can tell you, though, is that one was a tall, heavy-set fellow. They talked with the Indians for a while and then shoved off."

A tall, heavy-set fellow! The boys exchanged knowing glances. Could he have been Abdul?

Hamilton interrupted their thoughts by inviting the boys up to his villa for lunch. A few minutes later the group was seated in comfortable wicker chairs on the terrace enjoying lemonade, pineapple salad, and sandwiches of cold roast beef.

Aside from his staff of white-jacketed Puerto Ricans, Hamilton appeared to live alone on the estate. "It's nice to have company," he told his guests.

Lunch over, their host showed the boys his game room, decorated with huge trophies of marlin, sailfish, and barracuda. Then he suggested a couple of fast sets of tennis, which he refereed, on twin courts near the airstrip. Afterward, all of them cooled off with a refreshing swim in the gentle blue waters of the cove. By this time, it was late in the afternoon.

"You've given us a wonderful time, sir," Frank told Hamilton when the boys had finished dressing. "Now we'd better start back to San Juan."

"Nonsense!" The sportsman paused to bite off the tip of a fresh cigar. "As I told you, we don't have many visitors out here. Gets mighty lonesome. I want you boys to stay and be my guests as long as you like."

Chet and Tony, though eager to extend their visit, left the decision to the Hardys. Frank and Joe were excited about the possibility to do more exploring. But, to throw Hamilton off the scent, they deliberately hesitated in accepting the invitation.

"At least stay overnight," Hamilton urged. "If you get bored, you can go back tomorrow morning."

"Well, if you put it like that, Mr. Hamilton"— Frank grinned—"I guess we'll accept your invitation."

"Fine! Wonderful!" their portly host beamed. "I'll cook part of the dinner myself. I'm quite a chef in my spare time," he boasted. "I'm counting on some real appetites to do it justice!"

The dinner of rock lobster and red snapper proved to be delicious. Both Frank and Joe took only the snapper, which was broiled to a juicy turn. But Tony and Chet ate liberally of both dishes.

After dinner they strolled out on the terrace under the stars. Chet sank into a deep lounge chair and let his head loll back.

"O-oh," he groaned. "I must've eaten too much."

"Is that unusual?" Joe needled.

"No kidding," Chet replied. "My stomach feels like lead!"

Tony looked a bit unhappy too. "I don't feel so well myself," he confessed.

As the boys continued to feel uncomfortable, Durling Hamilton became concerned. "Just sit there and take it easy," he advised. "I'm sure it'll pass off. Too much excitement for one day, maybe —not good for digestion!"

Meanwhile, Frank and Joe decided to do some sleuthing around the southern end of the island. Saying that they needed exercise, they excused themselves and wandered off along the smooth, sandy beach.

Darkness had fallen, and a full yellow moon was rising over the water. A cool trade wind wafted through the palm trees.

Suddenly Frank gripped his brother's arm. "Look! A campfire!" he pointed.

The flickering orange flames were visible through the dark foliage a short distance back from the beach.

"Come on!" Joe whispered. "Let's see what's up!"

Creeping closer, they pulled aside some branches and saw a group of natives squatting about the fire. The Indians, clad in ragged shirts and trousers, were jabbering excitedly.

"They're sure upset about something," Joe murmured.

"Hamilton said they practice voodoo," Frank whispered. "Maybe they're getting ready for some kind of ceremony."

As the boys listened they caught several words spoken in Spanish. "Sounds more like an argument," Joe noted.

Presently a skinny brown dog that was curled up near the campfire got to his feet and began to sniff the night air.

"Oh, oh!" gulped Joe in a low voice. "Let's hope he doesn't pick up our scent!"

Slowly the dog began to circle the camp, coming nearer and nearer to the boys' hiding place. All of a sudden he stiffened and broke into a volley of barks.

The natives stopped talking immediately and grabbed up heavy sticks. The Hardys flattened themselves in the underbrush. Should they lie still, or try to make a break?

The decision was made for them when the Indians strode toward the spot. Encouraged by his masters, the snarling cur charged into the thicket.

Instantly Frank and Joe sprang up and started to run. But before they had gone a dozen paces, the fleet-footed natives overtook them. Several grabbed the boys, while others menaced them with clubs.

"Don't fight!" Frank called to his brother. "Maybe we can convince them we're friends."

Trying to appear calm, the boys allowed themselves to be dragged back to the campfire. One of the natives, a youth about their own age, was able to speak a little English.

"Me Fernando," he told them. "What you do here? You come to spy for rich white man?"

"No," Frank replied. "We're just visitors here on the island. We saw your campfire and wondered what was going on, that's all."

As the boy translated, there was an angry babble from the other natives. Fernando turned back to the Hardys.

"They say you enemies—you work for Señor Hamilton," he said accusingly. "Him bad man! Our people live here on island always. This our home. Then he come—try to drive us away!"

Frank and Joe denied this earnestly. Speaking in simple words, they tried to convince the youth that they wished to be friends and that Durling Hamilton had no designs against the natives. But it was clear from the Indians' scowling faces that the words were having no effect.

Finally Joe decided to speak out bluntly. "Look, Fernando," he asked, "is it true that your people believe in voodoo and worship something called Skeleton Rock?"

The effect of Joe's question was astounding. At the mention of Skeleton Rock, the natives seemed to go wild. Shouting and babbling in mixed Spanish-Indian dialect, they seized the two boys and hurled them to the ground!

When Joe asked about Skeleton Rock, the
natives seemed to go wild

Frank and Joe fought like wildcats but were soon tied hand and foot. Then the natives began to drag them down to the water's edge.

"They're going to throw us to the sharks!" Joe gasped to his brother.

"You two boys bad like Hamilton!" Fernando glared at them. "Now my people take revenge!"

The Hardys turned pale, their hearts hammering with fear as the Indians loaded them into a boat. Again and again, they pleaded to be released, speaking in both Spanish and English.

Finally their words seemed to take effect. There was a lot of babbling among the natives, then one spoke to Fernando.

He translated, "We let you go. But you must leave the island and never come back!"

"You have our promise," Frank assured him fervently. "We'll go tomorrow."

As soon as they were untied, the boys hurried off down the beach. Both were baffled by their close brush with death and its relation to Hamilton. Was he more deeply involved than the natives had indicated?

"And why did they get so excited just because I mentioned Skeleton Rock?" Joe puzzled.

Frank shook his head in bewilderment. "Search me, unless the smuggling gang fooled them into thinking that any outsiders are dangerous. Or, maybe 'Skeleton Rock' is a sacred name."

As they neared Hamilton's villa, they saw a

lighted cigar glowing in the dark on the front terrace.

"Have an interesting walk?" the sportsman greeted them.

"We sure did!" Frank said dryly.

A Puerto Rican servant escorted them to a guest room next to Chet and Tony's. Chet was moaning in distress when the Hardys went in to see him.

"Feeling any better, Chet?" Joe inquired sympathetically.

"Worse!" the plump boy replied. He was stretched out on the bed like a beached whale, in a pair of flowery pajamas provided by their host.

Tony was not so ill as Chet, but he looked worried. As soon as the servant was out of earshot, he whispered to Frank and Joe:

"Listen! I went out on the dock for some fresh air and noticed that Hamilton's red boat looked awfully shiny in the moonlight. When I touched it, the red paint came off on my finger!"

The Hardys' eyes widened with interest. "Was it blue underneath?" Joe asked breathlessly.

"Before I had a chance to find out, I heard someone behind me and turned around. It was Hamilton!"

CHAPTER XVIII

A Weird Vision

"HAMILTON!" exclaimed Frank. "Do you think he was spying on you?"

Tony shrugged. "I'm not sure. But he was right there watching when I tested the paint."

The Hardys, having heard what the natives had said about Hamilton, were not surprised. This latest information definitely seemed to put their host under suspicion!

Joe urged that the boys confront Hamilton immediately.

But Frank was more cautious. "Hamilton has a whole crew of servants. If they're part of the gang, they could do plenty!"

"What's the difference?" Joe said stubbornly. "If Hamilton is a member of the gang, we're in danger, anyhow. Maybe he even slipped something into those lobsters Chet and Tony ate!"

Tony gasped. "You mean we've been poisoned?"

"Not deadly poison, but something he hoped would make all of us sick enough so we couldn't do any investigation and have to go home."

Frank was still doubtful. "In that case, why did he invite us to stay on the island?"

"So he could keep tabs on us until he had a chance to report to the gang," Joe suggested.

In the end, Frank agreed to put the question of speaking to Hamilton to a vote. Chet was feeling too sick to care one way or the other, but Tony sided with Joe. So the three boys went off to find Hamilton. But they agreed not to arouse the man's suspicions if they could avoid it.

The sportsman was still on the terrace, finishing his cigar.

"Is Chet feeling better?" he asked affably.

"Not much," Frank replied. "But I don't understand it. Lobster never seemed to bother him before."

Hamilton grinned. "I think your friend had too much to eat. Lobster's very rich."

Tony, changing the subject, told Durling Hamilton about his boat *Napoli II,* and of several exciting adventures he had had in her. Then he remarked casually, "But she needs a new paint job right now. What did you use on your motorboat, Mr. Hamilton? I noticed before that it was freshly painted."

The sportsman smiled. "Not the whole boat. I had the bow touched up today because of rust spots on it. By the way, Tony, you seem to be feeling better now."

"Yes, thank you." Casually the boy added, "Lucky for me, though, that you came out to the dock before. I felt a little woozy."

"I was afraid of that," Hamilton said, giving him an ingratiating smile. "As host here, it's my duty to look after my guests, isn't it?"

Hamilton seemed so frank that the boys found it hard to remain suspicious. After chatting a few minutes longer, they said good night and returned to their rooms. Chet was asleep.

In spite of the cool trade winds, both Frank and Joe were unable to fall asleep. Their minds were overactive, and they were alert for any unusual happenings. About two o'clock they were roused from a fitful slumber by a humming motor somewhere in the distance.

"It's a plane!" Joe whispered.

The boys rushed to the window. As the drone of the engine grew louder, they saw the craft swoop down as if for a landing on the airstrip. Then it pulled up abruptly and circled around. Its green starboard light began blinking.

"A message!" said Frank as the light spelled "Okay H."

"What does that mean?" Joe asked.

"It could be Hamilton or Hardy," Frank replied.

As they stood watching, the plane soared off

and disappeared into the night. Thoroughly mystified, the two boys went back to bed, full of conjectures, mostly about their own safety. They had just fallen into a light slumber when a shriek from the next room made them sit bolt upright.

"Chet!" Frank said. "He must be worse!"

The Hardys dashed to the next room. Chet was quiet now, but trembling violently. He stood by a window, pointing.

Tony, sleepy-eyed, was already on his feet. " 'Smatter, Chet?" he asked.

"A g-g-ghost!" the boy quavered. "I just saw a ghost! O-o-o-oh, it was horrible!"

"A ghost?" Frank echoed blankly. "Good grief, what're you talking about, Chet?"

"It's true!" he insisted. "My stomach-ache got so bad I couldn't sleep, so I got up. Then I looked out the window and I saw it—a huge Indian war chief, shining all over with a white glow! I'd say the thing's somewhere up at the north end of the island."

"If it was that far away, how could you see the thing?" asked Tony.

"Because he was so big, that's why! I'm telling you, he towered way up over the trees!" Just thinking about the fearsome sight seemed to turn Chet's face a more sickly hue than ever.

"Chet's really ill," said Joe. "He's delirious!"

"I'm not delirious!" Chet insisted frantically. "Golly, can't you be—"

"Okay, okay, we believe you," Frank said soothingly. "But please go back to sleep and try to get some rest." After a while Chet calmed down and the Hardys returned to their room.

Early the next morning Frank and Joe leaped out of bed.

"Let's get down to the dock and take a peek at that boat!" said Frank.

Without waiting for breakfast, the boys dashed out of the villa and hurried down to the pier. They ran their fingers over the red motorboat. The paint seemed perfectly dry except for a few tacky brush marks near the bow.

"I guess Hamilton was telling the truth," said Frank. "This clears him."

"Thanks!" said a chuckling voice.

Whirling in surprise, the boys saw their host watching them from the inward end of the pier. He strolled out to join them, his ruddy face enveloped in a friendly smile.

"Don't think I'm spying, now," he said jovially, "but I couldn't help notice you test that paint. You're real detectives, yes sir! But you can trust old Durling Hamilton!"

Somewhat embarrassed, the Hardys asked about the plane they had seen the previous night.

"Oh, that!" Hamilton laughed heartily. "That was a friend of mine—fellow sportsman, you might say—named Steve Henry. He was just passing over on his way from Miami to Puerto Rico, so he stopped off to say hello. Always gives me that old blinker signal whenever he goes by this way."

Mentally, Frank and Joe had to admit that Hamilton's answer seemed reasonable. If his friend's name was Henry, that would explain the initial H at the end of the message.

Excusing themselves, the Hardys went back to the house to see how Chet and Tony were feeling. Tony was much better, but, to their dismay, they found Chet so weak he could hardly move.

"He's really in bad shape," Tony whispered.

Their stout chum lay almost motionless on the bed, moaning weakly from time to time.

"We'd better get a doctor, pronto!" Frank decided. "You stay here with Chet, Tony."

He and Joe hurried downstairs and reported their friend's condition to Hamilton. "We want a doctor right away," Joe urged.

Luckily the estate owner had a radiotelephone hookup to San Juan. He put through a call to the mainland immediately, then turned to the boys.

"There's a break!" he announced. "This doctor friend of mine I just called is taking the day off. He's fishing in his favorite spot about five miles from here. With luck, you can get back here in no time!"

He suggested the boys take his red motorboat,

which was faster than their own. Frank and Joe gladly accepted and he sent word to have it fueled and readied for the trip.

"Watch out for sharks!" Hamilton warned when the Hardys prepared to shove off. "These waters around here are infested with the brutes!"

Beyond the reef, the sea turned choppy as a spanking breeze whipped the water into white-caps. Frank and Joe headed south toward Puerto Rico, following their host's directions.

Several times they saw the fins of sharks knifing past. When their craft reached the fishing spot Hamilton had described, the doctor's boat was nowhere in sight.

Joe scanned the horizon anxiously. "Do you suppose Hamilton lied to us?" he muttered.

"Just what I was wondering," Frank replied. Suddenly he gave a cry of alarm. "Joe! The boat's leaking!"

A steady stream of water was gushing in from the motor compartment!

Hastily the boys whipped off their shirts and Joe crawled into the compartment with them to plug the leak. When he emerged a moment later, half-soaked and oil-smeared, his face was taut.

"There's a big round hole in the hull!" he reported. "Looks as if it was partly cut out with a saw, and sea pressure did the rest!"

"Hamilton!" gasped Frank.

"Sure looks that way. No wonder he was so eager to have us take this boat!"

There was no time to debate the matter further. They took off their slacks and stuffed them in the hole. But already there was too much water in the boat for them to do any good. To make matters worse, the engine suddenly stopped.

"Maybe there's a pump in the locker," Frank suggested hopefully. He opened the seat to look, then gave a startled cry as he dragged out a red, green, and white pennant.

It was the foreign flag, with a black skeleton added in the lower right-hand corner!

"Just like the one we found in Hugo's trailer!" exclaimed Joe. "Say, what *is* Hamilton's tie-up with that fortuneteller?"

Frank did not reply. The plugs in the hull suddenly gave way and more water gushed into the boat. Desperately the boys groped in the locker. There were three life jackets, but no pump.

Just then the drone of an airplane drew their attention. Waving wildly, they tried to attract the pilot. Once he dipped and the boys were sure he saw them. But the silver-colored plane went on.

"I'll bet that was Hamilton!" said Frank, clenching his teeth grimly.

"Yes," Joe stormed helplessly. "Everything those natives said about him was right! And he came out here to watch us battle the sharks!"

CHAPTER XIX

Skeleton Rock

"At least we have knives. That'll be some protection against the sharks," Joe said grimly. "If any of them want a bite out of me they'll have to fight for it!"

"Right!" Frank pulled out two of the life jackets and handed one to Joe.

They put them on. Then, arming themselves with their pocketknives, the two boys waited tensely. By this time, the water in the boat was up to their knees.

The boys had been so busy watching the water that they had not noticed a plane approaching the area.

"Hamilton again, I suppose," Frank said angrily as he looked up.

Suddenly Joe gave a happy shout. "It's *our* plane!"

The boys hardly dared believe their eyes.

"Do you suppose Dad and Jack are aboard?" Joe asked hopefully. "And they've come to rescue us?"

Frank and Joe waved their arms frantically, yelling as loudly as they could. The plane circled and swooped in low. Jack Wayne was at the controls.

"Yippee!" shouted Joe.

The pilot waved back to the boys reassuringly. Mr. Hardy was not in the plane. A moment later the cabin door opened and an inflated life raft tumbled down toward the water.

It landed with a splash several yards away from the boat, but Frank was overboard in a moment to swim to it. He climbed inside, then picked up Joe.

As soon as the boys were safely afloat, Jack dipped his wings, then began to circle the area.

"Too bad he couldn't haul us into the plane," Joe remarked.

A half hour of anxious waiting followed. Sharks bobbed up repeatedly, close to the raft. Finally a government patrol boat appeared and Jack flew off as soon as the Hardys were helped to the deck of the rescue craft.

"Lucky you're not minus a few toes," declared the captain with grim humor.

"How'd you find us?" Joe asked.

"Jack Wayne radioed an SOS," the captain replied. "Better go below, fellows, and get some hot soup. We'll have you back at San Juan before you dry off!"

Jack was waiting to greet them there at the dock. "Man, am I glad to see you two!" he exclaimed.

"Not half as glad as we were to see *you!*" Joe quipped as they shook hands. "Did you know it was Frank and me stranded on the water?"

"No. I saw that the boat was not moving and decided to take a closer look. What happened?"

Frank described their visit to Calypso Island and his suspicions about Hamilton. Jack flushed with anger. "The skunk!" he cried out. But a moment later he said, "I just had another thought. Maybe one of those natives who hates Hamilton put the hole in his boat."

"That's right," Joe agreed. "It seems as if every time we suspect that man there's a sound reason to excuse him."

But Frank was not so charitable. "I'm sure Hamilton was in that first plane which wouldn't give us any help. Well, Jack, what's the news from Dad? Where is he now?"

Jack's face became grave. "I'm worried about him," he replied. "After we took off from here, I flew your father to Centro, Tropicale. He said that if he didn't show up at the airport by twelve o'clock last night, I should go get you boys and try to find him. Well, he didn't show up!"

The news sent a shock of alarm through the

boys. Centro was the spot where they had tangled in the gunfight between police and rebels! Could the gang have sought revenge on their father?

"We ought to fly to Tropicale as soon as possible," Joe urged.

"And we must get help to Chet," Frank reminded him. "Let's stop at a doctor's on the way to the airport and talk to him."

A taxi driver they consulted took them to the office of Dr. Roberto Cortez, just a few blocks from the waterfront. After hearing their story, the physician reassured the boys.

"From the symptoms you describe, I am sure that your friend will be no worse. If he had been given a harsh poison, he would have been in great pain last evening. But I'll write you a prescription which should ease the young man's difficulties."

Greatly relieved, the boys thanked Dr. Cortez and hurried off to the nearest drugstore. While waiting for the prescription to be filled, they discussed what to do.

"We can fly to Calypso Island, give Chet the medicine, and make arrangements for the rented boat to be returned to its owner. Then all of us can go on to Tropicale," Frank suggested.

"Good idea," Joe agreed.

When they reached the airport, Jack Wayne refueled the Hardy plane for take-off. But as he started to warm up the engine, it gave a sputter and died. The pilot could not restart it.

Wearily Jack climbed out and went to work on the defective engine. "Plugs aren't firing," he announced after a brief inspection.

Impatient and worried, the Hardys stood by while Jack traced the trouble to a faulty magneto. Then came another long delay while he went off to hunt for a replacement.

It was late afternoon before the ship was finally ready for take-off. To the Hardys' relief, the engine purred smoothly as the plane soared off toward Calypso Island.

"What about Hamilton?" Joe asked Frank. "You suppose he'll give us any trouble?"

Frank shrugged. "No telling. I have a feeling that man is very slick."

Both boys took brief turns at the controls, and Joe brought the plane down on Hamilton's airstrip for a perfect landing.

The estate owner came out to greet them. "Welcome back!" He smiled. "I see you found a faster method for the return trip."

"We had to," Frank said curtly, introducing Jack. "Your boat sank."

"What!" Hamilton appeared genuinely shocked when the boys told him about the hole in the speedboat's hull.

"Sabotage!" he stormed. "Those confounded Carib Indians must have done it!"

For several minutes he ranted angrily against the natives. The sportsman seemed so genuinely upset that Joe glanced at Frank as if to say, "Maybe Hamilton is innocent after all."

"How's Chet?" Frank asked, interrupting the sportsman. "We brought him some medicine."

"I guess he won't need it," Hamilton replied with a cheery grin. "In fact, he and Tony were feeling so much better, they decided to go off and do a little spying on the Indians."

"Why?" Frank asked.

"Professional jealousy, I'd guess." Hamilton chuckled. "Your chubby friend figured the two of them might solve a mystery about the natives before you boys got back. Well, let's go up to the house and get some supper."

The Hardys were puzzled and uncertain what to do. Could they trust the estate owner's story and fly on to Tropicale? But, talking it over privately at the villa, they decided it was too risky to leave until they knew for certain that their friends were safe.

After a tasty supper, Frank asked, "Mr. Hamilton, don't you think Chet and Tony should be back by this time?"

"Perhaps so, but I shouldn't worry about them."

Frank and Joe could not accept Hamilton's suggestion. They had to find out where their friends were. Excusing themselves, they set out with Jack Wayne for the southern end of the island.

They made a point of avoiding the open beach

as they pushed their way through the palm groves and underbrush. It was dark now, but the rising moon shed enough light for them to see where they were going.

Soon the boys sighted the glimmering windows of a cluster of native shacks. Natives were milling about outside, jabbering excitedly.

"Something's up," Jack observed. "I wonder if Chet and Tony are being held prisoner."

As the pilot started forward, Frank grabbed his arm to stop him. "Joe and I have had one set-to with these Indians," he whispered. "Let's keep out of sight. We promised them we'd leave the island for good today."

Staying in the shadows, the three circled the village. Suddenly Joe caught sight of Fernando. By hissing, he managed to attract the youth's attention.

"Why have you come back?" Fernando exclaimed worriedly as he joined them. "You are in terrible danger here if my people find you!"

"We'll go quickly if you'll help us," Frank promised. "We only came back to find our two friends."

"Your two friends?" The boy looked puzzled.

Frank and Joe explained that their friends had come to call on the Indians. Fernando denied that he or his people had seen them.

The Hardys had fresh cause for worry! Where

were Chet and Tony? Was Hamilton making up the story of their whereabouts?

Before leaving, Joe asked one more question. "Tell me, Fernando, why did your people get so angry when I asked about Skeleton Rock?"

The young Carib shuddered. "It is a terrible place, *amigo!* It is at the other end of the island, but do not go there! Sometimes at night the ghost of an old cacique rises up to devour men's souls!"

The words were hardly out of Fernando's mouth when he turned pale with fright. "Look! Look!" he quavered, pointing northward. "He is there now!"

As the others turned, a fantastic sight met their eyes. Looming above the distant treetops was the huge figure of an ancient Carib chieftain. The specter glowed with a weird white radiance.

"Jumping cacti!" gasped Jack Wayne.

"So that's what Chet saw last night!" added Joe. "No wonder he couldn't sleep!"

The whole village seethed with turmoil as the natives wailed and quaked in alarm.

"What do you make of it?" Jack asked.

"I believe that ghost is a plant by the gang to keep these natives in subjection," Frank replied.

"Yes," Joe agreed, "and it might have been put into action right now to scare *us* away."

"I feel sure," said Frank, "that Hamilton is involved in this and in Chet and Tony's disappearance. Come on! I think we'd better radio a message for help from our plane to the authorities in Puerto Rico."

As they reached the airstrip, the three crept toward the plane under cover of darkness. Joe warmed up the radio and started beaming a message to San Juan. Finally the harbor police replied.

"Calling from Calypso Island!" Joe spoke urgently into the mike. "This is an emergency. Two boys—"

Joe got no further. A gunshot cracked in the distance. Then two more rang out as a horde of armed men rushed toward the airstrip from the villa. Though still out of effective range, they were shooting wildly at the plane. One bullet pinged off a rock near the craft.

"Hamilton's leading them!" yelled Frank, recognizing the man at the head of the gang. "Get going, Jack!"

The pilot grimly went to work. The starter whined, but nothing else happened.

"Mixture control is jammed!" he groaned. Jumping up, he dashed aft for the tool kit.

Frank grabbed the controls and managed to free the mixture control before Jack returned. With a roar, the engine thundered into action!

As the plane taxied down the strip, another volley of shots ripped the night air. A moment later they were aloft and gaining altitude.

"Wow!" Joe relaxed weakly in his seat and wiped the perspiration from his forehead. "If the police heard the shooting, they ought to get here pronto!" Nevertheless, he continued to send out a call for help.

Soaring over the northern end of the island, Frank looked for the cacique's ghost, but the figure had disappeared.

A moment later Joe pointed down toward the beach. "Look!" he exclaimed. "There's Skeleton Rock!"

Below, in the moonlight, a curious formation was visible in the coral reef. A portion of the rocky shore line protruded above the water in the shape of a crude skeleton. Even the arms and legs were clearly defined.

"Weird!" said Jack. "Enough to make a fellow feel creepy. Now what do we do?"

"What Beppo tells you to, *amigos!*" came a sneering voice from the rear of the cabin.

The Hardys and Jack whirled in dismay. A blond figure had just emerged from the luggage compartment, clutching a pistol. It was the youth who resembled Joe!

"Turn back and land on Calypso!" he ordered.

CHAPTER XX

The Ghost's Secret

As FRANK hesitated, the blond youth came a step closer. His finger curled menacingly around the trigger of his gun.

"Do as I say," he snapped, "or you'll be sorry!"

Jack, who was occupying a rear seat, made a lunge for Beppo's weapon—but not in time. Swinging his heavy automatic, the gunman caught Jack on the side of the head with a vicious blow. Jack groaned and slumped unconscious!

Joe started toward Jack, but Beppo motioned him to sit beside Frank.

"Now turn this plane around," the gunman ordered Frank, "before you two get the same treatment!"

Frank suddenly realized he was now on his own, with a gun at his back and no flight instructor to guide him! Determinedly he banked the plane and executed a neat turn.

As they winged back toward Hamilton's villa, a

daring plan occurred to the young pilot. He nudged Joe, to alert him that he would need help.

Suddenly Frank shoved the wheel forward! The plunging dive threw the gunman off-balance. As he lurched backward, Joe grabbed the gun.

"Don't move!" barked Joe.

When the craft leveled off, Frank set the automatic pilot. Joe pulled some rope from a locker, and in moments the two boys had the gunman tightly bound.

"No wonder this guy looks like me, Frank. His features have been changed with make-up putty!"

Joe now came forward and Frank whispered, "This time I'm going to imitate our prisoner."

As they neared the landing field, Frank turned up the two-way radio, "Calling Hamilton!" Frank rasped, disguising his voice to sound like that of the prisoner. "All okay."

The receiver crackled in reply. "Good work, Beppo! Now we have the whole Hardy gang at Skeleton Rock. We can strike at once!"

The brothers were stunned. So the smugglers had their father—and also Chet and Tony!

Frank gripped the controls, his brain working at top speed. How could they free Mr. Hardy and their friends? Stalling for time to find an answer to the dilemma, he swooped low over the field, then banked and circled.

Again the radio crackled. "Don't fool around, Beppo! Hurry up and land them!"

"Now what?" gasped Joe in a low voice.

Uncertain of his next move, Frank climbed for altitude and circled once more. The engine began to sputter, and with a final cough, died. Then the plane began bucking and plunging as it suddenly ran into severe turbulence.

Wildly Frank worked with the controls. What to do now? If they landed on the strip, they would both be captured. Hoping against hope that they would not lose altitude too rapidly, Frank glided for the northern end of the island.

"Maybe we can make the beach!" Joe cried.

With luck they could, Frank thought, as he eased the wheel forward. Both boys froze as the plane nosed downward in a normal glide.

At the tip of the island, a broad strip of wet sand lay exposed by the low tide. With a great jolt the plane hit the beach, plowed forward, and upended as its nose wheel gouged into the sand and collapsed. The craft was only a few yards from Skeleton Rock!

"Frank, you're a whiz!" Joe said shakily.

Frank smiled wanly, then said, "I hope the crack-up didn't make Jack worse."

At once they gently lifted the pilot's limp body out on the beach. There was an ugly bruise on Jack's right temple. Frank chafed his wrists and bathed his face with water. Jack stirred slightly.

"How is he?" Joe asked anxiously.

"Breathing okay. He should revive completely in a little while."

A sudden cry from his brother made Frank snap bolt upright. "Look!" Joe gasped.

From a nearby pit a huge phosphorescent figure was emerging. It was the Indian chieftain's ghost, glowing weirdly in the moonlight!

"It's some kind of plastic balloon covered with phosphorescent paint!" Frank exclaimed. "What a stunt for scaring the natives!"

"Well, that gang won't do it any longer!" Joe declared. Taking out his pocketknife, he darted forward and ripped the bag wide open.

There was a rush of escaping air. With a weak, moaning sound, the ghost balloon collapsed sideways in a brightly shining heap. As Frank watched it sink beside the pit, he cried out excitedly, "Joe! There's a trap door in that pit! I'll bet there's something else down there besides the balloon and gas machine."

"Loot, you mean?"

"Perhaps."

Together, the boys raised the door. A flight of stone steps led downward into the coral rock.

Frank flicked on his pocket flashlight, and the boys descended cautiously. At the foot of the stairway, the passage opened into an underground room.

Three familiar voices cried out, "Frank! Joe!"

The Hardys stared in astonishment. Before them, trussed up, were Mr. Hardy, Chet, and Tony!

"Thank goodness you came! We must get out of here before those killers seal us up for good!"

Quickly Frank and Joe untied them, telling of their own narrow escape. The group rushed up the stone steps. They had just reached the beach when Hamilton and his attackers swarmed into view through the shrubbery.

"We're outnumbered three to one!" Tony cried in dismay.

Mr. Hardy suggested that if they could subdue Hamilton, the suspected leader, perhaps the others would give up. As the smugglers closed in on them, he maneuvered his way toward Hamilton, who had stepped to the side.

Hamilton was ready. He was about to strike the private detective with a heavy stone, when Chet came to the rescue. Throwing his voice, he yelled, "Look behind you, Hamilton!"

The gang leader whirled in surprise, expecting an attack. Fenton Hardy acted instantly. He delivered a punch that knocked Hamilton backward and sent his weapon flying through the air.

Meanwhile, the four boys had gone into action. Blows were exchanged right and left as they ripped into the mobsters.

"Keep it up!" Tony shouted excitedly.

But the tide of battle was turning in favor of

the gang. Outnumbered, Mr. Hardy and the boys were being battered into defeat.

Then, just as the end seemed near, the fighters heard wild war whoops above the din. Through the darkness swooped a mob of Carib Indians! Fernando was with them.

"Fernando! Help us—the Hardys!" Joe shouted. "We are fighting your *real* enemies!"

The natives needed no urging. With clubs and sticks, they beat Hamilton's followers into howling panic.

When the battle was over, Frank rushed up to Fernando. "Thanks! *Muchas gracias,* Fernando!" he panted. "You sure saved the day!"

Among the captives the boys spotted Abdul and Hugo, and pointed them out to their father. Then they plied Mr. Hardy with questions as to what had happened to him in Tropicale.

The detective smiled. "Now the story can be told. I was working on a case involving subversives in the United States friendly to a gang of rebels in Tropicale who hoped to take over the government. Those in our country have been rounded up with the exception of a few, like Abdul and Hugo, who escaped down here.

"Unfortunately, in uncovering a hideout in Tropicale, I was captured. Two men flew me here last night," he explained, "but apparently something went wrong. The plane couldn't land."

Joe snapped his fingers. "No wonder! Frank

and I showed up here and Hamilton didn't want us to see you. Matter of fact, Frank and I read the plane's signal—'Okay H.' That must have been to let Hamilton know they'd captured you!"

The detective nodded. "The men finally brought me over this morning. I guess you two had left by that time."

"That's right," said Chet. "Then they tied Tony and me up and brought us to the dungeon. They planned to kill all of us and blame it on the Caribs. I'll say one thing, though," he added, chuckling. "Made me so mad I forgot all about my stomach-ache!"

At that moment powerful searchlights began to sweep the island.

"Patrol ships!" Joe exclaimed. "Must be the police arriving from San Juan!"

Soon a boatload of armed bluejackets and officers hit the beach. After Mr. Hardy had given a brief account of the affair, the officers escorted the prisoners, including Beppo, back to Hamilton's villa. By this time, Jack Wayne had revived and was assisted there by the boys.

At the house Captain Valdes of the San Juan police held an official hearing. Mr. Hardy cleared up the mystery.

"It was not until today that I learned who was masterminding a diabolical plot to overthrow the government of Tropicale. This man Hamilton is the one," the detective explained. "He organized an air-freight theft ring to seize various articles useful to his cause. Among these were isotopes to build an atomic weapon. Once completed, this would have given him and his gang absolute power over Tropicale. On the side, the men smuggled diamonds in dolls' or dummies' heads to help finance their crazy venture."

"It wasn't so crazy!" snarled the handcuffed Hamilton. "We might have pulled it off if that important Hugo dummy hadn't been sent to the very town where the Hardys live. Those nosy detectives and their pals upset our plans!"

"Tony and me?" Chet's eyes widened and his face glowed with pride.

"Yes, indeed," Captain Valdes praised them. "You all helped preserve peace in the Caribbean!"

"But how does the stolen drug, Variotrycin, come into the picture?" Frank asked his father. "And what about the brief case we found in the public locker in Eastern City? It was filled with the drug! In fact, after the man, who posed as Shanley, snatched it from us, we never saw him or the brief case again."

"The gang thought that stealing and selling the new drug would supplement their income in addition to the diamonds," Mr. Hardy explained. "However, not enough of it was being manufactured to make it profitable. After the man impersonating Shanley snatched the brief case from you boys, he suddenly got greedy. He was arrested in New York City trying to sell the stuff."

Numerous other facts were brought out. "Skeleton Rock" was the gang's identification, and they had used the same device on their revolutionary pirate flag. The pineapple tattoos helped the members recognize one another.

"So that's why the cook at *El Calypso Caliente* got so upset when he spotted my tattoo!" said Joe. "He thought for a moment I was Beppo."

Mr. Hardy nodded. "The restaurant was a regular meeting place for the gang."

Abdul, Hugo, and many of Hamilton's island retainers now talked freely in the hope of getting light sentences. They revealed that a new red motorboat had been switched overnight for the blue one which Hamilton had tried to disguise with a fresh coat of paint. They also admitted that some mild poison had been put in the lobsters served at dinner.

"Too bad we didn't make the dose twice as strong," growled Hamilton.

The mysterious "doctor friend" was just a ruse to send Frank and Joe to their doom. Abdul also admitted that he lived in the old pink stucco house in San Juan, and that the basket device had been used to pick up loot and messages.

"How about the Hugo dummy?" Frank asked his father. "Was the Mexican manufacturer involved?"

"No," his father replied. "Hamilton's gang put the purple turbans on the dummies, inserted the glass eyes, and acted as distributors. Radley discovered this and notified me shortly after I saw you boys last."

Frank snapped his fingers. "I get it now! As distributors, Hamilton and his gang substituted the old-fashioned glass eyes for the original plastic ones in the Hugos and concealed the contraband and messages inside."

"The changed instruction sheet, too!" Joe chimed in.

"Right!" Mr. Hardy said. "That code in Spanish was an extra precaution!" The detective added that the Hugos were shipped to bona fide customers in the United States, such as Mr. Bivven in Bayport. "Gang members were on hand," he said, "to purchase the purple-turbaned Hugos immediately and get the diamonds."

"Then why," Chet burst in, "did those hoodlums snatch the red-turbaned dummy at Mr. Bivven's place?"

Hearing this, Hamilton snapped, "Bivven, the old goat, fouled up the whole plan. He said that was his only Hugo, so my men figured I must have made a mistake in the color of the turban."

At this point, a seaman from one of the patrol boats brought a radio message to Mr. Hardy. It was a report from the Tropicale police, saying they had rounded up the remaining gang members from information relayed by Fenton Hardy before he was captured.

"Well, boys, I guess we can now get a good night's sleep!" The detective sighed.

"Believe me, you have earned it, señores!" Captain Valdes congratulated them. "I give you permission to use the villa. Mr. Hamilton won't need it tonight!"

In a few days the Hardys' damaged plane was repaired, and they took off for San Juan. Jack Wayne urged Frank and Joe to demonstrate their flying skill to their father.

After watching them, the detective grinned. "Looks as if I have a couple of budding air aces in the family!"

His grin grew wider as Joe made a beautiful landing. A crowd of officials and newsmen were waiting on the field to greet the passengers.

An envoy of the Tropicale Government stepped forward and pinned a medal on the private investigator. "In token of your distinguished efforts for the cause of peace and justice!" He beamed.

"Thank you," Mr. Hardy said, smiling, "but these boys here deserve it more than I do!"

"We know the part your sons played," said an airline official. "As a reward, my company is presenting them with this DME—Distance Measuring Equipment unit for the Hardys' private plane!"

"And for their friend Tony," said the Tropicale official, "we have a special boat trip in Caribbean waters."

With a broad smile Tony accepted, unaware of
the next exciting role he would play in helping
the Hardy Boys solve *The Mystery at Devil's Paw*.

One more gift was presented and unwrapped—
a whole family of ventriloquist dummies for Chet!

"Without diamonds, however," the official said,
laughing.

Excitedly Chet seized one of the dummies and
put on an impromptu act.

"Who cares about diamonds!" the largest one
squawked. "When do we eat?"

The Hardy Boys Mystery Stories®

THE STING
OF THE
SCORPION

BY

FRANKLIN W. DIXON

GROSSET & DUNLAP
Publishers • New York
A member of The Putnam & Grosset Group

CONTENTS

CHAPTER I

An Elephant Vanishes

THE roar of an engine passing overhead vibrated through the Hardy house on Elm street one June morning.

"What in the world is that?" said Frank Hardy, who had just finished breakfast. "Sure doesn't sound like an airplane!"

"Let's find out!" exclaimed his younger brother. Blond and impetuous, Joe Hardy leaped up from the table.

Dark-haired Frank followed. They rushed out on the porch to peer up at the sky. A gleaming silver airship was sailing over Bayport.

"It's the *Safari Queen!*" shouted Joe.

"She was never that loud before." Frank frowned. "I wonder if they've got engine trouble?"

Seventeen-year-old Joe shaded his eyes against the sunshine and watched the huge airship anx-

1

iously, while his brother hurried inside for binoculars. The *Safari Queen,* biggest craft of its kind since the ill-fated *Hindenburg,* had aroused the keen interest and hopes of all lighter-than-air enthusiasts.

Frank returned and focused the glasses. "Oh, no!" he cried out. "Something fell out of the gondola!"

A vivid flash dazzled the boys' vision. A boom like thunder reached their ears, and billowing clouds of smoke blotted the airship from sight.

"Maybe the *Queen* exploded!" Joe gasped.

But the dirigible soon became visible again as the smoke cleared. Something else could be seen —and it caused the boys to stare in horror.

An elephant was plunging from the sky!

"I d-don't believe it!" stuttered Joe, who could discern the creature even without binoculars. The words were hardly out of his mouth when another explosion startled the brothers.

"The elephant blew up!" Frank exclaimed in a shocked voice. He lowered the glasses and the two boys exchanged stunned glances.

"I heard on the TV news that the *Queen* was bringing a load of wild African animals on this trip," Joe said, "for that new animal park, Wild World. But I never thought one would fall overboard!"

"If it really did," Frank added thoughtfully.

"What do you mean? We both saw it happen."

"Yes, but I was watching through binoculars and, you know, there was something funny about that elephant."

"Funny? What's funny about an animal blowing up?" Joe demanded indignantly.

"Nothing. But I'm not sure that it was a real animal."

"You think we were seeing things?"

"Of course not. But somehow that elephant looked—" Frank paused and scratched his head, "Well, I don't know, sort of stiff and unnatural."

"You mean, like a dummy?" Joe asked with an expression of quickening interest.

Frank nodded, frowning. "I guess so—a stuffed animal, or something like that."

"But why would anyone pull such a trick?"

"Search me. A publicity gimmick, maybe?"

Joe snapped his fingers. "Hey, that's an idea. Wild World just opened recently. Maybe someone thought this would attract customers to the park."

"Could be," Frank agreed. "But if you're right, I'd say whoever dreamed it up has weird taste in publicity stunts."

The dirigible seemed to be proceeding smoothly on course with no further sign of trouble. But the two explosions and the loud engine sound, compared to the *Queen's* normally silent flight, were alarming. The falling elephant added an even stranger touch.

"Let's go watch her land, and find out what happened!" Joe suggested.

"Good idea!"

The Hardy boys were fond of mysteries, and this one looked intriguing. They were heading for their car when the mailman came along. He had watched the startling sky scene, as had several other people in the area.

"What did you make of those blasts up there, fellows?" he asked, handing Joe a batch of letters.

"We can't figure them out," Joe replied. "But we intend to go and see."

"Leave it to you two." The postman chuckled.

Frank and Joe, both star athletes at Bayport High, were the sons of Fenton Hardy, a former New York City police detective who had retired from the force and was now a world-famous private investigator. His two boys already showed signs of following in their father's footsteps. Their most recent mystery, *The Firebird Rocket,* had taken the young sleuths to Australia on the trail of a missing space scientist.

Joe glanced through the letters the mailman had handed him and plucked out one addressed to The Hardy Boys. He went inside and tossed the others on the hall table, then hurried to join his brother, who was already easing their car down the drive. Soon they were bowling along toward the Quinn Air Fleet terminal, just north of town, where the airship would dock.

"Too bad this had to happen," Frank remarked as he steered the car through traffic. "Those explosions may start people thinking all over again that dirigibles are unsafe."

"True," Joe agreed. "It could set back the whole lighter-than-air movement."

The fiery crash of the *Hindenburg*, decades before, had ended dirigible development for many years. But the successful maiden voyage of the *Safari Queen*, which was the first of several such craft to be built for the Quinn Air Fleet, had raised hopes for a new generation of airships. Today's incident might dash those hopes.

As the boys approached the terminal, the number of cars heading toward the scene increased to a massive traffic jam, with drivers and passengers gawking at the fenced-in grounds of the Quinn Air Fleet base.

The dirigible was now nosed into her mooring mast, a stubby domed tower especially designed for quick, convenient debarking of the passengers.

"Looks okay," Joe reported, craning out the car window for a better view.

"Thank goodness," Frank said in relief. "I'll bet half these people thought they might see another *Hindenburg* disaster!"

The lines of traffic crawled, bumper to bumper, toward the terminal entrance. Just as the Hardys reached the intersection fronting the gates, the light changed to red. A policeman waved all cars away from the terminal, and the boys realized that their trip had been wasted.

The officer spotted them and came over to exchange a few words while they were stopped.

"I'm afraid you're out of luck, fellows. Can't let anyone else inside. Too big a tieup."

"Was the *Queen* damaged?" Frank asked.

"Nope. They haven't figured out yet what caused the explosions, but apparently they didn't do any harm."

"What about the elephant that fell overboard?" Joe put in.

"The word I get is, all animals are safe and accounted for," replied the officer, taking off his hat to mop his brow. "The whole thing's a total mystery—right up your alley."

"Boy, *what* a mystery!" Joe agreed.

"Say hello to your dad for me," the officer added.

"Will do," Frank promised as the light changed and the policeman walked off.

The boys were just getting past the worst of the traffic jam when a light flashed and the dashboard radio buzzer sounded. Joe switched on the speaker and lifted the mike. "Hardy here. Come in, please."

"G calling F and J." It was the voice of their spinster aunt, Fenton Hardy's sister Gertrude.

"What's up, Aunty?" Joe inquired.

"I've just had a code message from your father.

"You're out of luck, fellows. Can't let anyone else inside."

He wants you two to stand by for a phone call at one-thirty."

"We'll be there," Joe replied. "Any idea what it's about?"

"Something dangerous, I suspect," Miss Hardy stated darkly. "He said to beware of the scorpion's sting!"

"Okay, Aunt Gertrude, we'll be careful."

"See that you are! Over and out."

"What's that about a scorpion?" Frank asked, puzzled, as his brother hung up the mike.

"Search me. But that reminds me, we got another message this morning." From his hip pocket Joe pulled the letter that had come in the mail, and he tore open the envelope. Inside was a colored folder.

"Who's it from?" Frank inquired, his eyes still on the road ahead.

"There's no name or anything. Just a brochure from Wild World, the kind they hand out to visitors. Wait a second," Joe added as he opened the folder. "There *are* markings inside."

"Like what?"

"Well, there's a map of the park layout, and someone penciled in a diagram of the area right near the lion enclosure."

Frank pulled over to the curb to look. "What's this X-mark for, labeled 'hollow tree'?" He frowned.

"Maybe something's hidden inside the tree,"

Joe suggested, "and whoever sent this wants us to go there and find it."

"Funny way to tip us off."

"Sure is. It could be a practical joke."

Frank nodded. "But I think we should check it out. It may be connected with a case Dad's working on."

"Right."

Wild World was located on the coast of Barmet Bay, between the town of Bayport and the Quinn air terminal. Summer vacation had begun just a few days ago, and the park was crowded with people.

After driving through the entrance gateway, Frank turned left into one of the parking areas. He and Joe were getting out of their car when once again their radio buzzer sounded.

"Hardys here," Joe responded, almost expecting to hear another bulletin from their aunt.

Instead, a male voice came over the speaker. It sounded disguised. "If you want an important crime tip, meet me as soon as possible!"

"Who's this?"

"Never mind. Are you interested or not?"

Joe shot a glance at Frank, who nodded. "We're interested," the younger Hardy replied.

"Then go through the woods near the park opposite the entrance. Head for Spire Rock. It's a tall pointy rock formation, sticking up through the trees."

"We see it."

"I'll meet you there. Make it snappy. And don't tell anyone!" The transmission ended abruptly.

As Joe replaced the microphone, he looked questioningly at his brother. "Another practical joke?"

"We'll soon find out," Frank declared. "Let's go!"

Crossing the graveled parking lot, the boys plunged into the wooded area their unknown caller had indicated. They followed a narrow trail, winding among the trees. Suddenly they heard a rustling noise behind them. Before the Hardys could glance around, each felt something hard jammed against his back.

"Freeze—both of you!" a gruff voice barked in their ears. "One wrong move and you're dead!"

CHAPTER II

X Marks the Spot

FRANK and Joe glanced at each other from the corners of their eyes. Both were wondering the same thing. Had they walked into a trap, or was this the punch line of a joke someone was playing on them? In either case, was it safe to turn their heads and find out?

As if reading their minds, someone behind them—a different voice this time—snarled, "We don't want to hurt you, but the first one who tries looking around will get *this* bounced off his skull!"

A hand slid between them, displaying a nasty-looking leather-covered blackjack to emphasize the speaker's warning.

"Okay, we get the message," Frank said curtly. "What do you want?"

"Put your hands on your heads, where we can see 'em, and start walking toward those beech trees over to the left of the trail."

The boys obeyed, pressing forward through the dense vegetation without a word, though they were sizzling with anger. Each was ordered to lean against a tree, supporting himself with his up-raised hands, as if for a police frisking.

"Now get this, and we'll only tell you once," the gruff voice warned. "You two keep your noses out of the *Safari Queen* trouble!"

"And don't take on any new cases," the second voice added threateningly. "Understand?"

"We heard you," Frank replied coldly, controlling his anger. "Is that all?"

"That's all for now, punk. Just remember what I said!"

The first voice chimed in again. "And don't turn around for the next five minutes. Just stay like you are—if you want to walk away from here alive!"

The Hardys listened as footsteps moved away from them through the underbrush. As soon as the sounds had faded, they glanced at each other, then lowered their hands and looked behind them.

"Those wise guys!" Joe fumed. "They may have been bluffing all along!"

"Maybe and maybe not." Frank shrugged. "They had the upper hand, and remember what Dad always says. No smart detective takes unnecessary chances."

"Think we should try to trail them?"

"And risk stumbling into another ambush? No thanks," Frank said. "With all this brush, we can see only a few yards in any direction. And think of all the people strolling around the park just beyond this screen of trees. How can we spot the guys who braced us when we don't even know what they look like?"

"You're right," Joe said bitterly. "But in that case, what chance have we to nail them?"

"Whoever they were, they must be mixed up in the *Safari Queen* mystery," his brother reasoned. "That gives us one lead to work on."

The Hardys decided to continue along the trail to Spire Rock, though it seemed certain the radio call had been a trick to set them up for what had just happened. The odd upthrusting rock formation was surrounded by a small clearing. Nearby was a public fountain at which a woman and two small children were drinking water.

No one else was in sight.

"Looks as if we wasted our time," grumbled Joe.

Just then three figures burst out of the bushes behind the boys.

"You wanted a crime tip—try this!" growled a voice, and the tip of a finger jabbed Joe hard in the ribs.

The Hardys whirled around, chuckling in spite of themselves. Both had recognized the voice of their chubby pal, Chet Morton. Two more of their high school buddies were with him, big rangy Biff Hooper and dark-haired, bookish Phil Cohen.

"Wow! Did you guys ever fall for that one!" Chet exulted. His plump cheeks jiggled as he bobbed up and down in sheer high spirits, poking Joe playfully.

"You're nuts!" Frank grinned. "You mean it was one of you who broadcast that phony radio message?"

"Who else?" Biff grinned back. "We saw you pull into the parking lot, and decided to feed you a little excitement."

"And you fell hook, line, and sinker!" Chet went on, rubbing it in. Then he paused to wipe the perspiration brought on by his cavorting from his moon-shaped face.

"After all," Phil added, "it's been at least a week since your last mystery, hasn't it?"

"That's what *you* think," Joe said wryly. "Matter of fact we've got a new one on our hands just since we left the parking lot."

Their friends were startled when they heard how the Hardys had been waylaid en route to Spire Rock.

"I don't get it," said Biff with a puzzled frown. "How could those hoods have known you'd be going through the woods just at that time?"

"They must have heard you broadcast the message," Joe deduced. "Where were you calling from?"

"The parking lot on the other side of the entrance you pulled into. Right after Phil spotted you, we used the CB radio in Tony Prito's pickup truck."

"Did you notice anyone eavesdropping?"

Biff looked at Phil and Chet. All three thought for a moment, then shook their heads.

"I guess not," Biff concluded. "But that doesn't prove much. There were people all around us, hopping in and out of cars. We were getting such a bang out of fooling you, we probably wouldn't have noticed, anyway."

"Where's Tony?" Frank inquired.

"He had to help his dad on some construction work." Biff explained that he and the others had come to Wild World to apply for jobs as park attendants in response to an ad in the Sunday paper. Although Tony had to leave as soon as they filled out their forms and were interviewed, Chet, Biff, and Phil had decided to stick around and enjoy the rides in the park's amusement area. "How about you guys?" he asked. "Did you come to apply, too?"

"Nope." Joe grinned, teasing. "We came to check out an X-mark on a map."

Their chums' curiosity was immediately aroused. When the Hardys showed them the mysterious folder that had arrived in the mail, their three friends insisted on coming with them to inspect the hollow tree.

Although Wild World was surrounded by a

high chain-link fence, the animal park proper was also partitioned off from the amusement area. To reach the spot indicated on the map, the Hardys' car would have to take its place in the line of vehicles cruising slowly along the road that wound through the animal range. A sign above the gateway warned spectators not to leave their cars.

"That X-mark better not be a gag," Chet grumbled as they paid their admission fare through the car window to an attendant with a coin changer on his belt. "This ride's costing us money."

"Don't worry. You'll get your money's worth just seeing the animals," Joe said.

"You bet!" Phil piped up enthusiastically. "I went through with my whole family a couple of weeks ago. It's almost like a trip through an African game preserve!"

His words were borne out as they passed in close view of grazing giraffes, ostriches, and gazelles. The sights were impressive. Many spectators pulled off the road to photograph the animals, and Joe wished he had brought his camera.

One ostrich gulped a peanut Biff tossed out the window. The creature seemed to take a fancy to him and raced alongside the car, keeping up easily with long loping strides of its knobby legs.

"Careful. I think it's fallen for you!" Frank joked. "Either that or it's hungry."

Biff hastily pulled back from the window. "Better get my head in before it gives me a peck on the cheek!"

"Serve you right for wasting good peanuts," said Chet, munching. He and Biff had each bought a bagful outside the gate, and the chubby youth was busily cracking the shells and popping goobers into his mouth.

"Boy, all you need's a good monkey suit, and you'd make a great addition to this park," Phil wisecracked.

"Listen, I haven't had a thing to eat since breakfast," Chet said defensively.

Joe glanced back from the front seat. "When was that, an hour ago?"

"Hey, we're coming to lion country!" Biff exclaimed, peering ahead over the Hardy boys' shoulders.

This area was enclosed by a fence of its own, and visitors were advised to keep their windows up. Frank, at the wheel, followed the cars ahead. Half a dozen or more of the big cats could be seen, including two males with flowing dark manes, several females, and at least one cub.

One male was fast asleep with his legs in the air, snoring audibly.

"Now that's what I call a real snooze!" Chet said enviously.

Frank grinned. "You should know."

He braked to a stop at the gate booth as they were leaving the lion enclosure.

"Can I help you?" said a black youth on duty in the booth. Pinned to the pocket of his green park attendant's uniform was a badge showing his name, Leroy Mitchell.

Frank took out the folder with the X-mark. "We're searching for a certain tree."

The youth glanced at the diagram, then looked up with an expression of puzzled interest. "Where'd you get this?"

"It came in the mail," Frank replied and showed him the envelope.

Leroy Mitchell's eyes widened. "Man alive! Don't tell me you're one of *those* dudes?"

"Which dudes?"

"The ones who solve all the mysteries—the sons of that famous detective."

"You guessed it. That's us," Frank said. "I'm Frank, and this is my brother Joe."

Leroy broke out in a friendly grin as he shook hands with the boys. "Wait till I tell everyone about meeting you two!"

"How about the tree," Frank asked, glancing around. "If I read this map right, it must be near here."

The black boy studied the diagram for a few moments. "Yeah, it's got to be that big old hollow oak." He pointed to a tree about a hundred yards off, on the right side of the road leading away from lion country.

"Okay if we get out and take a closer look at it?"

"Sure. I guess so. Nothing dangerous around there. But watch your step."

"Thanks, Leroy."

"Any time. Nice meeting you guys."

Frank drove near the hollow oak, then pulled to the side of the road. He and Joe got out.

"The rest of you had better wait in the car," Frank suggested.

Biff nodded. "Sure." He and his two friends in the back seat watched as the Hardy boys approached the oak.

"What do you think?" Joe asked his brother.

"Maybe there's something hidden in it." Frank stuck his arm in the hollow trunk.

"Anything there?" Joe asked eagerly.

"Yes, it feels like an envelope." Frank picked it up and withdrew his arm. As his hand came out, clutching the white object, Joe turned pale.

"Watch out!" the younger Hardy boy yelled. "Look what's on it!"

CHAPTER III

A Trumpeting Tusker

CLINGING to the envelope was a brown creature, several inches long. It had two crablike front claws, eight legs, and a tail ending in a stinger.

"A scorpion!" Frank gasped, his eyes widening in horrified disgust. The small animal's tail was curving forward over its back, ready to sting him in the hand. Frank dropped the envelope as if it were red hot!

The same question occurred to both boys.

"Is this what Dad was trying to warn us about?" Joe wondered out loud, still a trifle breathless.

Frank shrugged and ran his fingers through his hair. "Maybe, though I don't see how he could have known I'd stick my hand in this hollow tree."

"He might have known someone would use a scorpion sooner or later to harm us."

"Could be."

The loud sound of a put-putting motor caught the Hardys' attention. Turning, they saw a park guard speeding toward them on a trail bike. He had a visored uniform cap on his head and a holstered weapon on his hip.

Red-faced with annoyance, the burly officer braked his bike and swaggered up to growl at the Hardys. "What are you two kids doing out of your car?"

Joe started to explain, but Frank cut him short. "We got permission from one of the attendants."

"What attendant?" the guard demanded, as if he thought Frank were lying.

"Leroy Mitchell in the gate booth at lion country."

The guard turned to look in the direction Frank indicated. Leroy, evidently noticing that the Hardy Boys were in trouble, left his post and hurried toward them. Two or three passing cars slowed or halted so their occupants could see what was going on.

The guard started to bluster at the Hardys again as Leroy reached the scene.

"Take it easy," the black youth said to the officer. "I told them it would be all right to get out of their car just this once. They wanted to take a look at the tree."

"Don't you know it's against regulations for visitors to leave their cars?"

"Sure, but they only wanted to get out for a couple of minutes. And there's nothing dangerous around here."

The only animals in sight were a pair of mild-eyed gazelles, grazing and paying not the slightest attention to human goings-on.

"It's still against regulations," the officer said roughly.

"Okay. If I've done wrong, report me," Leroy said. "Don't hassle these guys."

The guard grunted and told the Hardys to go back to their car. "And from now on," he warned, "obey the park rules!"

Joe pointed to the brown creature crawling on the grass near the envelope. "If you're so anxious to protect visitors, better get rid of this scorpion before it stings someone."

The guard was taken aback and seemed reluctant to touch the odd creepy-crawler. Leroy grinned and brought an empty milk carton from his booth to scoop up the scorpion for safe disposal.

Frank retrieved the envelope, and after thanking the black youth, he and Joe rejoined their buddies in the car.

"What was that all about?" Biff asked.

Joe filled him and the others in as Frank peered inside the envelope. It contained a card bearing a seemingly senseless jumble of letters.

"Some kind of code," the elder Hardy boy declared and passed the card to his brother. "Guess we'll have to try cracking it later."

Joe studied the letters while Frank started the car and turned back onto the road.

"I wonder if the same party planted both this code message and the scorpion?" Joe mused.

"Good question," Phil agreed.

"There's another," Chet put in. "Would a scorpion sting kill you?"

"It would certainly hurt," Frank said, "and I think the venom of some species can be fatal. Matter of fact I intend to read up on scorpions in the encyclopedia when I get home."

"Likewise," said Joe.

"You really think someone planted that scorpion, and tried to set you guys up?" Phil inquired.

Frank shrugged. "I doubt that it got there on its own."

On either side of the road roamed zebras and several kinds of antelope, which the boys identified from the park folder as gnus, elands, and hartebeests.

Ahead, they were coming to a fenced-in elephant pen. Because the animals were big enough and strong enough to overturn a car, visitors were not allowed to enter their compound and could only drive past the fence, a few yards from the road.

Nevertheless, spectators were able to get an excellent view. Three of the huge beasts were drinking at a shallow creek that flowed through the enclosure. One was wading in the stream and scooping up water, then flipping its trunk backward for a do-it-yourself shower.

"I wouldn't mind cooling off like that," Chet observed enviously, fanning his chubby-cheeked face with the now-empty peanut bag.

"Why don't you get in there and join 'em?" Biff joked. "You'd look right at home—you're built along the same lines!"

"Don't knock it." Frank grinned. "That kind of beef makes a good football lineman."

Visitors' cars had slowed to a halt and everyone seemed to be enjoying the spectacle. In a foreign-made station wagon just ahead, a bearded man with a camera was waving and shouting to attract the elephant's attention, then hastily snapping pictures. Checking the rearview mirror, Frank noticed two men in sport shirts sitting in a blue car. They were wise-cracking loudly and chucking popcorn out the window at the elephants.

Suddenly one big tusker bellowed, taking everyone by surprise. The animal waved its upraised trunk to and fro as if sniffing the air, then charged toward the road, trumpeting loudly! When it reached the fence, the huge creature reared up on its hind legs, as if ready to batter down any obstruction!

"Oh, no!" Phil gasped. "Is that elephant powerful enough to break out?"

"Sure looks like it," Joe said, "if he gets worked up sufficiently."

The tusker's bellows of rage seemed loud enough to be heard all over the park. A guard speeded to the scene and summoned a trainer by walkie-talkie.

Presently a four-wheel-drive wagon appeared inside the compound. Evidently it had entered from the opposite side. It drove right across the creek and stopped about fifteen feet away from the angry elephant. The khaki-clad driver got out.

He began talking to the tusker in a coaxing, soothing voice and offered some tidbits on his outstretched hand. Gradually the enraged beast calmed down.

Chet glanced out the window. "Oh-oh," he muttered. "Here comes more trouble."

The guard who had scolded them earlier for inspecting the oak tree was striding toward their car. "Don't you guys ever learn!" he bawled at them angrily.

"What have we done now?" Joe demanded.

"I warned you once about obeying park rules! Now you're stirring up the elephants."

"Don't be ridiculous," Frank said, refusing to be bullied. "We were just sitting here, watching them."

"Yeah? And I suppose that big one got peeved because he didn't like somebody's face."

"Don't look at us," Frank said evenly.

"Don't get smart with me, kid!" the burly park guard stormed. "I'm going to teach you a lesson!"

"What's that supposed to mean?"

"It means you're all coming with me to the office. If I've got anything to say about it, this is a case for the police!"

He ordered the Hardys to follow him in their car while he escorted them across the grounds to a neat frame bungalow outside the fence. Here he made all five boys get out and took them into a room furnished with a desk and several file cabinets.

An elderly man with a tanned, weather-beaten complexion and white mustache listened calmly to the guard's ranting. Then he got up from his desk and shook hands with each of the boys.

"My name's Carter, fellows. Pop Carter, most people call me. I own Wild World. Glad you could come and see our animals today."

After the boys had introduced themselves, Mr. Carter added, "Is what the guard here says correct?"

"No, sir, it isn't," Frank replied. "It's true one of the elephants got worked up—"

The park owner nodded. "I know. I've already had a call from the trainer."

"But we didn't goad him in any way," Frank went on. "We were watching like the other spectators. If your guard was going to pick out anyone, why not the two men in the car behind us?

They were acting like wise guys and tossing popcorn toward the elephant pen."

"Not only them," Joe put in. "There was a black-bearded guy with a camera ahead of us, who kept waving and shouting at the elephants in a foreign language. He was trying to get them to face his way, I guess, so he could snap their pictures. Maybe that irritated them."

A strange expression appeared on the park owner's face. He glanced at the burly guard, who burst out, "They're trying to talk their way out! I think you should make an example of these smart alecks."

"All right, that'll do for now. I'll handle this," Pop Carter said calmly.

The guard left the office, red-faced and muttering. A moment later they heard his trail bike go put-putting off with a loud roar of exhaust.

Pop Carter grinned apologetically. "Sorry about that. He means well, but he has off days now and then. Got family problems, I guess."

The kindly old park owner tried to refund the boys' admission fares, but they refused his offer, having enjoyed their view of the animals despite the unpleasant episode.

"Mind answering a question?" Joe murmured hesitantly.

"I'll try, son," Pop replied. "Shoot."

"Why did you look so concerned when I mentioned the bearded foreigner?"

Mr. Carter eyed Joe in surprise and slowly filled his pipe. "You're quite a detective, my boy." Mention of the word detective seemed to strike him suddenly, causing him to do a double-take. "Wait a minute. You and your brother wouldn't be the sons of Fenton Hardy, by any chance?"

"We are, sir," Frank nodded. "Do you know Dad?"

"Met him once in Florida, when I was wintering there with the circus. Fine man. And I hear you two take after him."

Joe grinned. "Let's say we enjoy unraveling mysteries—or trying to."

Pop Carter seemed to make up his mind as he lit his pipe. "All right, here's one for you." He explained that the elephant, Sinbad, who had become enraged, was normally a peaceful, good-tempered animal and had only gone berserk once in the past. This had occurred when Pop was running a small circus and had hired a new trainer—a bearded Pakistani named Kassim Bey.

"Taking him on was one of the worst mistakes I ever made," Pop said, shaking his head reflectively. "Mind you, I've known other Pakistanis who were excellent with animals. But Kassim was just plain mean—he mistreated Sinbad and drove him crazy. I fired the no-good fellow as soon as I found out what had happened."

Kassim had reacted vindictively, cursing both Carter and Sinbad and vowing revenge.

"Said he was going to call down a Djinn or evil spirit to haunt us," Pop went on. "I paid no attention, of course, and Sinbad was a good elephant from then on. Behaved docilely at all times, up until a week or so ago, that is."

"Then what happened?" Frank asked.

"One night he started acting up again, trumpeting like all get-out. I live here, you see, and I could hear him, so I jumped out of bed and went to see what was wrong."

"What did you find?" Joe asked the elderly man.

"Nothing. Couldn't make out a thing, except —well, a dark shape soaring up and away through the trees."

"You don't mean one of those evil spirits that Kassim called down?" Frank inquired, half joking.

Pop Carter shrugged and looked at the Hardys with a sheepish grin. "I still don't know what to make of it. Maybe you two can solve the mystery."

CHAPTER IV

Wheel Trouble

THE boys were mystified by the park owner's story.

Pop Carter scratched his balding head and gave another helpless shrug. "Anyway, now Sinbad's thrown another tantrum. If it happens again, I may have to get rid of him," Pop added unhappily.

"Could those dirigible explosions this morning have upset him?" Joe suggested.

"I reckon it's possible. They were certainly loud enough around here. In fact, the airship was practically right over the park when it happened."

"Or maybe that bearded photographer reminded Sinbad of Kassim Bey," Frank put in.

"That's what I wondered at first," Pop admitted.

"Hey!" Joe snapped his fingers in sudden excitement. "Maybe that guy *was* Kassim Bey!"

Pop seemed momentarily startled by this idea. "What did this fellow you saw look like?" he inquired.

"Well, he had bushy black whiskers and a twirled-up handlebar mustache," Joe replied. "A big man, I think, although we never saw him out of his car."

The park owner shook his head thoughtfully. "Nope. Doesn't sound like Kassim. He had a slick black mustache that curved down on each side of his mouth and joined a neat little black chin beard. Above the mustache, he was clean-shaven."

Pop puffed on his pipe for a moment, then added with a sigh, as if annoyed at himself for taking the idea seriously, "Anyhow, it's impossible. I heard Kassim was killed in an accident after he left the circus."

From his worried expression, it seemed obvious to the Hardys and their friends that Mr. Carter had more on his mind than the elephant's misbehavior. The boys watched him as he moved away from his desk and stared out the window for a moment.

"Wild World seems to be quite a success," Frank remarked, breaking the silence. "Do you enjoy running an animal park more than a circus?"

"I love it," Pop said, turning back toward the visitors. "Put my life savings into this place. But now I'm wondering if I made a mistake."

"How come, sir?"

"Well, I opened the park in April, and I had Sinbad and his two mates brought here in May. Since then, it seems I've had nothing but trouble."

"What sort of trouble?" Chet inquired.

"First, someone tried to break into the park one night. The fence is wired, you see, so that set off an alarm. Upset all the animals and almost caused the giraffes and zebras to stampede. Terrible time we had getting 'em calmed down again. Then, later on, when the weather got warm, someone threw a stink bomb in the park on a real hot, crowded day. You can imagine what a commotion *that* caused!"

"I'll bet," Joe said sympathetically.

"Next, somebody started a rumor that the animals were rabid and might be dangerous to visitors."

"Hey, that's right. I remember hearing that," said Phil. "Did it lose you much business?"

"Sure did. Attendance fell way off for the next few days till I managed to get a full denial in the newspapers, and a clean bill of health from the State Wildlife Bureau." Pop spread his hands. "Why go on? It's been one thing after another. Sometimes I wonder if I wouldn't be smarter to sell out."

Frank's eyes narrowed with interest. "Has anyone made you an offer?"

"Sure. Matter of fact, two parties keep after me to sell."

"Mind telling us who they are?"

"One of them is Arthur Bixby. He owns several animal parks in other parts of the country, and now he wants to open one around here."

"Who's the other one?" Biff asked.

"Manager of a real-estate firm—fellow named Bohm. Clyde Bohm. Wants to develop this land around here as an industrial site, or some such."

Frank said, "Do you think one of them might be making trouble for you on purpose, trying to pressure you into selling out?"

Pop Carter tapped out the ashes from his pipe. "I won't say the idea hasn't crossed my mind. 'Course I can't prove anything. As far as facts are concerned, the whole thing's still a mystery."

"Joe and I will look into it," Frank promised.

"I'll sure appreciate it if you turn up anything."

Before the boys left his office, the elderly park owner insisted on giving them free passes to all the amusement rides.

Chet was ecstatic. "Wow! What a break! Let's try everything!"

His enthusiasm cooled, however, by the time they had sampled the first five. In fact, he appeared slightly green around the gills and decided to wait on a bench while his friends boarded the Ferris wheel.

Frank and Joe strapped themselves into one seat, with Biff and Phil facing them in the other. Presently the wheel began to turn.

"Wow! What a view!" Joe gasped. From the top of the wheel they could see not only the whole Wild World layout but most of Barmet Bay, with Rocky Isle clearly visible far out from shore.

"Know who invented the Ferris wheel?" Frank asked.

Biff grinned. "That's easy. A guy named Ferris."

"Wrong. It was William Somers, who built one in Atlantic City. Ferris copied it for an exposition in Chicago in 1893 and got all the credit."

To the boys' surprise, the wheel squeaked to a halt as their car reached the top for the third time.

"Something must be stuck," Phil said apprehensively.

Anxious minutes passed before the operator cupped his hands and shouted up that the drive mechanism had temporarily jammed but was now being fixed.

"Another headache for Pop Carter," Frank muttered.

The wheel soon began to revolve again, but the experience of being stranded helplessly in midair had been unnerving. Afterward, Biff and Phil went off in Chet's jalopy with a parting wave, while the Hardys drove home in their own car.

"Hmph! Late for lunch again," Aunt Gertrude observed as they entered the kitchen.

"We got hung up." Frank grinned.

The tall, angular woman was about to retort sharply when Joe added, "On a Ferris wheel."

"My stars! What happened?"

The boys described the amusement park mishap.

"Sounds suspicious, if you ask me," Miss Hardy commented. "If I'd been there, I'd have questioned the operator."

"We did," Frank told her. "He claimed it was just an accident, and that no one who doesn't work at the park had had any chance to tinker with the mechanism. We think he was telling the truth."

Their aunt eyed the boys shrewdly. "Are you two working on a new case?"

The boys winked at each other and nodded with a smile, well aware they had no chance of evading her cross-questioning. Besides, although Miss Hardy would never have admitted it, they knew what a thrill she got out of their detective work. They, in turn, enjoyed hearing their aunt's opinions, which more than once had given them a new angle on a mystery.

Over ham sandwiches and milk, followed by juicy wedges of apple pie, they told her about the anonymous letter and map that had led them to Wild World and the hollow tree incident. Miss Hardy was incensed when she heard how Frank and Joe had been waylaid in the woods when they first arrived at the animal park.

"I'd have taken a stick to those scoundrels!" she declared.

"I'll bet you would have," Frank said.

Just then the telephone rang, and he glanced at his watch. "One-thirty on the nose. That must be Dad!"

Both boys jumped up from the table. Frank hurried to the living-room phone, while Joe answered on the kitchen extension. Sure enough, it was their father, calling from St. Louis.

"What's up, Dad?" Frank inquired after switching on a scrambler to insure secrecy for their conversation. This synchronized with a portable device Fenton Hardy used whenever circumstances permitted.

The sleuth explained that he had been hired by the government to help round up a band of political terrorists known as the Scorpio gang.

"I've heard about them in the news!" said Joe. "They go in for bombings, don't they?"

"Among other things," Mr. Hardy replied drily. "But bombs are by no means their only weapons. They'll use any form of terror to hurt American companies or individuals they don't like." The gang's leader, he went on, was code-named the Scorpion.

"So that's what you meant by that warning in your radio message!" Frank exclaimed.

"Right, son. He knows I've been assigned to crack his gang, so he may well try to strike back at my family. I want you two to be on guard at all times."

"We will, Dad!" the boys promised.

Mr. Hardy related how he had zeroed in on the

gang's hideout in New York City more than a month ago, and had tipped off the FBI only to have the group escape moments before the police closed in. Since then he had been following up fresh leads in other parts of the country.

He was keenly interested when the boys told him of their morning adventures.

"I'd say there's no doubt the Scorpion himself was responsible for that park map you received in the mail," Fenton Hardy declared. "What's more, I believe the Quinn Air Fleet has been chosen as the gang's next target."

The owner of the airship service, Lloyd Quinn, he went on, had already received threatening messages. The messages called Quinn an imperialist tool and accused him of using the *Safari Queen* to help loot the resources of new African countries.

Mr. Hardy said he himself had been informed by the FBI about the dirigible explosions that morning, within minutes after they occurred.

"That's why I radioed you boys. I believe those explosions may be only the first move in the gang's war of nerves against Quinn. Now then, I'd like you to go out to the air terminal and talk to him. Scout for clues. You may be able to—"

The detective's voice broke off with a sudden gasp. "Hold it, sons! I think I'm being—"

Again his voice halted. The boys heard confused sounds, then a loud report.

Next moment the line went dead!

CHAPTER V

Queen of the Skies

"Dad! Dad!" Frank cried, jiggling the hook frantically. It was useless. The only response was a dial tone.

Hanging up, Frank went glumly back to the kitchen, where Joe greeted him with a worried look.

Noting their expressions, Aunt Gertrude demanded sharply, "What's going on? Is something wrong with your father?"

"He broke off the conversation suddenly, Aunty," Frank admitted, "but that doesn't mean he's in trouble."

Miss Hardy started to retort, then pursed her lips. "Hmph. Perhaps you're right. We'd better not alarm your mother."

Frank phoned the Quinn Air Fleet terminal and asked to speak to the head of the company, Mr. Lloyd Quinn. When he explained why he was calling, he was put through immediately.

Lloyd Quinn listened to Frank's opening remarks, then said, "The FBI told me about your father's investigation of the Scorpio gang, so I'll be happy to talk to you and your brother. If you can do anything to clear up this problem, believe me, I'll cooperate in every way possible."

"Could we see you this afternoon?" Frank asked.

"Any time. The sooner the better, as far as I'm concerned."

"Good. We'll be right over."

The terminal was a vast, sprawling complex of buildings, which included both an assembly plant and spacious maintenance hangars. It was also, in effect, an international airport. There was a reception building for passengers, with customs and immigration personnel to deal with incoming flights.

Dominating the whole scene was the mooring tower, with the huge, silvery, cigar-shaped *Safari Queen* floating majestically in full view.

"Boy, what a sight!" Joe exclaimed as they drove through the gate. "I wonder when the next airship in the fleet will be ready for its maiden voyage?"

"In a month or two, I think," said Frank.

Lloyd Quinn's office was in the reception building. After announcing themselves, the boys were whisked up by a private elevator and ushered in to see him. Quinn, a stocky, broad-shouldered man in shirt-sleeves, with a pug nose and a friendly grin, shook hands with the Hardys and invited them to sit down. His dress and manners were as plain as his office.

"What would you like to know, fellows?" he said, coming straight to the point.

"For one thing," Frank said, "have you any idea what caused those explosions this morning?"

"Grenades. Not much doubt about that. Someone aboard the *Safari Queen* dropped them just as she was arriving over Bayport."

"Any suspicions as to who that someone might be?"

Quinn shook his head. "Not really. But there are only two possibilities. Either a member of the crew was paid to do it, probably by this terrorist gang, or the grenades were tossed out by one of the passengers."

"How could a passenger throw something outside?"

"Through an emergency hatch. There are a number of them in the gondola. The *Queen's* not pressurized like a jetliner, you see. It cruises at much lower altitudes. In fact, it can drop down to rooftop height for sightseeing. That's one of the beauties of airship flight."

"What about the engine noise?" Joe put in. "It seemed a lot louder than usual."

Quinn smiled wryly. "It sure was. Normally she's as silent as a sky ghost. But some of the muffling came loose."

"Accidentally?"

"I'd be inclined to say yes if it hadn't happened just before those grenades went off. Under the circumstances, the answer may be sabotage."

Frank said, "Which would point to a crewman, right?"

"Right," Quinn agreed, with a troubled look.

"It fits in too neatly to be an accident," Joe pointed out. "First, the engine noise attracts people's attention and makes them look up at the sky, the way Frank and I did. Then they see and hear the grenade explosions."

"And the elephant falls out," Frank added. "Any idea how *that* stunt was pulled?"

"Not a hint," Quinn said, getting up from his desk to pace about angrily. "But the whole thing was fiendishly clever. It was purposely planned to give my air service a black eye and remind everyone of the *Hindenburg* disaster!"

Both Hardys had read about the fiery explosion of the famous German dirigible at Lakehurst, New Jersey, in 1937.

"That couldn't happen to the *Safari Queen,* could it?" Joe asked.

"Of course not. It wouldn't have happened to the *Hindenburg* if we'd let them have American helium gas, as they requested. We didn't, so they had to use highly flammable hydrogen. And even at that, what happened was no accident. More likely that, too, was caused by sabotage. But anyhow, the *Queen's* filled with helium, which can't burn. Most people don't realize it, but a helium-filled rigid airship is actually the safest method of air travel known to man."

"You really think dirigibles are coming back, sir?" Frank inquired.

"They're bound to," Quinn declared. "Not just because I'm a believer—the facts dictate it. Planes depend on airports, ships depend on seaports, and trucks depend on highways, but airships can haul anything anywhere, and do it cheaply, quickly, and safely."

"What about helicopters?" Joe questioned.

"Too costly and inefficient to operate, even if they were built big enough for real freighting. By comparison, the *Queen* can haul three hundred tons in a single trip, profitably." Quinn broke off with a boyish grin. "But don't get me started on all that. You're talking to a lighter-than-air enthusiast!"

He glanced proudly out the big picture window of his office at the *Safari Queen*, the first airship on the Quinn Air Fleet.

"Look at her. Isn't she beautiful? How would you fellows like to go aboard?"

"We'd love to!" the Hardys exclaimed.

In the elevator Frank asked, "By the way, were any of the African animals you were transporting here for Wild World harmed?"

"Not at all. They've all been inspected and safely trucked to the animal park."

The mooring tower was built with a projecting ramp, somewhat like the lip of a pouring spout. The nose of the dirigible rested atop this ramp, from which an extended walkway and conveyor led directly into the gondola, the cabin structure underneath the airship.

Quinn told the boys the *Safari Queen* was 600 feet long and could cruise at 150 miles per hour. It was powered by four turbines, which drove the main rotor and the blowers for the steering and hovering jets.

Frank and Joe were surprised by the spacious accommodations, which extended above the gondola well up into the main structure. The inside of the airship was not simply hollow and filled with gas, but divided into separate cells so that a sudden disastrous leak would be impossible.

As they went through the engine compartment, Joe noticed a young crewman who was eyeing them furtively. Without saying anything to the others, Joe snapped the fellow's picture with his miniature pocket camera, which he had brought along to photograph any clues that they might discover.

The aerial bridge, or flight deck, was a marvel of neatly arranged dials and control consoles.

"The ship can be flown from here to Africa entirely by autopilot," Quinn explained. "And the steering jets are computer-controlled to help counteract any crosswinds that might affect our course or stability."

The boys were thrilled at the view from the dirigible's wide cabin windows. "Sure gives you a lot better outlook than those peepholes on airliners!" Joe remarked.

Quinn smiled. "You bet they do! There's no finer sightseeing in the world than the view a traveler can enjoy on an airship voyage. And the Germans proved long ago that such trips can take place between continents on regular schedules, with no serious weather problems."

After showing the boys the *Safari Queen,* Quinn took them to his assembly plant, where a second dirigible, the *Arctic Queen,* was under construction.

"Where will this one fly?" Frank asked.

"To northwestern Canada, hauling supplies for a three-year pipeline project." Quinn's face darkened as he added, "That is, if what happened this morning doesn't cause the pipeline company to cancel our contract."

"You think they might, sir?"

"Who knows? Those explosions could arouse their fears about airship safety."

"Have you had any trouble before this?" Joe asked.

"Yes, two or three sabotage incidents."

Frank said, "Do you suspect anyone?"

Lloyd Quinn frowned and hesitated before replying. "Don't get me wrong. I'm not making accusations. But the only possible enemy I can

Joe snapped the fellow's picture with his miniature camera.

think of is a man named Basil Embrow. My former partner."

"The two of you broke up?"

"We had to," Quinn replied. "We were having too many violent disagreements, so I went ahead and formed this dirigible company on my own. Embrow may bear me a grudge."

After asking for and obtaining computer print-out data on the crew and passengers aboard the *Queen's* morning flight, the Hardys returned home.

Their mother informed them that they had received a phone call from Eustace Jarman, a well-known New York industrialist and head of a large corporation called Jarman Ventures.

"What did he want, Mom?"

"Actually, it was his secretary who called. She didn't say what it was about, but left this number. She wants you to call back."

Frank dialed the number, only to learn that Jarman was out. His secretary asked if the boys would be willing to come to New York City and talk to him. An appointment was set up for eleven thirty the next morning.

Afterward, Frank phoned Mr. Hardy's ace operative, Sam Radley, and asked him to trace Quinn's ex-partner. Frank also read him the names and other data on the twelve passengers who had arrived in Bayport that morning from Africa aboard the *Safari Queen*. All of them were foreigners.

"Would you please find out if the FBI has anything on any of them?" Frank asked.

"Will do," Sam promised and rang off.

Meanwhile, Joe had developed and enlarged his photograph of the crewman. He had no special distinguishing features, except for a mole near his left eye. A check of their father's crime files revealed no data on him or any other member of the crew.

"Looks as if we're up against a blank wall." Joe sighed.

"For the moment, anyhow," Frank agreed.

The boys now set to work on the code message they had found in the envelope hidden in the hollow tree at Wild World. It read:

HXTREXST OCHOXTEH ROXCFUTX SVSKIETH
EEHYVSLA SXOXEDER HNRIXAXD
OOESAYWY ERXLMXIS

"There are quite a few X's," Joe mused. "Those could stand for spaces between words."

"Right," Frank said. "If you'll notice, there are exactly eight letters in each group—so those groups almost certainly don't stand for individual words as the message is now laid out. Hm, let's see."

A lengthy silence followed while the boys racked their brains for a possible key. Each tried various transposition and substitution ciphers without success.

"Wait a second!" Frank exclaimed suddenly.

"There are nine groups and eight letters in each group, which adds up to seventy-two."

"Hey, I get it!" Joe said. "You mean this may be one of those 'twisted path' ciphers, laid out in a square."

"Right."

The boys tried arranging the letters horizontally.

"That's it!" Frank exulted.

CHAPTER VI

Jungle Man

WITH the nine groups of letters laid out in rows, side by side, the Hardys had the following box:

> HORSESHOE
> XCOVEXNOR
> THXSHOREX
> ROCKYXISL
> EXFIVEXAM
> XTUESDAYX
> SETTLEXWI
> THXHARDYS

"In this case, it's not really a 'twisted path' cipher at all," Frank said. "Just a straight-line path."

"Check." Joe agreed. "Follow each line straight across from left to right, one after another, with the X's representing the spaces between words. Let's see what that gives us."

The deciphered message read:

HORSESHOE COVE NORTH SHORE ROCKY ISLE
FIVE AM TUESDAY SETTLE WITH HARDYS

The brothers looked at each other, and Joe whistled. "Settle with Hardys!" he read aloud. "That sounds like trouble!"

"It sure does," said Frank, frowning uneasily. "Seems as if enemies of ours are arranging a meeting to plot how to get even with us."

"Or get rid of us!"

"Right. The place will be Horseshoe Cove on the north shore of Rocky Isle, at five A.M. Tuesday—tomorrow morning."

"And the ones holding the meeting," Joe added, "could be this Scorpio gang that Dad's after."

Frank looked puzzled. "But that would go against Dad's theory. Remember, he suggested that it might be the Scorpion himself who sent us the park map in the mail—hoping one of us would get stung when we checked the hollow tree!"

"Yes. I'd forgotten that," Joe said, scratching his head. "But that doesn't add up either, Frank. Why would the Scorpion warn us about a plot by our enemies?"

"Maybe the warning's a phony. I mean this code message may be just a trick to lure us into a trap."

"In other words, if that scorpion in the tree didn't sting at least one of us, the gang would still get us when we go over to the island tomorrow morning to spy on their meeting."

"Right," Frank nodded. "But I think we should check out this information in the message, Joe, phony or otherwise. Only let's not wait till tomorrow morning. Let's go right after dark and keep watch tonight so they don't get a chance to set up a trap."

"Smart idea. And we'll take a couple of the fellows with us for extra muscle, just in case."

The boys hopped in their car and drove to the construction project, where they found Tony Prito jockeying a wheelbarrow full of cement. Tony, a dark-haired youth who had taken part in many of the Hardy Boys' mystery cases, readily agreed to accompany them to Rocky Isle.

"And how about taking your boat instead of the *Sleuth?*" Frank added, referring to the Hardys' own motorboat. "If this tip-off in the code message is a trick, the gang may be keeping watch on our boathouse to see if we take the bait."

"Smart thinking, Frank. The *Napoli's* all set for a run. I topped up her tank this morning."

From the construction site, the boys drove to the Morton farm on the outskirts of town. They found Chet's slim, pixy-faced sister, Iola, curled up on the front-porch swing, reading a book.

"Hi, Iola," said Joe, who rated her the cutest

girl at Bayport High School. "Where's Chet?"

"Out in that patch of woods behind the barn." She smiled. "He's busy on a new project."

"What now?" Frank asked. "Training squirrels to gather nuts?"

Though he avoided most forms of exertion, Chet developed a new hobby every few weeks. He would work at it furiously till the first flush of enthusiasm wore off, or an obstacle arose that threatened to require too much effort to overcome.

Iola giggled. "Go and ask him."

The Hardys tramped around the barn and into the wooded grove behind it. They found their roly-poly chum in T-shirt and gym pants, holding on to a rope tied to the branch of a tall tree and swinging.

At the sight of the brothers, Chet dropped to the ground. He was sweating profusely, but his moon face was wreathed in smiles.

"Hi, guys. Meet Jungle Man!" he thumped his barrel chest and gave vent to an errie bellow that shook the leaves on the trees.

"What in the world are you up to?" Joe asked.

"Wait till I tell you. Boy, have I got a great idea!"

"I'll bet."

"No, really! That setup at Wild World, it's really a form of show biz, right? I mean, the animal displays, and the amusement rides to help attract crowds. Pop Carter himself used to run a circus."

Frank shrugged. "I suppose you could call it a form of show biz. So what?"

"So I have an act that'll top everything!" their chubby chum announced.

"Chet Morton as Jungle Man?" Joe stared. "Are you kidding?"

"No. Let me give you a sneak preview!"

Chet spat on his palms, which were red and blistered. "I ought to rub some chalk on my hands first, but never mind."

He grabbed the dangling rope, took a few steps backward, then launched himself with a running jump. As he swung back and forth like a pendulum, he pumped with his chunky legs to increase the arc of his swing.

Finally he was far enough out to touch a tree behind him with his feet. Using its trunk to give himself a fresh push, Chet swung high in the air, aiming for the branch of another tree some distance away.

Unfortunately, the branch was too slender to support his weight, or perhaps it was already cracked from too much use. Whatever the reason, it suddenly gave way, just as he managed to land on it precariously.

With a loud report, the branch broke off. Chet yelled in fright as he plunged to the ground.

Luckily Frank and Joe had dashed to his aid as

soon as they saw the bough start to bend, so they were able to break his fall. But Chet was badly shaken by his mishap. "I think I need some nerve tonic!" he gulped.

"I think you're right, pal." Joe chuckled, and the boys went into the house.

Over ice-cold glasses of cola, the Hardys told their friend of their plan to spy out a possible enemy move on Rocky Isle. Chet tended to get the jitters whenever their mystery cases became too exciting, but could always be depended on in a tight spot.

"Okay," he agreed. "But let's play it careful, huh, and not go asking for trouble."

"We won't," Frank promised. "Anyway, it can't be any more dangerous than your jungle-man act."

Shortly after eight o'clock that night, equipped with sleeping bags and camping gear, the four boys shoved off from a dock in Bayport Harbor aboard Tony Prito's boat, the *Napoli.* A cool evening breeze had set in across the bay, carrying a bracing salt tang toward the shore.

"Should be great sleeping tonight," said Tony as he steered a course across the dark, moon-dappled water, kicking up plumes of spray.

"I just hope we *get* some sleep!" Chet remarked nervously.

Frank grinned. "We'll take turns standing watch. I wish it weren't so bright. But maybe it's just as well. At least we won't have to use our flashlights much to find our way around."

"Hey!" Joe exclaimed softly. "Speaking of flashlights, take a look over there!"

He pointed toward the brightly lighted amusement park area of Wild World, which could be seen overlooking the waterfront just north of town. A green light was flashing on and off from the revolving Ferris wheel.

"Somebody's signaling!" Chet Morton gasped.

CHAPTER VII

Cave Camp

Tony slowed the *Napoli* so they could watch the flashes.

"They're signals all right," Frank agreed, "but not in Morse code."

The same thought was going through everyone's head. Were the signals in any way connected with their secret scouting expedition to Rocky Isle?

"I don't like this," Chet gulped. "Maybe someone spotted us leaving the dock!"

"That's not likely," Joe argued. "Why would they watch Tony's boat? But I'll bet it has something to do with the gang."

Frank nodded thoughtfully. "I agree. If you'll notice, the flashes only occur around the top half of the wheel's turn, so the signals could probably be seen by someone on the island."

"Especially by someone on the north shore," Joe added, thinking of the code message.

"Want to turn back?" Tony asked in a disappointed voice.

"Not unless you fellows do," Frank said.

"Not me!" Tony declared with an air of suppressed excitement.

The Hardys glanced at Chet, who hesitated a moment, then shrugged cheerfully. "Oh, well, we've come this far. May as well see what's out there."

"Good," Frank said. "But from now on we'd better watch our step and be extra careful."

The green light flashes had ceased while they were talking. The boys continued their cruise to Rocky Isle, with only the sound of the boat engine and the slap of water against the hull to accompany their passage. As they neared the island, Tony shut off the motor and they made the final leg of the trip with muffled oars.

On Frank's suggestion, they beached the boat on the southwestern shore and covered it with brush and driftwood.

Rocky Isle was a popular picnic and swimming spot by day. The boys had briefly used a Chinese junk to operate a ferry service between there and Bayport. After dark the regular ferry service ceased, and the lighthouse was now automated, which left the island in desolate loneliness during the night hours. Even the park guard's cottage was dark.

"Let's leave our stuff here and scout the north shore before we settle down for the night," Frank said, after they had lugged their camping gear halfway across the island.

"Suits me," said Chet, who was beginning to puff a bit.

The boys hiked the rest of the way with their hands free except for flashlights, and cautiously probed the northern portion of the tiny island. The terrain was rocky and vegetation sparse, affording few places for cover.

The horseshoe-shaped cove was fringed by a sandy beach, which in turn was overlooked by flat-topped cliffs, barren except for weedy clumps of dune grass and here and there a gnarled, stunted tree. There was no sign of any other human in the area.

"We must have beaten the gang over here," Tony observed, "if they're coming at all."

"Sure looks that way," Joe agreed. "Let's bring our gear and lie down."

They unrolled their sleeping bags in the tall grass on the bluff overlooking Horseshoe Cove. A few boulders and a nearby tree gave them a certain amount of cover, and from this vantage point they could see anything happening on the beach below.

"We'll stand two-hour watches, okay?" Frank plucked several weed stalks, broke off the tops, and clutched four uneven pieces in his fist with the ends sticking out. "Draw straws for turns," he proposed. "Shortest stands the first watch, second shortest takes the second, and so on. Okay?"

Joe drew the first two-hour sentry assignment, and Tony the next, followed by Chet. Frank, who was left holding the longest straw, would stand the last watch, by the end of which time, the boys figured it would be daylight.

In the peaceful night air, with the sound of surf in their ears and the occasional distant mewing of seagulls, the three boys soon fell asleep. Joe was left to study the stars and keep his eyes and ears trained for any suspicious comings or goings. The lighthouse beam swept intermittently out to sea.

Some time later, Frank awoke in the darkness. He had heard a faint noise somewhere in the distance. Cautiously he squirmed upright out of his sleeping bag and looked around him.

Chet, who was guard at the time, was slumped against a rock. A low, sawing noise issued from his open mouth!

"Oh, no!" Frank muttered to himself. He wormed his way through the tall grass toward the edge of the cliff and scanned the shore, where a fresh shock awaited him.

On the beach, not far from a point just below his own position, he could make out the figures of three men!

Frank wriggled back toward his own group and shook their sleeping sentry.

"Chet, wake up!" he hissed, then immediately

clapped a hand over the boy's mouth before he could utter a startled outcry.

"Wh-wh-whassa matter?" Chet managed to say in a muffled voice between Frank's fingers.

"You fell asleep at the switch, that's what," Frank whispered in his ear, "and now three of the gang are down on the beach."

With the utmost caution, the pair woke up their two companions, and Frank, Joe, and Tony hastily pulled on their sneakers. Then, as silently as Indians, the boys wriggled toward the edge of the bluff. The three men appeared to be digging in the sand.

"What are they up to?" Joe whispered in his brother's ear.

"Search me."

Tony wormed his way closer to the brink of the cliff for a better look. In doing so, he dislodged a few fragments of gravel, which skittered down the steep slope! Instantly the three men on the beach jerked to attention. One swung a flashlight beam in the boys' direction.

"Someone's up there!" he shouted.

Frank realized that he and his pals might be in a tight spot if the men were armed. Thinking fast, he called out, "There they are, sergeant!"

Joe immediately clued in and exclaimed loudly, "I'll go get the rest of the men!"

Their ruse worked even better than they had dared hope. The crooks appeared to panic.

"It's the law!" one of them cried. "Let's get out of here!"

All three broke into a run down the beach.

"What do we d-do now?" Chet stammered, excited.

"Go after them!" Frank blurted. "Maybe we can scare them into surrender, or at least get a good look at them!"

The boys slid and scrambled down the steep slope and took off in hot pursuit, though the sand slowed their pace. The crooks were already out of sight in the darkness.

The shoreline curved sharply beyond the cove. As the boys rounded the arc of the horseshoe and continued along the jagged beach, they could see no sign of their quarry. Finally they halted to look around.

"Where did they go?" Tony asked, puzzled.

"They probably went up the hill to cut across the island," Frank conjectured. "The slope isn't that steep here. It wouldn't take them long to reach higher ground. I imagine they beached their boat a safe distance away, just as we did."

The four boys clambered back up the hillside for a better view. The moon drifted out from behind a veil of clouds, but despite the increased brightness, they could see no one.

Joe snapped his fingers. "Wait a second. I'll bet I know where they've gone!"

"Where?" Chet panted.

"That cave you discovered when we solved the Chinese Junk mystery!"

Frank was less hopeful, but agreed the cave might be worth looking at in the absence of any better leads. It was located on the north side of the island, not far from their present position. The boys walked toward it through the moonlit darkness.

To reach the entrance, they had to climb several yards below the brow of the cliff. Here Frank called a momentary halt before entering. They strained their ears for the slightest sound from within but could hear nothing.

"Okay, come on!" Frank led the way, keeping his fingers over the lens of the flashlight so as to provide just enough illumination to see where they were going, without glaringly advertising their approach.

Even in the dim glow of his flash beam, the interior of the cavern looked awesome. Because of water seepage, it was a "living cave" with glittering icicles that thickened into stalactites and stalagmites as the boys probed deeper into the bedrock of the island.

Finally the passageway widened into a huge chamber with a vast, greenish scum-laden pool that gave off faint ripples as water bubbled up from below. Frank shone his flashlight around more boldly now, convinced there was no one hiding in the cave.

"What's that?" Joe exclaimed, snapping on his own beam to brighten their view of a spot that Frank's light had just swept over.

There were unmistakable signs that someone had recently been camping there!

Excited, the boys skirted the small underground lake and hurried toward the far wall of the chamber. Besides a camp cot and a beat-up, greasy-looking pillow with uncovered striped ticking, there were several cartons of canned food along with eating utensils, bottled beverages, a kerosene lantern, and a supply of candles and matches. Accumulated trash from a number of meals lay nearby.

"Whoever the guy is, or was, he must have been here for more than a few days," said Tony. "He left plenty of empties."

Frank picked up a book from the cot. Its title was *Elephant Lore*. "Joe, look at this!" he exclaimed. "The guy's been reading about elephants!"

The Hardys traded startled glances, each remembering what Pop Carter had told them about his recent difficulties with Sinbad.

"And that's not all," Frank added suddenly as he leafed through the book. "What do you make of these?" He pulled out two snapshots that had been stuck between the pages.

"Jumpin' catfish!" Joe gasped. "They're pictures of *us!*"

Tony and Chet crowded closer and stared at the photographs.

"Not very good shots," Tony observed.

"Don't worry. We never posed for them," Frank said wryly. "These are telephoto shots, snapped on the street when we didn't even know our picture was being tak—"

He broke off as Chet suddenly clutched his arm and hissed, "Shhh! I think I heard something!"

The Hardys instantly doused their lights. A moment later, a shot blasted the darkness!

CHAPTER VIII

A Dangerous Dummy

KAPOW! The bullet ricocheted off a stalagmite close by. The cavern rang with echoes and all four boys sank to the ground.

"Spread out!" Frank whispered urgently.

More shots followed, spraying the area where they had just been standing.

Joe snatched a hunk of rock from the floor and pegged it hard in the direction of the last gunflash.

He was rewarded by a yelp of pain and, almost at the same instant, the splashing sound of something falling into the water.

Silence ensued, the boys scarcely daring to breathe. Tense moments lengthened. Then suddenly the stillness was broken by footsteps running away through the cavern.

Was their enemy's retreat just a trick? The four teenagers wondered.

At long last, Frank groped for a rock and ventured to flash his light, ready to douse it again instantly and hurl his missile, should his beam reveal a glimpse of their unknown assailant.

There was no one in sight!

He played the light around thoroughly to make sure the gunman was not hiding behind a thick stalagmite or rock formation.

"All clear, I guess," he murmured.

The four boys rose warily to their feet, and Frank's companions switched on their own flashlights.

"Whew! Wh-what an experience!" Chet quavered. "I might have known something like this would happen, once you Hardys started chasing clues!"

"Thank goodness you heard the guy in time. You probably saved us," Frank congratulated their plump chum. He added to his brother, "Nice going on your part, too, Joe. I take it you heaved a rock at him. At least that's how it sounded."

"Right. I guess I hit him."

"Yes. And then he must've dropped his gun in the pool."

"So he decided to get out fast before we got him." Tony chuckled in relief.

The boys retraced their steps to the cavern entrance, moving carefully, ready to react at any moment if their enemy was lying in wait.

As they emerged into the night air, the faint drone of a boat engine reached their ears. They listened as the sound slowly faded in the distance.

Joe glanced at his brother. "Think that was the crooks leaving?"

Frank nodded. "Probably."

The Hardys went back into the cavern long enough to retrieve the elephant book and snapshots, as well as the eating utensils, the lantern, and one of the empty soft-drink bottles.

"These should be enough to give us some clear fingerprints of the man who was hiding in the cave," Frank declared.

They ripped open the pillow ticking and used it as a makeshift bag to carry the evidence. After the Hardys rejoined their pals, the boys trekked back to Horseshoe Cove. Here they shone their flashlights around the site where the three men had been digging.

A seated figure startled them momentarily, but Frank waved reassuringly. "Relax. It's only a dummy."

The dummy's back was propped against the cliffside, in a slight shallow recess formed by two projecting rocky outcrops.

"Why did they plant *that* here?" Joe wondered. He started to move forward to examine the seated figure, when Frank stopped him, flinging his arm across Joe's chest.

"Hold it! There's your answer!" Frank pointed

to a round disklike object that Joe had almost stepped on.

It was made of green plastic and was about the size of a small Frisbee. Apparently the men had been burying it in the sand when Tony's move had alerted them to the presence of watchers on the cliff.

"What's that?" Chet blurted.

"A land mine, unless I miss my guess." With cautious fingers, Frank unearthed the device. Under Mr. Hardy's expert training, he had learned how to recognize and disarm such contrivances. He took no chances, treating this one with the utmost respect.

Luckily he saw a pressure switch lying in the sand close by and realized the crooks had not had time enough to rig a detonator.

"A booby-trap setup?" Joe questioned, shaken.

"Right. That's why the dummy was put here. To arouse our curiosity. After walking up to examine it, one of us would have stepped on the mine, and—*boom!*"

"Whew!" Joe wiped his forehead. "And I almost did!"

"It wasn't fixed to go off yet," Frank reassured him.

"Thank goodness!"

"Also, from the looks of this," Frank went on, "I'd say it doesn't contain enough explosive to do more than stun us, or at worst, injure us slightly."

"Then what was their angle?" Tony asked.

The older Hardy boy theorized that the code message had been carefully planted as bait for the booby trap. "They figured we'd know enough about secret codes to decipher the note. Then when we got here, the mine would either scare us off the case or disable us enough to be captured without a fight."

"In which event," Joe added, "they would have held us as hostages to force *Dad* off the case."

"Correct," Frank agreed.

There was silence as the four youths digested the grim significance of their find.

Finally Tony stretched and sighed. "What do we do now?" he asked. "Hit the sack again or go back to Bayport?"

"May as well go back," Frank advised. "We've accomplished what we came to do."

"That suits me fine," said Chet. "I've had enough of this creepy place!"

Before leaving the island, the boys stuck a note under the park guard's cottage door, informing him that a man who might be involved in criminal activities had been hiding out in the cave. Then they lugged their camping gear to the *Napoli* and climbed in. As they headed back across the bay, the first pearly light of dawn streaked the horizon.

Joe was silent and thoughtful as they entered the harbor. "Do you suppose those three hoods came to Bayport after they left the island?" he asked his brother.

Frank shrugged. "Hard to say. They seemed to be heading down the coast, but the way sound spreads out over water, it's hard to judge direction. Why?"

"Remember why we went in Tony's boat instead of our own?"

"Sure. We figured the gang might be watching the *Sleuth* to see if we took the bait."

"Right," said Joe. "So if those hoods didn't come back here and report what happened, our boathouse may still be staked out!"

Frank's eyes narrowed. "That's an idea! If we move fast, maybe we can nab the guy who's keeping watch!"

"And make him talk," Joe added grimly.

As soon as they had entered the marina and tied up at the dock, the Hardys left Tony and Chet to unload the *Napoli* while they themselves hurried off along the waterfront to check out their hunch.

They were still fifty yards or more from their destination when Frank suddenly flung out his hand in warning. "Joe, look!"

A man was tampering with the lock of their boathouse door!

CHAPTER IX

Sky Show

IN unspoken accord, Frank and Joe quickened their pace, preparing to grab the trespasser before he could get away. But he evidently heard their footsteps pounding across the wharf.

The man turned with a startled expression. Then he let go of the lock and darted away. The boys got only a quick glimpse, but noticed that he was dark-complected and had a black mustache.

The two young sleuths gave chase.

Their quarry was heading for a dockside warehouse. Barrels, crates, and empty oil drums were crowded against the front wall. Just before rounding the corner of the building, the stranger knocked over two of the drums with a sweep of his arm and sent them rolling toward the boys.

"Look out, Joe!" Frank yelled.

The younger Hardy tried to sidestep hastily,

lost his balance, and fell, sprawling headlong on the wharf! Frank himself had to dodge the rolling drums, and by the time the boys resumed the chase, the fugitive was out of sight.

"Come on. We've got to catch him!" Frank urged.

As they ran around the side of the warehouse, they suddenly saw the intruder.

"There he goes!" Joe yelled.

The mustached man sprinted across a parking lot and then an open field, heading for a street that ran parallel to the waterfront.

Just then a bus came into view, filled with workers on their way to early-morning jobs in Bayport. The man turned toward a bus stop straight ahead.

"Oh, no!" Joe groaned as the boys redoubled their speed.

The bus rolled to a halt and the man leaped aboard.

"Stop, thief!" Frank shouted at the top of his lungs.

But apparently his words failed to carry. The bus doors swung shut, and despite the Hardys' frantic waving, the vehicle sped off toward town.

The Hardys skidded to an angry halt. "Of all the luck!" Joe fumed, socking his fist into his open palm. "Think there's any sense getting out our car and trying to follow the bus?"

Frank shook his head in disgust. "It's already out of sight, and our car is way over at the marina.

By the time we catch up, if we ever do, the bus will be unloading downtown. And for all we know, that guy might jump off at the first stop."

Glumly the young sleuths rejoined their two chums, loaded their sleeping bags and other items into their car, and drove home.

Aunt Gertrude, as usual, was up bright and early, and so was their slender, attractive mother. Both women listened attentively while the boys recounted their night's adventure.

"What about that explosive whatchamacallit the crooks were hiding in the sand?" Aunt Gertrude inquired.

"We dropped it overboard in the deep water on the way back to Bayport," Joe informed her.

Miss Hardy nodded approvingly, then pursed her lips. "Those criminals may strike again."

"You're right," Frank agreed. "That's why we've got to nail them. If we can identify any fingerprints on this stuff we brought back from the cave, at least the police will know whom to look for."

"Smart work," Mrs. Hardy said. "I'll make breakfast now. Then you two had better get some sleep."

"I could sure go for bacon and eggs," said Joe. "But I don't feel like turning in just now. Guess I'm too keyed up."

"Same here," Frank said. "We have to go to New York this morning to see Eustace Jarman, the business tycoon. We can doze on the bus."

Both brothers wolfed down a hearty breakfast, then set to work in their basement lab, dusting the objects from the cave with powder. Much to their surprise and disappointment, there were no fingerprints on any of them.

"That guy must've wiped everything he touched," Joe grumbled.

Frank nodded. "He was playing it safe and taking no chances in case anyone discovered his hideout."

"Which means that he must be a pro."

"I'd say there's no doubt about it."

The boys showered, changed their clothes, and started out for New York City. It was only a few minutes after eleven o'clock when their bus rolled into the Port Authority Terminal, which gave them ample time to keep their eleven thirty appointment at Jarman's midtown office. The weather was bright and sunny.

"Let's walk," Frank suggested.

"Good idea."

The sidewalks were filled with the usual bustling crowds. Noting the bumper-to-bumper crosstown traffic, Joe chuckled. "We're probably making better time on foot than we would by taxi."

A ripple of gasps and excited remarks ran through the throng of pedestrians, and the boys suddenly noticed people stopping to stare skyward.

"Hey, look!" Joe exclaimed.

A sleek, silvery airship was gliding majestically over Manhattan!

"The *Safari Queen!*" said Frank.

Awed, excited comments could be heard all around them.

"I'll bet Quinn sent her here to prove that nothing serious happened yesterday," the older Hardy boy guessed, "and to show everyone his dirigible's as good as ever."

"If that's his idea, it's working," Joe said. "Listen to the way everyone's admiring her."

The words were hardly out of his mouth when two baby blimps suddenly soared up into view.

"Hey! Where'd they come from?" Joe asked.

"A skyscraper up ahead," said Frank. "They must have been berthed on the roof."

"The two mini-airships headed straight for the *Safari Queen.* They looped and swooped and maneuvered about the larger craft like baby whales frolicking around their mother. The sidewalk observers chortled with delight at the spectacle.

"What a show!" Joe chuckled.

"I doubt if the *Queen's* pilot appreciates their company," said Frank. "But the crowd really goes for it. I wonder who thought *this* one up?"

"I don't know, but I intend to get some pictures while the show's on!" Joe took his miniature camera from his pocket and began snapping photographs rapidly.

The boys finally walked on as the dirigible

sailed southeast toward Brooklyn and Long Island. At the Jarman building, they took the elevator to the industrialist's penthouse office. A smiling, beautifully dressed secretary ushered them in.

Jarman was a tall, intense-looking man with long dark hair and a hawklike profile—the perfect picture of a hard-driving business executive. He got up from behind his huge modern desk to shake hands with Frank and Joe.

"Glad you fellows could come. I'm sorry I was out when you returned my call yesterday."

"What was it you wanted to see us about, Mr. Jarman?" Frank asked when they were all seated.

"My security department's been in touch with the FBI about the activities of those confounded terrorists, the Scorpio gang," Jarman explained. "I gather you Hardys are working on the case."

"Dad is, sir. We're helping unofficially," Frank replied.

"That's good enough for me. From what I've heard about you two, your 'unofficial help' is often mighty effective."

"Did you want us to investigate something, Mr. Jarman?" Joe inquired.

"Yes," the businessman said emphatically. "If you're not already working full time to run down those terrorists, I'll pay you to do so."

"Thank you, sir, but there's no need for that," said Frank. "In fact, I doubt if it would be right

"I wonder who thought this one up?" Frank asked.

for us to accept such an assignment from you, since Dad's already in charge of the case. But, as I say, we're working with him, and Joe and I intend to do all we can to help catch the Scorpio gang. May I ask what your interest is in the case?"

"Jarman Ventures is a vast corporation. We do business in many fields, and we've already had several brushes with terrorists. But that's not all." Jarman clipped off the end of a long cigar, lit it, and eyed the boys with a thoughtful frown as he blew out a cloud of smoke. "I'm sure anything I tell you will be kept confidential."

Frank and Joe nodded. "Of course."

"The fact is, Jarman Ventures is moving into the lighter-than-air field."

"You're building a dirigible yourself?" Joe asked with keen interest.

The businessman nodded. "My aircraft division has already laid the keel of one even larger than Quinn's. It'll be called the *Globe Girdler* to indicate its worldwide flight range. So naturally I'm pretty angry over what happened yesterday."

"You mean," Frank said, "the bad publicity?"

"Exactly. Anything harmful to *his* dirigible is bound to affect my project, too. That's why I want to do anything I can to help nab these filthy terrorists. And that's why I contacted you two."

"Believe me, sir," Frank declared, "we're as anxious to round up the Scorpio gang as you are. And we'll be happy to follow up any leads you can provide."

"Good. Then I'll instruct my security department to pass along any clues they uncover."

"What got you interested in the lighter-than-air field, Mr. Jarman?" Joe inquired.

"The tremendous future I see for it. Matter of fact, we've been building blimps, which are non-rigid airships, for several years."

The Hardys exchanged surprised grins.

"Those little ones we saw this morning wouldn't be yours by any chance, would they?" Joe inquired.

"You bet they would!" Eustace Jarman replied with a pleased smile. "I keep them berthed right here on the roof of this skyscraper."

He got up from his desk again and strolled across the room to gaze out the huge floor-to-ceiling window of his penthouse office.

"Here they come now!" he said.

Frank and Joe both joined the industrialist. Looking east, they could see the two little craft over Manhattan.

"I got the idea of sending them up on the spur of the moment, when the *Safari Queen* appeared over New York," Jarman related proudly. "Then I had my public-relations department phone all the news agencies and TV networks."

"It made a terrific spectacle," Frank said, genuinely impressed.

"I knew it would," the tycoon boasted. "Unless I miss my guess, that scene will show up in news photos clear across the country. I expect it to generate as much publicity as those dirigible explosions yesterday morning."

Jarman glanced at his watch, and the boys got the impression they were politely being dismissed. "I wish I could have lunch with you fellows, but I'm booked with some European manufacturers. You'll have to excuse me. This is a high-pressure schedule I work under."

He strode to his desk and picked up a pen. "Let me write you a check, though, to cover your time in coming here today."

When the Hardys declined, Jarman promised to take them for a ride personally in one of his baby blimps on Thursday, and asked them to meet him at Bayport Airport at noon.

"We'll really enjoy that, Mr. Jarman," Frank said, shaking hands.

After leaving the tycoon's office, the Hardys went down to the lobby.

"There are phone booths up ahead." Joe pointed. "Maybe we ought to call home and see if anything's happened."

"Good idea. I hope they've heard from Dad!" Frank found enough coins in his pocket to cover the call and dialed the Hardys' area code and home number. After depositing the amount of money requested by the operator, he was put through.

Aunt Gertrude's voice came on the line. "Hardy residence," she said crisply.

"This is Frank, Aunt Gertrude. We're still in New York."

"Well, make it brief. These long-distance calls cost money!"

"You're telling me." Frank grinned as he looked at his depleted stock of coins. "We just wanted to find out if anything has come up while we were gone."

"Yes. You had a call from Sam Radley. It sounded important. He wants you boys to phone him right away!"

CHAPTER X

Mole Mystery

"OKAY, Aunt Gertrude, I'll ring Sam as soon as I hang up." Frank hesitated uneasily before adding, "No word yet from Dad, I suppose?"

"No, indeed—we've heard nothing so far." Miss Hardy's voice reflected her own anxiety. Then she reverted to her usual tart tone, like a top sergeant bracing up recruits. "But I don't want you boys to worry about him. Do you understand? Just mind your own p's and q's, especially in a city as big as New York. The streets are dangerous these days, from all I hear. As for Fenton, he can take care of himself!"

"Thanks, Aunty, we'll bear that in mind," Frank said, comforted in spite of himself by her brisk, no-nonsense manner. "Tell Mother we'll be home soon. 'Bye now."

He replaced the receiver in its cradle and shook his head in response to Joe's questioning glance.

"She says they haven't heard from Dad. But we're to call Sam Radley, which means I'd better get some more coins."

After breaking a bill at a drugstore news counter, just off the lobby, Frank returned to the phone with his brother and rang his father's long-time operative.

"Hi, Sam. This is Frank," he said when the detective answered. "Aunt Gertrude gave us your message. Got something for us?"

"Sure have," Radley replied. "I've traced Quinn's ex-partner, Basil Embrow."

"Nice going. What's the scoop?"

"He's now running a business called Embrow Exports in Manhattan. I figured you two might want to check him out while you were there."

"Right. We'll do that. What's the address?"

The operative read it over the phone and Frank copied it down. "Thanks a lot, Sam," he said and hung up.

"Lower Manhattan," Joe noted, glancing at what Frank had written. "We can take the subway."

Leaving the building, the boys were thrilled to see the two baby blimps directly overhead. The minicraft were just about to settle into their berths on the penthouse deck, high atop the skyscraper.

"Boy, I can hardly wait to ride in one of those things," Joe said eagerly.

"Right. They're tubby little cigars, but they do look like fun."

The Hardys took a subway train downtown. Embrow Exports occupied a tenth-floor suite of offices in a dingy area, but the firm looked busy and prosperous.

"I'm not sure Mr. Embrow can see you," a receptionist told the boys. "Have you an appointment?"

"No, but give him this, please," Frank said. He wrote something on a slip of paper and handed it to the young woman, who excused herself and took the message to her employer.

Joe shot his brother a quizzical glance. "What did you write?" he asked in a low voice.

"Just 'Quinn Air Fleet.' Let's see if it works."

Apparently it did. The receptionist soon returned and said that Mr. Embrow would see them.

The businessman wore a puzzled frown as the boys were ushered into his office. "What's this supposed to mean?" he asked, flicking his fingernail at the paper.

"Nothing in particular. It's the only thing I could think of that might get us an interview," Frank replied.

Embrow, a balding, raw-boned man, responded with a smile to Frank's boyish grin. "Fair enough. At least you're honest. Sit down and tell me what I can do for you. Am I mistaken in thinking you two are the sons of that famous detective?"

"No, sir, you guessed right," Joe replied. "Fenton Hardy's our father. In fact that's why we're here. We're helping him on one of his cases."

"Indeed? What sort of case?"

"It has to do with those dirigible explosions yesterday morning," Frank replied.

Embrow sighed, nodded, and settled back in his chair. "I see. I thought there might be some connection." He rolled a pencil back and forth between his palms for a moment and frowned. "Well, what would you like to know? Do I take it I'm under suspicion?"

"Why should you think that?" Frank inquired.

"Look! Let's not play games. I'm sure you've found out by this time that I used to be Lloyd Quinn's partner and that we broke up after a quarrel. Why else would you be here?"

"Naturally we have to check out every angle," Frank said.

"Sure, I understand that. But if you think I had anything to do with those explosions, you're barking up the wrong tree."

"Any comment you'd care to make about the case, Mr. Embrow?"

"Just one. No. Make that two. First, I hope you Hardys catch whoever's responsible. And second, I wish Lloyd Quinn nothing but good luck." Embrow grinned at the boys' wary expressions and added, "Does that surprise you?"

Joe grinned back. "Well, it's not exactly the sort of attitude we were led to expect."

"I can imagine. Lloyd and I are both hot-tempered guys. We went at it hammer and tongs before we busted up. But that's water over the dam. I've got too much going for me right here to waste any time harboring grudges."

"How did you two meet?" Joe asked curiously.

"We served in the Navy together," Embrow replied. "In blimps, on Atlantic-patrol duty. That's what got us interested in dirigibles. We both made up our minds that someday we'd go into the field commercially."

"Do you regret leaving?"

"Frankly, sometimes I do. It's an exciting field with a great future. On the other hand, my export business has been highly successful, and I must say, I don't envy Lloyd any of his present head-aches."

Joe nodded at a framed desk photograph that Embrow had been toying with as he spoke. It showed a youth in an academic cap and gown. "Is that your son?"

"Yup, it's his high-school graduation picture." Basil Embrow smiled proudly. "Quite a lad if I do say so, though I don't see much of him these days." He moved the photograph aside with a brisk back-to-business gesture and said, "Well, is there anything else I can tell you fellows?"

"No, sir. You've answered all our questions," Frank replied, rising. "We appreciate your frank-ness."

"And thanks for your time," Joe added.

The boys shook hands with Embrow and left. Outside the building, they headed back to the subway entrance, a couple of blocks away.

"What do you think?" Joe asked his brother.

Frank shrugged. "Hard to say, but he seems a decent enough guy."

"I agree. He's not my idea of a sneaky saboteur."

"By the way, why did you ask him about that high-school picture?"

Joe's eyes twinkled. "Don't tell me you didn't spot it?"

"Spot what?"

"That mole next to the boy's left eye."

Frank stopped short with a gasp. "Now I get it! Just like that Quinn air crewman you photographed who was giving us the once-over!"

"Check. I snapped a shot of Embrow's desk photo, too, with my pocket camera."

"Good work!"

As soon as the boys arrived in Bayport, Joe developed his roll of film. Then he enlarged the picture of the youth in the desk photo and compared it with his shot of the air crewman.

"Hmm. The mole's in the same place," Frank mused, "and their faces are similar, but I'd hate to bet they're the same person."

"Ditto," Joe agreed. "Besides, there's at least five or six years' difference in ages, and neither one of these blowups is ideal for identification purposes. Also, the name stenciled on the crewman's coveralls isn't Embrow. It's H. Maris."

"Which could be phony," Frank pointed out. "He'd hardly apply for a job under his own name if there were enmity between his father and Quinn, especially if he were planning to sabotage the *Safari Queen.*"

"True, but it's not that easy to get the kind of fake ID he'd need, like a social-security number and maybe a birth certificate and so on. Unless— wait a minute!" Joe snapped his fingers. "Do you suppose there might have been someone else filling in yesterday, doing some temporary maintenance work, and wearing Maris's coveralls?"

"Let's find out." Frank picked up the phone, dialed the Quinn Air Fleet number, and was soon talking to Lloyd Quinn himself. But the air-fleet owner said no temporary help was ever employed, partly for security reasons and partly because of the high degree of specialized training needed for dirigible work.

"I had a call this morning from that pipeline company," Quinn added glumly. "The one my next airship was supposed to haul supplies for. Needless to say, they heard about the midair explosions yesterday, and the way they're talking now, they may cancel our contract, just as I feared."

"At least it hasn't happened yet," Frank said,

refusing to be discouraged. "We'll do our best to crack the case before it does happen."

He hung up without mentioning his family's fears for his father's safety.

Meanwhile, Joe was studying the computer printout data on the crew.

"Look. It says here Maris attended Ardvor College," he remarked after listening to Frank's report. "Why don't we drop over there tomorrow and see what we can find out about the guy?"

"Good idea."

Just then the phone rang. Frank picked up the handset and answered. His face burst into a happy smile as he heard the voice at the other end of the line.

"Dad! We've been worried about you. Are you all right?"

"Yes, son. I'm calling from Cleveland. Sorry I had to end our last conversation so abruptly."

"What happened, Dad?" Joe put in. He had realized that Frank was speaking to their father and now he eagerly crowded close to the receiver.

"I discovered I was being watched," Mr. Hardy replied.

"By whom?"

"A known terrorist. At least that's who he looked like. I was calling on an airport phone. When he saw I'd spotted him, he snatched a traveler's bag and hurled it at me, and then got away in the confusion."

"You think the guy's a member of the Scorpio gang?"

"It's possible. The odd thing is, he was reported to have fled this country over a year ago. He's a Hindu named Jemal Raman, and at that time I was investigating him for acts of terrorism against his own government's embassies over here."

Fenton Hardy explained that he had gathered enough evidence against Raman so that the U. S. Immigration Service was preparing to deport him. But before a hearing could be held, the Hindu escaped aboard a freighter, evidently fearing arrest.

After listening to the boys' report of their own activities, the detective advised them to keep an eye out for Raman. "He could be vengeful and dangerous. Better check him out in my files."

"Will do, Dad," Frank promised. After hanging up, he got Jemal Raman's dossier from the crime file in his father's office so he and Joe could study its contents. These included three long-range telephotos, snapped without the subject's awareness. They showed Raman to be dark-skinned, with a drooping mustache.

"Do you suppose this could be the snoop we spotted at our boathouse this morning?" Frank asked, with a glance at his brother.

"Sure looks like him." Joe was startled as he examined the photos closely. "Jumping catfish!

Notice how his mustache curves down on each side of his mouth?"

"What about it?"

"With a black chin-beard, this guy might even fit Pop Carter's description of that elephant trainer, Kassim Bey!"

Before Frank could reply, a scream rang through the house!

CHAPTER XI

The Knobby-Nosed Peddler

"THAT's mother!" Frank cried.

Joe dropped the photos and both boys dashed into the kitchen. They found their mother backing away from a huge scorpion!

The horrid-looking creature, now poised on the kitchen counter, was brown and hairy and about six inches long. Mrs. Hardy, pale, stared at it with a shocked expression, holding one hand over her mouth. In her other hand she held a widemouthed plastic container.

"Out of the way! I'll swat the nasty thing!" exclaimed Aunt Gertrude as she burst in from the dining room. Brandishing a fly swatter, she advanced on the scorpion with lethal intent.

"No. Don't kill it!" Frank protested. "It's an interesting specimen."

"Interesting, my hat!" sniffed Aunt Gertrude. "That creature may be deadly!"

"I'm not so sure. Where did it come from?"

"Out of here," Mrs. Hardy replied in a shaky voice, holding up the plastic container.

Frank and Joe examined the label, which bore the name *Vinegareen*. But no manufacturer's name or address was shown.

Joe glanced at his mother, puzzled. "Where'd you get this, Mom? At the supermarket?"

"Certainly not!" Aunt Gertrude cut in, in a scandalized voice. "I got it this morning from a door-to-door peddler."

"Some phony!" said Joe angrily. "What did he tell you?"

"That he was handing out free samples of a new food product. Said it was highly condensed, and mixed with water, it would give a particularly rich, flavorful form of vinegar."

The spinster paused to examine the plastic container. "Hmph. Empty, is it?"

"It is now," Frank said drily.

"I might have known there was something wrong with such an offer. I thought at the time the fellow looked suspicious. 'That man's got a criminal type of face,' I said to myself. 'He'll come to no good end!' "

Miss Hardy seemed as annoyed about being cheated out of the expected free sample as she was about the sinister trick that had been played.

The boys smothered grins, then Frank turned anxiously back to their mother. "It didn't sting you, did it?"

"No, but it frightened me out of my wits."

"I don't blame you. That thing really looks scary."

With a shudder, Mrs. Hardy went on, "When I opened the container, it crawled out on my hand! I had to shake it off in the sink."

"It's a wonder it didn't sting you," Joe said.

"From what I read in the encyclopedia," Frank said, "I've a hunch this is a whip scorpion called a vinegaroon, a kind that's found in the southwestern United States and Mexico. It's called that because it emits a vinegary odor when aroused, just as this one's doing. Many people think they're highly venomous, but the scientists who study scorpions say they are not."

Aunt Gertrude described the peddler as a knobby-nosed man with sideburns, wearing a yellow knit sport shirt and checked summer slacks.

"Neat description," Frank said approvingly. "You make a good witness, Aunty." He added with a slight frown, "Funny thing is, the guy sounds familiar, somehow."

Unfortunately, with no photographs of the Scorpio gang to go on, there was no way to identify the man as a member.

The boys managed to corral the scorpion back into the plastic container and delivered it to the home of Thomas "Cap" Bailey, their science teacher and track coach at Bayport High, with whom they had once searched for fossils out West in a place called Wildcat Swamp. Cap verified Frank's guess that the creature was a vinegaroon.

"It'll make a great specimen for our science collection," he added. "Thanks, boys."

"Too bad we didn't see those guys who ambushed us in the park yesterday," Joe remarked as they drove home.

"Or those creeps on Rocky Isle last night," Frank said. "Then we might know for sure whether Aunt Gertrude's phony peddler was one of the gang."

"I'll bet anything he was," Joe declared.

"Likewise. But definite evidence would be better. Which reminds me, Joe, speaking of the park, we still haven't checked out those two guys Pop Carter mentioned."

"You mean the ones who've been trying to buy him out?"

"Yes."

"Let's call them as soon as we get home," Joe suggested.

After phoning, the boys made an appointment for an interview the following morning with Clyde Bohm at his real-estate office. The animal park magnate, Arthur Bixby, agreed to see them Thursday.

After dinner that evening, the Hardys decided to find out whether or not there was anything in Joe's notion that the mustached terrorist, Jemal Raman, might actually be the fired elephant trainer, Kassim Bey, who was believed to be dead.

"I know it sounds far out," Joe admitted, "but there must be some connection between these two cases we're working on—the Scorpio gang causing the dirigible explosions and Pop's trouble at Wild World. Take that pair who ambushed us in the woods. They warned us to keep out of the *Safari Queen* mystery, but the ambush happened at the park."

"Check. And that's also where the hollow-tree code message was planted, along with the first scorpion," Frank added. "And don't forget the gang member who was hiding out on Rocky Isle. He was reading up on elephants!"

"Right. Plus the fact that those green-light signals being flashed toward Rocky Isle came from the Ferris wheel at Wild World."

"I agree, Joe, there must be some connection; otherwise we're up against too many coincidences. It won't hurt to check out your hunch with Pop Carter."

As they drove down Elm Street, away from their house, Frank, who was at the wheel, suddenly muttered, "Oh-oh!"

"What's the matter?" Joe asked.

"That parked car we just passed back there on the left. The guy in it had a mustache like Raman's!"

"Jumping catfish! You mean he's got our house staked out?"

"Could be. He's not just sitting there for his health. But I didn't want to slow down for a closer look. It might put him on guard, and then he'd take off before the police got here."

"Circle around the next block," Joe proposed, "and come back on the same side he's parked on."

"I intend to," Frank said. "You give him a good once-over as we go by."

Much to the boys' frustration, the car was gone by the time they returned.

"He must have realized you spotted him," Joe grumbled.

When the Hardys arrived at Wild World, they were surprised to see Tony Prito and Phil Cohen on duty near the gate in the green-jacketed uniform of park attendants.

"What are you fellows doing here?" Frank asked.

"Three guesses." Phil grinned.

"We all got calls this morning," Tony said.

"What do you mean, 'we all?'" Joe inquired.

"Chet, Biff, Phil, and I, all four of us."

"Chet and Biff are here, too?" Joe asked, gazing around.

Phil shook his head. "Not now. They work in the afternoon, while Tony and I have the evening shift. We each put in four hours a day."

"Nice going. Congratulations!" Frank said.

"What about you?" Tony asked. "What brings you here? Just out for fun?"

"Nope."

"I didn't think so. What cooks?"

Frank took out the photographs of Jemal Raman and explained Joe's idea. "Even if Joe's wrong, the guy might turn up in Bayport. In fact, he may be here already, so watch out for him. Dad spotted him in St. Louis and thinks there's an outside chance he may be working with the Scorpio gang."

"We'll keep our eyes peeled," Phil promised.

Pop Carter was glad to see the Hardy boys, but after glancing at Raman's picture, he shook his head. "No. This fellow looks nothing at all like Kassim Bey."

The elderly park owner sighed and fingered his thinning white hair. "Anyhow, I'm sure Kassim's dead."

Nevertheless, he thanked Frank and Joe for their efforts and was glad to hear that they would be checking on Clyde Bohm and Arthur Bixby.

Next morning the boys went to keep their appointment at Bohm's real-estate office. Joe backed the car out of the garage and started down the drive. But as he was turning into the street, Frank suddenly exclaimed, "Hey, hold it!"

"What's the matter?"

"Look at those white marks on the front door!"

Joe frowned. "Somebody scribbled something in chalk." He stopped at the curb, and both boys hurried up the porch steps to inspect the strange marks.

"These aren't just scribbles," Frank declared. "It looks to me like some kind of Oriental script. This must mean something!"

"True." Joe nodded. "And something tells me the meaning's not pleasant!"

CHAPTER XII

Green Shadow

FRANK had the same foreboding as his brother about the strange inscription chalked on the door. "Who do you suppose wrote it?" he wondered aloud.

"That's easy," Joe said. "It's got to be that mustached guy you spotted in the parked car last night."

"I think so, too, which makes me more certain he must've been Raman. He could have sneaked back here after we left for Wild World."

"Right. It was dark when we got home, and we went in the back door after you pulled into the garage, so we wouldn't have noticed."

"Maybe we can find some professor at Ardvor College who can translate it for us," the older Hardy boy suggested.

"Smart thinking, Frank. Here—I've got some paper. Let's copy it down."

It was nine fifteen when they arrived at the

downtown offices of the real-estate firm of which Clyde Bohm was the local manager. He eyed them suspiciously as they were shown into his office, and, without rising, gestured curtly for the boys to sit down.

"What is it you want to see me about?"

Frank decided blunt frankness was the best policy. "About the Wild World animal park," he said in a clear, firm voice.

His words seemed to take Bohm by surprise. The manager snuffled nervously and retorted, "What about it?"

"We'd like to know why you've tried so hard to buy Mr. Carter out."

"What business is that of yours?" Bohm demanded, blinking and squinting rapidly through his steel-rimmed glasses.

"Mr. Carter's been having certain troubles at Wild World," Frank replied. "We're investigating them for him, and we're trying to get an overall picture of the situation. You seem to be part of the picture."

Bohm fiddled with his glasses and squinted at the boys more suspiciously than ever. "Exactly what is that remark supposed to mean?"

"You've tried desperately to buy Wild World. Do you mind telling us why?"

"Certainly not. I've made no secret of that. My company believes that land could be more profitably developed into an industrial site, or perhaps a shopping plaza."

Bohm suddenly rose to his feet and sniffed again. "You'll have to excuse me a moment," he said and went abruptly out the door.

The Hardys looked at each other. Joe rolled his eyes, and, pointing to his head, twirled his forefinger rapidly. Frank grinned.

Presently Clyde Bohm returned, still squinting and snuffling. He made no move to sit down, as if to make it clear to the boys that the interview was over. "Now then, I'm a busy man," he said. "If you've nothing more important to talk about, I'm afraid I have other things to do."

"Just one more question, Mr. Bohm," Frank persisted. He was determined to apply more pressure in the hope of extracting a possible clue from Bohm's reaction. "Can you suggest any reason why someone might harass Pop Carter and try to drive him out of business?"

"I've no idea," snapped the real-estate man. "But you'd better not make any such charges against *this* company, if that's what you're implying, or you may find yourself facing legal action!"

Frank rose from his chair calmly. "Mr. Carter may also have to consider taking legal action, if the harassment continues," he said, leaving Bohm gaping open-mouthed at the Hardy boys as they walked out of his office.

Outside, Joe chuckled. "You really took the wind out of his sails with that last crack, Frank!"

"I hope so. He strikes me as a first-class creep!"

"What do we do next?"

"See what we can find out about Bohm and his real-estate company."

The boys got into their car and Frank drove several blocks through the business section to the Bayport Bank and Trust Company, where Fenton Hardy kept his professional accounts. In the lobby, he asked to speak to Henry Dollinger, the vice-president, who knew all the Hardys.

"Howdy, boys." Mr. Dollinger, a shrewd-eyed man with a gold watch chain across a slight paunch, greeted the brothers with a friendly smile and handshakes in his office a few moments later. "Can I help you?"

"Hope so, sir," Frank said. "We're working on a case that involves a tract of land outside of town. We've just been talking to a real-estate man named Clyde Bohm. Is that name familiar to you?"

Mr. Dollinger nodded. "Bohm, eh? Yes, I know him."

"Can you tell us anything about him? Is he an honest, reputable businessman?"

The banker pursed his lips and frowned thoughtfully. "Well, let's say I've never heard anything against him. But suppose I check with our credit department."

Lifting the phone, he dialed a number and carried on a low-voiced conversation for several minutes. Finally he hung up and turned to the Hardy boys again. "The real-estate company

Bohm works for is a fairly large firm. He simply manages their local office, which was opened recently. From all reports, it's a profitable, well-run business with no black marks on its record."

"What about Mr. Bohm himself?" Joe inquired.

"That's a little harder to say," the banker replied. "He came to Bayport a month or two ago to take charge of the company's new office here, so we have nothing on him before that. However, he does have a private account at our bank. So far none of his checks have bounced, and he hasn't run up any bad debts that we know of."

The last words were spoken with a slight waving gesture and an offhand smile.

Frank grinned back. "Thanks a lot, sir. We appreciate what you've told us."

As they drove off, Joe remarked, "Bohm may be a creep, but apparently he operates inside the law."

"So far, anyhow," Frank agreed, "or at least so far as the bank knows. But that doesn't clear him completely. It doesn't prove he didn't have some kind of sneaky part in causing Pop Carter's troubles, like the stink bomb or the phony rumors about the park animals being rabid."

"You mean, trying to ruin attendance at Wild World so Pop would have to sell out?"

"Right."

Joe nodded thoughtfully and scratched his

head. "I guess it's a mistake to judge a person's character from the way he acts the first time you see him, but Bohm sure *looks* the part. I wouldn't put it past him. What's next on the schedule?"

"How about running out to Ardvor College?"

"Suits me." Joe noticed his brother watching the rearview mirror. "Anything wrong?" he asked.

"Don't look now," Frank said, "but I think we've got a tail."

"Since when?"

"A green sedan with a radio antenna on its right front fender was behind us all the way from the real-estate company to the bank. Now it's following us again."

"I'd say that's no coincidence."

"So would I."

Frank pulled to the curb sharply and braked to a stop. As the green sedan went by, the boys caught a fleeting glimpse of a driver with a crew cut.

Frank hastily started up, turned into an alley, emerged onto a residential block, then zigzagged through several side streets. When he finally headed for Ardvor College via a different route, there was no further sign of their shadow.

"Looks as if you've shaken him," Joe said, with a glance out the back window.

"For the time being, anyhow."

Ardvor College was located in a nearby town. The Hardys drove to the administration building in the midst of a pleasant, tree-shaded campus. A secretary told the boys the dean was busy, but would see them in a few minutes.

While they were waiting, Frank slipped out to the corridor on a sudden impulse and called Sam Radley from a phone booth.

"What can I do for you?" the operative responded good-naturedly when he heard who was calling.

"Does the name Clyde Bohm ring any bells?" Frank asked.

"Not offhand," Sam replied. "Who is he?"

"A real-estate man who keeps pressuring the owner of Wild World to sell out. A middle-sized guy with glasses. Very ordinary-looking, except that he has this nervous tic—he keeps snuffling and squinting at you when you talk to him."

"Wait a minute," Radley said in a slow, thoughtful voice. "That tic does ring a bell."

"Somebody in a case you and Dad have worked on?"

"No. I doubt if you'd find him in Fenton's crime files. But I recall some crook with a snuffling, squinting tic who was wanted a few years back on an out-of-state fugitive warrant. Let me check with the FBI and get back to you later."

"Thanks, Sam. I'd appreciate it."

When Frank returned to the office, the boys were told that the dean would see them. He was a tall, distinguished-looking man with a thick mop of silvering hair and a brisk, friendly manner. The Hardys had consulted him more than once before.

"Another mystery?" he asked with a twinkle in his eyes as they shook hands.

"You've guessed it, sir," said Frank. "It has something to do with those dirigible explosions Monday morning. One of the crew is named Maris, Hector Maris, and according to the personnel records, he went to Ardvor College. We wondered if you could tell us anything about him."

"Maris, hmm." The dean frowned briefly. "Oh, yes, Hector Maris. I recall him now. Very nice young chap. Graduated a year ago. He's not under suspicion of anything, I hope?"

"Not exactly," Joe said. "In fact we're wondering if there may be a mixup in identities."

"I see. Well, the Hector Maris who attended Ardvor got very good marks as I recall. He was a pre-med student. Also on the swim team."

"A pre-med student?" Frank echoed and exchanged a puzzled glance with Joe. "Why would a pre-med student apply for a job on a dirigible crew?"

"Good question," said the dean, pinching his upper lip thoughtfully. "Maybe he couldn't raise the money to continue his education. Or perhaps he wasn't accepted at any medical school. There's intense competition among applicants, you know. But let me just check our files."

The dean pressed a switch on his intercom and spoke to his secretary. A few moments later, she brought in a folder bearing the name Hector Maris.

"Now then, let's see what we have on him," said the dean, opening the folder. "Ah, perhaps this picture of him would help to clear up any confusion. All students here at Ardvor are required to include a photo with their entrance application."

Frank and Joe were startled as they looked at the form the dean handed them. The young man shown in the attached photo was blond and stocky. But the Hector Maris Joe had photographed aboard the *Safari Queen* was *dark and slender!*

Frank scanned the application data hastily before handing the form back to the dean. "Thanks, sir. You've cleared up one question, at least. This isn't the fellow we're investigating."

"He's the only Hector Maris who attended Ardvor," the dean reported after having his secretary double-check the files.

Frank nodded. "Which means either someone's goofed in the Quinn Air Fleet personnel department, or somebody's trying to pull a fast one."

"There's one other thing you might be able to help us on, sir," Joe put in, handing the dean the piece of paper on which he had copied the inscription chalked on the Hardys' front door. "We think this may be some kind of Oriental script."

The dean studied the odd markings. "Yes, I agree."

"Could someone please translate it for us?"

"Hm. Yes. I think our professor of Oriental studies may be able to help." Picking up the phone, the dean arranged for the boys to meet Professor Meister, who proved to be an elderly, pipe-smoking man with bushy eyebrows. He needed only a brief look at the markings to translate them.

"These are three words in Hindi, a language spoken in India and written in the Devanagari script. *Hoshiar! Bura kismet!*"

"What do those words mean, sir?" Frank asked.

"I suppose you could call it a warning. They stand for *Beware! Bad luck!*" The professor brushed some ashes off his vest and flashed the Hardys a quizzical look. "Where did you run across them?"

"On our front door," Joe replied with a wry smile.

As the boys were driving away from the college, Frank said, "I guess this practically proves that our unknown caller was Jemal Raman. He's a Hindu."

"Could be," said Joe. "But the language might also apply to that elephant trainer, Kassim Bey. That is, assuming Pop Carter's mistaken and Bey is still alive."

"Pop said Kassim Bey was a Pakistani."

"Sure, but Pakistan used to be part of India, and the two countries are right next to each other. It wouldn't be surprising if he could read and write Hindi."

"Guess you're right," Frank conceded, scratching his head. "But if Pop Carter says Kassim's dead, let's leave him that way unless we find out otherwise. Jemal Raman's a big enough headache!"

When they reached their house, the Hardys decided to phone the airship crewman who called himself Hector Maris and give him a chance to explain why the photograph on his college application differed so drastically from his appearance.

"Of course it's still possible there are two Hector Marises," Joe mused.

Frank shook his head. "No chance. I took a good look at the data on his college application. It matched the Quinn Air Fleet personnel data all the way."

After dialing the air-fleet terminal, Frank was told that Maris had not reported for work that day. Nor had he answered the telephone.

"Looks as if we're up against another blank wall," Frank remarked. His hand was still on the receiver when the phone rang. He answered, "Hardy residence."

"Frank?" said a voice at the other end of the

line. "This is Leroy Mitchell, the park attendant at Wild World. I met you and your brother on Monday when you went through lion country."

"Hi, Leroy," Frank said, recalling the black youth instantly. "Good hearing from you. What's new?"

"I understand you Hardys are looking for a man with a mustache."

"How did you know?"

"Your friend Phil Cohen told Chet Morton, and Chet told me when I was talking with him at the hot-dog stand."

"Well, it's true," Frank confirmed. "Have you seen the guy?"

"No, but I have something else that may interest you," Leroy reported. "Did you notice the two dudes in the car just behind you, when the elephant started kicking up all that fuss?"

"Yes, two wise guys in sport shirts, munching popcorn."

"Right, they're the ones. I came to see what was going on just as the guard pulled your car out of line and took you to see Pop Carter. They were laughing and carrying on like it was all a big joke."

"It probably was, to a couple of loudmouths like them," Frank said wryly. "Why? What about them?"

"Well, I saw those two even before that," Leroy said. "They were in one of the cars that pulled up to watch when you stopped to check out that hollow tree. And that's not all."

"What else?"

"Those same fellows drove through the animal park again today, and they sure don't look like nature lovers! I felt they were up to no good. When my partner relieved me at the gate booth," Leroy continued, "I went to tell Chet. Believe it or not, I spotted them again. They were skulking among some bushes, snapping a picture of Chet!"

CHAPTER XIII

The Sea-Faring Stranger

FRANK was alarmed. He at once thought of the snapshot of himself and Joe that they had found tucked between the pages of the elephant book in the cave on Rocky Isle.

If a gang member had photographed the Hardys unaware so the others would recognize them and harass them, maybe they were now planning to annoy the boys' friends.

"Are the two guys still in the park?" Frank asked.

"Yes. Chet's keeping an eye on them." Leroy explained that their chum had been temporarily assigned to clean up candy wrappers, soda bottles, and other litter, which gave him the opportunity to keep the suspects in view at all times.

The black youth added that he himself would be working for the rest of the afternoon in the amusement park area, and that he would look for the Hardys near the salt-water-taffy booth.

"Good! We'll be right over. And thanks for calling, Leroy!"

Frank filled Joe in on the phone conversation, then the brothers hopped into their car and headed for Wild World. On the way, Joe said, "If Leroy's hunch is right, those two guys could be the ones who jumped us in the woods!"

"Just what I'm thinking," Frank agreed. "And later they followed us to see if we got the message in the hollow tree."

But a bitter disappointment was in store for them. When the Hardys reached the park and went to the amusement area, they found Chet waiting, long-faced, with Leroy.

"What's the matter?" Joe asked.

"I lost them," the plump youth reported.

"How come?"

It turned out that Chet's help had been enlisted by a frantic mother trying to find her lost child. By the time the little boy had been located, watching the roller coaster and smearing his face with a huge tuft of pink cotton candy on a stick, the suspects had disappeared.

"Never mind, Chet," Frank said. "At least you lost track of them for a good cause."

"That's what *you* think," Chet retorted glumly. "When I tried to take the kid's arm and lead him back to his mother, the little brat kicked me in the shins."

The Hardys could not help laughing at the sour expression on their pal's moon face. But Leroy shook his head, obviously much disappointed that his first detective effort had misfired.

"It's a tough break," he grumbled. "I'm sure there was something fishy about those guys. They seemed to be a couple of hoods, you know, completely different from the people who normally drive through the animal park. Most of our customers are families with children or high school students with their friends. But these two were toughies. They looked like they couldn't care less about wild animals. Yet they not only showed up on Monday, when you fellows were here, they came back two days later for another visit!"

"Don't worry, you don't have to convince us, Leroy," Frank told him. "I'm sure your hunch is right. The fact that they were snapping Chet's picture practically proves they're part of the gang we're after."

"And I'm sure glad you tipped us off," Joe added. "This opens a whole new angle on the case."

Leroy brightened under their appreciation. So did Chet.

"What did these men look like?" Frank asked. "Getting a full description of them could be a real break."

"Well, one was wearing a denim jacket and jeans," Chet said. "He was dark haired with a big underslung jaw and a dimple in his chin."

Frank nodded. "That jibes with what I remember from those glimpses in the rearview mirror when we were watching the elephants."

"And the other one," Leroy added, "was wearing a turtleneck shirt and black-and-white checked pants. He had long sideburns and a big bumpy nose with a bulge on the end of it."

The same thought clicked in both Hardy boys' minds. Joe snapped his fingers. "The peddler who gave Aunt Gertrude that Vinegareen container!"

"Check," Frank nodded. "No wonder her description of him rang a bell!"

Chet and Leroy were astounded to hear how the vinegaroon scorpion had been slipped into the Hardy household.

Before either could comment, a voice called out, "Hey, Frank! Joe!"

The boys turned around and saw Biff Hooper hurrying toward them in his green park-attendant's uniform.

"What's up, Biff?" Frank asked.

"Pop Carter wants to see you."

"What about?"

Biff shrugged uncertainly. "Search me, but it must be important. He seemed worried. He just said, 'Try to find the Hardy boys, Biff, as quick as you can. They must be somewhere in the park.' "

"How would he know that?" Joe wondered.

"The quickest way to find out is to ask him," Frank said logically.

The Hardys hurried toward Pop Carter's bungalow. They found the white-mustached park owner in his office.

"Biff said you wanted to see us, sir," Frank greeted him.

"That's right, boys. I had a mighty strange telephone call just a few minutes ago."

"From whom, Mr. Carter?" Joe inquired.

"Wouldn't give any name, but it must be someone at Wild World because he knew you were in the park. Said he'd just seen you himself, near the rides."

"What did he want?" Frank asked.

"Wanted me to get a message to you, but not to call out your names over the public-address system. He was very insistent about that."

"And what was the message?"

"He wants you lads to meet him—alone—in that little clearing between the boat pond and the animal fence. Said you're to look for an old man with a cap, that he's got some important news for you."

"Thanks, Mr. Carter!" Joe exclaimed. "Let's go, Frank!"

"Hold it, fellows!" the park owner blurted. His usually cheerful face appeared agitated. "I'm not so sure you should go there, at least not alone."

"Why not, sir?"

"How do we know it's safe? Something mighty funny's going on around here, and there may be a criminal angle to it. I wonder if I did right, unloading my troubles on you. Maybe some enemy of mine's trying to get back at me and give the park a bad name by hurting you boys."

"I doubt it, sir," Frank replied, a little more confidently than he felt. "If your caller were planning something underhanded, surely he wouldn't advertise it in advance, or try to do it right in the center of the park."

Pop Carter paced back and forth, worried. "At least take a guard along with you!"

"That might spoil everything," Joe argued. "You said yourself he wants us to come alone. If he really does have information for us and spots a guard, he may be scared off."

After a hasty discussion, it was agreed that a guard would keep a distant watch on the boat pond. The Hardys would pass there en route to the meeting spot, and if they did not return within fifteen minutes, he would raise an alarm and the park gates would be closed.

Frank and Joe hurried off to keep the rendezvous. The clearing was well screened by trees and other vegetation. There was no one in sight. The boys seated themselves on a lone bench and waited.

Presently the bushes parted and an old man hobbled out. He was stooped and wore the battered white cap of a ship's officer, with the visor pulled low over his forehead. His clothes looked shabby, and, instead of a shirt, he had on a seaman's jersey under his blue jacket. His face, stubbled with a grayish growth of beard, was twisted into a permanent scowl by a long scar down one cheek.

The fellow glared at the boys intently as he came toward them, looking around suspiciously. Frank and Joe felt a twinge of uneasiness.

"So you weren't afraid to meet me, eh?" the stranger cackled. Then his voice became twenty years younger as he added, "I'm glad you came, sons!"

"Dad!" both boys exclaimed in astonishment.

"Excuse the disguise," Fenton Hardy said with a chuckle, "but I didn't want to take a chance on the Scorpio gang finding out I was anywhere near Bayport." He shook hands warmly with Frank and Joe, and added, "From what you've told me, I figured you might turn up at Wild World, and luckily you did. I spotted you as you came into the park."

The boys exchanged detailed reports with their father, bringing him up to date on their activities.

"You really think the Scorpio gang's in the Bayport area?" Frank asked.

"I'm sure of it," Mr. Hardy declared, "especially after what you two have just told me. I'd better go now, sons, but I'll keep in touch. You carry on as you've been doing, but be cautious at all times. And take care of your mother and Aunt Gertrude."

"We will, Dad," Frank and Joe promised.

Frank and Joe felt a twinge of uneasiness.

On their way out of the park, they passed Chet and Leroy again.

"Everything okay?" Leroy inquired, searching their faces.

"Sure is," Frank assured him with a grin.

"Listen," Chet said, "We were talking to Biff, and we decided to have a picnic here tomorrow evening. Biff and Leroy will bring their girl friends, and you two can ask Iola and Callie."

"Great idea," Joe said.

"How about Phil and Tony?" Frank asked.

"They'll just be coming on duty," Leroy said, "but I'm sure they can eat with us."

"I'll talk to them," Chet promised. "Another thing. How about coming out to the farm later on this afternoon, when I get off work? I have something terrific to show you."

"Okay," the Hardys agreed.

Driving home, Frank suddenly muttered, "Oh, oh!"

"What's the matter?" Joe asked.

"That green sedan's on our tail again!"

"Are you sure?"

"Definitely. Same driver, same radio antenna." As he spoke, Frank suddenly slammed on the brakes in the middle of the street.

"What are you doing?" Joe exclaimed.

"Having a showdown with this guy!" Frank leaped out of the car and started toward the green sedan behind them.

But its driver evidently panicked at the sight of the boy's determined face. He backed up, U-turned illegally, and sped off with a roar of exhaust.

"Take the wheel and pull over," Frank instructed his brother hastily as horns began to honk.

"Did you get his license?"

"I sure did. I'm going in that drugstore to call Chief Collig."

Phoning police headquarters, Frank quickly checked out their shadow's license via computer hookup with the State Motor Vehicle Bureau. Then he looked up the owner's name and address in the phone directory and dialed his number. A woman's voice answered. Frank asked to speak to the owner.

"I'm sorry, he's not here," she said. "Who's calling, please?"

Frank deliberately slurred his own name in replying and asked, "Can I reach him in Bohm's office?"

"Certainly," the woman said. "He doesn't get out of work until five."

CHAPTER XIV

The Yelping Lion

JOE saw the triumphant look on his brother's face as Frank returned to the car. "Any luck?" he asked.

"You bet!" Frank grinned. "It was Clyde Bohm who sicked that guy on us." He explained how he had found out.

"Nice going," Joe said. "We might've known it was Bohm. The shadowing started right after we left his office."

"Sure. Not only that, but remember how he excused himself for a few minutes? He probably went to tell the guy to wait in his car and follow us."

"What are we going to do about it?"

"Wait'll we hear from Sam Radley," Frank replied. "Then we'll put pressure on Bohm."

Later that afternoon, the Hardy boys drove to the Morton farm as Chet had requested. Mrs.

Morton told them with a smile that their pal was out in the barn. Chet was not alone. Iola and Biff Hooper were with him, and so was Biff's huge Great Dane, Tivoli. Iola wore a pretty blue-and-white terry-cloth beach jacket, and Chet's barrel-chested figure was encased in a red bathrobe. He was tying what looked like a black string mop, or several of them, to Tivoli's head, while Biff clutched the Great Dane's collar.

The Hardys eyed the scene with mystified grins.

"Mind telling us what you're doing to that poor pooch?" Frank inquired.

"This is no pooch," Chet retorted. "He's Simba the lion, king of the jungle, and this black wig will be his mane."

"I thought *you* were the king of the jungle," said Joe.

"No. I'm Jungle Man. Get down, you idiot!" Chet blurted as the huge dog reared up on its hind legs and began lapping his face. Standing erect, Tivoli was taller than the boy.

"That critter's really gotten enormous," Frank remarked in awe.

"Right. He'll probably make a pretty good lion at that!" Biff chuckled proudly.

"What do you feed him?"

"Better ask what we *don't* feed him. He'll eat anything he can wrap his jaws around, possibly including Chet!"

"Listen! Jungle Man can handle *any* kind of

wild beast!" the plump performer boasted as he finished tying the black mop under Tivoli's chin.

"What have you got in mind, Chet?" Joe asked.

"Stick around and you'll see."

Joe turned to Jungle Man's sister. "Are you part of the act, too?"

Iola giggled, looking a bit embarrassed. "Chet talked me into it. I owe him five dollars, but he promised to cancel the debt if I'd be his assistant."

"Sounds like blackmail to me," Joe cracked.

"Go ahead and make fun, wise guy," Chet said confidently. "I'll bet we get offers from television once our act premiers, and maybe even from Hollywood!"

"You mean they'll offer you money to keep the act out of sight?"

"Very funny!"

"On second thought," Joe corrected himself with a glance at Iola, "at least part of the act will be worth looking at." She blushed.

Chet sniffed and turned to her with a dignified air. "Just ignore the remarks from the peanut gallery. Let's get ready for costume rehearsal!"

He flung off his robe and Iola did likewise. She was wearing a bikini swimsuit, but despite her attractive costume, the boys couldn't help goggling at Chet. His beefy figure was revealed by a suit of fake leopard-skin tights that strapped over one shoulder.

"Sufferin' snakes! Where'd you get that?" Joe exclaimed.

"I made it for him on Mom's sewing machine," Iola confessed, giggling again.

"You'll bring down the house!" Frank told Chet.

"Think they'll like it?" Chet asked eagerly, preening himself proudly before an imaginary audience of thousands.

"That's not quite what I meant."

"I get it. You've no confidence in the act." Chet snorted. "Well, this didn't just happen overnight. I've been working on the show for weeks. I got the idea long before Pop Carter hired us at Wild World, and it's been developing ever since."

"Maybe you should have squashed it when it first hatched," Biff said with a wink to the others.

With another disdainful sniff, the leopard-skinned boy led the way out of the barn and into the wooded grove at the rear. Long ropes were dangling from several trees. Chet grabbed one, and with remarkable agility, swung himself up onto a high branch.

Despite their teasing a few moments earlier, his school chums broke into spontaneous applause.

"Not bad, Jungle Man!" Joe called out.

Chet sketched a pleased professional bow, teetering precariously on the branch as he did so. "Okay, white princess and Simba!" he shouted down. "This is your cue! Go get her, Simba!"

Biff let go of Tivoli's collar, but the huge Great Dane merely stood there, panting and gazing around contentedly.

"What's he supposed to do?" Frank inquired.

"Leap at Iola with fangs bared," Biff explained, trying to keep a straight face. "Then Chet will swing down to her rescue and grapple with the ferocious man-eating lion."

After several encouraging slaps of the flank, Tivoli finally ambled toward Iola, tongue lolling and tail wagging amiably.

"Trying to keep that mop out of his eyes," Frank deduced.

"Go on! Snarl at her, you dumb cluck!" Chet berated the dog from his tree branch. "Act ferocious!"

"Gr-r-r!" Iola growled, trying to get Tivoli to imitate her. Instead, he licked her hand.

"Oh, never mind!" Chet fumed in disgust.

At that moment, Tivoli suddenly reared up on his hind legs and began to slobber kisses on Iola's face.

"Hey, that's great! Hold it!" Chet yelled.

"Well, hurry up!" Iola cried frantically, covering her face with her hands in a vain effort to protect it from Tivoli's moplike tongue.

"Here I come!"

With a jungle bellow, Chet swung down from his perch. As he did, his leopard-skin snagged on a projecting branch, threatening to strip him down to his underwear!

Desperately Chet let go of the rope with one hand and tried to hold his costume in place. But his hefty weight was too much to support. Losing his grip, he slid down the rope and, with a plop, landed heavily astride the Great Dane, who bounded off into the underbrush, yelping loudly!

Jungle Man wound up sprawling among the dead leaves on the ground, with his costume half off.

His audience staggered around and leaned against nearby trees, rocking with laughter.

Chet got up sheepishly, brushing himself and examining his torn clothes. "I guess the act needs a little more work," he conceded, then burst out laughing, unable to control his own mirth.

Joe flung an arm around his plump pal. "What a sense of humor! Chet, you're wonderful!"

The Hardys escorted their pal into his house, then left for home. When they arrived, the telephone rang. The caller was Sam Radley.

"I just heard from the FBI," he reported. "Clyde Bohm's got a record, all right."

"No kidding!" Frank exclaimed. "What for?"

"Fraud and embezzlement. He served two years behind bars in Kansas and got out a couple of months ago. But the Bureau's got nothing on any of the foreign passengers who flew in Monday on the *Safari Queen.*"

"What you just told me about Bohm is news enough," Frank said with an eager smile. "And that's not all, by the way."

He informed the operative about the car that

had shadowed them that afternoon and how he had discovered that their shadow was one of Bohm's employees.

"Good work, Frank," Sam Radley congratulated him. "Are you going to confront Bohm with all this?"

"You bet! I think Joe and I will drop around to his place tonight. Want to come along?"

"Wouldn't miss it for the world!" Sam chuckled.

After dinner that evening, he accompanied the Hardy boys to Clyde Bohm's home, which they found by consulting the latest phone directory. It proved to be a rented flat on the north edge of town.

The real-estate man was at first indignant that the Hardys should bother him after hours. "What right have you got to come snooping around here at this time of evening?" he ranted, snuffling and squinting at his three visitors. "I'll report this to the police!"

"You do that," Frank said calmly. "And while you're at it, maybe you'd better tell them how you've been employing *this* fellow lately." He held out a piece of paper bearing the name, address, and license-plate number of their shadow, which he had obtained from the police that afternoon. Bohm turned pale as he read the information.

"Maybe they'll also be interested in your record

as a con artist and embezzler," Sam Radley added.

Gulping and stammering, Bohm stepped back from the door. "M-M-Maybe you'd better come inside."

Wringing his hands after they had entered and sat down, the real-estate man went on, "My reputation could be ruined here in Bayport if all this comes out. Remember, I'm new on this job, gentlemen. Surely you won't find it necessary to make the information public?"

"That depends on how well you cooperate," Frank said.

"I'll tell you anything you want to know," Bohm whined. "Anything at all!" He then revealed that he had been ordered to buy out Pop Carter's interest in Wild World, using available means.

"Did that include harassing him with stink bombs and nasty rumors?"

"No, no! Nothing like that!" Bohm assured them.

"Where did your orders come from?" said Frank.

Bohm claimed they had been passed down by some unnamed official higher up in the holding company that owned his real-estate firm. "We're just a subsidiary!" he stressed.

After the trio left, Sam Radley promised to trace the owners of the holding company. "But it may not be easy," he added. "The financial structure of corporations can get complicated these days. Often holding companies are used to mask the real owners of a business."

The operative was amazed to hear about the Hardy boys' investigation of the dirigible crewman, Hector Maris. "If he turns out to be the son of Quinn's ex-partner, he may be the saboteur behind the *Safari Queen* explosions," Sam conjectured, "trying to avenge his father's breakup with Quinn."

"That's the angle we're working on," Frank said.

After dropping Sam Radley at his house, the Hardys drove to their own home on Elm Street. As they turned up the drive, Aunt Gertrude suddenly appeared in the glare of their headlights. Waving a broom, she appeared to be in a state of high excitement.

"Help me!" she cried. "I've caught the culprit!"

CHAPTER XV

Aunt Gertrude's Prisoner

FRANK slammed on the brakes, and both boys leaped out of the car.

"What culprit, Aunt Gertrude?" Joe demanded.

"Over there!" she replied, jabbing the air with her broom in the direction of the back porch. "He may be the head of that Scorpio gang Fenton's after! Or at least the rascal who chalked those marks on our front door!"

Joe had snatched a flashlight from the car's glove compartment, and aimed it in the direction in which Miss Hardy was pointing.

A man was slumped on the back-porch steps, clutching his head in both hands. He looked up groggily. The Hardy boys gasped as they recognized his mustached face.

"It's Jemal Raman!" Frank exclaimed.

The man shook his head. "No. I'm not."

"Tell us another story," Joe scoffed. "How'd you catch him, Aunt Gertrude?"

Miss Hardy explained that she had been home alone and had noticed a suspicious-looking mustached stranger lurking on the corner when she went out to the drugstore to buy some indigestion pills.

"When I came back, he was no longer in sight," she went on, "but I remembered what you had told me about that terrorist Fenton had mentioned, so I decided not to take any chances."

"Smart thinking, Aunty," Frank approved.

After scouting the front of the house, she had circled around through a neighbor's yard and had glimpsed a dark form huddled outside one of the Hardys' rear basement windows.

"I retreated to the front porch," Aunt Gertrude related, "and armed myself with a broom I had left out this morning. Then I tiptoed around the house and attacked the intruder. I whacked him good and proper!"

"Aunt Gertrude, that's the bravest thing I've heard in a long time," Frank declared, hugging her.

"You said it!" Joe chimed in, planting a kiss on her cheek.

"Hmph! Well, anyhow," she continued, trying to maintain her poise, "I was just about to go in and call the police when you boys drove up."

"We'll attend to him," Frank said.

After herding their prisoner inside and frisking him, the boys made him sit down on a kitchen chair while Joe checked the contents of his wallet. To their surprise, the man's ID showed his name as Gopal Raman.

"I'm Jemal's brother," he confessed. "I've been a student in your country for three years."

Gopal explained that he had happened to see Fenton Hardy at the St. Louis airport and had recognized him from news photos. This gave him the idea of coming to Bayport during the detective's absence and trying to break into his office.

"What for?" Frank asked.

"I wanted to find out exactly what evidence he had gathered against my brother. You see, Jemal wants to apply for re-entry into the United States on a student visa. So I thought if I could find out what your father has against him, it would help him prepare his case."

"And what was the idea of trying to break into our boathouse?" Joe prodded.

"I learned you two had a boat while talking to some fan of yours on the plane flying into Bayport." Gopal Raman said he had hoped to find something useful in the boathouse, perhaps even a spare set of keys to the Hardy home, which would enable him to slip in easil· when everyone was out or during the night.

His spying and the chalk mark on the door were intended to unnerve the family. "That way, if I *were* spotted breaking in," Gopal confessed glumly, "I hoped to scare the women into letting me go without a struggle."

"Boy, you sure didn't count on our broom-toting aunt!" Joe chuckled.

The prisoner was so depressed and woebegone, the Hardy boys hardly had the heart to turn him over to the police. They both felt that Gopal Raman had proved himself a rather bumbling, inept villain.

"P-please don't hand me over to the authorities," he quavered. "I shall be totally disgraced and disowned by my father if I am kicked out of this country and sent home without completing my education!"

Joe scratched his head and glanced at Frank. "What should we do with him?"

Frank turned to their aunt. "He's your prisoner, Aunt Gertrude. What do you think? Should we give him another chance?"

Gopal's large dark eyes fastened hopefully on Miss Hardy. He placed his palms together in the praying *namaste* gesture of India. "P-p-please, Madame!"

"Hmph!" Miss Hardy frowned and fussed uncomfortably. Despite her tart, forbidding manner, she was soft-hearted. "Use your own best judgment, Frank," she decided.

"Okay. Joe, take his driver's license, his car registration, his passport, and any other I.D. he's carrying."

Joe nodded. "Right—I've got them."

Frank turned to the prisoner. "Where are you staying here in Bayport?"

"At the Regent Hotel."

"Our father should be home in a day or two. If you'll promise not to leave town, and to remain in your hotel room until he's able to interview you, we'll let you go for now."

"Oh, I shall! I shall!" Gopal Raman promised fervently, sounding as if he were on the verge of tears.

"Okay, then beat it!"

As the Hindu disappeared into the darkness, Frank shut the door behind him and headed for the hall phone.

"What are you going to do?" Joe inquired as his brother consulted the telephone directory.

"Call his hotel and make sure he doesn't pull any fast ones." Frank dialed the Regent Hotel's number and spoke to the manager. After explaining the situation, he asked the man if he would notify the Hardys at once if Gopal tried to check out.

"You can depend on it!" the manager promised.

Next morning the Hardy boys left home early to keep their appointment with Arthur Bixby, the second party who had tried repeatedly to buy Wild World. The animal-park magnate had opened a temporary office in Bayport while he conducted negotiations.

Bixby was a stout, jolly man, built along much the same lines as Chet Morton. Throughout most of the interview, a king-sized cigar tilted upward from one corner of his mouth, filling the office with wreaths of blue smoke.

"So you two are the Hardy boys, eh?" he said, rocking back in his desk chair. "Heard lots about you, but I never expected you to come calling on me!" He chuckled and slapped his thigh to emphasize his surprise. "What can I do for you, lads?"

"Not to beat around the bush," said Frank, "we'd like to know why you're bidding so hard for Wild World."

"Because it's a good investment. Why else?" Bixby boomed.

"If you're so eager to own an animal park around here," Joe probed, "why didn't you open one yourself?"

"I intended to, but old man Carter beat me to it. I may still have to, if he won't sell out. That's why I've opened this office, so I can scout the area and pick out a good location."

"You don't really think this area would support *two* separate animal parks?" Frank challenged.

Bixby chuckled, but his eyes remained cold. "You're a smart young feller, me lad! No, between the two of us, I don't think so. That's why I've been trying to buy Wild World."

Joe said, "Do you believe it's fair to pressure

Pop Carter into selling out after he's worked so hard to get the park started and invested all his life savings in it?"

"Business is business, son. Besides, I'm offering Pop a good price. I'd even be willing to let him stay on and run the park. After all, I'm a showman. So's he. A good one. We'd get along!"

"Wouldn't be quite the same for Pop, though, would it," Frank pointed out, "working as a hired hand for someone else, compared to running his own show?"

Bixby unclamped long enough to wave his cigar through the air. "Ah, what's the difference? I treat all my employees right. They *love* working for Arthur Bixby. Talk to them if you don't believe me."

"May I ask you a blunt question?" Frank said.

"Shoot!"

"Do you want Wild World badly enough to resort to dirty tricks to crowd Pop into selling out?"

"Dirty tricks?" the stout impresario cocked a perplexed eyebrow at the Hardys.

"Like having someone toss a stink bomb in the park on a hot, busy day," said Joe, "or spreading scare stories about the animals' being rabid."

"I've never resorted to such tactics in my life, and I don't intend to begin now!" Bixby thundered, thumping his fist on the desk. A moment later, his little blue eyes twinkled and his double-chinned face burst into a sly smile. "On the other hand, I play to win!"

Frank glanced at Joe, who shrugged and smiled faintly.

"Thank you, sir," Frank said, rising. "No need to take up any more of your time. I guess we've learned all we're likely to."

"Oh, no, you haven't, son! If you're smart, you'll go on learning all your life, just as I try to do. And just to make sure you don't forget old Arthur Bixby, let me present you each with a little memento of this cherished meeting!"

Bouncing up from his chair, he extracted two small plastic animals from a box on his desk and handed them to the boys—a giraffe to Joe, and an elephant to Frank.

"What are these?" Frank asked, slightly mystified.

"Read what's on them, son!"

Both boys examined their presents carefully and discovered the words, *Souvenir of Arthur Bixby, Animal Parks, Inc.* stamped into the plastic base.

Bixby roared with laughter as he ushered them out the door.

"Quite a character!" Joe remarked drily as the Hardys drove off in their car.

"Don't let him fool you," Frank said. "Under that jolly mask, he may be as hard-boiled and ruthless as they come."

At home, Frank made another call to "Hector Maris" at the Quinn Air Terminal. Once again he was told that Maris had not reported for work.

"Where's he gone?" Frank pressed.

"Don't ask me," the crew chief rasped over the phone, "but if I don't hear from him in the next twenty-four hours, he's going to be out of a job!"

Frank shook his head at Joe as he hung up. "Still missing."

"What do you make of it?" Joe asked.

The older Hardy boy shrugged uneasily and plowed his fingers through his dark hair. "I don't know, but if Maris doesn't show up by tomorrow, maybe we should notify the police." After an early lunch, the boys sped to the Bayport airfield for the blimp ride Eustace Jarman had promised them. Both were eager to try out one of his mini-aircraft.

Apparently the baby blimp had touched down shortly before they arrived. Jarman was proudly holding forth about the craft to a crowd of admiring onlookers. To the Hardys' amazement, its gas envelope had shrunk to less than half its normal size as compared to the gondola cabin, which rested on well-sprung landing gear.

"How come it's deflated?" Joe asked.

"Come aboard, boys, and I'll show you," the industrialist replied.

Once they were seated inside the luxurious cabin, Jarman explained that the helium gas had been compressed and pumped into a storage cylinder. This decreased the lift and enabled the blimp to land.

"For takeoff, we do just the opposite, valve the gas back into the cigar-shaped envelope and let it expand again."

Frank and Joe were excited at the spectacular view as the baby blimp rose into the air, then cruised over Bayport and along the coast. Below, on the blue-green waters of the Atlantic, they saw pleasure boats and commercial ships as well as a warship steaming out to sea.

The Hardys were even more thrilled when Jarman let them try their hands at the simple controls. At the magnate's suggestion, Frank steered the craft inland again. When they approached Wild World, he cruised lower, so they could glimpse the spectators and the herds of animals.

"Hey! What's that?" Joe exclaimed suddenly.

"What's what?" his brother inquired.

"That sign!" Joe said, pointing downward. "It's painted on the ground, right outside the fence!"

Frank gasped as he saw the odd, bright-orange marking. "That's the astrological symbol for Scorpio!"

CHAPTER XVI

The Scorpio Symbol

"WHAT? Let me see!" blurted Eustace Jarman, craning.

Frank gestured toward the spot below. The symbol had been splashed so boldly and brightly that it was clearly visible from the air. It looked like a lower-case *m* with the tail of the letter curved sharply to the right and capped with an arrowhead.

"You say that's the symbol of Scorpio?" Jarman demanded, turning back to Frank with a frown.

"Yes, sir. It's one of the signs of the zodiac."

"And you think this may have something to do with the Scorpio gang of terrorists?" The tycoon's glance flicked sharply back and forth between the Hardy boys.

Frank nodded. "There's no doubt about it."

"That's the Wild World animal park down there, Mr. Jarman," Joe added. "We've already had half a dozen other clues connecting the gang with the park. That symbol's got to be more than a coincidence!"

"Then let's descend and take a closer look!" Jarman said with an air of tense excitement. "Perhaps you'd better let me handle the landing, son."

The remark was directed to Frank, who promptly surrendered the controls. Jarman took over and deftly brought the baby blimp to a gentle, well-cushioned landing just outside the park fence.

He and the Hardys leaped out of the cabin, one by one, and hurried to inspect the strange mark. The symbol was made up of lines almost a foot wide, in brilliant orange phosphorescent paint that looked as if it had been slapped on with a whitewash brush over the grass, stones, and bare earth.

"Wow! I'll bet this could be seen from the air even at night!" Joe exclaimed.

"You're right," Frank agreed, rubbing his jaw thoughtfully. "The question is, what does it mean?"

"Any ideas?" said Jarman, watching the boys hopefully.

"Not really." Frank frowned. "Unless that arrowhead on the tail of the symbol is supposed to be pointing at something."

"Hmm, let's see." Jarman turned in the direction indicated by the arrowhead, then emitted an excited whoop. "By George, you're right! Look over there—under that tree!"

The boys hurried after the tycoon as he strode

toward the tree. Screened from aerial view by the overhanging tree branches was another mark on a bare patch of ground. This one, a wiggly, jagged line that was only about the width of a man's finger, was in white paint and was much smaller than the Scorpio symbol.

"This one is surely no zodiac symbol," Eustace Jarman mused as he studied the white line.

"Definitely not," Frank agreed. "But don't ask me what it is."

"Beats me, too," Joe admitted, after copying it on a piece of paper. "It doesn't look like writing, and it's not a picture of anything, either, at least not that *I* can recognize."

His brother was equally baffled. Jarman glanced at his watch—once again the hard-driving, tightly scheduled businessman. "Maybe an idea will occur to you later. Meantime, I'm afraid I have to get back to New York, but I'll drop you at the airport first."

The Hardys were silent and thoughtful on the way back to the Bayport airfield, each racking his brain for a solution to the odd mystery of the painted markings. Nevertheless, both enjoyed the brief flight.

"These baby blimps are really nice!" Joe said effusively. "They're a lot more fun to ride than a regular airplane."

"And safer," Jarman boasted.

"What do you call this model, sir?" Frank inquired. "Got a name for it?"

The industrialist smiled proudly. "I have, indeed, the Jarman *Hopscotch*. It's delightful for short hops, and very tight on fuel costs."

Both boys nodded politely.

"Eventually," Jarman went on, "I plan to develop this into a road car, so that it can be driven as well as flown, and even have an amphibian hull. It'll then be a true all-purpose vehicle."

"And how!" Joe said admiringly.

"With living facilities like a present-day camper, it would be ideal for family vacations."

"Let us know when it hits the market." Frank grinned. "We'll order the first one off the production line!"

After landing, the Hardys thanked their host and watched him take off again. Then they headed for their car in the parking lot.

They had just paid their fee and were turning onto the airport exit road when a buzzer sounded and the light flashed on their dashboard radio. The caller was Miss Hardy.

"What's the good word, Aunt Gertrude?" Frank asked.

"I don't know how good it is," her tart voice crackled over the speaker, "but you and Frank just had a call from someone named Hector Maris."

"The dirigible crewman!" Joe exclaimed with an excited glance at his brother.

"So he told me," Aunt Gertrude said.

"What did he want, Aunty?"

"He wants to drop in this evening at eight thirty for what he calls a *confidential talk* with you two."

"Great!" said Joe. "If he calls back again before we get home, you tell him we're eager to see him!"

Sometime after five o'clock, the Hardys picked up Frank's date for the picnic. She was Callie Shaw, a pretty blond girl with brown eyes. Then they drove to the Morton farm to get Iola.

"Hi, everyone!" Chet's sister smiled as she climbed into the car with a large basket over her arm.

"Did you bring enough to feed Chet?" Joe asked.

"I brought enough to feed *everyone!*" Iola giggled.

"We'll really have a feast, then," Callie said gaily. "I have a hamperful of sandwiches and cookies, and the boys brought some of Aunt Gertrude's fried chicken and a chocolate cake."

"Think we'll be able to stagger home?" said Frank.

"We may have to," Joe wisecracked, "if none of us can squeeze in behind the wheel."

It was not yet six when they pulled into the parking lot at Wild World. They soon found Chet, Biff, and Leroy in the picnic area of the park. The boys, who were now off duty, had shucked their green jackets and cleaned off one of the tables. They were bringing armloads of soda bottles and a plastic tub full of ice cubes to keep their drinks cold.

Biff's date, Karen Hunt, and a pretty brown-skinned girl who proved to be Leroy's girl friend, Elgine Brooks, were laying out place mats. Then they set the table with items from their own picnic baskets.

"Hey, look who's coming!" Joe exclaimed as they sat down and began eating.

Phil Cohen grinned as he walked up to the table in his park attendant's uniform. "Got a handout for a hungry man? Tony'll be along later."

"Help yourself, pardner," said Frank with a wave of his hand. "We've got enough here to feed an army!"

"Just a drumstick will do. And how about one of those pickles?"

"Anything your little heart desires," said Biff, passing the pickle bottle.

Silence fell for the next minute or two. Suddenly they were all startled by a loud whistling beep that seemed to come from Frank.

"Jumpin' Jupiter!" Chet exclaimed. "Don't tell me you're carrying a portable burglar alarm?"

"Not that I know of," Frank replied. He was as puzzled as everyone else. Hastily he groped in his pockets and pulled out the toy elephant Bixby had given him.

The sound was coming from the small plastic animal!

"Where did you get that, Frank?" Callie inquired, intrigued.

"From a guy named Arthur Bixby, who's trying to buy Wild World. Joe and I saw him this morning. But don't ask me what *this* is all about!"

"He gave me a toy giraffe, but I left it in the car," said Joe. "I wonder if it's beeping, too?"

A look of dawning comprehension passed over Elgine's face. "Wait a second!" she murmured. "I've been to one of Bixby's parks near Washington, D. C. Those animals are sold as souvenirs. He calls them *Bixby's Beasts*."

"But why the beep?" put in Leroy.

"There's a sound device inside," Elgine explained. "I guess it responds to a radio signal— you know, like one of those pocket-phone alarms that doctors carry to let them know a patient's trying to get in touch."

"Funny thing to put in a toy animal."

"Not when you hear why. It's an advertising stunt. The people who buy the souvenirs are supposed to keep them handy, where they can hear them, and two or three times a week, the park broadcasts a signal that makes the animals sound off."

"Then what?" Iola asked.

"When you hear it, you're supposed to call right away, and the first ten people who phone in get free tickets to the park, including all rides."

"Hey, that's quite a gimmick!" Joe said.

"But Bixby has no park around here," Frank

pointed out thoughtfully, "so what made *this* elephant sound off?"

The loud whistling beep, which had attracted the attention of other picnickers also, had now ceased. It was followed by several shorter beeps.

The Hardys wondered if the signals had anything to do with the Scorpio gang.

"Maybe we ought to call Bixby and find out!" Joe suggested.

Frank nodded and they hurried to a public telephone. After trying Bixby's office number and getting his answering service, they were finally able to reach him at his apartment hotel.

"Yep, you guessed it, son!" The man chuckled when asked about the beeping. "I got me a portable transmitter and broadcast those signals so you'd see what a live-wire showman I am. Take it from me, I can double the attendance at Wild World. You tell Pop Carter that."

Frank made a polite rejoinder and hung up with a glance at Joe, who had listened in.

"What a gimmick!" Joe chuckled wryly.

Back at the picnic table, they found Chet eagerly explaining a brand-new idea, which sounded as if it might nudge his Jungle Man act into second place. "Animal balloons!" he exclaimed to the Hardys. "If I could get a concession at Wild World from Pop, I could make a fortune!"

"Wait a minute!" Frank said slowly. "I think you've got something there."

"Sure, I could design them myself and get a balloon company to—"

"No, I mean you've given *me* an idea! Joe. I'll bet I know how that dirigible saboteur pulled his falling-elephant trick. You know those big animal-balloon floats that are used in some parades?"

Joe's eyes lit up. "You've got it! He dropped a rolled-up balloon, and it was inflated in the air, by a CO_2 cartridge!"

"Maybe we should ask Sam Radley to check out specialty-balloon manufacturers," Frank said.

"Good idea," Joe said. "I'll bet it will lead us straight to the crooks."

Leroy snapped his fingers. "Hey! Talking of crooks, that reminds me." He reported that he had seen one of the two suspects at the park again that afternoon. Although unable to trail the man immediately, he had observed him drop a crumpled piece of paper, which Leroy later picked up.

The Hardys examined it eagerly, then passed it around. It bore the name Sandy P.

"Who's Sandy P.?" Iola inquired with a puzzled frown. "One of their pals?"

"Maybe and maybe not," said Joe, who seemed quietly excited. "I've got an idea about this, Frank. We'll check it out later."

When they finished eating, the Hardy boys went to lock the picnic baskets in their trunk. As they neared the parking lot, Frank's eyes widened. *A man was crawling under their car!*

CHAPTER XVII

A Saboteur Surfaces

THE stranger held a wrench in one hand! Frank cried out, startled. Evidently the man heard him. He glanced at the approaching boys with fear in his eyes, then sprang to his feet and darted off through the trees bordering the parking lot!

The Hardys chased him, but soon lost him in the gathering dusk.

"That creep!" Joe fumed. "I never even got a good look at his face. Did you?"

Frank shook his head grimly. "But he saw *us,* all right. We were just passing under a lamp when I spotted him."

"Trying to sabotage our car, no doubt."

"Sure, he was probably going to tamper with the steering or the brakes. Maybe we'd better check and make sure he didn't have time to do anything."

Their car doors were still locked, and after carefully examining the undercarriage, the boys were relieved to find no sign of damage.

"Think our would-be saboteur was one of the Scorpio gang?" Joe asked his brother.

"Could be, but the time angle's interesting," Frank mused.

"What do you mean?"

"That elephant beep went off, so we called Bixby. And you remember I mentioned to him that I was calling from the park. How long ago would you say that was?"

Joe shrugged. "Twenty minutes, half an hour, as long as it took us to go back to the picnic table and finish eating."

"Also, just long enough for Bixby to send a man here to Wild World and find our car on the lot."

Joe whistled. "You think that's what happened?"

Frank frowned and shook his head uncertainly. "Not really. Bixby strikes me as a guy who gets fun out of showing off with publicity stunts and outwitting his competitors in business deals. Resorting to force or out-and-out crookedness doesn't fit, somehow. But we have to consider all the angles."

"Well, I think *I've* got an angle on that Sandy P. note," Joe declared.

"You figured out what it means?"

"I have a hunch it stands for Sandy Point, but

that's not all." Joe unlocked the car and got a large-scale map of the Bayport area out of the glove compartment.

"You mean that spot on the coast called Sandy Point?" Frank asked as Joe spread out the map.

"Right—and look here." Joe reached in his pocket and produced the paper on which he had copied the odd white markings they had found near the orange Scorpio symbol outside the park fence.

The wiggly, jagged line exactly matched the coastline around Sandy Point!

Frank was excited. He clapped his brother on the back. "Joe, that's terrific! You solved it!"

"But we still don't know how Sandy Point figures in the gang's plans."

"No, but we're going to find out. Let's take the *Sleuth* and investigate after we call Sam and talk to Maris."

"Suits me," Joe agreed, "but that's quite a run. Maris isn't due at our place til 8:30. Considering the time back and forth, we wouldn't get home before midnight."

"All the better! The darkness will give us good cover while we look around."

Frank and Joe locked the baskets in the trunk and helped the others clean up their picnic table. Then they called Sam Radley from a public telephone, asking him to check out balloon and novelty manufacturers.

Later the boys and their dates enjoyed the rides. The free passes Pop Carter had given them would be good throughout the summer. The group had so much fun that Frank and Joe were sorry to leave the park before closing time.

After dropping off Iola, Chet, and Callie, the Hardys returned home to await their visitor. Shortly before eight thirty the doorbell rang. Joe answered and admitted Hector Maris.

The young dirigible crewman, clad in chinos and a zippered jacket, was clearly nervous. He ran his fingers through his dark hair and sat down awkwardly in the chair Frank offered.

"I suppose you know why I'm here," he began.

"Why not tell us?" Frank replied. "Including why you're going under the name of 'Hector Maris.' "

Their caller gave a guilty start. "I figured you were on to me. Well, you're right. I got my job under a false name. The real Hector Maris is a good friend of mine, who's attending medical school in Europe."

Frank nodded. "And your real name is— Embrow?"

The young man gulped, his eyes opening even wider. "Yes, I'm Terry Embrow—though I can't imagine how you found out. My father, as you probably know, used to be Lloyd Quinn's partner, but they had a fight and broke up."

"So why do you work for Quinn?" Joe asked.

"Believe it or not, I'm an ardent lighter-than-air buff. I got that from my father, I suppose. He used to fly blimps for the Navy and always wished he could have flown in the *Hindenburg*. When Mr. Quinn started hiring a crew for the *Safari Queen*, it seemed like the chance of a lifetime. But I knew perfectly well he'd never take me on if he recognized me as Basil Embrow's son. So Hec Maris agreed to let me use his name while he was out of the country."

Frank said, "Did anyone else know about this arrangement?"

"Nobody," Terry replied. "Not even my Dad. He thinks I'm working for a trucking company. That's what made the call so mysterious."

"What call?"

"Sorry, I'm getting ahead of my story," the young crewman apologized. "Just before we took off for Africa on our last trip, I got an anonymous phone call. Whoever it was, somehow he'd found out my real identity!"

"What did the caller want?"

"He threatened to expose me to Mr. Quinn and tell him who I really am, unless I agreed to—to do those things that happened Monday morning," Terry ended lamely.

"Better spell it all out," Frank advised.

"Well, he—he wanted me to loosen the muffling, so it would sound as if the *Queen* was having engine trouble, and then drop two items from the gondola as we sailed over Bayport."

"What two items?"

"A smoke grenade and a tightly packed balloon in the shape of an elephant. The balloon was designed to inflate automatically in the air after it was released. Obviously it contained a small grenade or destruct charge in it, but he didn't tell me that beforehand."

Joe gave Terry a scornful look. "Is that supposed to be an excuse?"

"No, of course not." Terry Embrow shifted uncomfortably in his chair. "I realized what bad publicity all this might cause for the Quinn airship fleet, and I didn't want that. I'm as eager as Mr. Quinn to see dirigibles come back. On the other hand, I had to weigh those bad effects against losing my job. I was sure he'd fire me once he found out I lied on my application and was really his ex-partner's son."

"So you went along?"

Terry nodded guiltily. "I had to—at least that's what I told myself."

"How did your anonymous caller get the grenade and the balloon to you?"

"They were dropped outside my apartment door the night before we took off. I found them the next morning. But whew! I was sweating icicles all during the flight to Africa and back, for fear I'd be caught. Then when I saw Mr. Quinn showing you around Monday afternoon, I figured the jig was up."

Joe said, "You knew who we were?"

"Sure. I heard him introducing you to the crew chief. And I remember seeing your pictures in the paper a couple of times in connection with mysteries you've solved."

"Where have you been since then?" Frank inquired.

Terry rubbed his hand over his forehead. "I panicked. I was sure you suspected me, but I had no idea how much you knew. Then I began to wonder whether I should give myself up. So I decided to think things over. I knew of an old cabin in the Ramapo Mountains where Hec and I used to go sometimes. That's where I've been staying for the last couple of days—until this morning."

"And now what?" Joe pressed.

Terry Embrow shrugged and swallowed hard. "I decided to talk to you and make a clean breast of everything."

There was an awkward silence. Then Frank said, "If you're hoping we'll intercede for you with Mr. Quinn, you're out of luck. We don't have any special influence with him, at least not as far as crew-hiring goes."

"I'm not asking you to do that. I'm not asking for anything," Terry retorted proudly. "I came here to tell you the truth, and that's what I've done. If you want to turn me over to the police or report me to Quinn, that's up to you."

After drawing Joe aside for a brief consultation,

Frank returned to the young crewman and said, "We're not going to do anything yet, Terry, until we've cleared up this whole mystery. In the meantime you're free to do as you like about telling Quinn."

Terry Embrow heaved a deep sigh and rose to his feet. "Fair enough. And thanks for listening, both of you." He shook hands with the boys and left.

The Hardys immediately drove to their boathouse. Soon they were chugging across Barmet Bay in their sleek motorboat, the *Sleuth*. They talked little, each occupied with his own thoughts about the case.

Finally Joe remarked, "You think Terry was telling the truth?"

Frank gave a thoughtful nod. "Yes, I don't believe he'd be a good enough liar to fake such a story. Besides, why would he?"

"But how did the gang find out his real identity?"

"That wasn't hard. They probably checked out the whole crew, looking for a weak link. Once they started probing the background of 'Hector Maris,' they realized what was up."

"Guess you're right," said Joe. "And they took advantage of it. Well, at least we've solved part of the dirigible mystery."

"But we haven't helped Dad capture the Scorpio gang yet," Frank pointed out wryly.

"Or unraveled the animal-park mystery, either," Joe added.

Moonlight silvered the Atlantic rollers as the boys emerged from the bay and rounded southward down the coast. At Sandy Point, they beached the *Sleuth* quietly and began to reconnoiter the area. Frank pointed to an old weather-beaten cabin, visible among the pines. Its windows were partly boarded up or patched with cardboard, but a light gleamed from inside.

"That shack could be the gang's hideout," Frank murmured in a low voice.

"And someone's there!" Joe said tensely.

They approached cautiously. A beaten path led up to the cabin through the trees.

"Wait!" Frank hissed suddenly. "We'd be smarter to close in from two directions. That'll give us a better chance to see what's going on inside."

They tossed a coin. It landed heads, which meant that Joe would approach from the front, while Frank would come through the trees on the left. They agreed on flashlight signals, then separated.

Step by step, Joe moved closer, pausing from time to time to listen for sounds from within. He almost held his breath as he covered the last few yards. Suddenly a cry of alarm escaped his throat as he felt the ground giving way beneath him. Next instant he was plunging down into darkness!

The boys beached the Sleuth *quietly.*

CHAPTER XVIII

A Fast Fadeout

FRANK heard his brother's scream, and, glancing around in the moonlight, saw Joe being swallowed up by the earth.

"A covered pitfall!" he realized.

But there was no time to pull Joe out. When the trap was sprung, a buzzer sounded inside the cabin. An instant later a man rushed out, clutching a poker.

"Got ya now, you punk!" he gloated.

Apparently he intended either to finish Joe off or take him prisoner. Frank did not wait to find out which. He had picked up a hunk of wood that he had stumbled over earlier, and now dashed through the brush to his brother's rescue.

The man from the cabin was just raising his poker to strike. Frank hit him over the head from behind, and the man's legs buckled!

But he buffered the impact of his fall with his hands as he went down on all fours. Levering himself upright, the now-disarmed poker-wielder swung around and knocked the driftwood out of Frank's hand. Then he launched himself with a bull-like rush and butted Frank in the stomach!

This time Frank went down. Swinging his legs upright, he stopped his opponent's rush with two well-placed shoe soles in the solar plexus. As the man staggered back, gasping, Frank surged to his feet and belted him in the jaw.

By then Joe had managed to claw his way out of the deep pit. Without bothering to raise himself from his sprawling position, Joe grabbed his enemy's left ankle, yanked his foot off the ground, and upended him!

The man landed flat on his back, cursing. Before he could struggle up again, the Hardy boys were looming over him menacingly. Joe was now clutching the poker and Frank the hunk of driftwood.

"One wrong move, mister," Frank said coldly, "and you'll be spitting out a mouthful of teeth."

"Hey!" Joe exclaimed. "This must be the knobby-nosed man that Aunt Gertrude described."

"Right. And also one of the guys who braced us in the woods. I can tell by his voice," Frank added. Then he looked at their prisoner. "Roll over on your chest and hold your hands together in back of you."

"Try and make me!"

"You want a broken nose?"

The man obeyed. Frank and Joe ripped some tangled vines from the underbrush and bound his wrists.

"You can get up now," Frank ordered. "Then walk ahead of us into the cabin."

The shack contained a potbellied stove, two bunks, a rickety table and chairs, and a shelf of canned goods. The only light came from a burning candle jammed into the mouth of an empty bottle. A few magazines and paperback novels were scattered about.

"You want to talk to us," Frank asked with an edge to his voice, "or the police?"

"Talk about what?" the prisoner sneered. "You got nothing on me. All I did was dig a trap to protect myself against prowlers like you. No law against that!"

Frank realized there was a measure of truth in the man's bluster. Without having seen their ambushers' faces, Joe and he could not prove that this fellow was one of the men who had waylaid them in the woods.

The knobby-nosed crook seemed to sense Frank's frustration and chuckled nastily. "You goofed all the way tonight. While you're here at Sandy Point, wasting time on me, you'll be missin' the real show near Bayport!"

"What kind of show?" Joe challenged.

"Wouldn't you like to know, sonny boy! All I can tell you is that there's gonna be a lot going on tonight!"

Frank turned away in disgust. "Watch him, Joe. I'll look around and see if the gang left any clues."

The prisoner kept teasing and making fun of the boys as Frank searched. Joe boiled and was barely able to control his hot temper. Finally he averted his glance to avoid giving the crook the satisfaction of watching the effect of his mockery.

"Hey, look at this!" Frank exclaimed suddenly.

"What is it?" Joe moved toward his brother.

Frank had picked up a battered paperback bearing the title *Elephant Boy*. The colorful picture on its cover showed an Indian mahout driving his elephant through the jungle, with a snarling leopard poised to spring on him from a tree branch.

"True story or a novel?" Joe inquired, looking over his brother's shoulder.

"True, I guess," Frank said, flipping through the pages. "It probably tells about how elephants behave, just like the book we found in th—"

He broke off suddenly and whirled around to check on their prisoner. "Joe! He's gone!"

The man had sneaked through the open door while the boys were occupied with Frank's find!

Groaning and berating themselves for their carelessness, the Hardys dashed outside in pursuit. The man was nowhere in sight and the young sleuths realized that he could easily lose himself in the surrounding brush, with the darkness for added cover. Carefully they probed among the shadowy trees. Then a disturbing thought hit Joe. "Frank, our boat!"

"You're right!" Frank muttered angrily. "Come on, let's see if that's where he's gone."

The boys hurried toward the beach. Clouds partially veiled the moon, but far ahead, at the water's edge, the Hardys could see the figure of the fugitive. He was crouching in the cockpit of the *Sleuth!*

"Trying to hotwire the ignition!" Frank blurted.

"He must have had a knife in his pocket to cut himself free!" Joe fumed. "We should've frisked him!"

Their voices carried and the man in the *Sleuth* straightened up. Next moment he snatched what looked like a hammer from their tool kit and swung a hard blow at the instrument panel. Then he leaped out of the cockpit, ran a few paces out into the water, and dived from view!

The Hardys' pulses were pounding with anger and exertion as they reached the scene. "He's smashed our radio!" Joe cried, then peered into the darkness. "Can you spot him, Frank?"

"Don't even waste time looking. He could swim underwater along the point and sneak ashore anywhere among the reeds."

"But he'll get away! There's a highway back inland. He may have a car stashed there."

"Probably does. He tried to swipe our boat and leave us stranded. We've got to get back fast!"

"You think those remarks he made meant something?"

"I'm sure of it." Frank worried. "He said 'near Bayport.' That sounds as if the gang may be planning a raid on Wild World!"

"Leaping lizards! And we haven't even got a radio to warn Pop!" Joe realized.

"Exactly, so come on!" Frank urged. "Let's get the *Sleuth* out in the water and shove off!"

Planing up a bow wave, they sped north along the coast to Barmet Bay, then headed inland to the boat harbor. When they finally berthed the *Sleuth* in her boathouse, more than an hour had elapsed since their departure from Sandy Point.

Frank ran to a phone booth on the wharf, inserted a coin, and dialed the animal-park number.

"No answer!" he reported after lengthy ringing.

"Call Chet!" Joe suggested. "Tell him to rouse the gang and meet us at Wild World!"

"Roger!"

Minutes later, their car was speeding toward the animal park. All seemed peaceful as they drove to the entrance. The boys leaped out, gazing through the moonlight at Pop Carter's bungalow, which was dimly visible in the distance beyond the amusement area.

"No sign of troub—" Joe started to say, but his voice broke off as the frame building suddenly exploded into white-hot geysers of flame!

"It's a fire bomb!" Frank cried.

CHAPTER XIX

A Fiery Trick

THE Hardys were frantic with worry for Pop Carter's safety. "He may be in there, unconscious!" Joe exclaimed. "Maybe that's why he didn't answer the phone!"

"I know," Frank said tersely. "Come on, there's no time to find the watchmen. We'll have to go in over the gate."

The words were hardly out of his mouth when a loud *boom* shattered the night. The ground reverberated beneath their feet. As the echoes died away, a cloud of smoke could be seen billowing on their right.

"Part of the fence is down!" Frank cried.

Rather than waste time running along the park boundary to the section of wrecked fence, the boys scaled the gate as Frank had originally proposed. Dropping down on the other side, they raced across the grounds toward Mr. Carter's bungalow.

The crackling sound of the flames grew louder as they neared the building. Its walls were ablaze and tongues of flame licked toward the sky from every window.

"Hold it! Someone's coming!" Joe told his brother.

A running figure emerged from the darkness. It was Pop Carter, his wispy hair flying in all directions. Apparently he had pulled on trousers and suspenders over his pajamas.

"Thank goodness!" said Frank. "Are you okay, sir?"

"Yes, yes! But how did this blaze start?"

"Magnesium firebomb, from the way it looked." Frank hastily related the circumstances that had brought the Hardy boys rushing to the park. "We tried to call and warn you but got no answer," he added.

Pop explained that he had been roused from sleep by a call from one of the park's two night watchmen, who reported glimpsing an intruder inside the grounds. Pop and the other watchman had hurriedly joined the one who called. Then all three had spread out to search the area.

"Soon as I saw the glow from the flames, I came back to see what had happened. This is terrible!"

The heat from the blaze was intense, adding to Frank's suspicion that it was a magnesium fire bomb. "Another bomb exploded right after your bungalow ignited," he told the park owner. "It wrecked part of the fence."

Both bombs, Frank speculated, could easily have been planted during the day or evening by one of the visitors, with timing devices to make them go off during the night hours.

"What about that prowler the watchman sighted?" Joe put in. "Wouldn't he have touched off an alarm when he broke into the park?"

"He should have," Pop Carter replied, shaking his head in puzzlement. "As I told you fellows the other day, the fence is wired. I can't figure out how he sneaked in!"

"Well, never mind now, sir," Frank said, sympathetically putting a hand on the old man's shoulder. "The first thing is to fight this fire. You're outside the Bayport city limits, so you'll have to rely on the local volunteer fire brigade till they put through an official call for assistance. What about your two watchmen?"

"They should be along soon," Pop said anxiously. "Wherever they are, I'm sure they can see the fire by now!"

"Good! And our gang's coming to pitch in. Why don't you go to the nearest phone and call for help, while Joe and I open the front gate for our friends."

Pop agreed gratefully and gave the Hardys a key before hurrying off. Chet's jalopy was already rumbling up to the entrance by the time Frank and Joe got the gate open. Phil and Biff were with Chet. Tony Prito's pickup arrived moments later, with Leroy Mitchell in the cab beside the driver.

Luckily, hydrants had been installed when the park's water system was put in, along with a water tower to maintain adequate pressure. One of the hydrants was located halfway between Pop's bungalow and a nearby cluster of buildings, which included supply sheds, a veterinary clinic, and half-completed winter quarters for the tropical animals.

The boys quickly unreeled a fire hose, and soon were spraying a lively stream of water over the blaze. They also used buckets to dampen the surrounding brush to keep the flames from spreading.

"Hey!" Joe exclaimed as the Hardys refilled their buckets. "Do you hear that?"

Frank paused and caught the distant sound of an elephant trumpeting. "It's Sinbad!"

"Do you suppose he's just excited by the fire?"

"He's pretty far away to get *that* excited!" A look of dismay came over Frank's face. "Joe, I think we've been tricked!"

"How come?"

"That second bomb, the one that wrecked the fence! It would also knock out the alarm circuit!"

Joe gasped as he caught on. "Which means someone else could have broken into the park. Maybe near the elephant compound!"

"Right! And the whole purpose of the fire bomb," Frank went on tensely, "was to divert everyone's attention to this area, while the crooks carried out their real raid unnoticed!"

Joe nodded. "Let's see what's going on over that way!"

Dropping their buckets, the Hardys jumped into Tony's pickup truck and sped off toward the animal area.

They leaped out at the gate, scaled over it, and continued down the road leading past the elephant compound. In the moonlit darkness, they could sense the restless movement of animals disturbed by Sinbad's trumpeting.

As they neared the elephant enclosure, a strange scene met their eyes. At least three men with flashlights groped about the low rocky hillock that bordered the creek running through the compound. Some distance away, a fourth was holding Sinbad and his mates at bay with fiery squirts from a flamethrower!

Frank and Joe were thunderstruck. But neither hesitated. They scrambled over the fence and charged toward the trespassers on the rocky rise. The men saw them and turned to fight. Soon fists were flying.

Though outnumbered, the Hardy boys were well trained in boxing, karate, and other forms of unarmed combat. Nevertheless they quickly realized that they were up against tough, professional thugs. The melee began to go against them.

Then two newcomers joined the fray. One, a

pudgy roundhouse swinger, rushed in like an angry bear. The other threw lightning punches at a big-jawed crook who had tried to edge around the Hardys and attack from behind.

"Chet and Leroy!" Joe cried to his brother. With fresh spirit, the Hardys pressed their own attack.

"Look out!" Leroy shouted suddenly. "That dude with the flamethrower's coming!" He decked his opponent with a right hook, snatched a hefty rock, and hurled it with all his might as the fourth crook started up the hillock toward them.

The rock hit the man in the arm, knocking his flamethrower into the creek below. With a bellow of rage, he charged up the slope at the boys. The free-for-all took on fresh fury.

Once again, the outcome wavered. Frank, who was trading punches with the nearest intruder, glanced toward the elephants as Sinbad filled the night with a fresh trumpet blast.

A dark figure was running toward them past the three angry tuskers.

CHAPTER XX

Stalled Takeoff

FRANK felt a momentary surge of dismay. If the newcomer was one of the gang, he would tilt the odds against them and the fight might be lost!

The man dashed up the slope with long strides, his fists cocked for action. Moonlight gleamed from the visor of his battered white cap. Suddenly Frank realized who the man was.

"Dad!" he cried happily.

Mr. Hardy's arrival brought fresh hope to the hard-pressed youths and glum despair to the gang as the detective's fists began crashing among them. One by one, the criminals were knocked to the ground or gave up. Soon they were lined up with their hands in the air.

Just then Tony, Phil, and Biff appeared.

"You're too late," Chet crowed, waving his fists overhead like a match-winning boxer. "We've rounded up the whole gang!"

"But we could use some light," Joe said. "How about going back and asking Pop to turn on the lamps in the compound?"

"I think there's a switch panel in the gate-house," Tony reported. "I'll go see."

"Good. And look for rope while you're at it, so we can tie these creeps up!" Frank called.

As Tony ran off, Frank turned to his father. "How did *you* get here, Dad?" he asked.

"I had a strong hunch the gang was planning something at Wild World tonight," Fenton Hardy replied, "especially when I spotted a boat pulling in just below the amusement park area."

"Then you must be the man the watchman saw," Frank said. "But how did you get over the outer fence without setting off the alarm?"

Mr. Hardy chuckled. "Good question. It's twelve feet high. But you see, I cleared sixteen as a college pole-vaulter."

Presently the lights flashed on in the elephant compound, giving a better view of the prisoners. Among them was the dark-haired, heavy-jawed crook with the dimple in his chin who had been one of the two park lurkers described by Chet. Another was the knobby-nosed bruiser whom the Hardy boys had encountered at Sandy Point.

"You were right, Joe," Frank said. "He must've had a car stashed near the cabin."

Joe nodded. "Yes. He was just trying to swipe our boat so we'd be stuck out there all night."

"Too bad you didn't both wind up in that pit-fall!" the man growled. "I'd have finished you off then and there."

"Pipe down!" Mr. Hardy warned, shoving him back in line, "or I'll finish *you* off right now!"

The gang had been looking for a satchel hidden in the enclosure. Only a moment before the fight started, they had retrieved it from one of the deep crevices honeycombing the rocky rise along the creek.

The satchel contained explosives and timing devices as well as several letters and other written material. But there was no time to examine them. Tony returned with rope, and Mr. Hardy super-vised tying-up the prisoners. Meanwhile, the boys were occupied with another problem.

"How do you suppose these guys got in?" Frank wondered.

"They probably chopped out a section of the rear fence with wire cutters after the second bomb went off and killed the alarm system," Joe rea-soned.

"But that's wild, mountainous terrain in back of the park. How did they expect to get away afterwards?"

"Maybe some kind of off-the-road vehicle. Once they got back on the highway, they could escape fast enough," Joe offered.

Frank shook his head doubtfully. "I'm not so sure. They'd be taking an awful chance of being spotted by firemen or police directing traffic. There'll probably be TV crews and all kinds of gawkers on the road before very long."

Tony, in fact, had reported that firemen and a highway patrol car had now reached the scene.

"The best way to avoid being trapped would be an aerial getaway," Joe remarked.

Frank's eyes suddenly lit up. "You're right! And I'll bet that's exactly what they planned!"

He dashed out of the elephant enclosure. Joe followed, exclaiming, "You mean they've got a helicopter waiting outside the park?"

"Not a copter. Something a lot quieter. And talking about getting trapped—remember how *we* got steered into that pitfall setup at Sandy Point?"

"Well, first we sighted the Scorpio symbol, and then that white line painted on the ground nearby—"

"Right. And remember who thoughtfully made sure we'd see it?"

Joe gasped as his brother's meaning sank home. But he did not waste time replying. The two hopped into Tony's pickup, which their friend had driven up, and sped off toward the outer fence enclosing the rear of the animal park.

As expected, a small section had been cut open. Outside this gap in the fence, the glare of their headlights picked out the dark form of a baby blimp!

The boys leaped out of the pickup and ran toward it. The blimp's gas bags began to fill, and the craft started rising slowly off the ground. But the Hardys struggled to hold it down with their added weight! Joe clung desperately to its landing gear while Frank opened the cabin door and yanked the pilot away from the controls.

Squirming aboard, the older Hardy succeeded in switching on the compressor pump. As the airship's envelope swiftly deflated, the blimp settled back to earth with a bump!

The pilot fought frantically, his face a mask of rage. But, between them, the Hardys finally overpowered and frisked him. He was *Eustace Jarman!*

"You confounded pests!" he exploded as the boys gripped his arms.

"Speaking of pests." Joe chuckled, "I'd say a certain scorpion has stung his last victim!"

"You don't have any idea who the scorpion is," Jarman jeered.

"Yes, we do," Frank answered. "And we'll be sure when Sam Radley tracks down the firm that made the elephant balloon for you."

The boys drove Jarman to the elephant enclosure, using his own weapon to keep him cowed. Then all prisoners were taken to the park entrance, where State Police had arrived and were talking to Pop Carter.

The satchel contained crucial evidence. Realizing their position was hopeless, the men broke down and talked freely, despite Jarman's angry protests.

Several weeks earlier, when Fenton Hardy had discovered the terrorists' New York hideout, they had fled the city by car. A breakneck chase ensued. For a long time it appeared that they had lost their pursuers, but the police caught up with them again, and the gang desperately turned into Wild World.

It was a gray day with few visitors, so the terrorists seized the opportunity to dump the satchel with its damaging evidence. One of them spotted the rocky crevices near the creek and jumped out of the car long enough to hide the satchel in one of them. They planned to retrieve it as soon as possible, but when they returned to the park about ten days later, they found the site occupied by the newly set-up elephant compound.

Jarman, the gang's leader, was furious at this turn of events. The written material in the satchel identified the various members and incriminated him as the Scorpion. Though well out of sight in the rocky crevice, the satchel might be discovered by a trainer or park attendant. Jarman realized it must be retrieved at all costs, or he might face disgrace, ruin, and a possible life sentence for his terrorist activities.

"What was a big-shot businessmen like Jarman doing, leading a terrorist outfit?" asked one State Trooper.

"He was sympathetic to a foreign power and

was aware of the dirigibles' military capabilities. The gang was financed by this power, and he used them as a weapon to attack and ruin competitors," Mr. Hardy replied. "One of them was the Quinn Air Fleet."

"He wanted to make sure his fleet would have the only serviceable airships in the country," Frank explained.

The gang had first tried to retrieve the satchel by breaking into the park at night, but had been frustrated by the alarm. Later they had flown in aboard a baby blimp, but again they had drawn a blank when Sinbad's angry trumpeting brought Pop Carter and the watchmen to investigate.

Joe snapped his fingers. "The blimp was that 'dark shape' Pop saw soaring up and away through the trees!"

"And when we came here Monday," Frank added, "Sinbad must have recognized those two crooks in the car behind us. That's why he kicked up a fuss!"

"Reckon you're both right." Pop chuckled.

Desperate to recover the satchel, Jarman had tried every way possible to force Pop Carter to sell out, including ordering the real-estate firm Bohm worked for, a subsidiary of Jarman Ventures, to buy Wild World.

The Hardys posed a fresh obstacle. The phony code message luring Frank and Joe to Rocky Isle and the Scorpio symbol trick to get them to Sandy

Point had both been attempts to use the boys as pawns to force Fenton Hardy off the case.

The detective chuckled. "I'd say they turned out to be considerably more than pawns!" he said ironically.

Jarman's response was an angry glare at the boys. The dropped note picked up by Leroy had been a deliberate part of the tycoon's scheme. And the attempt to sabotage the boys' car, as well as the vinegaroon episode had been other moves to harass the Hardys.

Following their flight from New York, the gang separated and went under cover. Jarman flashed green light signals from the park Ferris wheel instructing the crook hiding out on Rocky Isle to come ashore and transmit the boss's orders to the other gang members.

With the case closed and all terrorists in custody, Fenton Hardy, his sons, and Chet Morton went to talk to Lloyd Quinn the next day.

When they arrived at the air-fleet terminal, they found Terry Embrow seated glumly in Quinn's office.

"We're wondering if you couldn't see your way clear to keep Terry on," Mr. Hardy asked the airship owner.

"What? This sneaky young thug!" Quinn roared angrily, glaring at Terry. Then he grinned and added in his normal tone of voice, "He's one of the best men in my crew! If he can assure me that there will never again be another incident, I'll keep him on!"

Terry could hardly believe his good luck. He promised good behavior and tried, with a dazed expression, to thank his boss.

"Don't thank me—thank the Hardys," Quinn said. "And by the way, fellows, that pipeline company wants to sign a contract right away, chartering the services of our new *Arctic Queen,* now that they know the real story behind those explosions!"

"Then the sky's the limit for the dirigible business!" Chet exclaimed enthusiastically. "Speaking of which—how about a sky-high malt, fellows?"